Book Two: Foundations Series

PAULA WISEMAN

MINDSTIR MEDIA

Refined: Book Two: Foundations Series
Copyright © 2013 by Paula Wiseman. All rights reserved.

Published by Mindstir Media
1931 Woodbury Ave. #182 | Portsmouth, NH 03801 | USA
1.800.767.0531 | www.mindstirmedia.com

ISBN-13: 978-0-9890288-6-8

Library of Congress Number: 2013935734

Visit Paula Wiseman on the World Wide Web:
www.paulawiseman.com

To Alan, a mighty man of valor

"Beloved, do not think it strange concerning the fiery trial which is to try you, as though some strange thing happened to you."

1 Peter 4:12

One

Wednesday, August 12, Mombasa, Kenya

"International call from the United States of America. Please wait." Julie Bolling sat in the rocking chair blinking away the haze of sleepiness. She squinted at the clock on the mantle. A quarter till two, so it was almost six p.m., yesterday, back home. Their friends and extended family called first thing in the morning stateside, so they got most phone calls in the late afternoon or early evening. This felt wrong. Something was up. "Go ahead, please," the operator said with a click.

"Mark? This is David Shannon."

Julie immediately got a knot in her stomach. One of Mark's closest friends, David pastored one of their supporting churches in St. Louis. Had something happened with Mark's dad there in St. Louis?

"This is Julie. Mark and Peter were in Mapenya all day. I don't expect them back until tomorrow, or today, I mean. What's wrong?"

"One of our church members works at the courthouse, and she called me as soon as she got off work. In fact, I just got off the phone with her—"

"David, what's wrong?" Julie demanded.

She heard him take a deep breath. "Mark's father has filed a lawsuit to get protective custody of your children. Doug Bolling is suing you for your kids."

The bewildered nausea of betrayal seized her. Doug . . .

was suing . . . how could he do something so despicable? They had endured sixteen years of bitter conflict over Mark's faith, over his call to preach, over his decision to go to seminary and his surrender to the mission field. Doug's decision to live with a woman caused Mark to sever their relationship and Doug hadn't seen the kids since they'd been in Kenya.

But all that was supposed to be over. They were coming home. Mark was giving up the mission work. Just two months ago, he admitted to her that God never called him to Kenya. He chased it, trying to win approval, or validation or respect. He was working to get all the ministries on solid footing so he could leave. Surely Doug knew that. And if he did, what would prompt him to sue?

She pushed aside the swirl of questions in her mind long enough to ask, "On what grounds?"

"I don't know. I've left messages with a couple of lawyers. I'll get one of them to call you as soon as I can."

Lawyers? Like in court? They were going to court? Is that where this is headed? She gripped the arm of the rocking chair. It felt firm, real. If it were a dream, she wouldn't be able to feel the chair or smell the light, lingering scent of spaghetti from last night's dinner still hanging in the house . . . but it couldn't be real either.

It was another moment before she realized David was still talking.

"We'll try to handle as much as we can here for you, and I'll call back tomorrow. God help you, Julie. I don't know what else to say."

"Me either. I'm sure Mark . . . he'll call you. Thanks David." Julie eased the phone onto its cradle and hung her head, coaching herself to breathe. Mistake. This had to be a mistake. Maybe there was another Doug Bolling and it was just a mix-up. She hugged herself and leaned back in the chair, afraid she might faint and pitch forward out of the chair.

"Dear God in heaven, I don't know where to start . . . I can't . . . " Tears choked off her words. Doug loved the kids. She believed that. How could he subject them to the trauma of a lawsuit? He couldn't. He wouldn't. She closed her eyes and wished Mark was home.

When she felt the gentle touch on her arm, she snapped upright in the chair. "Mark?"

"I'm sorry." Her oldest son, Matt, withdrew his hand. "I heard the phone. Is everything all right?"

Julie swallowed hard and smoothed her hair, trying to appear in casual control. "Yes . . . yes, fine."

The fourteen-year-old dropped his eyes and nodded. He wasn't buying it. "Matt, please try to understand. I need to discuss it with your dad first. No one is sick and nobody has died or anything like that, but something really serious has happened back home. Let us get the details first, okay?"

"Sure," Matt shrugged.

"Thanks." She squeezed his hand, and tried to smile, hoping it didn't look like a smirk.

"You want me to sit up with you?"

"No, you go on back to bed. You need your sleep."

"Like you don't." Matt kissed his mother lightly on the cheek, and slipped back down the hall.

Matt stole a glance at his mother before he shuffled into the bedroom he shared with his younger brother, Ben. "What'd she say?" Ben whispered hoarsely.

"Nothing. She wants to talk to Dad first."

"I bet it's Grandpa."

Matt shook his head. "Mom said nobody died or was sick or anything. Besides, Dad always calls him."

"But I gotta gut feeling."

Matt dropped on his bed and huffed, "You may as well go to sleep. We're not gonna find out anything till she talks to Dad."

"Like you can sleep," Ben muttered.

"What else can we do?" Any other night, the volume and frustration in Matt's voice would have been enough to get a parental warning.

"Email Grant Shannon. See if he knows anything."

"I can't get to the computer without Mom seeing me. They'll tell us soon enough."

"Doesn't it bug you?"

"Yeah, but I can't do anything about it."

"Sometimes I hate being a kid," Ben grumbled.

Even after seven years, Mark marveled at how dark the night was. Far away from any towns, the blackness swallowed the beams from the headlights mere yards in front of them. Peter Bakari drove faster than Mark would have, but he trusted Peter's driving and his knowledge of the road. If it had been daylight, Mark would've settled back and slept the rest of the way home, but he felt obligated to keep Peter company.

Sometime soon, he needed to sit down with Peter and explain that they were going to head back to the United States. In spite of the success he seemed to have, the truth was, this wasn't where God wanted him. It was where he wanted to be, where he thought he could make a name for himself. He dreaded that conversation, that admission. Maybe that's why he couldn't let go of the ministry in Mapenya.

"You are deep in thought, Pastor Mark," Peter said. Even in the dim light from the dashboard, Mark could see Peter's smile.

"Honestly, I was trying to stay awake."

"Sleep if you are tired. We have hours yet."

"Aren't you tired?"

"I will rest when I am old."

"I doubt you will."

"There is much work to be done. I sometimes wonder if God has chosen the right man."

The openings didn't come any bigger than that one, but he balked. "Peter, about that . . . I think God is calling me back to the States." That was a lie, and he knew it.

"Then you must obey God's call. He has other plans here."

Mark felt heat rise from his shoulders to his ears, and a throbbing pain thumped at his temples. "God never called me to Kenya. I made it up. He's not calling me home, I just can't carry on the act any longer."

Peter nodded slowly. "God redeemed your work here. He has done mighty things."

"I think God was blessing your work, not mine."

"It is His work."

"I've learned a lot from you, Peter."

"And I from you." Peter was silent for several moments, but then he glanced toward Mark. "It takes great courage to do what you are doing."

"Tucking my tail and running?"

"You are facing your true self. Few men will dare to do that."

"It isn't pleasant. I can tell you that much."

"It never is. But when men face their true selves at last, that is when they see God."

Soft morning light filtered into the kitchen as Julie emptied the remains of the tea kettle into her cup. In four hours it seemed she'd worn a groove between the kitchen and the front window. Surely Mark would be home soon. A few times, she was tempted to take their SUV and head north, to look for Peter's Jeep, but she couldn't leave Matt, Ben and Jane.

With nearly every pass through the living room, she tried to pray, but her prayers always collapsed into bitter mental tirades against Doug Bolling. How could he betray them and attack them this way when he got what he'd wanted for years? Mark was moving back to St. Louis. Was this punishment? Was he trying to prove something or teach Mark a lesson? Was the woman he lived with behind this? Had she somehow pushed him into it?

It made no sense. At the end of April, Mark arranged for Matt, Ben and Jane to spend a week with his dad. A week! Doug even called and talked to the kids to make preliminary plans. Then before May was over, Mark decided they needed to leave Kenya and began working to wrap things up. Why couldn't Doug hold on a few more months?

Julie heard Peter's Jeep crunch to a stop outside. She so hoped things had gone well. She didn't want to deliver her news on top of a disappointment. She waited by the front door, and in the quiet, she could hear Mark, boisterous and exuberant, talking to Peter. She took a deep breath and put on her best smile. He deserved a few moments to savor his victory.

"It was incredible!" Mark beamed, letting the screen door slam too loudly behind him and Peter. "The chief, the one Mbogo knows, he listened, and then he asked how to become a believer! The chief! Then he got everybody outta bed! The whole tribe!"

"Mark, that's wonderful!" She hugged him tightly, and swallowed hard. *God, why now? It will just suck the life out of him when I tell him.*

"Pastor Mark, God is good," Peter said. "I want to tell Helene. She was praying." He took a step toward the door. "Miss Julie, peace and mercy. Good morning to you."

"Thank you, Peter." He couldn't know how much she and Mark would need that peace and mercy. "Give Helene and the kids my love."

"We'll get together in the next day or two and talk about getting regular teaching out there to the chief," Mark said with a wave. Peter nodded, smiled broadly and slipped out the door. "Julie, it was the most amazing thing I've ever been a part of. There were, I don't know, fifteen, eighteen people that believed in Jesus, that want to be baptized."

"Mark, I knew you'd get through to them."

"It was God. Plus Peter's a great translator. He's got a great heart." Mark sighed and dropped into one of the living room chairs. "I'm exhausted, but I'm not. Does that make sense?" Julie nodded. "Man, there's so much to do now. Wonder if Peter's son is ready to teach? This would be a great opportunity for him."

"But you're winding things down, right? We're heading home, aren't we?"

"Yeah, just as soon as I can see some closure."

In that pause, she delivered the blow. "David Shannon called." She watched the joy in Mark's eyes dissolve and she tried hard not to hate Doug Bolling.

"It's my dad, isn't it?" There was an odd resignation in Mark's voice, an expectation almost. Julie nodded. "Is he okay? What happened?"

"He's filed a lawsuit. Mark, he wants our kids."

Two

"A lawsuit? He's lost his mind! He can't. That doesn't even make sense." Mark jumped up from the chair and paced. "What kind of idiot would take his case?"

"I don't know. All David knew was that a suit had been filed. He was going to call some lawyers for us—"

"We can't afford a lawyer! My dad knows that!"

"The children will hear you." Julie glanced past him down the hall.

"Why would he want the kids?" Mark waved his hand toward the bedrooms. "He didn't want to raise me!" He strode across the living room to the kitchen and yanked the telephone receiver off its cradle. "He can't get away with this." He furiously punched in numbers. "The United States, please."

Julie pushed the switch on the telephone down, disconnecting the call. "You can't talk to him. At least not right now. "

Mark collapsed into one of the kitchen chairs and buried his face in his hands. "My mother would be so humiliated."

"This would have never happened if your mother was still living."

"For a whole bunch of reasons," Mark muttered. He closed his eyes and took a deep breath. "So what did David say? Word for word."

"He said one of the church members works at the courthouse and she called him. Doug filed a protective custody suit—"

"Protective custody? Like he thinks the kids are in danger? That's ridiculous!"

"I don't know what it means, exactly. That's why we need to wait until we can talk to a lawyer—"

"How are we going to pay a lawyer? It's going to take everything we've got to move back home."

"And that's what I don't understand. Why is he doing this now when he's won? We're moving back to St. Louis like he wanted all along." She watched the color drain from Mark's face as he shifted awkwardly in his chair. "He knows we're moving back, right?"

Mark drew his limbs in tightly, and without lifting his eyes, he whispered, "I . . . when I called him on his birthday, he was headed to the airport. We didn't have time to talk."

Venomous accusations exploded in Julie's mind, each one fighting and clawing to find an outlet. She clenched her fist as if she could physically hold it all back. He . . . never . . . told Doug. "You haven't talked to him in the two months since then?"

"You have to understand—"

"What did you say to him? Or not say to him? Did you push him to this?" She was yelling. The children would hear.

"He found out about Jane breaking her arm."

"And he was furious, wasn't he?" When Mark didn't respond, she turned and paced away from him. "I told you. I told you not to keep that from him. I offered to call him myself."

"I know."

She sighed and turned to face him. Shame and humiliation pulled his shoulders down, and redness rimmed his eyes. Whatever was between them would have to wait. They had to be united for the children's sake. "I think you'd better call David back and figure out a way to get us out of this mess." Mark nodded. "He's expecting your call."

When he reached for the receiver, she faded back to the living room and listened in on the other phone. "I am so sorry," Mark whispered. She couldn't respond. None of the standard answers fit. It wasn't okay. She wasn't sure everything would be all right. She wasn't even sure she forgave him.

The call connected and David's phone rang at last. She heard Mark clear his throat, and as soon as David answered, he spoke with fake confidence. "David, what's going on?"

"I'm not sure we should even be discussing it. It may all be confidential, but it was officially recorded that a lawsuit was filed by your dad today. I don't know what he claimed, but he's asking for custody. I've called a lawyer—"

"We can't afford a lawyer."

"Don't worry about that. You're covered."

"You can't afford a lawyer either," Mark said.

"He's a good guy, from the church my dad pastored for years before he died. Name's Chuck Molinsky. He's a business lawyer, but he said he'd take care of finding you a good family attorney."

"He's not going to do it for free, though."

"If Chuck said he'd handle it, he will. I'd trust him with my life."

Julie shook her head. It wasn't David's life. What would a business lawyer know about finding a family lawyer? Just because it was a buddy of his didn't mean he'd be competent.

"That's good enough for me," Mark said. "I guess we're stuck until we have a lawyer and actually see what's in the suit."

"Maybe so. I can have Chuck call you. He may have some idea what you're up against."

"Only if he's got time."

Julie rolled her eyes. Why was Mark so passive? Why didn't he feel the urgent threat the way she did? Was there something else he'd neglected to mention to her?

"Listen, David, I really appreciate you letting us know, and doing the legwork for us, but Peter and I were up north all night and I am exhausted."

"Sure thing. I'll have Chuck call. What time is it there?"

"Five-thirty in the morning."

"I'll have Chuck call you late afternoon, or early evening."

"Sounds great. Take care, David."

"Mark, I gotta tell you. I don't know if I could be as calm as you are if I was facing this."

"If it's what God asked of you, I'm sure you could. Thanks again and God bless."

Julie slammed the phone down and stormed back to the kitchen. "What God asked of you? I thought God asked you to pack up and go home! What . . . what happened to that? Have you even told Peter we're going home?"

"I told him tonight."

"Tonight! You've known for months. How long did you know before you told me?"

"A month maybe."

"So you lied to your dad—"

"I didn't lie to him. There are some things that are best discussed in person."

"Did you plan to show up on his doorstep one night?"

"I don't even know where he lives now," he muttered.

"Is that where you get it then? This shutting everyone out of your life?"

"You know I could really use your support right now."

"Works both ways, Mark. Do you understand your father is trying to take our children away from us?"

"Yeah, I get that." He pushed away from the table and stood up. "And so you don't have to say it, it's my fault. I made a promise to my mother two days before she died to make sure my dad came to faith in Christ, and I ran from that because it was hard. Ran all the way to Kenya, hiding from that one call. God told me to go back home and face that, and I filled my calendar so we couldn't possibly leave anytime soon."

"Mark, I didn't mean—"

"Doesn't matter what you meant. Truth is, God's gonna get me home to deal with my dad. I'm sorry you and the kids have to suffer because of it."

Tuesday, August 11, St. Louis, Missouri

Doug Bolling stood on his deck, staring out across the swimming pool, absently sipping from a glass of tea. This was Mark's fault. He was the one who delivered ultimatums, passed judgment, prevented contact with the kids, lied to him about their well-being.

Ten days ago, he caught Mark in an ongoing lie about Jane breaking her arm. That was the last straw. If Mark had backed down, had admitted he was wrong, had made any kind of concession . . . but ten days. Nothing. No phone call. No apology. No explanation. Not even an email to the office.

All day long he heard recriminations in his mind for what he'd done, all in Judy's voice. The only way he could quiet them was with his own constant refrain—He had no choice. Mark forced his hand. He had to do this for the kids. He took a long drink from the tea and wished it was something stronger.

He flinched in surprise as arms gently encircled his waist. He never heard Cassandra Grayson steal in behind him. "You didn't say two words at dinner," she said softly.

"Just tired."

"It's only Tuesday." She dropped her arms and he turned to face her.

"I'm old."

She crossed her arms across her chest, a smile in her eyes. "You need to come up with a better one than that."

"I filed the lawsuit today. There's no turning back now."

"Second thoughts?"

He shook his head. "Mark will hate me regardless of how it turns out." He grabbed the rail and lowered himself to the deck steps, and began his refrain. "It was a choice between him and the kids. They're innocent. They don't have a voice. They shouldn't have to live that kind of life when they can't choose, especially when they have other options."

Cass dropped in beside him. "He and Julie wouldn't lis-

ten to your concerns. I don't know what else you could've done
to get his attention." They sat in silence for several long moments until she leaned over and kissed his cheek. "I'm going
on up to bed."

"I'll be up in a minute." He took her hand before she
could get away. "You think I'm doing the right thing?"

She smiled gently. "When have you ever been unsure
about what you were doing?"

"You know, if we end up with the kids, it'll be a big
change for us."

"We can handle it. We're in this for the long haul, aren't
we?"

He nodded and she kissed him again, then walked back
into the house.

Doug listened to the back door click shut and gulped
the last of his tea. Cass never doubted him. She understood
him at a gut level, maybe more than Judy did. Their eighteen,
almost nineteen, year age difference didn't bother her, and she
stuck with him even as her friends all married, some of them
for the second or third time.

He took a deep breath and pulled himself to his feet. He
was doing the right thing. If Mark and Julie wanted to live like
natives and claim Jesus told them to, that was their business.
Matt, Ben and Jane deserved a normal life.

———————

Cass switched on the television, but after a few moments of the drone of a cooking show, she clicked it off and
changed into her pajamas. She loved Doug. She believed in
him, supported him, but this was going to be a mess.

She stepped into the master bath and rummaged
through the drawer between the sinks until she found the Tylenol. She shook two pills, then a third, into her hand and
quickly swallowed them, chasing them with a gulp of water.

Doug's only son. Her first meeting with him would be in
a hearing room in family court. Not how she envisioned it. She

didn't have a chance of being part of the family now. It would always be 'us' against 'them,' and she was doomed to the role of the wicked step-mother. Step-grandmother, actually. Grandmother. At thirty-seven. To a fourteen-year-old. She shook her head, and sighed. If they didn't all end up in therapy after this, it would be a miracle.

She moved down to the last drawer in the vanity. She pushed the tubes of lipstick out of the way and retrieved a case of birth control pills. She snapped the lid open and stared at the partial ring of pills. People miss doses all the time.

She studied her reflection in the bathroom mirror. She wasn't that old yet. She could still have children, Doug's children. In fact, if she went downstairs and announced she wanted a baby he'd blink and smile and say, "Okay." Then he would marry her. He was just that way.

He didn't want a baby, though, and she couldn't trap him like that. She dutifully popped today's pill in her mouth, and swallowed it with another gulp of water. Now somehow she was supposed to go get a good night's sleep in spite of her complicity in this scheme to steal Mark's children.

Wednesday, August 12, Mombasa

When the phone rang just after midnight, Mark snatched it from its cradle. After the hours he'd spent alone in his study avoiding his family, he'd welcome it, even if it was more bad news. Before he said hello, he heard the telltale click as Julie picked up the other receiver.

"Mark? This is Chuck Molinsky. David Shannon called me."

"We were expecting your call. Were you able to find out anything?"

"First of all, Mark, I'm a business lawyer. I can give you some basics, but you need someone better qualified—"

"David trusts you, that's good enough for me."

"I appreciate the vote of confidence, but if it were me, I'd want Fletcher Durant. He's got thirty-some years' experience and specialized in helping dads keep custody of their kids."

"Sounds like exactly what we need."

"I'll firm things up with Fletcher, then. We'll contact the clerk and have them serve the papers. That will give us thirty days. We'll ask for thirty more to give you time to get here—"

"But here's what I'm up against. The last time we flew home, the tickets were seventeen hundred dollars each. If I have to buy open-ended tickets, there's no way."

"David's been on the phone all day. He's already raised over four thousand dollars. You choose your flights and charge them to my law firm. I'll have my secretary get in touch with you to work out the details. We'll take care of it one way or another."

"I can't let you do that." He heard Julie huff, and hoped Chuck dismissed it as a quirk of the international connection.

"We're going to file a countersuit to have your father reimburse you for the expenses since he started all this."

"I can't do that, either."

"Mark!" Julie said and Mark coughed loudly.

"Are you still there?" Chuck asked.

"Yeah, sorry."

"We can argue about the countersuit later." The aggravation in Chuck's voice was hard to miss. "The money will take care of itself. Now, do you have a fax machine?"

"I can find one in town somewhere."

"Email?"

"Yes."

"I'll email everything to you, then. Hang in there. This will work out."

"Is there any way . . . does he have a case?"

"I haven't seen the filing, but I know courts are very reluctant to take children away from their parents. I think your worst-case scenario is court-ordered visitation. It's far more likely that the thing gets thrown out before it gets started."

"So what do we do in the meantime?"

"Keep ministering, keep an eye on the airline flights and

Fletcher or I will be in touch as soon as we have any more information."

"Thanks, Chuck. Thanks for everything." He eased the phone back on its cradle. A few moments later Julie appeared in the doorway of his study.

"So we have thirty days," she said.

"Or sixty. Either way, I can't shut things down that quickly. We'll have to come back. I'll have to come back at least." She frowned and crossed her arms across her chest. "I can't just drop these people. I've made commitments to them."

"Whatever." Her eyes were cold and dark. "We need to tell the children. Do you want to do it or should I?"

"I will. First thing tomorrow." She didn't soften. "I know I've really messed things up, but I need you."

"No, you don't. You need my approval, but you don't need me."

Julie lay in bed, alone, staring at the ceiling, too angry and frustrated to cry. Mark had to step up. He had to defend them. He couldn't stand by, protecting his reputation as the 'perfect' pastor, and let his father take their children. He couldn't, he just couldn't.

David had spent the day raising money for them. What had Mark done all day? Nothing. He couldn't shut down the ministry in sixty days if he couldn't function.

The lawyer sounded cautiously optimistic, but family law wasn't his field. She'd feel better when they heard from the expert. And what was Mark thinking? Why wouldn't they want his dad to reimburse them for the expenses? Wasn't that customary that the loser paid the winner's costs? Not the moving expenses, but the lawyers and the plane tickets. That was reasonable, wasn't it?

For a moment she considered calling her mother in Italy. Maybe she had some wisdom, some insight into Doug. Or even Mark. What should a wife do when her husband . . .

wouldn't?

She turned away from his side of the bed and sighed. She'd pray. Wasn't that what she was supposed to do?

Lord, help him. Give him the strength and the courage he needs to fight this battle. I know I need to be supportive of him, and not someone else picking at him, but I'm afraid. Mark is a good man. I know he loves us, but his father has always bullied him. Lord, how do we put a stop to it once and for all?

———

Still feeling the sting of Julie's words, Mark escaped outside to the back step. Stars twinkled in the clear night sky and the sliver of a moon hung delicately in its appointed spot. Peter's son, George, nodded as he guided his German shepherd, Joe Jr., around the yard, following close to the fence.

Mark leaned against the back door and picked out the few constellations he recognized. When he was ten or twelve he wanted to be an astronomer, but physics class shot that dream full of holes. Back in high school, he told everyone he wanted to be an accountant, not because that's what he wanted, but because it was a good answer; an acceptable, approved answer.

He'd chased approval his whole life. His mother and grandparents meted it out in the tiniest, most volatile doses, ever ready to withdraw it on a whim. His father was no freer with his approval, but at least his dad never showed him the contemptuous disapproval his mother was so good at.

When his mother got sick, and found Jesus Christ, everything about her changed, but what caught his attention was that he was finally good enough for her. He measured up at last. That kind of change was worth investigating. Within a year, he'd become a believer, too.

He met Julie and between his faith and her connections through her father, the preacher, he finally found a place. The more serious he became in his faith, the more he fit in, the more approval he garnered. It was addictive.

He promised his mother he'd make sure his father became a believer. That proved impossible, and it seemed the more effort he put into it, the more distant their relationship became. It was pointless to pursue it, especially since preaching and pastoring were so much more gratifying. Self-gratifying.

The sky lightened with the first hints of dawn. Dawn always came. There was always a new day. He resisted the temptation to run back to his study and declare that he had the answer. Instead, he kept watching. One by one the stars faded, and finally the glow of the moon itself was overtaken by the morning sun.

He'd always pictured himself like one of the stars, a bright light in a very dark world. The fact was, he was more like a star clinging to the darkness because it made his own light brighter. He was called to show people Jesus, but he'd settled for showing them what a fine job he did being a believer.

God tried to tell him months ago, years ago, really. He did his best to ignore it. Now his family would pay the price. He gazed back up at the sky, straining to find the moon, but it had disappeared in the sun's glow. Disappearing was not an option. "Lord, how do I fix this?"

No answer came and after a few more moments, he went back inside. The clock on the stove was set for Central time. Not too late. He picked up the phone and dialed David Shannon's number. "I need some advice, some wise counsel. How do I do this?"

"I'm not sure there are too many precedents for what you're facing. What are you struggling most with right now?"

"This is my fault. God is punishing me for not coming home when He told me to."

"I seriously doubt that's what's going on. What about your dad?"

"Trying to grasp how he could muster that level of bitterness and vindictiveness."

"You can put it in words. That counts for a lot."

"Forgive my skepticism."

"Listen, you know your Bible as well as I do, but every time I've thought about you or prayed for you, First Peter keeps coming to mind. Maybe your answers are there."

"That's the one that's all about suffering, the 'fiery trials,'" Mark muttered. "Great."

"Yes, but it's also the one that talks about 'joy unspeakable,'" David's voice grew quiet. "I don't presume to know or understand what kind of pain this is causing for you and for Julie, but I have hope. We've all been praying for your dad for years that something would wake him up, that somebody would get through to him. Maybe this is it. Maybe God is letting Doug be his own catalyst."

"Chuck told me you were already raising airfare for us. Thanks."

"Hey, we're in a partnership. The ones who go and the ones who stay have to help each other out."

"I still appreciate it. I'll be in touch." He hung up the phone and walked back to the tiny glorified closet that served as his study. He switched on the desk light and sat down, resting his head in his hands.

"Lord, I have to face everybody and tell them all the truth. Please . . . I need some reassurance that You aren't through with me, that I haven't somehow gone too far. I really do want my dad to be a believer. If this is what it takes, I'll do it." He pulled his Bible down and read through First Peter slowly. As Peter closed out the epistle, he sent greetings from his fellow ministers, ending with "so does Mark, my son."

Mark, my son.

He checked the clock again. "I need to call my dad."

Three

Tuesday, August 11, St. Louis

Doug locked the back door, activated the security system, then turned out the kitchen light anxious to head upstairs to Cass. When the phone rang, he was tempted to ignore it. He didn't know anyone who'd be calling at this hour of the night. Even so, he grabbed the phone from its cradle. "Doug Bolling."

"Dad, it's Mark."

Doug's mouth went dry. Of all the reactions to the lawsuit he'd anticipated, a quiet phone call wasn't on his list. Unsure of Mark's motives, or even how to respond, he went with his standard question. "Are the kids all right?"

"We'll be coming home as soon as I can get everything arranged. I want to talk to you, just the two of us, without lawyers, before we go to court."

"Mark—"

"I'm giving you the benefit of the doubt, that somehow what you're doing makes sense to you, that you have a good reason—"

"I can't discuss this with you, Mark. I've tried. You never wanted to hear me, so I had no choice but to take action."

"This is not action! This is taking my children away from me!"

"Wonder what that feels like?" Doug slammed the phone down, and leaned over the counter. Mark didn't want to talk. He wanted to deliver a lecture.

"Hey, I thought you were coming right up." Cass had slipped silently into the kitchen.

Doug turned to face her. "Mark called."

"You're kidding! From Africa?"

"Yeah, he wants to talk to me privately before we go to court."

"Do you think that's a good idea?"

"It won't fix anything. I'll talk to the lawyer about it. Let him say no." He leaned against the counter and folded his arms across his chest. "Do you believe in God?"

"I don't know. I think having faith in something is good, but I'm not sure religion works the way people say it does."

"How do you think it works?"

"Why are you asking me this all of a sudden?"

"You're smart, college-educated, reasonable, thoughtful."

"Why, thank you, Mr. Bolling," she smiled.

He allowed himself a slight smile in return. "I trust your ideas, Cass."

"I'm not sure I have any. I've never really thought about what I believe."

"You ever go to church or anything when you were a kid?"

"Not really. My aunt took my brother and me to Bible school and we sang all the little songs, but that's about it."

"Judy said she never understood faith until she experienced it. That's a cop-out. How can you believe in something that doesn't make sense?"

"You don't want the kids to grow up with faith? Is that what this is about?"

"I just want them to be free to choose. Mark and Julie have force-fed them that there's only one right way to do religion, only one idea about God that's right."

"Then what's your idea about God? You think heaven is real?"

"Maybe, but they all say that the things you do don't

matter. That's not how you get there. If that's the case, what's the incentive to do anything good? Shouldn't we just serve our own selfish interests?"

"And you don't do that now?" Cass teased, raising an eyebrow at him.

"No. I worked to provide for my family."

She tilted her head and almost smiled. "I think people are generally selfish. We're all looking out for our own interests first and foremost."

"Mark accuses me of that all the time. He thinks I'm a money-hungry workaholic."

"You have done pretty well for yourself."

"There," he said, pointing a finger. "Case in point. Why would God 'bless' me with money when I couldn't care less about Him or what He says?"

"You usually get offended at the suggestion that you've been blessed."

"Because I worked for everything I have. I've done it myself." He pushed away from the counter and added quietly, "In my experience, God only takes. He doesn't give."

Wednesday, August 12, Mombasa

Julie stood over the stove scrambling eggs for the kids' breakfast. Mark never came to bed last night. Each time Julie turned the spatula, she breathed a prayer. For wisdom, for grace, for her husband and for their marriage. They went through a season of distance after she miscarried several years ago. Awkward grief tangled the communication between them and unvoiced guilt and fear stole their intimacy. She could feel it creeping in again and that unnerved her almost as much as Doug's lawsuit did.

God alone knew Doug's motives and only He had the answers they needed. They had to hold on to that fact if they hoped to weather this storm.

She heard the long squeak of the screen door and

turned to see Mark come in from the backyard. "You didn't sleep, did you?" she asked.

"No." He rubbed his eyes and yawned. "Are the kids up?"

"They're in the living room." She laid the spatula on the counter. "I'm sorry. I feel helpless and fear is making me turn on you."

"I deserve it," he muttered. Was he trying to win her sympathy? "I, uh, called my dad this morning."

"Mark!"

"He thinks he didn't have any other option. If I can understand what he's trying to accomplish—"

"He thinks he's getting back at God by hurting you."

He shook his head. "He still loves me in some weird way. And I believe he really loves the kids. Maybe we should've gone back to St. Louis after Mom died."

"See, this is what happens every time you talk to him. You end up blaming yourself for his bitterness."

"I'm not blaming myself. I just, I think I should've handled things differently."

"If we had gone back, he would've completely undermined your faith. You never would have pastored or gone to seminary or done any of the other things God called you to do."

He shook his head and rolled his eyes. "I never listen to my dad."

"That is absolutely not true. You internalize everything he says about you. You always have."

Mark forced himself to eat a breakfast he didn't want only because he knew the children were watching him closely. Ben glanced at Matt after every bite but neither boy said a word. Even Jane was quiet. The only sounds were the occasional scrape of a fork or a slurp of milk.

After Ben and Julie cleared away the dishes, Mark motioned them back to the table. Ben glanced at Matt once again, then took his seat.

Mark avoided Julie's eyes, and focused on his sons. "Boys, you've already figured out something was up. We need to go home for a while. I'm going to start looking for a flight out today." Mark looked at Janie, but she was blissfully unburdened by the announcement. The boys remained silently unsatisfied by his declaration.

He shifted and leaned forward. "Your grandfather has filed a lawsuit and we have to go back and go to court."

"Grandpa's suing us?" Ben asked, and Matt's eyes darkened.

"He . . . uh . . . he wants custody of you guys. All three of you."

"Custody?" Matt sat up straight in his chair. "He wants to take us away from you?"

Mark's silence was answer enough.

"He can't!" Matt shouted. "I'm not going! And neither are they!"

"Matt, calm down. I've talked to a lawyer already. He says this will probably be thrown out before it even goes to trial—"

"Trial? We have to have a trial? With a judge?"

"I'm not handling this very well," Mark said, looking to Julie, but she dropped her eyes. He was on his own. "I don't think it will be a big deal, but we have to go or I could be arrested the next time we do go home."

"What about the Sukumas?" Ben asked.

"Peter can work with them. They like Peter."

"But you did all that work. Don't you want to see how it turns out?"

"Of course I do, Ben, but sometimes there are things you just have to do. We don't have a choice in this."

"Is the lawyer good?" Matt asked.

"Pastor David recommended him. He's a good guy."

"But is he a good lawyer?"

"I'd say so. He has his own law firm."

After a few moments of silence, Mark was about to get up from the table, but he saw Ben's frown. "What's the matter?"

"I can't decide. Does Grandpa like us or not like us?"

"What are you talking about?"

"Well, does he like us and he wants us to be with him, or does he not like us and he wants to make us miserable?"

Mark could see Julie subtly shake her head. "Of course Grandpa likes you. He loves all of you. He thinks he's doing what's best for you."

"Does he think you're bad parents or something?" Ben asked.

"That's stupid," Matt said. "Completely stupid."

"Matt, please. You don't have to like what he's done, but we have to conduct ourselves in a way that honors God. As a testimony to your grandpa and everybody else."

Matt frowned and clenched his jaw. "How could he even think something that stupid?"

"I'm not sure what he thinks. We don't have the actual papers from the lawsuit, yet. The lawyer is going to get them and email them to us. Until then, we stick with what we know." Mark leaned forward and looked Matt in the eyes. "Son, I need you to trust me to handle this. Can you do that?"

"Yeah," he mumbled, then he glanced across the kitchen at Julie. "Yes, sir."

"Thanks, Matt." Mark reached across the table and took his daughter's hand. "Janie, you understand what I said?"

"We're going to see Grandpa?"

"Yes, and there is a small, tiny possibility that you may be staying with Grandpa for a while."

"Can we swim in his pool?"

"No, Janie," Matt interrupted. "We don't want anything he has."

"Matthew!" Julie said sharply, then she smiled at Jane. "Sweetie, I don't think you'll have to worry about that. You may not even go to Grandpa's. We'll just pray and see what God does."

Four

Monday, August 17, St. Louis

Doug Bolling hop-stepped to keep up with the secretary as she ushered him into his attorney's office for a late afternoon appointment. Vic Wiley met him at the door, and pumped Doug's hand. "I've got good news! We got the judge."

"What?" Doug backed away, hoping the lawyer would sit down.

"The hearing date puts us on Henry Whitmire's docket. He's got a reputation for being very hostile on religious issues. He's our best shot."

"So you've got a date?"

Wiley nodded and rounded the desk. He peered over the rim of his glasses at his calendar. "October thirteenth. The other guy says your family is getting in late on the tenth of September. We can meet them at the airport and get the kids that night."

"Get the kids? You mean take them right then?" An unwanted image of SWAT teams flashed through Doug's mind.

"Yeah, although . . . " Wiley licked his lips slowly and leaned back in his chair, speaking mostly to himself. "We don't want media . . . the last thing we want is to get the evangelicals in a snit. We'll get them that Friday. That's better anyway. You'll have them all weekend until the hearing on Tuesday."

"You lost me," Doug said. "I thought we were going to court in October."

"October is when we finish them off. We're going to ask for temporary protective custody. Since you're a grandparent and are obviously capable of providing for the children, that will be a slam dunk."

Temporary protective custody? Doug scowled and crossed his arms across his chest. "Are you sure about this?"

"Doug, I do this all the time. I'm used to working with the D.A. and Child Services. It will go off like clockwork."

He was less than reassured. "Okay, so we get the kids Friday night, have them all weekend, and Tuesday the judge will say what?"

"That you will have temporary custody of the children until the adjudication hearing on the thirteenth of October."

"You're sure."

"Completely."

"What about visitation? Mark will be allowed to see the kids, right?"

"I don't think that's wise. I want it kept to a minimum, court supervised."

"Vic—"

"Look, they've got passports. I think they're a flight risk. They could take the kids and disappear to some foreign country. I mean, look what we've already had to go through to get them here."

"Mark and Julie aren't criminals."

"You love these kids, right?"

"Yeah, but—"

"And you'll do whatever is best for them, right? And what is best for them is that they're raised by someone other than their narrow-minded, judgmental, fanatical parents, who are causing deep psychological and emotional damage."

"It just seems harsh," Doug said.

"Custody is a blood sport, not for the weak at heart." Vic leaned back in his chair. "That's why I'm the best. I have the guts to do whatever it takes."

Whatever it takes. But Doug knew what it felt like to have your kids taken from you. When Mark was a toddler, Judy took him for a couple of months. He still remembered the empty powerlessness. That wasn't exactly what he was aiming for with the lawsuit. "So what do I do in the meantime?"

"Remodel your extra bedrooms."

"Seriously." Doug rolled his eyes.

"You don't have to do anything. I'm waiting on all the papers from the other guy—the house plans and pictures, the kids' medical and school records, Mark's financial records and work history, that kind of thing."

"Do I have to testify?"

"Not unless they call you or the judge wants to talk to you. Even if that happens, it's no big deal."

"Mark called—"

"You didn't talk to him, did you?"

"He asked to meet with me before we go to court."

"Absolutely not!" He jabbed a finger toward Doug. "Under no circumstances are you to talk to him without me there."

"Why not? He's my son."

"He's not your son now. He's your adversary. Don't give him any openings."

Adversary? Granted, they weren't on the best terms, but he never thought of Mark as his enemy.

"Doug, everything changed once you filed this lawsuit. Everything."

"I guess so," Doug said. "One more question. What about Cass?"

"What about her?"

"Does she affect the case at all? Does it hurt my case that we're not married?"

"You planning on getting married?"

"No."

"Won't matter. Whitmire's pretty liberal. You'll be good for the kids. You have a loving, stable relationship. It's just like the home they're in, except that you guys are normal."

"All right then. I'll see you in court."

"Just sit tight until that Friday night when the sheriff

delivers the kids to you."

"The sheriff?"

"Yeah, but it'll be an unmarked car. I'm telling you, Doug, we don't want any media attention. It will kill us if a bunch of church ladies show up and picket the courthouse, or Fox News puts Mark on television or something. There'll be a feeding frenzy and you'll be vilified."

"Great," Doug mumbled. "It's enough that Mark hates me."

"None of that is gonna happen. We're gonna keep this as quiet as possible." Victor Wiley stood and shook Doug's hand again. "Don't hesitate to call me if you have other questions or concerns, but I think you'll be pleased with how smoothly this goes."

———

Cass scanned the waves of people jostling down the mall concourse, looking for Doug. She sipped her tea and smiled at the janitor as he pushed in the chair across from her. He smiled back and for an instant she thought she recognized him. Then she caught sight of Doug, his plaid shirt, the unmistakable strides, and his unrelenting scowl. He hated the Galleria, but she was scouting for furniture all day and this was the easiest place to connect. Surely he didn't expect her to wait until tonight to hear how things went.

He mumbled a hello and jerked out the chair the janitor had just straightened and dropped into it. "You got any aspirin or anything?"

"Yeah." She pulled her purse from the chair back. "That bad?"

"The meeting went okay. We have a court date and the judge he wanted and everything." He took the pills from her hand and she pushed her tea across to him. "Thanks." He gulped and swallowed the pills then handed the tea back. "I don't know . . . I can't explain it."

"Is it Vic?"

"No he's . . . he's out to win this. I mean, that's what I want."

"You think he's unethical?"

"No." Doug shifted and frowned again. "I just . . . I don't think of this like he does. He's saying Mark's my enemy and . . . ."

"That's not what you think."

"No, but it's too late now. I started it, and I gotta see this through."

She reached across the table and took his hand. "You know I am on your side, but what did you expect would happen when you filed this suit?"

Doug's jaw tightened and he turned his head, looking anywhere but her eyes. He said nothing.

She sat for a moment, debating whether to push him any further when he spoke. "I didn't think it would go this far. I thought . . . he'd come around."

"He's as hardheaded as you are." She smiled gently but Doug didn't return the smile the way he usually did.

"This is about the kids, not Mark. It's never been about Mark."

"It's always been about Mark. It's about Mark and his decisions, his lifestyle." She left unsaid, *his rejection of you.*

"Only as far as his decisions have dictated that ridiculous idea of raising the kids in Africa. They deserve better than that and no one else will speak up for them. There is no objective, outside voice in their lives."

"Outside?"

"Non-religious."

"So it's about religion, then?"

"Cass, why are you doing this? I already have a headache. I already feel like a jerk."

"I want to understand. I want you to understand and be sure you've done the right thing and not bought into some lawyer's line in a moment of anger."

"I didn't. I just didn't realize how custody cases worked, and how they have to be handled."

"Like?"

"Like temporary protective custody. We're getting the kids on that Friday night after they get into town."

"Wait, protective custody? Like witness protection?"

"I don't think it's that big of a deal, but we'll have them for the weekend and after a Tuesday hearing, we'll have them until the real hearing."

"Then it could be permanent."

"Yeah."

Cass sighed deeply. She understood exactly where that headache-y jerk feeling came from. "What about Mark? Did he say you could talk to Mark?"

Doug shook his head. "Strongly advised against it."

"What if Mark calls or comes to see you and says, 'Dad, what would it take to call this all off? What do I have to do?' How do you answer him?"

Doug just frowned.

"Come back to St. Louis? Leave the ministry? Divorce his wife?"

"It's not that simple," Doug said. "It's not a simple action-reaction thing. There is a lifetime's worth of issues that have to be dealt with."

"Such as?"

"Look, that guy you were with a long time ago—"

"Donovan."

"Yeah. You told me he was abusive in every sense, right?"

"Yes."

"Well, how would you feel if your very best friend, the only one who understood, the one who grieved with you when you were hurt, started dating him?" Doug blinked several times. "And then they got married and berated you because you wouldn't come and help them celebrate."

"I'd feel betrayed, cast-off."

"Yeah, and then it's all somehow your fault because you won't forget what he did to you."

"Mark's done that to you."

Doug sniffed and almost smiled. "That makes me sound like some petty, vindictive . . . ex-girlfriend or something." He folded his hands and took a deep breath. "I don't want his kids to look back and realize he never loved them either, that he was chasing this religion thing and they were just items on the list. This is intervention."

"You really don't think he loves the kids?"

"He puts himself ahead of all of them." He began counting off on his fingers. "Julie losing the baby. Moving to Chicago. Moving to Africa. Jane breaking her arm, and then not taking her to the hospital until the next day. All of it happened because he could only see his agenda. He couldn't leave his church, so Julie was stuck with some idiot doctor in Springfield. He had to have a seminary degree, so instead of sticking with his job—even though he couldn't feed his family on what he was making—off he went to school. I'm still trying to figure out what possessed him to go to Kenya, but there was no talking to him. There's never any talking to him. You just listen."

"Hasn't Julie ever stood up to him?"

"Julie created him. She's just reaping what she's sowed."

"Does she love the kids?"

He stopped and dropped his eyes. "I guess." Then he seemed to recover his fight. "But she's in this, too. He wouldn't make a move if she didn't approve."

Cass nodded, leaned back in her chair, and took a long sip from her tea. Victor Wiley thought this was just a custody battle. He had no idea.

Doug was not used to getting home before Cass, and immediately he began rehearsing a list of reasonable explanations for her delay. She always called or sent a message when she was late. Think. Was there another appointment she mentioned? Or an errand? He grabbed his phone and pushed her speed dial when he saw her car turn onto the long drive to the house.

Her sleek Jaguar whispered to a stop in the driveway and she got out with a sheepish smile on her face. "I totally lost track of time."

"I thought I had forgotten something."

"No, I stopped at the bookstore."

Which was not unusual. Doug had never seen anyone read the way she did. Constantly. Big, thick books. The descriptions on the back were enough to make him nod off, but she devoured them. This time, though, she was way over her limit. She pulled two large bags with handles from the backseat.

"You, uh, expecting a blizzard or something?"

"No," she said. "It hit me after lunch today that there is a good possibility that we will end up with children in the house and I know absolutely nothing about them."

"So you're going to read?"

"Yes."

Doug smiled and shook his head.

"What?"

"You'll be fine without all the research."

"You don't know that." She dropped the books at his feet. "What are you supposed to do if a kid wakes up with a fever of a hundred and two."

"Are they throwing up?"

"Does that matter?"

"Sometimes."

"See, I didn't know that. I am in so much trouble." She reached for the bags again, but he picked them up for her.

"Cass, you had a mother. I suspect you have a pretty good idea what's involved."

"But my mother was horrible."

"Then do the opposite."

"But boys. What am I supposed to do with boys?"

"Feed them."

She rolled her eyes and shoved him gently. "There's more to it than that."

"Maybe, but that's the one that matters."

She turned to go inside and he fell in step with her. "Seriously, aren't you nervous about this at all? I mean the responsibility for molding another human being . . . I don't know how parents do it."

"Most of them fail."

"And that terrifies me."

"That's why you will be great at it. You understand how important it is."

She held the door while he stepped through. "Did you get it when you were raising Mark?"

"Not starting out, and after a while his mother had shut me out." He set the bags of books at the foot of the stairs. "I did the best I could within the boundaries she set."

"What if the kids think I'm like the wicked stepmother or something?"

He smiled again. "They will love you. They'll probably like you better than they like me. You're not as grouchy."

"I might be. I've never been around kids. I don't think I've held a baby even."

"We won't be dealing with any babies. You just have to love the kids and that comes naturally."

"You know, no offense, but I'm not sure I trust the parenting advice of a guy who hasn't spoken to his son in seven years." She smiled and kissed his cheek.

"We've spoken. It would take both hands for me to count all the times."

"I'll stick with the books." She left him and headed for the kitchen.

"Fine, let some stuffy psychologist flake teach you how to raise robot children," he called after her. "Mark and Julie probably read books to raise the kids!" He shook his head and pulled the books from one of her bags, held each at arm's length and squinted. *Boys to Men, Raising Teens and Tweens, Taking the Wicked Out of Stepmother.* Cass worried too much. She would be the best thing to ever happen to those kids.

Monday, September 7, Mombasa

Mark shuffled down the aisle away from the pulpit where he'd preached for the last seven years. If he closed his eyes, he could still see the folks packed in yesterday, hanging on his every word as he tried to explain why he was leaving.

He read from Jonah and confessed that God gave him a mission, one that was hard, one that he didn't want to take on. Since he ran from that call a great storm had arisen, and he had to surrender now before he and his family were thrown overboard and swallowed up.

Of course, no one in Nineveh used the legal system to try and strip everything from Jonah.

"Would the fish be easier?"

Mark opened his eyes to see Peter Bakari standing in the doorway. "If it would be over in three days, I might consider it."

The older man squinted and smiled. "Is our idea of easier truly easier? I am not so certain."

"I don't know, not going to court with my dad and his lawyer, having my wife smile at me again . . . I'd be willing to risk it."

"Julie is afraid."

"So am I."

"Of your father?"

"Not exactly." He slid his hands into the pocket of his jeans. "I'm . . . this sounds really obnoxious, but I'm afraid I've messed this up badly enough that God won't trust me with anything else. I'm afraid my ministry is over."

"It is changing, but it is not over." He leaned against a bench. "Do not worry for anything here. I have Moses, Simon and Jonas to help me. We will fast and pray."

"Thank you." Mark knew he meant to reassure him, but it hit him wrong. It felt like Peter and the church here didn't need him anyway, so it was just as well that he was taking off. Even entertaining that idea made him feel like a whiny, self-absorbed brat. *Lord, if you bring us through this . . .*

"Peter, I have every intention of coming back to help wrap things up, but if the judge orders visitation, or . . . I don't know what to expect."

"God knows. He will keep you. He will keep us. And He will bring us together again, whether here or before His throne."

"I know that, but my choice is to be back here as quickly as possible."

Peter frowned and tilted his head. "I have one question, though. How is it your judges can take children away from their parents?"

"They are terribly deceived. They think they're doing the right thing. The courts rule against God and His people more and more all the time."

Peter kicked at a small rock that had found its way inside the building. "Your father is a wicked man."

Wicked? Was he? He never thought of his dad that way. Was that the problem? "My father is deceived as well. He's his own god. He doesn't understand evangelism, and he believes it is abusing my children to raise them here. That I'm endangering their lives."

"He said this?"

"His lawsuit says that."

"He is wrong."

"My father is never wrong," Mark muttered. Peter scowled in confusion. "It's sarcasm."

Peter nodded, then he hugged Mark tightly. "I will keep in touch with you on the computer. You must tell us how things proceed."

"I will. Keep praying."

Thursday, September 10, en route to St. Louis

Julie Bolling tried in vain to stretch her legs out in the narrow aisle. The closer they got to St. Louis, the smaller the planes became and for this last leg from O'Hare, they were on a commuter. Janie sat beside her, watching carefully out the window, fascinated by the lights below. Mark dozed across the aisle and Ben and Matt sat in the row in front of him.

The kids were great travelers, real pros, but in the thirty hours they had been on busses, planes or in airports, none of them had mentioned what they might be facing once they landed. She couldn't blame them. To let the lawsuit into her thoughts meant it would drag with it the perverse possibility that Doug Bolling would somehow end up with her children.

God would not let that happen. He would show Doug that it didn't pay to interfere with God's work or to persecute His children, especially if they were blood relatives. *Just this morning, or no, yesterday . . . whenever, Lord, I read in Psalms where David asked You to vindicate him. That's what we need, Lord. We need You to step in, in a dramatic and miraculous way, and stand up for us.*

She heard Mark breathe deeply. *How can he sleep? He's been so calm through all this.* Maybe it was because he was more accustomed to dealing with his father. That had to be it.

She glanced at her watch and quickly counted ahead to Naples time. It was early tomorrow morning, like middle of the night early, there. Maybe one of her parents was awake, or maybe both of them. Maybe they were praying and that's why she was thinking about them. When Julie told her mother about Doug's lawsuit, she couldn't find words to respond. Her mother had always liked Doug, seemed to connect with him. This grieved her like losing a close friend, she said. She ached for what they were going through but she never dreamed Doug could betray all of them this way.

Oh, but he had.

The captain came on the loudspeaker announcing their final approach into St. Louis Lambert Airport. Janie shifted in her seat, and grinned broadly at her mother. Landings were almost as much fun as takeoffs in her mind.

Mark roused and smiled. Julie reached across the aisle and took his hand. They always held hands during takeoffs and landings. She admitted it was superstitious, but she felt better knowing he was there.

The pilot eased the plane down onto the runway smoothly and gently. Knowing the trip was over at last unleashed a wave of heavy exhaustion on Julie's mind and body. She wanted to curl up somewhere and sleep for ten or twelve hours, but she'd have to be charming and diplomatic for David Shannon instead.

He and his wife were meeting them at the airport and giving them a place to stay. It wasn't that she was ungrateful. No, she deeply appreciated the sacrifices David and Jan were making on their behalf. She just . . . she wanted to go through this in private. Staying with someone would mean they were always "on," that their guard could never drop, that they had to be the perfect picture of grace.

Tomorrow afternoon they would have their first meeting with Chuck Molinsky and Fletcher Durant, their lawyers. Maybe then it would seem real. Sitting in a lawyer's office discussing what they could do to keep their children . . . it didn't get much more intense than that.

Matt had protested that he should be allowed to go to the meeting since he was fourteen. In some states, that would get him his own representation and a completely separate proceeding, he claimed, then produced a stack of papers from his research. They, nonetheless, adamantly and unswervingly refused.

When the plane finally came to a stop, Julie looked over to her husband. "Welcome home," she said.

"Is it?" Mark answered, as he worked to unwedge his carry-on from under the seat in front of him.

"I thought you were the one with faith and resolve."

"I'm tired, Julie, and the battle hasn't even started."

"Daddy, will Grandpa be here to meet us?" Janie asked as she stepped into the aisle in front of her mother.

"No. I'm not sure when you'll see Grandpa."

"Do we have to wait till court?"

"Maybe. I'll find out more tomorrow when I talk to Mr.

Molinsky." Mark took Janie's hand as she bounded down the jetway to the gate area. Julie fell in line behind the boys, after they yawned and stretched. The airport was quiet and relatively empty so it wasn't too difficult to keep the family together, unlike JFK and Heathrow, and they didn't have to rush anywhere. The only connection was meeting up with David and Jan Shannon.

The Shannons were waiting just on the other side of the security checkpoint, smiling and waving. "Janie! You are so big now!" Jan bent down and scooped Jane up into her arms, and Julie felt the slightest twinge seeing someone else with her baby.

"I'm seven going on seventeen Mommy says."

"You may not want that," Jan said. "I have a sixteen-year-old girl. She's a handful." Jan hugged Julie and whispered, "This will work out. I've seen God do amazing, incredible things."

Mark and David shook hands, then David turned to shake hands with Matt and Ben. "Are you hungry?"

"Always," Mark said, answering for his sons, and Ben rolled his eyes.

"Let's grab your luggage and get out of here, then," David said. "I'm sure you're sick of airports."

"You may be sorry you came to get us when you see our luggage," Julie said.

"Nonsense," David said. "Besides, I brought a church van, so it's not a problem." The only advantage of flying on a smaller plane was that it didn't take as long for the luggage to be offloaded, but it was still after eleven before they were all in the van. As soon as David got away from the airport, he pulled into a Wendy's. "It's not much, but it's open."

"Doesn't matter," Ben said. "They have French fries!" He scrambled out of the van with Janie and Matt close behind. "And Matt, stop trying to act so cool. We all know you're as excited as Janie and me."

Soon everyone was settled, with the kids at one table and the adults nearby. Mark and David delivered with trays, burgers, fries and Frostys to Julie and the rest of her jet-lagged family.

David glanced at the children, then leaned up to the table and asked quietly, "So where do things stand?"

Julie wanted to scream out, "Can we have a few hours of peace?" but she silently chewed her hamburger and let Mark answer.

"I'll find out more tomorrow," Mark said. "Chuck and Fletcher have all the supporting documents my father filed. He's not claiming Julie and I are unfit, just that the environment is detrimental to the growth and development of the kids."

"How? What's his evidence?"

"Mostly that it's a third-world country and supposedly the kids are denied access to adequate schooling and medical care. I think Janie's broken arm was what set him off. We had to send copies of her x-rays and medical charts."

Julie dropped her eyes and hoped David and Jan didn't notice she was picking at her baked potato without really eating any of it. Mark knew good and well that it was Jane's broken arm, or rather, his decision not to tell his father that sparked this.

"But it healed, didn't it?" Jan asked.

"Pcrfectly. They couldn't have done any better at Barnes." Mark took a long drink from his Coke. "My father has a lot of money, and nothing else to do with it. I'm sure he's hired some high-powered attorney who's going to nitpick his way through our lives looking for anything he can find to make us look bad."

"Just like Daniel," David said. "The only accusation against him they could find was his religion."

"We're not quite that spotless, David, thanks anyway." Mark smiled the perfect pastoral smile, full of deferential humility—or something else—and took another drink from his Coke.

"I still think this is an opportunity for you," David said. "I hate that you have to go through it, but I really believe God is going to turn this into something tremendous."

Julie knew she was supposed to agree, and join in with some pious affirmation about how God was going to move in a mighty way, but she was empty. Empty of affirmations, headed toward empty of faith. If God was going to do something tremendous, she needed some reassurance before she'd believe it.

Friday, September 11

Mark squeezed Julie's hand before sliding his hand up the steering wheel of David Shannon's compact car. He carefully turned into the parking lot at Benton, Davis and Molinsky just before two o'clock. All morning he'd tried to encourage her to stay positive. They had prayed. Her parents were praying along with everyone else they knew. God was listening, he said.

She knew he was right, but in her heart she battled the most smothering fear she'd ever known. What if they lost their children? Granted, the chances were so small as to be nonexistent, but there was still a chance. Mark had his ministry. All she had were the children.

She pasted on the smiling face everyone expected and caught up with Mark at the outer door. He reached for her hand before opening the door for her. The receptionist was a lively blonde woman who smiled broadly as soon as they stepped inside.

"Good afternoon, Mr. and Mrs. Bolling?"

Mark nodded and reached across her desk to shake her hand. "Mark and Julie, please."

"Mr. Molinsky and Mr. Durant are anxious to see you. Mr. Molinsky's office is right over there." She pointed to a large glassed-in office off to her left. "Just go right in."

"Thank you," Mark said, and Julie relaxed ever so slightly.

Before they reached the office, a man opened the door

for them and extended his hand. She immediately recognized Chuck's voice from the telephone. He was about her mother's age with close-cropped gray hair like her father's. She relaxed a little more. His shirt sleeves were rolled up and his tie was slightly loosened at his neck. A suit jacket hung on the rack just behind the door. She suspected that Chuck's suit and shoes cost more than all the suits Mark had ever owned put together. Still, Chuck was warm and friendly and his blue eyes twinkled.

"Please, come in and have a seat. This is Fletcher Durant." He motioned to a man wedged into an office chair, dressed in a white suit and black string tie. All that Julie could think was, 'If Colonel Sanders had been a whale, he would be our lawyer.' Then she was eternally thankful Ben wasn't with them. The lawyer wore heavy black-rimmed glasses with thick lenses. Every breath brought a soft wheeze and perspiration beaded across his forehead.

"Is this them, Charlie?" he bellowed. Apparently he was deaf, too.

"Yes, Mark and Julie Bolling."

The man made no effort to stand, so Mark crossed in front of her to shake hands.

"I'm Mark."

Durant leaned forward and squinted. "You need to firm up that handshake, son."

"Yes, sir. This is my wife." He gave Julie a guiding push toward Durant and she smiled graciously and reached for his hand.

"Good heavens, boy. Your wife's got a better grip than you do. Does she run things?"

"No, sir," Julie answered. "Mark runs the household."

"But he lets you talk for him." Durant snorted and settled back in his chair. If he was their best hope, they were doomed.

Julie followed Mark's lead and took a seat across the desk from Chuck, keeping a watch on Fletcher Durant out of the corner of her eye.

"Do you know what time zone you're in yet?" Chuck asked as he spread folders out on the desk.

"Not really," Mark answered. "My body says it's ten p.m., so don't be offended if I drop off."

Chuck grabbed a pair of glasses that lay on the desk as he sat down. "I think we are in very good shape," he said opening a thick folder that lay in front of him.

"You think?" Julie asked. "Mr. Molinsky, I need you to be more confident than that."

"Don't you worry about Charlie," Durant piped up and pointed at Chuck. "He knows what he's about."

She was not reassured.

"I am extremely confident, Mrs. Bolling." He slid some papers across the desk. "These are the results from the academic testing firm we hired. Your children are at or above grade level in every subject, sometimes two grade levels above average." He snapped another folder open. "We have the orthopedic surgeon's statement on your daughter's arm. He looked at the x-rays and said the Kenyan doctors did everything properly."

"That's a relief," Mark said, glancing through the paperwork. "That was his main complaint." He handed the papers to her and she made a show of studying them.

"Your house is well within the average range size-wise." He slid his glasses off and leaned back in his chair. This is where he would say, 'but there's a problem.' He waited for Mark to lay the papers aside and look up. "Mark, your father has a girlfriend."

"I know."

"Are you aware she lives with him?"

"Yes."

"How old are you, Marcus?" Durant asked.

"Thirty-six."

Durant whistled and then almost giggled. "Well, now, Charlie. Papa Bear done found him a honey."

"What's . . . he talking about?" Mark glanced between Chuck and Fletcher.

"You haven't met the girlfriend?"

"No, why?"

"She's your age, like thirty-seven, I think." He dropped his glasses down and pulled another folder closer. "Yeah, here it is."

"Is she okay?"

"She's fine, college-educated, not so much as a traffic ticket."

"But there's no way a judge would take children from a stable home and place them with an unmarried couple. Is that what you're saying?" Julie asked.

"Especially not with a gold digger," Fletcher said.

Chuck nodded. "You have to make a very extreme case to take a seven-year-old from her mother. Whether Mark's father can provide a better home is not the issue. He has to prove, irrefutably prove, that you and Mark cannot provide a good home. I don't think he's done that. Not by a long shot."

"You keep saying 'think,'" Julie said.

"Nothing in life is certain, especially not the courts—"

"Mr. Molinsky, this may be just another case for you, but these are *my* children, this is *my life*, and frankly, I'm a little concerned about your lack of experience, nor am I adequately impressed with your so-called expert."

"Julie!" Mark turned to face her. "Chuck, I'm sorry."

"No, I understand completely if you want to hire another attorney, but if it were my children, I wouldn't want anyone else but Fletcher. He will win this."

"He's just sat here the whole time! Making these off-the-wall comments! The other lawyer will make a fool out of him!"

Durant laughed and slid off his glasses. He pulled a large handkerchief from the pocket of his suit jacket and began polishing the lenses. "Mrs. Bolling, you have trust issues. You don't trust me, or Chuck, or your husband. I have never lost a custody case. Never. And I don't intend to start now." His voice was calm and measured. "Mr. Bolling, you act as if you're a guilty man, like you have nothing to win. Tell me, how does one become a successful minister and missionary when he's already given up?"

Mark sat in stunned silence for several moments. Finally, Julie spoke. "So this was all an act?"

"Think of it as a test. One that you failed." Fletcher slid his glasses back on. "I was looking for weaknesses, measuring your responses, trying to discover any avenue or attack that might be used against you. You both need to confront and correct these items before we walk into court. Victor Wiley will show no mercy. He will make outrageous charges, outlandish statements and Henry Whitmire will not rein him in. You must endure it all with grace and dignity. Am I clear?"

Julie nodded sheepishly.

"The victory is already yours, Mrs. Bolling. You must decide if you will ride into battle as more than a conqueror." He cleared his throat and the chair squeaked as he leaned forward. "Mr. Bolling, your father does not want your children. He wants something else. Figure out what that is, and this will be done."

"So I should try to meet with him? Because I asked once and he turned me down."

"He'll meet with you. He's a good man."

"How do you know?"

"I've talked to dozens of people who know him. People living in homes he's built, people who worked for him. It's a very consistent picture."

Mark smiled and shook his head. "But they don't know the real Doug Bolling."

"What makes you certain that you do?" Mark scowled, but said nothing. "Now, I have several ideas about your father and his legal situation if you'd care to hear them." When no one spoke, Fletcher continued. "He's a self-made man. It bothers him deeply that he's had to turn to a stranger, a lawyer, for help. He didn't choose Wiley because of his reputation. He chose Wiley because Victor works in the law firm his lover uses."

Mark bristled in his seat.

"It's pure dumb luck he ended up with the second best

REFINED   47

custody lawyer in St. Louis." He smiled.

"How do you know all this?"

"His lover had a restraining order against an ex-boyfriend. Harrison Crawford handled it for her." He paused. "Then Crawford defended the ex-boyfriend. I haven't quite resolved that yet." He clucked his tongue twice and stared across the office. "But that's irrelevant to us."

Chuck began closing and stacking the folders on his desk. Julie had almost forgotten he was in the office with them. "So the meeting is over?"

"We can stay the rest of the afternoon if you'd like," Chuck answered. "You have other questions?"

"As a matter of fact, I do. What's your angle? You don't do family law. Why are you even part of this? Why aren't we at Mr. Durant's office if he's the expert?"

"Fletcher doesn't have an office. He's losing his eyesight and only consults these days. I've done the legwork, and paperwork, but it's all been at Fletcher's direction and for the record, he is your attorney. I got involved because David Shannon called me. His father was my pastor for years. I owe Phil more than I could ever explain. I'll take any opportunity I can get to pay him back."

"We're grateful to have you on this," Mark said, diplomatically. "Both of you."

"Thank you," Durant said, "and Mrs. Bolling, don't worry. I will be properly attired for our court appearance."

"Why are you being like this?" Mark asked, even before he put the car in gear.

"Like what?"

"All . . . I don't know . . . belligerent."

"I'm belligerent? Because I want to know what's going on with our case? Because I asked questions?"

"You were demanding."

"And that guy is a flake!"

"He's on our side. He clearly knows what he's doing and he's not going to be intimidated by anything my dad or his lawyer tries." He backed out of the parking place and began mentally reviewing what Fletcher said, dwelling on the lawyer's pronouncement that he acted like a guilty man who'd already lost.

"But I don't feel safe with him. This is too important for me to have doubts."

"You don't trust him. Just like he said."

"Mark, I just met him, and considering how he acted when we got there, I think it's justified."

"Do you trust me?"

"Of course I do." And she dropped her eyes.

"When I asked you to marry me, I asked if you trusted me to take care of you. Do you trust me to take care of you and the kids?"

"Why are you asking me this now?" Again, her eyes darted away.

"Because we have to be on the same side through this. We can't let this conflict with my dad come between us."

"It won't. How could it?"

"Matt, Ben, there's plenty more spaghetti, if this doesn't fill you up." Jan Shannon set a heaping plate in front of each boy. Julie smiled at their unabashed enthusiasm. At least they felt like eating. "Just make sure there's a little bit for Maddie to warm up when she gets home."

"How late will she be?" Julie asked.

"The game's a couple of hours away, so I don't expect her until midnight. She'll call when they get on the road."

Julie felt her stomach tense. Yes, it was perfectly normal for a high school student to go on a trip to an away game. Yes, Mark was gone like that all the time, but Julie wasn't sure she could ever muster such a casual attitude toward her children being gone. No, she didn't trust the lawyer, and she deeply wanted to trust Mark, but, after he'd lied to her about his call to the ministry, and kept the struggle to himself to maintain appearances, she had reservations. After this court thing resolved itself, they needed some time, probably some counseling too, before they moved into the next phase of marriage and ministry.

"So Maddie plays football?" Ben asked.

"She plays flute," Jan answered, then added with a smile, "it's a lot safer." She took the seat next to Jane, at the opposite end of the table from David.

David glanced around the table, then bowed his head. "Father, thank You. Thank You for this meal, for Jan and Julie and Janie who prepared it for us. I know that the circumstances are not what we would have chosen, but what a blessing it is to share this meal together. Bless the Bollings during this time and help them to feel Your presence. In Jesus' name. Amen."

After swallowing his first bite, Mark said, "Chuck seems like a good guy."

"He is. Did he tell you his story?"

Mark shook his head. "He was all business."

"I've heard him tell it in public, so I don't think it's a big secret anymore. Chuck had an affair several years ago, but he and his wife were able to work through everything. Then years later the other woman showed up with a boy that turned out to be Chuck's son."

Julie glanced at Mark, then the children. David should've saved the story for an adult audience, but Mark just smiled and winked at her.

"The boy's mother was killed in an automobile accident and Chuck and Bobbi are raising Jack. They are such a tremendous example of grace and forgiveness, and a testimony to God's power to heal." David took a drink from his glass of water. "You should have Chuck tell you."

"All he said was that he owed your dad."

"That was one of the last things my father did. In fact, he died without getting to see them reconciled, but Mom said he always knew they would."

Julie dropped her head. Great. The lawyer who's not a flake is an adulterer. An adulterer who has no experience in family law.

Thankfully, David asked Ben what he liked to do, and the boy launched into an intricate explanation of cricket. He smiled at Jane every time he called it "bug-ball" and she dutifully winced. Typical dinner time chatter. That little hint of normal life helped Julie push the thoughts of attorneys, lawsuits and courtrooms to the back of her mind.

They lingered over the pie Jan had picked up until at last she stood and began stacking the dishes. The doorbell's chime stopped her cold. "Who in the world?" David left the dining room to answer it.

Moments later, he returned, pale and wide-eyed. Jan set the stack of plates back on the table in very slow motion. "David? Is Maddie . . . "

David didn't make eye contact with her, though. He swallowed and gripped the back of his chair. "Mark, Julie, it's a sheriff's deputy. He's got a court order. He's here for the children."

Five

Mark's brain told his feet and his legs to stand up and go see for himself, but the shock paralyzed him. "For the children? Why?"

He felt Julie's hand on his arm. "He . . . he can't . . . can he?"

Across the table, Matt threw down his napkin and slid his chair back, his eyes narrow and his jaw tight with determination.

"Matt, stay here," Mark said without ever making eye contact with the teenager. He took Julie's hand and led her into David's living room, to the unreal sight of a deputy sheriff standing with his hat in one hand, a folded court order in the other.

"I'm Mark Bolling," he said without extending his hand.

"Sir, I have a court order to take Matthew Bolling, Benjamin Bolling and Jane Bolling into protective custody. If you'll have the children get their personal belongings—"

"Wait," Julie interrupted. "You're here to do what?"

"To take the children into protective custody."

"Where? Where are you taking them?"

"Ma'am, I can't tell you that. A court-appointed guardian will look after them—"

"For how long?" Mark asked.

"Sir, you are scheduled to appear in court Tuesday morning at ten o'clock."

He dropped Julie's hand and took a step toward the phone on the end table. "Wait, I want to call my lawyer—"

"Sir, interference with the execution of a court order is a crime—"

"I'm not interfering . . . I'm trying to understand." He had read First Peter again this morning. Submit yourself to every ordinance of man for the Lord's sake, it said. Submit. Surrender. But his kids . . . he looked back toward the dining room, then into Julie's eyes. She wouldn't understand. He had to start following God, though. Following and not simply asking God for a rubber stamp on his plans.

"Call Chuck, then get the kids' things together." His voice wavered. "I'll be right there to help you."

"What am I supposed to tell them?"

"Tell them it's only for a few days. It'll work out."

"How can you be sure?"

He couldn't respond. Julie yanked her hand away from his and turned back to the dining room.

The deputy relaxed his stance slightly.

Mark took a deep breath and tried to quell the dizziness and the quiver in his stomach. "We're . . . my father has sued us for custody of the kids, but we haven't been to court yet. Do you have any idea what prompted this?"

"A protective custody order is issued when the children need to be removed from a domestic situation for their safety."

"Safety! We're their parents, for crying out loud!"

"Sir, it's not up to me to decide whether the order is reasonable or justified."

Mark leaned on the arm of the nearest chair to steady himself. "Can I see the order?"

The deputy handed the paper over and Mark slowly unfolded it. The seal and signatures looked official enough, but this was insane. Insane and wrong. "I can't fight this?"

"Not tonight, sir."

"So he can steal my children, keep them until Tuesday, and there's not a living thing I can do about it?"

"I'm sorry, sir."

Julie had to make her legs move to get her out of the living room. Doug couldn't be this cold-hearted, this . . . evil. He just couldn't. He and Mark had their issues, but this . . . nothing that had ever happened between them justified this. This was unforgivable.

The woman. She had to be the one behind this. Doug loved the kids. They all agreed to that. Didn't the lawyer say Doug hired a guy the woman knew? That was too easy. Didn't things really break down between Mark and Doug once he started seeing that woman? Why would she want the children, though? She had Doug and his money. Why bother with them? What was she after?

Jan and David had gathered Matt, Ben and Janie in the kitchen, putting an extra room between them and the sheriff's deputy. Jan leaned against the counter with Janie up in her arms. The boys hovered close to Jane, the way they always did.

"Is this for real? Do we have to go with him?" Matt's jaw was set in righteous indignation.

"Yes."

"I'm not going," he said. "I don't need anybody's protection."

"You have to go or we will all go to jail." Julie snatched up the cordless phone without bothering to ask and punched in numbers. "This is serious." In spite of the ringing, her mother's ears were attuned to the hushed voices of her kids.

"Do we have to go to jail?" Janie whispered to Ben.

"We haven't done anything wrong."

"Where do we have to go?"

"I don't know, yet. They'll tell us."

She heard the click as someone picked up on the other end. She didn't wait for the 'hello.' "This is Julie Bolling," she shouted into the phone. "There is a deputy sheriff here to get my children! Why didn't you stop this?"

"One moment. I'll get Chuck."

Julie kept talking anyway. "He's got a court order to take them into protective custody! How can he do this? How can you let him do this?" Then she dissolved into tears.

Matt stepped over and took the phone from her. "Goodbye," he said then clicked it off. "Let's get our stuff," he said quietly to Ben and Janie.

"We all go together, don't we?" Ben asked. "'Cause I'm not leaving Janie."

Julie felt a wave of nauseating tightness. She never considered . . . surely the children wouldn't be separated. Surely.

Mark came into the kitchen, and motioned for the children to come close. He pulled a chair over and lifted Janie onto his knee. "This sounds much worse than it is. The deputy couldn't tell me where he's taking you, but he let me ask him some questions to try and figure it out. He's taking you to Grandpa's house."

"Why would Grandpa—" Matt began, but Mark cut him off with a raised hand.

"I can't believe that Grandpa would do this just to hurt us," Mark said. Julie couldn't suppress a huff, and he turned to look at her as he spoke. "This is something his lawyer told him to do."

"But Mark . . . " Julie tried to speak, to protest, but tears choked off her words. Where will it end? What will he do next?

"Now, today is Friday." Mark turned back to the children. He reached for Janie's hand and counted off on her little fingers. "You'll be there Saturday, Sunday and Monday. Three days. Then Tuesday morning, we'll go see the judge."

"With you?" Janie asked.

"Grandpa will take you, but we'll meet you there."

"Does Grandpa really think you're abusing us?" Ben asked.

"Of course not, but lawyers sometimes do dramatic things to try to win their case."

"But he's lying," Matt said. "How can you win when you lie?"

It happens all the time, Matt, Julie thought. *It happens all the time.*

"The judge will figure that out. You know, I've been reading First Peter a lot lately and he talks about how important it is to endure unfair treatment like Christ did, without talking disrespectfully or threatening to get even or anything like that. Jesus let God handle it."

"But Dad—" Matt protested.

"No buts, Matt. This is completely unfair, the accusations are false, and the only reason this is happening is because we've chosen to live our lives in obedience to God's call. I know that, but we can't walk away because it got hard."

"Aren't you upset?"

"Matt, I've never been betrayed like this. I'm devastated."

"You don't act like it," he said with a suspicious scowl.

"Well, my first reaction was to go punch your grandpa in the face, but I can't do that."

I wish you would, Julie thought.

"So are we supposed to just go act like it's a sleepover?" Ben asked. Julie wouldn't correct him for the sarcasm in his voice. Not this time.

"You don't have to pretend like everything is okay, but you can still be respectful." Mark patted Janie's knee. "It'll all work out." He kept saying that. So far nothing had worked out.

"Who's going to tuck me in?" Janie asked. "And does Grandpa even know how to say prayers?"

"Maybe you can teach him."

"He's a grownup," Janie said.

"Grownups learn some of their biggest lessons from little kids."

"Really?"

"Really. Now let's get your things together. Remember, it's just three days."

"It's five," Matt corrected then he trudged out of the kitchen. Mark lifted Janie off his lap and led her out with Ben following.

"He acted like this happens every day," Julie said quietly, ignoring the fact that the Shannons were still in the room. "He can't let him get away with this." She pushed back from the table and followed her family out of the kitchen.

The children had hardly unpacked yet, so gathering their belongings consisted of repacking their pajamas and toothbrushes. Mark carried Janie's suitcase to the living room with Matt and Ben following, lugging their bags. He handed the suitcase to the deputy. He hugged Matt, then kissed the boy on the top of his head. Mark then leaned over just slightly to hug and kiss Ben. "I think you've grown since we got here." Finally, he knelt down and Janie ran to him, throwing her arms around his neck. He squeezed her tightly, and then kissed her cheek.

Julie also hugged and kissed each of the children, but she couldn't bear to tell them goodbye. She had to turn away when the deputy escorted them out the front door. Before Mark could reach out to hold her, she collapsed in the floor and sobbed.

———————

Ben eased himself into the front seat of the deputy's unmarked car. He always, always sat in the back with Jane, but when Matt growled at him to sit up front, he decided this wasn't the time to argue. Glancing in the rearview mirror, he saw Matt buckle Janie in, her eyes wide with intimidated wonder. When Matt slumped back to his own seat, he caught Ben's eye and just shook his head slowly.

The whole time they packed up their stuff, Matt never let up from his low grumbling drone. "This is stupid," he said. "How can they do this without our knowledge or consent? Protective custody? Protected from what? Why don't we get a say?" And on and on.

If Matt had ever let him talk, he would've said, "For once, just accept it. For Jane's sake. For Mom and Dad's sake." But Matt never took a breath.

As the deputy rounded the car, Ben turned to Jane and quickly crossed his eyes. She gave him a faint smile and then stared out the window. He hoped she'd be okay. It was only for the weekend. Besides, everybody whispered that Grandpa was rich. He did send some very cool presents at Christmas and on birthdays. That's it. Just relax and enjoy the weekend. No reason to get all upset.

The deputy slid in behind the steering wheel. "All set?" Ben nodded as if it made a difference. They rode in silence for several minutes, then Ben decided this may be the only time he would ever be in a police car so he might as well enjoy it. He studied every detail of the car's interior and the deputy's uniform. Maybe he should be a cop when he grew up. There had to be worse things than carrying a gun, and the deputy's was huge. The polished wooden grip was shinier than any piece of furniture Ben had ever seen.

"It's a .38," the deputy said, startling him.

All right, since the guy knew he was curious, he might as well ask him. "You ever shoot anybody?"

"No."

Ben didn't hide his disappointment. "Ever been shot at?"

"A couple of times."

"But you didn't shoot them back?"

"Sometimes it does more harm than good to return fire. Innocent people can get hurt."

"Is it fun being a cop?"

"I like it. There's a lot of paperwork, though. I don't like that very much."

"Me either." In the rearview mirror, Ben saw Janie slip her thumb into her mouth. She hadn't done that since she was four. "So, you haul little kids around a lot?"

"Not too often."

The deputy turned onto a long residential street, and

Ben thought they might be getting close. "My mom and dad are good parents," he blurted out. Matt huffed from the back seat.

The deputy turned his head, and looked Ben in the eyes. "I know."

Ben nodded. Everything would be okay. At the end of the winding street, sheltered from the other houses by distance and by full maple trees, sat a large, tan brick home. A lighted chandelier was visible through the huge windows over the front doorway.

"It's like a castle," Janie said softly.

"It's just a house," Matt corrected.

The deputy pulled into the driveway, up to the three-car garage, and turned off his car. "Matthew, Benjamin and Jane, your grandfather, Douglas Bolling, is your court-appointed temporary guardian. If you have problems here, your parents cannot come and get you. That will be violating a court order." He shifted and pulled out his wallet and handed Ben and Matt each a business card. "Call me. I will come and get you."

"Then where will you take us?"

"Someplace safe. I don't think you'll have any problems, though." He reached for his hat, and turned to Matt and Janie. "Are you ready to go in?"

"Can we have a minute alone first?" Matt asked. "Just here in the car?"

"Sure," the deputy answered. He got out of the car and waited by the front bumper.

"I think we should pray," Matt said. Ben shrugged and reached around his seat for Janie's hand, hoping he got the dry one. "Heavenly Father . . . "

Ben opened an eye and looked at his brother. "What's the matter? Why'd you quit?"

"I don't know what to pray for."

"Then why'd you want to pray?"

"It's what Mom and Dad would do."

"But they know what to say."

"Not always, I bet." He looked out at the deputy leaned

against the front bumper. "I don't want to keep him waiting. I think I've got it." He closed his eyes, and cleared his throat. "Heavenly Father, we don't know what we're getting into. It sounds like things have gone completely crazy. Help me and Ben and Janie take it. Help us do the right things. Help us not miss Mom and Dad too much and help them not worry about us too much. Amen."

Matt opened his eyes and looked over to his sister. "Are you ready for this?" She shook her head, then looked from Matt to Ben. Ben smiled at her. Janie looked back at Matt and nodded. "Let's go in, then."

———————

Doug was more nervous than he would have admitted, watching from the dining room window as the sedan eased into his driveway. The deputy got out, but the kids didn't. "Do you think he's waiting for me to go out there and get them?"

Cass leaned up until her chin rested on his shoulder. "He'll come and get you if that's what he wants. They're probably scared to death. Did the sheriff have to go get them?"

"The lawyer said this was how it had to be done. They're here. That's what's important." The rear passenger door of the sedan swung open. He swallowed hard. "They're getting out of the car." He pointed out the window. "Matthew is practically a man now. Look at him. And Ben. Oh . . . and there's Jane."

"She's adorable. How long has it been since you've seen them?"

"Since they left for Africa."

"How could Mark keep the kids away from you like that?"

"Supposedly, he's protecting them from my evil influence."

"But shouldn't he want to be a good influence on you?" She smiled and took his hand.

"You'd think that, wouldn't you? I guess I'm a lost cause."

"Maybe the kids can rescue you."

"I thought I was rescuing them."

The deputy rang the doorbell then took a step back, and Ben followed his lead. Matt crowded him from behind. He was about to turn around and tell Matt maybe he should stand in the front since he was older when the door swung open. Jane gasped softly.

Ben didn't remember very much about his grandfather. He was pretty sure there were some pictures in his baby book, but if he hadn't been told this was his grandfather's house he wouldn't have recognized the man at the door. Except for his eyes. When he smiled, Ben knew.

"It's so good to see you kids." Ben heard a sniff behind him. Matt wasn't buying it.

The deputy handed over Janie's suitcase. "Mr. Bolling, you're aware of the hearing Tuesday at ten?"

"Yes, of course."

"Kids, you have my card." The deputy tipped his hat, then turned and left.

"Come in, come in." His grandpa patted him on the back as he stepped through the door. Ben could see into the formal dining room off to his right. The railing for the staircase in front of them became the rail for the second floor hallway. He figured with a good enough running start, he could slide in his socks from the stairs to the front door. His agenda for tomorrow was set.

"You've all changed so much. Matt, what are you, fourteen now?"

"Yes, sir." Matt took Janie's hand and stepped through the doorway into the entry hall.

Their grandpa carefully knelt down to Janie's eye level. "Baby, you don't even know me, do you? Last time I saw you, you were just sitting up good." Ben thought he saw tears in his eyes, so he looked away. It was rude to look at a guy if he was crying.

"Do you really have a pool?" Janie asked.

"Yeah, I do. Do you want to swim in it?"

"Now? At nighttime?"

"Why not? Do you have a swimsuit?" Janie shook her head. "We can fix that." He winked at her, then stood and shook Ben's hand. "Benjamin Douglas, you've become a fine young man, I see."

"Yes, sir." Ben set his bag down, then he noticed the woman. She was really pretty, taller than his mom probably and blonde. But she seemed shy, almost like she was afraid to participate in the hellos. Ben looked at his grandfather, to the woman, then back to his grandfather.

"Oh, I'm sorry." His grandfather stepped back, took the woman's hand and drew her closer. "This is Cassandra Grayson."

"Is she your girlfriend?" Ben asked.

"She's much better than a girlfriend."

"Hi, Ben." The woman reached out and shook his hand. She smiled and waved at Janie, and Janie smiled back. Then the woman held out her hand toward Matt. He stood up straighter, and put a hand on Janie's shoulder to pull her closer to himself.

"She lives here?" Matt asked.

"This house would be a big empty cave if she wasn't here," his grandpa answered.

Matt's eyes narrowed and he glanced at Ben. Oh boy. Here we go.

"We're not, like, restricted or anything while we're here, are we?" Matt asked. His fist was already clenching.

"What do you mean?"

"We're allowed to use the phone, aren't we?"

"Of course. The house is yours. There's a phone in here." He led Matt into the room off to the left.

Ben hated to leave Jane, but he had to talk Matt out of whatever he was thinking. He leaned down and whispered, "Be right back. Gotta keep Matt from being Matt." Janie nodded.

Before Matt picked up the receiver, he looked at their grandfather. "May I have some privacy, please?"

As soon as they were alone, Ben whispered, "What are you doing? You're not calling that deputy, are you?"

"I can't stay here," Matt muttered as he flipped through the phone book. "Not if he's living with her. That's just wrong. She's like, Mom's age. It's sick."

Ben glanced back out to the hallway, watching for Jane and the grown-ups. "Are you crazy? You can't leave!"

"What am I supposed to do?"

"Make this easier on Mom and Dad."

"Staying in the house with a harlot is making things easier on Mom and Dad? Explain that one to me."

Ben sighed deeply. "Well, for starters, I don't think you should call her a harlot—"

"Mom would."

"Dad wouldn't." Ben took a deep breath. "Dad expects us to ride this out. Here." Ben forcefully pointed at the floor. "We're safer here than with whatever strangers that deputy might stick us with. At least here we're with family."

"*She* is not my family."

"Matt, God knows this is not where you want to be. He's not going to take away some of your good-boy points for staying."

"Ben, you're compromising with evil—"

"I am not! I'm a kid."

Matt set his jaw and put a finger in Ben's chest. "You're supposed to be an example—"

"So are you!" Ben lowered his voice. "Janie will freak out if we go."

Matt stood for a moment, glaring at Ben, his jaw tightly clenched. "I'm not sleeping in this house."

"Whatever." Ben rolled his eyes, then turned and left his brother alone in the office.

"Is everything okay?" his grandpa asked.

"Yeah, it's just Matt being Matt," Ben muttered. "Ignore him."

"You want to see the rest of the house?"

"Sure," Ben checked with Janie, and she nodded. "We'd like that."

His grandpa picked up Janie's suitcase. "We'll start with the bedrooms, then. They're right upstairs."

David Shannon slumped on the sofa and buried his face in his hands. The Bollings were his guests and he hadn't protected them the way he should have. They were supposed to have a few days of rest before the custody ordeal began. Instead, the assault was immediate and malicious.

"Lord, have mercy on them. Mark's trying his best to get Julie calmed down, but—"

The doorbell rang again, and David hesitated to answer it. Surely this wasn't another blow to the couple.

He was relieved when he opened the door and saw Chuck Molinsky on his front porch. "Chuck, thanks for coming over so fast. Mark and Julie are in the kitchen."

"Where are the kids?"

"Mark said the deputy took them to his father's house." David closed the door behind Chuck. "Is that legal?"

"Maybe. I need to see the court order."

"Let me get Mark," David said.

Mark was on one knee in front of the kitchen chair where Julie sat. He had Julie's hands clasped in his, pleading, but she was shaking her head. Neither seemed to notice when he walked in, so he cleared his throat. "Chuck's here. He asked to see the court order."

Julie pushed Mark's hands away and charged past David into the living room. "Mr. Molinsky, send us a bill. We won't be needing your services any longer."

Six

"Of course, that's your prerogative, Mrs. Bolling, but I wish you'd at least let me see the court order," Chuck answered.

Mark was two steps behind his wife. "She doesn't mean it—"

"Yes, I do, Mark! He doesn't know what he's doing and Doug took our kids because of it!"

"Here, Chuck." Mark handed over the court order.

Chuck slipped on his glasses and chewed his lip while he read through it. Then he sighed and refolded the paper before he handed it back. "He's had to exaggerate or mislead the judge to get this thing through."

"Which is illegal?"

"At least unethical. Anybody who saw your kids would know they were loved and cared for."

"So we can get them back?" Could it be this easy? He glanced at Julie and she had new hope in her eyes.

"Not until Tuesday. There has to be a hearing within forty-eight hours, but Saturday and Sunday don't count. He played this very well."

"But you didn't see this coming," Julie said.

"Nobody could've seen this," Chuck said.

"What else is there that nobody expects?" Julie snapped. "How much worse is this going to get?"

"I'm not a prophet, Mrs. Bolling, but Fletcher and I

won't fight lies with more lies. We will present your case honestly and truthfully and depend on God to vindicate you."

"That's what I want, Chuck," Mark said. "Exactly."

He swallowed hard. "I cannot tell you how sorry I am. I haven't felt like this much of a failure in long time."

"Maybe this is a time saver. If my father sees that my kids are thriving and they aren't impressed by his money, this thing may be over before it starts."

"You really think so, Mark?" Julie asked. "You think this is what God is doing?"

"Of course," he nodded. "God is doing something. Something big."

"I hope you're right."

"Wow, something smells great!" Ben said as they finished the tour in the kitchen.

Doug smiled and pointed to the counter. "Cass made dinner."

"I had no idea what you guys might like," she said as she slipped around him. "It's breaded chicken over spaghetti with a tomato sauce, all covered with cheese. But I saved some of the chicken out, in case—"

"We already ate," Ben said.

"Oh . . . " Cass's eyes darted from the kids to Doug and back. "Sure . . . it's late. I mean, we eat late. I forget other people eat at normal times." She pulled a plate from the cabinet. "Doug, you still need to eat something."

"You aren't gonna eat?"

"I'm fine," she said, and scooped out a helping of the pasta and chicken. "Water or tea?"

"Water." Doug looked at Ben when she turned to fill a glass for him, then he nodded in Cass's direction.

Ben cleared his throat. "Um, I'll take some of that. If you have enough, that is. Just a little."

Cass spun around. "Really?" Her eyes shone brightly,

and Doug smiled. Ben was all right. They'd gotten him in time. Matt may be a different story.

"Yeah, but not a whole lot."

"Jane?" The little girl shook her head. "Fair enough." Cass opened the refrigerator. "How about chocolate milk?" Jane gave her a bashful smile and nodded. Cass stepped around the island and patted one of the bar stools, then she slid a glass of chocolate milk toward Jane's chair.

Jane looked at Ben, and he nodded, so she climbed up on the seat. Ben took the seat next to hers and Cass slid a plate in front of him.

"How long have you lived here?" Ben asked.

"I built it and we moved in seven years ago," Doug said. "Cass designed the interior without knowing it was going to be her house."

"How did you guys meet? No offense, but you're a lot older than she is."

Cass smiled broadly and handed Doug a plate of food. "We met at a home show, then I did the interior for a house Doug was building," Cass answered. "Now we work together. He builds and I work with the clients on the insides."

"And you worked with him to finish out his own house?"

"He told me he knew nothing about interiors and to just fix it however I wanted."

"It's very cool," Ben said. "It's huge."

"I don't know why I built it this big," Doug admitted. "You guys will help fill it up."

"We're not staying that long," Ben said. He nodded at Jane and took a bite of the pasta.

"Not this time," Doug said. "Maybe some other time you'll get to stay longer."

Ben finished chewing, then laid down his fork. "Do you hate my dad?"

"You don't mess around, do you?" Doug set his plate on the island and took a deep breath. "Ben, I love your dad very much. I don't understand him, though."

"I don't think he understands you either." He looked from Doug to Cass. "I think it's because he's a Christian and you guys aren't."

"That's exactly it." Doug picked his plate up again. "He has no patience with me, but I guess I don't have much patience with him, either."

"Matt's the same way. He's flipping 'cause you guys are living together."

The words rolled off Ben's tongue, but Doug saw Cass step away from the counter, and slide her arms up, almost hugging herself. "Does that bother you, too, Ben?" she asked.

"I don't think so. You seem nice." He looked at Doug. "I don't get why you don't get married."

"It's complicated, Ben," he said softly.

"You know, that's usually what grown-ups say when they don't want to do what they know they should do."

"Are you this smart with everybody?" Doug asked.

"Pretty much," Ben admitted. "My mouth gets me in trouble all the time." He looked around the kitchen for a clock. "Janie, it's past your bedtime. Want me to help you get ready for bed?"

She nodded, and slid down off the barstool. "Thank you for the chocolate milk."

"You're welcome, sweetheart," Cass said.

"We'll be right there," Doug said, watching, waiting until the kids were out of earshot. "Don't say anything. Not a word."

"Out of the mouths of babes." She rinsed Janie's glass and put it in the dishwasher.

"Do you want to get married?"

"No."

"You'd tell me if you did, wouldn't you?"

"No."

"Why not?"

"Because you'd be marrying me out of obligation, and not because you loved me."

He knew she was waiting for him to respond, to affirm that he did love her. "Cass . . . " He rounded the end of the island toward her, but she stepped back away from him.

"Doug, please. I'm not angry, I'm just pragmatic." She absently refolded the dishtowel and laid it across the sink. "I understood years ago that there would always be a limit, an emotional line that you would never cross again." She reached over and switched off the lights under the cabinet. "But you might reconsider if that's what you want, especially if your plan doesn't work out, and it's just us again."

Cass headed upstairs, leaving Doug alone in the darkened kitchen. "I do love you, Cass," he whispered.

———

Julie sat on the sofa in the Shannons' living room, her eyes tightly closed in a vain effort to ease the pain that seemed intent to split her forehead. Less than forty-eight hours ago they had walked away from their ministry in Kenya with absolutely no plan for the future. Mark had no job waiting, no prospects and they had very little savings to fall back on.

Moments ago, her children were escorted out by a deputy sheriff because they were dangerous, unfit parents. Unreal. It was worse than a nightmare or a movie because it was so easy. Bang, bang, boom and her kids were gone. And according to the lawyer, it was all legal.

The lawyer. The best thing she could say about their lawyers was that they were working pro bono.

She felt the jostle of someone joining her on the sofa. She opened one eye and Mark held out a cup of hot tea. "Thanks . . . I . . . " She sat up straighter and took the tea from him.

"We've got an international card. You should call your mom."

She shook her head. "I can't . . . I don't have words." She sipped the tea, then set the cup gently on a coaster on the end table. "I can't wake her up and just . . . you know."

"Yeah." He reached for her hand. "I know you're—"

"Stop. You don't know. You don't know what's gonna

happen. You don't know what I feel like. You don't know it's gonna be okay."

"But God knows all those things—"

"And you suddenly believe that? Everything is out of your hands and you're trying to convince me that you're okay with that?"

He dropped his head, but didn't respond.

"I know you, Mark. You have to be the one to push, and drive and make things happen—"

"And I was wrong. I got us into this mess because I had to set the agenda. I had to make a name for myself, my own way, and not the way God wanted me to."

"So how much more will God have to torment me before you've learned your lesson?"

Again he didn't answer.

"It's not fair. It's not right. I don't understand how God could let this happen."

"I think God is getting ready to do something amazing, and He's making sure we have all the junk out of our hearts and our lives before He takes the next step."

"So our kids are the junk in our lives?"

"Of course not!" He closed his eyes and took a deep breath. "How can I help you? What do you want me to do?"

"Get our kids back."

———————

Before Doug could head upstairs and untangle the mess he'd made with Cass, he remembered he'd left Matt in the office. The teenager stood by the desk, his duffel bag still hanging from his shoulder. "Matthew, can I show you to your bedroom?"

"I'd prefer to sleep outside, sir."

"What are you talking about? I can't let you sleep outside."

"I can't sleep here in the house."

"Why? Because of Cass?"

"I can't be a part of that."

"You've got some very strong convictions, Matt. God forbid that I should make you compromise them." Doug spoke slowly, focusing on his words, trying his best to push down his rising temper. Matt sounded exactly like Mark and Julie. Exactly. He felt his shoulders tightening so he crossed his arms across his chest trying to keep them stretched out. "Can I ask you some questions about this faith of yours?"

"Of course," Matt said. He stood a little taller, almost eye level with Doug.

"Does your religion teach you that you can only associate with people who are good enough?"

"I shouldn't allow myself to be influenced by anything worldly."

"I see," Doug said. "Does Jesus love me, Matt?"

"He loves everyone."

"Then why don't you?" Matt didn't immediately answer, so Doug seized the chance. "See, you're being raised to be judgmental and hard-hearted. There is no love in your religion, Matt, only judgment and condemnation. That so-called wicked woman upstairs loves me more than you or your father—"

"That's not true!" Matt sputtered.

"I only know what I see. Now, everything I have is yours, but if I'm not good enough to have you sleep in my house, then you are more than welcome to sleep outside. Be my guest." He swept his hand in front of him in a wide arc, then left Matt alone in the office.

———

Cass paced in the bedroom, trying to decompress. The kids had been in the house less than an hour and things were already weird. Matt wouldn't even shake her hand. He was just a kid, but if it was like Doug said, and he was parroting what his parents believed, she didn't want to know what they thought about her. Was living with Doug that evil?

Yes, she wanted Doug to marry her, but because he chose to, not because she wanted him to. She loved him, and she knew he loved her more than his own life, and that was all that mattered, right?

And dinner. What a disaster. She should have known better. She couldn't blame the kids for not wanting to eat. And the food was strange. Probably nothing like what they were used to, nothing like what their mother made. She wasn't trying to replace their mother. Not at all. She just wanted to make things comfortable, easier.

If that was possible.

Doug strode into the bedroom and as soon as she saw his furrowed brow and frown, she tensed. "Are you mad at me?"

"What? No, of course not." He sighed and sat down on the edge of the bed. "Matt wants to sleep outside so we don't taint him with our immorality."

"He said that?"

"Not verbatim, but yes, he said that." He shook his head. "He sounds just like Mark and Julie. How can a kid get so self-righteous? Unreal."

"Ben seems to have escaped."

"For now. Another couple of years and he'll be spewing the same kind of condemnation." He lay back on the bed and rubbed his temples. "I didn't teach him that. Mark, I mean. Judy didn't teach him that, either. For her, religion was about comfort and peace."

"What if they're right?" Cass sat on the bed next to him.

"What?" Doug sat back up and faced her.

"What happens if they're right?"

"Don't you start on me, too."

"I'm not. I just . . . I don't know."

"Yes, you do. You can tell me. I can handle it."

She smiled at him. "What's the difference? With the boys, I mean. Ben and Matt both disapproved of us living together. Ben made me uncomfortable, but Matt made you angry."

"Ben didn't judge us. He said he didn't understand it, but he was personable. He wasn't getting his soul dirty like Matt was."

"Then what do we do if Ben is right?"

Just then, a wail erupted from Janie's room, and Cass followed Doug down the hall. Janie was huddled in the corner of her bed, almost completely hidden by her pillow. "You try first," Doug whispered.

"Sweetheart, what's wrong?" Cass asked, gently pulling the pillow away from the little girl's face.

"Mommy," she sobbed.

"I think she's asleep," Doug said.

Cass reached over and lifted Janie onto her lap and cradled her in her arms. "It's all right, sweetheart. Shhh." She smoothed the little girl's hair and rocked her back and forth. The crying continued, though, with great, heaving sobs.

Doug knelt in front of her and tried patting her back. "Janie, you're still asleep. Honey, look. You're safe." It was no use. Janie would not be consoled.

"You think Ben could help?" Cass asked.

"I'll get him."

Moments later Doug returned with Ben, and the boy called out to his sister, "Janie! It's just a dream. It's Ben. Wake up!"

"I want Mommy, Ben! I want to go home!" She started another round of tears.

Cass held Janie tighter, and with tears forming in her own eyes, Cass looked up at Doug, "Can't we take her home?"

"Not with the court order."

"This isn't protecting her, it's torturing her. What does this prove?"

"I know it's hard on everybody, but it's best in the long run."

Cass kissed Janie's forehead. "Sweetheart, you'll be all right."

"Mommy," Janie whimpered. "I miss Mommy."

"I know you do. Grandpa's here and the boys are here."

"I can't hear the boys." She buried her face against Cass's neck.

"They're too far away?" Janie nodded without raising her head.

"I'll sleep in here," Ben said. "Janie, if I sleep in here with you, will that be better?" Again, Janie nodded without raising her head. "I'll get my stuff," Ben said as he walked out of the bedroom.

"You have a good brother," Cass said gently. Janie nodded, and slipped her thumb in her mouth. "Can I get you a tissue?" Janie nodded again, and shifted to sit up on Cass's lap. Cass reached over to the nightstand, and pulled out two tissues. She gently wiped the tears from Janie's cheeks, and brushed the girl's hair back from her face, working around the thumb still in Janie's mouth. "Here, blow." Janie dropped her thumb and blew her nose weakly. "No, blow it like Ben," Cass said. Janie managed a smile, then took a deep breath and blew her nose loudly.

"Hey! That sounded like me," Ben said as he came back in the room.

"It was you," Janie said, smiling at last.

"No, mine is more like this." Ben made loud, honking sounds. "Or maybe more like—" He put his hands up to his nose and squeaked and honked to Janie's delight.

"I think you sound like an elephant, or a rhinoceros."

"I don't even know what a rhinoceros sounds like. How could you?"

"He sounds like this!" She put her hands up to her nose and mouth and made the loudest honk she could.

"You win!" Ben announced. He threw his pillow on the floor by her bed.

"Baby, will you be able to sleep now with Ben here?" Doug asked, and Janie nodded once again. Doug knelt down to her eye level. "I tell you what. We'll go shopping tomorrow and get some things that will make this more like a Janie room. How about that?"

"How?"

"Cass is the expert, but we'll get some sheets and a new comforter. Things like that."

"With ponies?" Janie asked, and Ben rolled his eyes.

"You can pick them out," Doug said. "Will that make it better?"

"Uh huh." She twisted off Cass's lap and flopped back on her pillow. "Papa, will you say prayers with me?"

"Uh, yeah . . . okay," Doug stammered. He traded places with Cass, and took Janie's hand.

"You go first," Janie said.

"Baby, can I be real honest with you?" Doug asked, patting her hand.

"Uh huh," Janie said.

"God doesn't listen when I pray."

"He listens to everybody. That's what Mommy and Daddy say."

"I know that's what they believe, but a long time ago, I prayed for something really hard. It was the only thing that mattered to me. I promised God I would do anything He wanted if He would just answer that one prayer."

"He didn't answer it?" Janie asked.

"No. He did the opposite of what I asked for."

"And you never forgave Him?" Ben asked, startling Doug.

Cass gently put a hand on Doug's shoulder.

"Makes sense," Ben said, dropping back down on his pillow.

"What did you say?" Doug asked.

"I said it makes sense. I don't blame you." He reached up for Janie's other hand. "Here, I'll go first, E-Jane." He bowed his head and closed his eyes. "Father, bless Janie. Help her sleep, and not miss Mom and Dad. Bless Grandpa and Cass and work out this custody thing . . . " He opened his eyes. "Sorry, Grandpa, but you know."

"Pray however you want, Ben," Doug said.

Instead of closing her eyes like the others, Cass watched Doug. She knew him well enough to recognize that flex in his jaw. He wasn't listening to the prayer at all. He was turning Ben's comment over in his mind.

She absently listened as Ben finished and then Janie took her turn pronouncing a blessing on everyone she knew. Doug kissed Janie's forehead and switched off the light. "Goodnight, guys." He followed Cass back to the bedroom. "I don't think I'm sleepy yet. I may go sit out on the deck. You want to come?"

"It's Ben, isn't it?" Cass asked. "He shook you up."

"He sounds like Judy, like Julie's mother." He sat on the edge of the bed again. "You know, Julie's parents are missionaries, too. This whole Kenya thing was her idea." Cass sat down on the bed close to him. "Mark was a mama's boy and after his mother died, he found some other woman who could run his life for him."

"That's harsh."

"Wait until you meet her."

"We'll be on opposite sides of the hearing room. I doubt there will be much chitchat."

"Maybe not."

In the quiet, Cass couldn't help but think of the little girl down the hallway. Would she be able to sleep? Had they already caused some kind of psychological damage? "Doug, what do we do tomorrow night when Janie gets hysterical again?"

"She'll be fine."

"What if she's not? You know, I felt like the wicked witch, keeping a little girl away from her mother."

"It's the court, not you. And if her mother wasn't so—"

"Her mother can't be that bad. She obviously loves her, and don't you think young children need to be with their mother?"

"Her mother is the problem."

"I thought Mark was the problem, or religion was the problem, or Africa was the problem."

Doug let a long, deep breath escape. "Mark would be happier, the kids would be happier and God knows I would be happier, if he just divorced her and came back to St. Louis."

"You're not happy now?"

"Cass, that's not what I said," Doug moaned, hanging his head.

"I was just checking," she teased. Cass slipped her arm around his and laid her head on his shoulder. "You were very sweet with Janie."

"You did most of the work."

"But she asked her Papa to pray with her, not me."

"Yeah," he whispered. "She did, didn't she? That just leaves Matt. Tomorrow, we'll work on Matt."

Seven

Saturday, September 12

Even as a boy, Doug had been an early riser, so he was well-suited to the life of a building contractor. Weekends were no different on his internal clock. Today, like every other day, he woke between four-thirty and five, shaved, showered, and dressed.

Before heading downstairs, he looked in on Ben and Janie. They were sleeping soundly. He checked the other bedrooms, but there was no sign of Matt. He wasn't in the office, the TV room, or the kitchen, and his duffle bag was nowhere in sight either. "He actually slept outside," Doug muttered. "Unbelievable."

Doug checked the front porch, but the only thing out there was the morning paper. He picked up the paper and frowned. Doug walked back through the house, dropping the paper on the kitchen counter as he passed, and stepped out on to the back deck, but Matt wasn't out there either. The teenager was gone.

His wristwatch showed five-thirty. Think. Where could Matt be? What kind of religion would drive a kid to behave so irrationally? Matt was brainwashed. Pure and simple.

Had he called the deputy sheriff? The deputy wouldn't take him without letting someone know. There was the court order to consider, after all. The court. The lawsuit was in serious jeopardy if he didn't find his grandson soon. What kind of guardian was he if he lost his charges?

Taking the stairs two at a time, he strode into his bed-room and woke Cass up. "Matt's gone. I'm going to take the four-wheeler and check the woods."

"You don't know how long he's been gone?"

"No." He pulled a set of keys from the dresser and dropped them in his pocket.

"He doesn't know anybody in town, does he?"

"Just the preacher he was staying with. Julie's from Springfield, so I don't think she has any friends or family here that he could connect with."

"You really think he would leave the other two kids be-hind?"

"I don't know what to think," Doug sighed. He kissed Cass on the cheek. "I'll be back in a little while. If he's not out there . . ."

"Doug, I'm sure he's okay. He's used to living in Africa. He's probably more than capable of handling Kirkwood."

"Was that the doorbell?" Chuck Molinsky asked through a yawn. He squinted, trying to make out the numbers on the clock. "What time is it?"

"Seven-eighteen," his wife, Bobbi, said. "Who's out this early on Saturday?"

"Nobody I know." Chuck threw the covers back, slipped on a pair of old sneakers he kept by the bed, and grabbed his robe. "I'll take care of it. You go back to sleep."

"Fat chance," Bobbi said. "I'll be right there."

Chuck peeked in on Jack and Shannon, but the teen-agers hadn't stirred. He looked out the window before opening the door, but there was no car in the driveway. "Strange," Chuck mumbled. He swung open the door and was quite sur-prised to find a teenage boy on the porch.

"Mr. Molinsky?"

"Yes?"

"I'm Matthew Bolling. I need your help."

"He's not anywhere on the property," Doug said, as he came into the kitchen from the garage.

"Now what?" Cass asked. She pushed a cup of coffee across the island to him.

"I don't know." Doug rubbed his forehead as he gulped the coffee. "Are Ben and Janie still asleep?"

"For now. What do you want me to tell them?"

"Tell them the truth," Doug said. "Ben may have some insight, some idea where Matt may have gone."

"And you're sure he'll tell you?"

"Why wouldn't he?"

"Because we're the enemy."

"That's ridiculous," Doug frowned, and set the cup on the counter. "Matt and Mark are the only ones who think that."

"Let me get this straight," Chuck said, rubbing his temple. "You walked all the way over here from your grandfather's house because his girlfriend lives there, and you can't stay there."

"Yes, sir," Matt said. "You're my mom and dad's lawyer. I figured you could help me."

"Help you do what?"

"Get me out of there."

"Matt, I can't do that. In fact, I need to take you back as soon as possible."

"Why?"

"Because I'm interfering with a court order. Your grandfather can make a lot of trouble over this if he chooses."

"So he just wins?"

"He hasn't won anything yet." Chuck's mind raced, trying to figure out how to explain everything to the boy, and get him back to his grandfather's house without inciting his wrath and making things more difficult for Mark and Julie. Apparently his negotiating skills would come in handy after all. Before he could begin, he felt Bobbi slip her hand around his elbow.

"Good morning," she said. "Are you a friend of Jack's?"

"Bobbi, this is Matthew Bolling," Chuck said. "He walked here from his grandfather's house."

Bobbi's eyebrows arched in surprise. "Can I get you a snack or a drink, Matthew?"

"Actually, that would be great, ma'am, and it's just Matt."

"Come in the kitchen, Matt, and I'll see what I can find." Chuck closed the door behind Matt, then they followed her, and she motioned for them to sit at the breakfast table. "Juice, milk or coffee?"

"Juice, please," Matt answered. Bobbi set a large glass in front of him and he gulped half of it before taking a breath. "Do I have any options at all? Does God expect me to just stay there?"

"Have you discussed this with your grandfather?" Chuck asked, taking the cup of coffee Bobbi offered him.

"He wasn't very understanding. He's all about 'just love me, don't tell me I'm doing anything wrong.'"

"He has a point."

"What?"

"Matt, you want to be like Jesus, don't you?" Chuck asked, and Matt nodded. "Then think. Who did Jesus hang out with?"

"His disciples," Matt answered.

"He did, but the religious establishment criticized Him because He ate with sinners. Prostitutes, even."

"But I don't want them to think that what they're doing is okay," Matt protested. "Besides, you're coming at it from the other side."

"What are you talking about?" Chuck asked.

"Pastor David told us your story. You've committed the same kind of sin my grandfather has. It's no wonder you're sympathetic."

"I see," Chuck said, then he turned to his wife. "Bobbi, if you wouldn't care, fix him a bite to eat. I'm going to get dressed."

"What are you going to do?"

"I'm going to take him back, before we all go to jail."

Cass watched Doug stalk through the kitchen and TV room, pausing each time he passed the island to gulp more coffee. "You need to call Mark," she said.

"And tell him what?" Doug snapped. "That I've lost Matt? Absolutely not!"

"Doug, they're his parents. They deserve to know he's missing." Doug scowled. "Matt has to come back here. There's a court order. No matter where he is now, he has to stay with you until Tuesday."

"I'd be giving them ammunition."

"No, it would show that you really are putting the children's safety and welfare ahead of your own vendetta."

"It is not a vendetta," Doug muttered, but he picked up the phone from the kitchen counter, and pulled the phone book closer. He flipped pages, squinting the whole time. "This is crazy. I don't even know the preacher's name where they're staying."

"His father did your wife's funeral," Cass answered gently.

"Yeah," Doug whispered. "Shannon . . . David Shannon." He punched numbers in and waited for an answer. "This is Doug Bolling. I need to speak with Mark."

"My dad?" Mark took the phone from David Shannon,

with Julie watching anxiously. "What's going on?" Mark asked.

"Matt is gone," his father said, without trying to hide the worry in his voice. "I've searched the woods around here and up and down the street. He's not anywhere around. Has he ever done anything like this before?"

"No," Mark said, "but this is new territory for all of us." He held the phone against his shoulder, and Julie rose from her seat at the kitchen table. "Matt's gone."

"He's gone? Since when?"

"Dad didn't find him this morning when he got up at five."

"So he's been out all night?"

"We don't know that," Mark said. He held the phone back to his ear. "Dad, have you called the police or anything?"

"Not yet. I was hoping you could give me some ideas about where I should look for him. If I call the police, it will make this rougher on all of us."

"Have you called your lawyer yet?"

"No, of course not." His father didn't bother to hide his sharp indignation either, then his voice dropped. "Look, just let me know if he contacts you, all right?"

"We will. Let us know when you find him." Mark clicked off the phone.

"Aren't you going to go find him?" Julie asked.

"Yes, but I have to take him back to my dad."

"This is insane." Julie shook her head. "How could your dad let Matt run away?"

"He's torn up about it—"

"He should be! It's his fault! Besides, this hurts his precious custody case."

"I don't think he cares about that right now."

Then Julie's eyes grew wide and she grabbed Mark's forearm. "What if he orchestrated this? What if he wants you to find Matt and get caught with him, so he can take the kids away from us for good."

Mark shook his head. "I'm going to say this is the voice of a distraught mother. My dad isn't like that."

"He's suing us for custody of our children! He's capable of anything."

Mark peeled Julie's hand from his arm. "David, can I borrow your car?"

———————

When Matt finished his breakfast, Chuck handed him the phone. "Here, call your father."

The boy perked up and smiled. "You're taking me to my dad?"

"No, but I want you to tell him what you did. I want him to hear it from you so he gets the real story."

Matt nodded slowly. "You think my grandpa will lie."

"No." The beginning throbs of a headache drummed at Chuck's temples. This one obviously took after his mother. "You need to take responsibility for your actions and the first step is owning up to them." He pointed at the receiver. "Now, make the call."

The teenager eyed him for several moments then he picked up the phone, swallowed hard, and punched in the numbers. "Hello? Pastor David, I need to speak to my dad. This is Matt."

———————

Julie smoothed out a city map David had brought from his study while Mark leafed through their stack of legal papers looking for Doug's address. "He's not on the map," Mark frowned. "No wait, there it is."

David stood at Mark's elbow and pushed a second set of keys toward Julie. "You can take Maddie's car. I'll grab the church van, and with Jan, that'll make four of us. We can cover a lot more ground that way."

Julie took the keys, grateful for David's help. Before she could ask which direction she should head, the phone rang. "Maybe that's Doug. Maybe he's found him." She whispered a prayer while David answered the phone.

"Matt!" David smiled broadly. "He's right here. Hang on."

Julie intercepted the phone before Mark could take it. "Matt! Are you okay? Where are you?"

"I'm okay, Mom. I'm at Mr. Molinsky's house—"

"What were you thinking, Matthew? Don't I have enough to worry about?"

"Mom, I'm sorry—"

"I'll be right there." She stuffed the car keys in the pocket of her jeans.

"What about the court order?"

"What about it? I'm not afraid of your grandfather."

"Mom, I left Grandpa's house because I couldn't stand to be there with him and his girlfriend. They didn't do anything wrong." He lowered his voice. "This was a bad idea, a really bad, really stupid idea. I need to go back for Janie and Ben."

"Did they do all right? Is Janie okay?"

"They're fine." There was a pause on the line, then Matt said, "Mr. Molinsky said he'd take me back to Grandpa's. Just put Dad on. I need to talk to him."

"Matt, call me tomorrow," Julie pleaded. "I need to hear from you."

"Sure thing. I love you, Mom."

"I love you, too, Matt," Julie whispered.

She handed the phone to Mark, and sank into one of the kitchen chairs. Everything, her whole world was going completely insane. Nothing was predictable anymore. Nothing was secure, and no one else understood. Mark refused to believe the truth about how ruthless his father had become. He didn't seem to grasp the danger the family faced.

She wanted him to take action, to slay the dragon, but Mark was content to react, to let Doug call the shots and drive the crisis. What would it do to Matt and Ben to see their ungodly grandfather as more confident and assertive than their father? Would it undermine their faith? Would it turn them against faith altogether?

David handed her the cordless handset with a knowing smile. She mouthed 'thank you,' and clicked it on.

"Matt, what's going on?" Mark asked.

"Dad, I didn't know what else to do."

"Start at the beginning. Tell me the whole story."

Julie listened as Matt recounted the conversation with Ben in the office, how he didn't want to compromise with evil, and wanted to be an example. Mark offered no encouragement or reassurance. Then Matt detailed the confrontation with his grandfather. "And he was like, 'why don't you love me?' but Dad—"

"He's right, Matt."

"What?"

Julie wanted to ask the same question. Mark was taking has dad's side. They hadn't spoken for years over his father living with that woman, but when Matt makes a stand, it suddenly became the wrong thing. How could he expect Matt to understand that?

"Read the gospels, son. Jesus didn't refuse to associate with sinners, and He didn't make it a point to list their sins, but He never shied away from the truth."

"But Dad—"

"Listen to me, Matt. Is God still in control or not?"

After a moment, Matt mumbled, "He is."

"Then it's no accident that you're there with your grandfather. There's no question that you are a good and godly young man, but you have to love people where they are, and that means loving your grandfather." Then Mark added, "And loving the woman he lives with."

"Do you love him?"

"Of course I do."

"He doesn't think so."

"I know that. I've handled things very poorly with him, and maybe this is my opportunity to make it right. Maybe you can help me out."

So Mark's plan was to let his dad win in order to make

up for the last fifteen years? God help them all.

"So what do I say when I go back?" Matt asked.

"You apologize for acting like such a jerk, and ask your grandpa not to hold it against Christ because His followers mess up so often. We're not perfect."

"Is this going to hurt your court case?"

"I don't think so. Dad called here looking for you. He was worried."

"Really?"

"Matt, he loves you. He just doesn't understand how he can show you that. He's doing it his way. He does everything his way."

"Yeah. I'm sorry I worried you and Mom."

"You're safe. That's the most important thing."

"Mr. Molinsky's gonna take me back. I guess I'll talk to you later."

"Hey Matt, this didn't work out the way you wanted, but I'm proud of you for having such a strong sense of right and wrong."

Finally. Some encouragement.

"Thanks," Matt mumbled.

"Learn from it. Experience brings wisdom."

Matt clicked off the phone, and pushed it across the kitchen table to Mr. Molinsky. "I guess we should go back."

"You think we should call your grandfather and let him know you're on your way?" he asked.

Matt sighed and took back the phone. "Can I have the phone book?" He didn't rush looking up the number, but he found it soon enough and dialed. On the second ring, the woman answered. Great. God wasn't going to cut him any slack. "This is Matt. Can I speak to my grandfather?"

"Are you okay? Do you need us to come and get you?"

Matt was surprised by the frantic worry in her voice. She sounded almost as upset as his mother. "I'm fine. Mr. Molinsky is going to bring me back. I'll be there soon. Could you let my grandpa know?"

"He'll be so relieved. He's out looking for you right now."

"Thanks." He clicked off the phone and looked across the table to Mr. Molinsky. "Is there anybody else I have to call?"

The lawyer smiled. "No, I've humiliated you enough."

Mrs. Molinsky stood and began gathering his dishes. "Thank you for breakfast," he said.

"You're welcome." She smiled warmly. "Matt, we're praying for you and your family."

"Thanks, we need it."

Matt sat in silence in the front seat of Mr. Molinsky's car, with his duffle bag wedged between his feet. He dreaded facing his grandfather and that woman. They would think they had won, that they were right and what they were doing was okay.

His dad couldn't have been much plainer about how he was supposed to behave, though. Respectful. Apologetic. All right, but only because his dad asked him to.

It's just three more days, he told himself. *God, can You just let things go smoothly until Tuesday? I'll go along with whatever Grandpa says if you just get me through these next few days.*

"Your grandpa has a nice place," Mr. Molinsky said as he pulled into the driveway.

"Yeah, I guess so."

Mr. Molinsky turned off his car. "Do you want me to walk in with you?"

"No."

The lawyer twisted slightly in his seat and smiled. "Matt, you remind me of my son Brad."

"Brad? I thought his name was Jack."

"Brad is my oldest. He's in ministry now. He has this

tremendous sense of justice and right and wrong, just like you. Instead of trying to fix the world himself, though, he gave that passion over to God, and God gave Brad his heart's desire—to make a difference in the lives of the people around him. An eternal difference."

Matt stared out the front window of the car. He wasn't trying to fix the world. He was trying to do the right thing, for what it was worth. Nothing apparently. When Mr. Molinsky didn't say anymore, Matt looked over. "Thank you for the ride." He reached up to open the car door.

"One more thing. Anybody can hand out justice, but only a good and godly person is capable or willing to extend grace."

Matt nodded and got out of the car. Good and godly. His dad had just called him that. That couldn't be an accident. He always thought he was good and godly, but the rules were changing. If the rules changed, he wasn't sure if he could play the game anymore.

———————

When the doorbell rang, Doug scrambled to the front door, getting there a step ahead of Cass and before the last chime faded. He yanked the front door open and as soon as he saw Matt, he pulled the teenager close and hugged him tightly. "Matt, I was worried to death—"

"I know, I'm sorry Grandpa," Matt gasped.

Doug let go with a sheepish smile. "Sorry. I guess that was a little much."

Matt took a step back, set his bag down, and looked at each of them, then took a deep breath. "Grandpa, Ms. Grayson, I acted like a complete jerk. I was disrespectful to both of you, and I'm sorry."

"Apology accepted," Cass said, and she extended her hand. This time he shook it, and she smiled at him.

"I talked to my dad and I was looking for him to take my side, you know? He didn't." He forced a slight smile. "Just don't hold it against Jesus that Christians, like me and my dad, do things the wrong way sometimes."

"It takes a man to admit he's wrong," Doug said. "I'm impressed. I'm proud of you."

Matt nodded, but didn't smile. "If it's okay with you, I'm exhausted. Do you care if I grab some sleep, especially before Janie and Ben wake up? That is, if the bedroom is still available."

"Of course it's available," Doug said. "I'm glad you're safe, Matt."

"Thanks. Don't worry about fixing me breakfast. I ate at Mr. Molinsky's house."

Once he had disappeared upstairs, Cass shook her head and murmured, "Wow. I'd like to know what Mark told him."

"So would I," Doug said.

Eight

"Hey! You're snoring!" Ben threw a wadded up t-shirt at his brother, hitting him square in the face. A perfect toss.

Matt groaned and rolled over onto his back, but didn't open his eyes. "That's because I'm asleep."

"Grandpa wants to take us to lunch, Janie's choice. Do you want to go or sleep?"

Matt sighed and rubbed his eyes. "I'll go. What time is it?"

"Almost noon, ya lazy bum," Ben said. "You gotta give up this wild party lifestyle of yours."

""What's that supposed to mean?" Matt snapped upright. "Did Grandpa say something?"

"He said you were still asleep. What was he supposed to say?"

"That's all he said?"

"Yes . . . "

"No explanation of why, or anything else?"

"Is this paranoia a teenager thing? Is this what I have to look forward to?"

"This is important, Ben. He didn't say anything else about what I'd done, or where I'd gone?"

"You were gone? When? Overnight? Did you sneak out?" This was too good. Ben crossed his arms across his chest, and grinned. "You sneaked out, didn't you?"

Matt dropped his eyes and muttered, "I walked to the

lawyer's house."

"You what?" Ben's jaw dropped. He wouldn't have guessed that one in a million years. Well, maybe a thousand or a hundred years. Actually, the way Matt was pouting in the office last night, Ben would've come up with that answer in two days, tops. Oh, but Matt sneaking out because he wouldn't sleep in the house with his grandpa's girlfriend . . . Matt . . . Matt . . . Matt . . . "Are you insane?"

"Yeah."

That was disappointing. Matt just agreed so there was nothing to tease him about.

Matt ran his hand back through his hair, then rubbed his chin. "I need to shave—"

"Quit bragging," Ben said. "Now, back to the good boy gone bad. What were you doing?"

"Trying to get out of here. The lawyer made me call Dad, and Dad told me we were here because God wanted us here, and that I should love Grandpa and Cass the way Jesus does."

"Hmmm, that sounds vaguely familiar."

"Shut up, all right." He threw the t-shirt back at Ben. "I've had enough grief for today."

"So when did you leave?"

"I don't know, three-thirty maybe." He leaned down and untied his sneakers. "But Grandpa didn't say anything about it. He had the chance to really stick it to me." He stopped messing with his shoes, and looked at Ben. "He showed me more grace than I showed him. That's bad."

"Well, you've got a second chance now."

"Yeah, but what do I do with it?" He pushed off his shoes, stood and stretched. He pulled his duffel bag onto the bed and slowly unzipped it. "I need a way to show both of them that they matter, that we're not all about rules and regulations. Something that would seem to be out of character, or at least unexpected."

"You could act normal," Ben suggested. It was too easy.

"I will when you will."

"Now see, that shows no imagination or creativity as an

insult. It's like what a five-year-old would say."

"I've got it!"

"Got what? A better comeback?"

"I know how to fix this. Six Flags!"

"Going to Six Flags will be loving Cass and Grandpa the way Jesus does? I don't get it. Plus, he doesn't seem like the Six Flags type, you know, easy-going . . . fun-loving . . . how are you gonna convince him?"

"What if we go tomorrow?"

Ben clutched his heart. "On the Sabbath? What will Moses say?"

Matt stood speechless for a moment. Ben took special satisfaction rattling him that way.

"He'll know I'm willing to give up something very important to me in order to take advantage of this time with him."

"If that's really what you're doing. He'll be able to tell if you're faking. I'm not convinced you aren't faking."

"It's what I want to do. We need to do it." Matt pulled a change of clothes from his bag. "You know, we don't even know him, really. Dad doesn't talk about him much and we haven't seen him since we moved."

"I thought that's why we were supposed to spend a week here this summer, so we could get to know him, but that fell apart and he decided to sue us."

"Jane broke her arm. That's why we couldn't go."

"Jane got her cast off in May," Ben said. "We could have still come."

"So something else happened. Maybe Six Flags is where we get to the bottom of it."

"You're going to bug him all day at Six Flags? That's your plan?"

"Nah," Matt grinned. "He's afraid of heights. Maybe we can just keep him on the coasters until he talks."

"Torture. Seriously?"

"You have no sense of humor, Ben."

"I know it when I see it, Matt." He raised a hand to his

eyes and peered around the room. "Nothing in here."

"You're so annoying."

"It's a shame that's not a spiritual gift." He smiled and shuffled to the doorway. "Maybe Six Flags will work. If nothing else, it will help Jane out."

"Why does Janie need help?"

"Well, Sir Judge-A-Lot, while you were hiding in the office refusing to associate with us, she freaked out last night. Went all hysterical, crying for Mom. I slept on the floor in her room."

"What'd he do about it?"

"They tried their best to calm her down, but there's only so much strangers can do."

"Great, I told Mom she was doing just fine."

"Mom doesn't need to know." Ben turned to leave. "I'll tell Grandpa you're getting a shower."

"Don't say anything about Six Flags, all right? Let me do it."

"Whatever," Ben said, then he smiled. "Sir Judge-A-Lot. I like that. I'm gonna use that again."

Julie sat in the corner of the sofa at the Shannons' trying to fight off the rising tide of very negative, very un-Christian emotions. Matt never did anything wrong. Never. But less than twelve hours with Doug and he was sneaking out in the middle of the night. He could have been mugged, hit by a car, or who knows what. And he had lied to her about Jane. She knew it. Admittedly, he didn't want her to worry, but he had lied.

She tried to convince herself that this was what Doug needed. If he saw with his own eyes the pain he was inflicting on a sweet, innocent baby girl, he'd have to drop his legal action. Even if he had no qualms about hurting Mark and her, surely he'd have some compassion on his granddaughter.

God, I feel like You've abandoned us, like You aren't

hearing any of our prayers. I am begging You . . . You have to step in and fix this. This is more than I can handle. These are my children.

She flinched when Mark took her hand. She hadn't heard him come into the room. "Come on," he said. "I need to get you out of here for the afternoon."

Julie pulled her hand back. "I don't feel like going anywhere. Jan, David and Maddie are gone. I just want to be alone."

"But Julie—"

"Mark, do you grasp what is happening? Your father is stealing our children! I can't go out and have a vacation day with this going on. How can you even suggest that?"

"I'm not," he said, taking a seat on the sofa beside her. "I'm trying to take care of you so we can fight this battle together. I need you with me on this."

"I am with you. I've always been with you." She hoped she wasn't lying.

"I know you keep saying that, but I feel like there's an undercurrent between us."

"The undercurrent's name is Doug Bolling. How could he do this to us?"

Mark looked into her eyes for a long uncomfortable moment, then he spoke with careful quietness. "You mean, how could I let him do this? This is my fault somehow, isn't it?"

"That's not what I said, Mark."

"Then say what you mean. Stop hedging."

"All right." She slapped the arm of the sofa in frustration. "You want to know what I think? You won't stand up to your father. You never have. I don't know if you're looking for his approval or what, but you have always let him walk all over you."

Mark said nothing. She knew she had wounded him, perhaps irreparably, but the stakes were too high. She couldn't risk his inaction.

He stood and slowly crossed the room to the front door,

but he turned back toward her. "You're mistaken."

"Then show me."

He dropped his eyes and slipped out the front door without another word.

"Lord, I could really use some reassurance right now," Mark said, gazing up at the sky as he walked. He knew Julie didn't mean the things she said. She was upset and scared, and he was safe to vent it all to. After the mess he'd created, the least he could do was take that kind of heat.

As he continued to walk, though, the doubts began to creep in. What if she did mean it? What if she had already lost all respect for him? What if she truly believed he was afraid to stand up to his father?

What if he was afraid?

No, he wasn't afraid. It was just like he had told Matt—either God was in control or He wasn't. Since God *was* in control, He was doing something, something that would benefit them in the long run and glorify Him. He was holding on to the words in First Peter. "Therefore submit yourselves to every ordinance of man for the Lord's sake, whether to the king as supreme, or to governors, as to those who are sent by him for the punishment of evildoers and for the praise of those who do good. For this is the will of God, that by doing good you may put to silence the ignorance of foolish men."

He was putting his father's ignorance to silence by submitting to this legal process and trusting God for the outcome. If they could just hang on and see it through, everything would turn out all right. He'd walk a little longer, give Julie some time to cool down and then try to explain it to her.

Julie ran cold water in the bathroom sink and then splashed some on her face. She was ashamed, angry with herself that she'd allowed those words to come out of her mouth. That wasn't how a Christian was supposed to act, not to mention a preacher's wife. Mark needed support now, not recrimination. She couldn't let Doug get the added victory of driving them apart. Mark was doing his best, and she knew that.

But what would happen if that wasn't enough?

No. Stop thinking like that. She trusted Mark. She trusted God. This was just something they had to go through. God was preparing them for the next ministry He had lined up. It would all make sense in time.

There was that time, though, when Mark claimed that God was punishing his disobedience. If that was the case, how long would it be before God was satisfied?

God, what is the answer to this? What are You trying to teach me? How can I support Mark, protect my children and honor You all at the same time? I need someone to help me, to show me what I'm doing wrong, because I'm getting more frustrated with my husband. I'm bitter at my father-in-law. I don't want to be like that, but each time it gets harder to fight it off.

I don't understand what You're doing with us. I thought we were obedient to You, that we were doing good things in Mombasa, but it doesn't seem to matter now.

Listen to me. I don't even know how to pray, Lord. I'm terrified for my children, and now my marriage is under attack. I don't want to oppose Mark. If he's doing this the right way, then show me. Otherwise, show him what he needs to do.

When Mark returned to the Shannons' house, he found Julie on the sofa where he had left her. She immediately crossed the room to him and hugged him tightly.

"Mark, I'm so sorry. I don't know what got into me. Those words were so hateful, so ugly."

"I knew you didn't mean them," he said. "We're exhausted, and we've both been stretched to the limit on this."

She pulled away from him, and glanced between his

eyes and the floor as she spoke. "I'm not handling this the right way. I'm failing you. I'm failing my kids. I'm failing God, and I don't know how to fix it."

He took her hands and smiled gently. "First of all, based on past experiences, your definition of failure is everyone else's idea of great success. Second, this is a very unique test. I don't know if there's an example for you to draw on exactly."

"Then how are you doing it? You are so calm."

"It's like I told Matt. God's still God. He's in control of everything."

"That's too simplistic, Mark. I need more."

"All right, Peter and David both told me to read First Peter. I read it at least twice a day. Just now the part about submitting ourselves in order to silence the ignorance of foolish men ran through my mind. I believe God's telling us we'll win if we don't fight."

Julie didn't argue with him, but she didn't agree either.

"You want to try to talk to your mother?"

"I can't bring myself to tell her Doug has the kids. Besides, I don't want to run up David and Jan's phone bill just to hear her tell me the same thing you just did."

"We've got an international card. You can call her."

She shook her head. "I'll save it until this is all over."

———

"Finally," Doug said, with a teasing smile when Matt shuffled into the kitchen where everyone was waiting. "I have to eat on schedule, son. I'm old and I have diabetes."

Matt rolled his eyes. "I won't wash next time."

"It's worth the wait, Grandpa," Ben said, hopping off his bar stool. "Trust me on this."

"Janie said pizza for lunch." Doug lifted Janie down from the barstool at the island counter and turned off the light.

"Sounds great," Matt said.

"The garage is through that door. Go on out past the mudroom. My car is the black one."

"You have a room for mud?" Jane asked.

"He has a room to keep the mud from getting in the rest of the house," Cass said, reaching for Jane's hand. The little girl looked up at her for a moment, then slipped her hand inside. Doug smiled at Cass. Jane was settling in. Perfect.

"Can I talk to you for just a second?" Matt asked once Cass and Ben guided Janie through the doorway.

"Sure, what's on your mind?" Doug eased the mudroom door closed.

"I acted like a jerk and you really could have made things tough on me—"

"Matt, I love you. In spite of what you may believe or may have been taught to believe about me, I love every one of you and I only want what is best for you."

"Well, I wasn't very Christ-like."

"Who is these days?" Doug turned to leave, but Matt wasn't finished.

"You seem to have some idea what Christ is about."

"Your grandmother told me all about Jesus when she was dying."

"But you don't believe any of it."

"Not the way she did. I let her talk because it helped her, brought her some comfort, but here's the thing. If God is all-powerful like you say, then He can stop that kind of suffering. Why didn't He? Why doesn't He?" He lowered his voice and looked past Matt. "I'm not sure He has all that power."

"Grandpa, God is not Santa Claus, and He's not a genie sitting around waiting to grant wishes—"

"But what is the purpose of being God if you can't or won't use what power you do have for good?"

"Would you want a God that you could completely figure out? A God whose plans weren't any more complex than what you could lay out yourself?"

"Ah, the third path," Doug said, opening the door to the mudroom.

"The what?" Matt asked following him.

"The third path. God is neither *this* nor *that*, but somewhere in between."

"Not in between," Matt said. "Far beyond."

Matt was a smart kid. It was a shame he'd never been challenged. "Have you ever heard anything different about God than what your father has taught you?"

"He's taught us the truth. We don't need to hear from anybody else."

"Matt, even the Amish let their kids decide for themselves. I think you, Ben and Janie should have that opportunity, too."

"What if we decide we don't want to change?"

"Then at least you'll know."

Doug opened the rear passenger door on his Escalade for Matt then walked around the rear of the car and got in. "Janie, do you still need a booster seat?" The little girl nodded. Doug looked at Cass. "Add that to our list." He adjusted the mirror so he could see Ben and Matt in the backseat. "Do you guys need anything? Clothes, shoes, stuff like that?"

"Grandpa," Ben answered, "our other grandparents are missionaries in Naples. I bet I have more Italian-made shoes than Cass does."

"We need to talk, Ben," Cass said with a smile as she slipped on a pair of sunglasses.

"Well, just speak up if you think of anything," Doug said. He readjusted the mirror, punched the button for the garage door opener and pulled out.

"So how much money do you have, Grandpa?" Ben asked and Matt punched him in the leg.

"Just tell him to shut up," Matt said. "He's way too nosy."

"It's a fair question," Doug said. "Truth is, Ben, I don't know. Most of it is tied up in investments, and in my house. I do know that I don't have any debt and I have plenty to live on, so I'm fortunate to be able to do about anything I want to."

"And you did it all yourself?"

"Yeah, I started with nothing but a truck and some tools. And some ambition, I guess. At first, I was a drywaller, working for somebody else, but eventually I got out on my own."

"So, you have sports cars and boats and stuff like that?"

"I have this car, a truck, and a couple of four-wheelers, two boats."

"What about Cass?" Ben asked. "Don't you take care of her, too?"

"Cass is a very independent, self-sufficient woman. She doesn't need me to take care of her." He expected Cass to add her two cents or at least nod . . . something, but she kept her eyes facing forward and with her sunglasses.

Apparently, this made twice in two days that he'd said the wrong thing. He couldn't blame her for being on edge after the way Matt treated her last night. That had to be it. Surely she didn't doubt him.

An uneasy silence hung over them the rest of the drive to the restaurant. Cass fought the idea that Doug had sarcastically thrown those words at her in the presence of the children so she couldn't respond. Had she misjudged him? He said 'my house,' and he kept saying 'I' and not 'we.' Was he revealing his hand?

Had she been just someone to occupy his time until he got his grandkids back? She watched his eyes through lunch and in spite of the lingering awkwardness from the lawsuit, he was in his element. He hung on every word they said, especially Jane.

As the afternoon dragged on, Cass felt more and more like the outsider, the intruder on this intimate family time. Tonight, after the kids went to bed, she needed to get things settled with Doug. This upcoming legal battle was too much to invest herself in without some reassurances from him, reassurances that she still had a place in his plans, in his future.

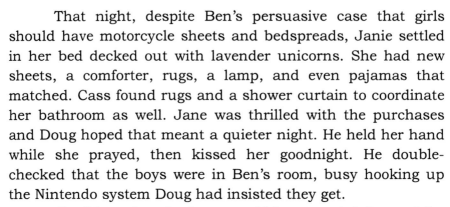

That night, despite Ben's persuasive case that girls should have motorcycle sheets and bedspreads, Janie settled in her bed decked out with lavender unicorns. She had new sheets, a comforter, rugs, a lamp, and even pajamas that matched. Cass found rugs and a shower curtain to coordinate her bathroom as well. Jane was thrilled with the purchases and Doug hoped that meant a quieter night. He held her hand while she prayed, then kissed her goodnight. He double-checked that the boys were in Ben's room, busy hooking up the Nintendo system Doug had insisted they get.

Confident that the boys would be occupied for a while, he headed downstairs to find Cass. She was in the kitchen, seemingly waiting for him. He casually opened the refrigerator door. "Do you want a beer?" he asked, pulling a bottle out and twisting off the cap.

"Not tonight," she said.

"Where should we go?"

"What do you mean?"

"We need to talk," Doug said. "Where do you feel the most comfortable talking?"

"Here's fine," she said. "What's on your mind?"

"What's on yours? I said the wrong thing again, didn't I?"

"No," she said with the slightest smile. "I guess I'm losing sight of how I fit into everything."

"Let me remind you, then." He set the bottle down on the counter, stepped over to her, and took her hands. "Cass, I depend on your judgment, your presence. You understand where I'm coming from without making me explain myself. My life would be pointless if I didn't have you to share it with."

"So you do love me?"

"Of course I do."

"Then what's going to happen if you do get the kids?"

"Nothing will change between us. I promise you that."

"Nothing?"

"You are the reason things will work. You're a perfect example of how things can work differently than the way they've been taught. You're showing them that a woman isn't limited to one set of choices, to one formula for happiness."

"I'm showing the boys that?"

"Yes, Matt and Ben can see that women are their equals in every way, and that women don't need some patronizing system that boxes them in and prevents them from becoming what they want to be."

"I had no idea you were such a feminist," Cass teased, but then her smile faded. "What if a woman wants to be a wife and a mother?"

"If it's her choice and not someone else's expectation of her, then that's exactly what she should be."

Cass pulled her hands away suddenly and Doug turned and saw Matt in the doorway.

"Hi, Matt." Doug picked his bottle up again. "You want a beer?"

"Uh, no, sir."

"Relax, I was kidding. You're too young to drink." He took a long drink. "Your dad was at least sixteen before he had one."

"What?"

"He never told you that?"

"I don't think so."

"Well, he drank his share when he was a teenager. I think he gave all that up though once he got religion. What can I get you?"

"Nothing, I guess." Matt shoved his hands deep into his jeans pockets. "Um, I was thinking . . . Grandpa, do you think we could go to Six Flags tomorrow?"

"Tomorrow? On Sunday?" Doug squinted and took another long drink from his beer. "Won't you go to hell or something if you do that?"

Matt rolled his eyes. "That's not how you end up in hell,

but if you don't want to go, it's no big deal."

"No, Matt, if you want to go to Six Flags, then that's what we'll do. We didn't have any plans, did we?" He looked to Cass, and she shook her head. "I'll have to find out when they open." He took another long drink. "This'll be a new experience."

"You've never been to Six Flags?" Matt asked.

"Never had a reason."

"Then you're due," Cass said. "I'm sure they're open by eleven, maybe earlier."

"See, she knows everything," Doug said, but Matt didn't comment.

Cass, however, read Doug's mind. "What brought this on?" she asked.

"Ben and I were talking. We really don't even know you. We were little kids the last time we saw Grandpa and you weren't even around then. God put us here for a reason, and we may as well take advantage of the opportunity."

"Forgive me, but that sounds a hundred and eighty degrees different from last night," Cass said. "Which one is the real you?"

Doug was anxious to hear the answer to that question himself.

"Both, I guess. My dad told me I was looking at things all wrong."

"How so?"

"I don't know if I should say."

"I won't hold it against you."

"See, that's what I mean. I was holding everything against you because you live here. I like you and all, but it's just wrong to live with somebody without being married."

"And I disagree," Doug said. "We have everything married people have except the paperwork."

"Anyway," Matt said, turning back to Cass, "I was judging you, and that wasn't fair."

"Your dad told you that?" Doug asked in stunned disbelief. "That it was judgmental to criticize me for living with

Cass?"

"Not exactly. It was more like I need to love you anyway, and not let living with her get in the way of that."

"So you still think it's wrong?"

"It's not just me. It's in the Bible."

"One of the 'thou shalt nots'?" Doug asked, finishing off the bottle of beer.

"Yes, sir."

"You believe the whole Bible?"

"Yes, sir."

"Even that Jonah and the whale business?" Doug opened the refrigerator and pulled out another bottle.

"Jesus believed it."

"That story is ridiculous," Doug said, twisting the cap off the bottle.

"Have you ever read it? The whole thing?" Matt asked.

"No," Doug admitted.

"Well, then let's read it. Both of us, all three of us, and we'll talk about it tomorrow."

"Whatever, Matt." Doug took a long drink.

"You have a Bible?"

"Someplace."

"Great. I'll see you tomorrow morning." He turned and left with an extra spring in his step.

"Do you know what you're getting yourself into?" Cass asked.

"What? He's a kid. He wants to show off what he knows. There's nothing wrong with letting him think he can convert me."

Suddenly a wail erupted from upstairs. "Janie," Cass said quietly and started for the stairway.

"You wanna bring her down here?" Doug asked.

"Then put the beer away," Cass said as she headed upstairs. Moments later, she returned with Janie bundled up in a new blanket.

Doug took her from Cass's arms. "Baby, I thought you liked everything in your bedroom now."

"Mommy," Janie whimpered. "I want Mommy."

"I can't get Mommy right now," Doug said, grasping for an explanation Jane would accept. "Maybe God wants you to learn how to be brave, you know, so He's giving you some time away from Mommy."

"But I don't want to be brave," she said dissolving into tears again.

"I know, being brave is very hard," Doug said gently as he walked toward the sliding glass door that opened onto the deck. "Want to sit out on the deck and look at the stars with me?" He slid the door open, and waited for Cass to follow him, but she motioned that she would leave the two of them alone this time.

"You need your insulin bag?" she asked softly.

"I don't want to do it in front of her. We won't be out here that long." He closed the door behind him and pulled a lounge chair around so that they could look out across the manicured backyard.

He stretched out on the lounge chair and wrapped Janie in her blanket, snuggling her in close beside him. "Now, if it's too scary to sleep without Mommy, we just won't sleep."

"I don't have to go to sleep?"

"Nope," Doug said. "Hey, look. See those blinking lights? That's an airplane."

"Just like my airplane?"

"Exactly like your airplane." He eased down slightly in the lounge chair. "Let's watch for the next one." Before they reached the first dozen, he felt Jane relax against him, and soon her deep breathing confirmed that she had fallen asleep. After being shut out of her life, he was in no hurry to get her inside. He brushed a wisp of hair from her cheek and kissed her forehead.

Cass and the kids. That's all he needed, all he wanted. He wouldn't ask for anything more. But in the quiet darkness, he couldn't shake a feeling deep inside, a cold resignation that God would never let him have even that much.

Nine

Sunday, September 13

When Doug awoke, it took several moments for him to get his bearings, to grasp that he was out on his deck and to remember why. Janie was still nestled in close, leaving his arm stiff from cradling her all night.

He carefully, slowly twisted to pull out his arm without disturbing her. As he shifted to sit up, he discovered his back and knees were almost as stiff as his arm. He kneaded his shoulder and upper arm. His upper arm. His shot site. He never took his insulin shot last night.

And I agreed to go to Six Flags today.

He twisted and stretched his back and ran through a half dozen scenarios and calculations for the day. Dinner was covered by the pill . . . then one light beer after dinner . . . a fast-acting shot now . . . he'd have to pack an insulated bag—three kinds of insulin, the meter, snacks. Breakfast this morning—eat now or wait and eat with everybody else? What a mess. He never missed his shot.

He cautiously stood and stretched once more, and reasonably confident his body would cooperate, he scooped Janie into his arms and carried her upstairs. She breathed deeply, but didn't stir when he laid her in her bed and tucked in the comforter around her.

He checked his watch out of habit, and it confirmed what his internal clock told him—it was a little after five. He ducked into his bathroom and tested his blood. High, but not terrible. Back downstairs for a shot, then instead of heading straight for the shower, he broke his routine. He stole into his bedroom where Cass still slept and retrieved a small box from the back corner of the closet. He carried it to the wingback chair by the window. He unfolded the tissue paper and reverently eased Judy's Bible out of the box.

The sharp antiseptic smell of the hospital still clung to the leather and stirred the memories of the last time he read from Judy's Bible. It was a Thursday morning and he'd struggled through one of the Psalms. He'd held her hand rather than try to keep his place on the page, and it was a mess. He missed lines, reread others, stumbled over pronunciations, but she smiled and faintly squeezed his hand when he got to the end.

Two days later, he packed the Bible in this box, and tucked it in their closet. The day he and Cass moved into the house, he wouldn't let the movers handle it. He personally carried it from closet to closet. Cass never asked him what it was. He would have told her if she had. It wasn't a big secret, but Cass understood without him having to explain it. That meant more to him than she would ever know.

He delicately opened the cover, and his chest immediately tightened. In those first few months after her death, he almost gave the Bible to Mark. Grief was making him crazy, though. Judy never gave him a wedding band, but she gave him this Bible. Regardless of what he thought about God or religion or the words in here, it was priceless because it was hers.

Now, Matt had challenged him, and he couldn't let that go unanswered. He pulled a pair of reading glasses from his shirt pocket, and put them on. There was a table of contents somewhere, and he leafed through the pages until he found it. Running his finger down the list, he got the page number for Jonah and flipped the pages to the prophet's story. He pulled the drapes back, and tipped the Bible to catch more of the early morning light.

He followed each line, carefully mouthing the words. Every few paragraphs, he stopped and rehashed what he'd read so he could remember and understand. After two pages the story ended abruptly. So what was he supposed to get from this? What was Matt's point?

The disobedient prophet got swallowed by a fish? No, the story would've have ended there if that was the point. Jonah got a second chance.

"Hey," Cass said, raising up on her elbow. "I never knew when you came to bed."

"That's because I didn't." Doug slid the glasses off and eased the Bible back into its box. "I, uh, I fell asleep out on the deck with Jane."

"If you're gonna be out all night with another girl, we need to talk."

"I don't think you have anything to worry about." He sat down on the bed and kissed her.

"I don't know. She's very cute, and seems to feel very safe and secure with you."

"She never roused, even when I brought her upstairs."

"You're a good dad."

"Grandpa."

"What'd I say?"

"You said 'dad.'"

"I'm not awake yet," Cass yawned. "Let me get a shower and I'll get breakfast started."

"Just eggs. My sugar's screwed up this morning."

"When did you take your shot?"

"I missed it."

"Doug!"

"I'll be okay. I'll just have to watch everything real close today."

She pressed her fingers against her temples. "I shouldn't have gone to bed without making sure you'd taken your insulin."

"Cass, I'm a big boy. It's my responsibility."

"Next time, I'm sticking you myself."

He grinned. "And who's picking you up off the floor?"

"You'll have to do that, but at least I'll know your sugar will be good before I pass out."

"All right, Matt, teach me." Doug passed a plate heaping with pancakes to the teenager. "I can't eat these so you guys have some work to do."

"You read? Really?" Matt pulled several pancakes off for himself and then got one for Janie, before passing the plate to Cass. "You better get yours before you give this to Ben."

"I said I would, didn't I?" Doug said, drawing Matt back to the conversation.

"Well, yeah."

"You church types aren't the only ones who keep your word."

"That's not what I meant. I just didn't think you were that serious about it." He glanced at Ben and Janie. "Do you mind if we pray first?"

"No, go ahead." Doug laid down his fork.

"Ummm, we usually hold hands," Matt said, then he reached for Cass's hand and Janie's.

"Papa, get Ben's hand," Janie said as she slipped her hand into Doug's.

Doug mumbled, "Sorry," and did as he was told.

Matt bowed his head and closed his eyes. "God, thank You for this food. Bless it and give us a good, safe day. In Jesus' name. Amen."

"At least it was short and sweet," Doug said, stuffing a bite of eggs in his mouth. He checked his watch and made a mental note.

"Did you read, too?" Matt asked Cass.

"I confess, no, I didn't."

"That's okay. It was short notice." He turned to Doug. "So what'd you think?"

Doug saw Cass watching him and he gulped his coffee

before he tried to answer. "I'll concede that there's more to the story than just a whale, although I still have trouble believing it really happened."

"What do you think it's about?"

It was another challenge, only this was more like the kind Mark levied, the kind designed to unmask his ignorance. Doug felt a flush like he was back in the sixth grade and the teacher had called on him and he was unprepared as usual. "Punishment for disobedience."

"That's part of it, I guess." Matt took a drink from his glass of milk. "It's also about prejudice, and telling God who He should save and who He should judge."

"Is that what all that stuff about the vine was about? He lost me there."

"Yeah, Jonah was more upset that the plant died than he was about the whole city that was about to face God's wrath."

"Jonah really believed that? That the whole city would be wiped out?"

"Yeah, that's what he was waiting to see. He wanted a front row seat for the destruction."

"He doesn't sound like much of a preacher." Doug took another bite. Was Mark like Jonah? Was Mark waiting to see him wiped out? Was he angry that God hadn't already destroyed him? Was Africa Mark's time in the fish's belly?

"So was that your point, Matt?" Doug asked. "To show me that Christians are a sorry, vindictive bunch waiting for God to destroy the rest of us like we deserve?"

"No, it was to show there's more to the Bible than you think." Then the teenager laid down his fork and looked at Cass first, then he locked his eyes on Doug's. "Nobody is ever too far gone. Whether you're a believer stuck inside a fish or a hardcore unbeliever, God knows where you're at and He'll do amazing things to reach you."

What if he didn't want to be reached, though?

As Doug followed the line of cars to his assigned spot in the parking lot, he glanced at Janie and the boys in the rear-view mirror as often as he could. She squirmed with excitement, and the trip to the theme park was worth it for her sake alone. Ben and Matt tried to hide their anticipation behind a veneer of teenaged coolness, but Doug wasn't fooled.

He turned off the car, and grabbed a baseball hat from the gear shift. "So what's the plan?" he asked Cass.

"How's your schedule?"

"Oh . . . an hour, hour and a half before I have to go through the whole routine."

Cass twisted in her seat to face the kids. "Miss Jane, are you a fearless, daredevil, roller-coaster riding—"

"Uh, no," Ben said. "Merry-go-rounds are more her speed."

"I thought you were a tree-climbing, brother-chasing tomboy."

"Trees don't move," Jane said.

"I see," Cass smiled. "Sounds like we better split up."

Doug nodded. "Why don't you take Jane and I'll follow the boys around."

"You're not gonna ride, Papa?"

"Not today."

"Papa doesn't like high places," Cass said and winked at him. She climbed out of the car, then helped Jane out of her seat.

"But Papa's been in a plane and they go very, very high."

"Papa never sits by the window," Doug said scooping her up into his arms. "That way it's just like a bus."

Jane pointed at Matt and Ben, now several yards ahead of them. "The boys are winning!"

"The boys don't have tickets. They'll have to wait for us."

Jane smiled with satisfaction and so did Doug in spite of a twinge of bitterness, and a whisper deep inside, *He's kept*

them from you all these years. See what you've been missing.
Yes, but he had them now.

Inside the main gate, Doug kissed Cass and double-
checked the charge on his phone.

"You remember how to text, right?"

"Yes," he muttered with irritation.

"Send me your numbers when you test. I want to
know."

"Go ride something," he said with mock annoyance,
waving them off. "So where to, gentlemen?" Doug scanned the
park map and the skyline in each direction, looking for landmarks. Everything was laid out to keep a person wandering in
circles. Naturally.

"You seriously aren't gonna ride anything?" Ben asked,
peering over Doug's elbow at the map.

"I'm seriously not."

"The biggest coaster's right there. Let's go."

Of course the biggest coaster was farthest away. Doug
checked his map one more time then stuffed it in the pouch of
his cooler bag. The boys walked at a good clip, chattering and
pointing as they went.

"This is really your first time here?" Ben asked.

"Yours too, isn't it?"

"Yeah, but I'm a kid. Plus we've been to other theme
parks. But Dad never came when he was a kid?"

"Oh, he came. His mother brought him. Her parents.
School groups."

"So what'd you do for fun when you were a kid?" Matt
asked.

"Hung out by the river. I grew up north of downtown
real close to the river. I fished, threw sticks in the water, that
kind of thing."

"You didn't have any brothers or sisters?"

"Is this where your line starts?" Doug asked.

"Oh, yeah. Doesn't look too long."

"I'll meet you over there somewhere." Doug pointed to a
bench. "In the shade."

"Sure thing," Matt said.

Doug watched them bound up the ramp, and he shook his head. If there was going to be an interrogation in between rides, he'd hope for longer lines.

―――――――

Jane skipped and danced all the way back to the corner of the park where the kiddie rides were located. She squealed and clapped her hands at everything she saw—shops, souvenirs, even the snack vendors, but Cass was astonished that the child never asked for anything. It seemed to be enough just to see it all. After riding airplanes and swings, Cass suggested they get ice cream, and Jane hopped and jumped to the ice cream shop. She chose birthday cake ice cream, and swung Cass's hand while she waited on Cass to choose.

"Peanut butter, mud pie or strawberry?"

"Don't get mud," Jane said. "I've tasted it. It's not that good."

"You don't like the nuts?"

"No, the dirt."

Cass smiled and ordered peanut butter, then followed Jane to a table by the window. After a few spoonfuls, Jane eyed Cass carefully. "Are you married to my papa?"

"No, sweetheart." Apparently Jane missed it the first hundred times it came up.

"But you kissed him on the lips. I thought only married people kissed on the lips."

"I love your papa very much."

"He loves you, too. His eyes get all gooey when he sees you."

"Gooey?"

"Like this." She rolled her eyes and batted her eyelids.

"I've never seen him do that."

"He does it on the inside." She took a big spoonful of ice cream, then shivered.

"I see. Does your daddy get all gooey at your mommy?"

"Not very much. Daddy studies a lot and preaches and works on important things."

"He has a big job, I guess."

Jane nodded. "He says any work you do for God is important."

"What does your mommy do?"

"She does our school, and all the house things and she plays with me some."

"That sounds like an important job, too."

"Mommy says that's what she was made to do. What were you made to do?"

"Uh . . . I draw . . . I help people fix their rooms up so they'll be special."

"Like my room?"

"Yes, only whole houses."

"Wow. That's a lot of work."

"Sometimes."

"No wonder you don't have a little girl or boy of your own."

A couple of rides later, Doug checked his sugar and coaxed the boys into a pizzeria that also had some salads on the menu. "You guys know how to send a text message?"

"I thought you told her you knew how," Matt said.

"I do." He handed Matt his phone. "Here. Tell her my sugar was one-twenty, I took my shot and I'm having a . . . salad with pepperoni." He watched as the teenager's fingers flew over the key pad, then a moment later his phone buzzed.

"She said she's proud of you and she'd make pasta tomorrow."

"Lemme have the phone." Doug took it, and typed in 'thanks,' then dropped the phone in his pocket "Just to prove I could do it."

"I believed you," Matt said. He and Ben agreed on a supreme pizza and Doug settled at a table in the corner. By now he knew to wait until they prayed before he took his first bite.

"So do you have to do all those shots and everything all the time?" Ben asked.

Doug shook his head. "Usually it's two pills and a shot, but things are messed up today, so I have to test more and adjust more and really watch what I eat."

"Is that why you're not riding anything?"

"Partially. Heights bother me."

"So how do you build houses?"

"I hire roofers and framers."

"Framers?"

"The guys that build the wooden structure. I've got a house going up. I can take you to the site tomorrow if you'd like to see it."

"That'd be cool." Ben stuffed a half slice of pizza in his mouth which meant it was Matt's turn. At least Doug got another bite in.

"You know, we did this family history project when I was in the sixth grade, and Dad didn't even know your parents' names," Matt said.

"John and Mary Ann Ross Bolling. Ross is my middle name. My dad worked construction. My mother left when I was eleven. My dad died when I was seventeen. I got married when I was nineteen and became a dad three weeks after I turned twenty. Anything else you wanna know?"

Matt blinked several times. "Who took care of you?"

"Nobody. Once my mother left, my dad became a drunk, but when he wasn't drunk he was abusive, so I preferred drunk."

"So you had to cook for yourself and stuff?" Ben's eyes were wide with disbelief.

"I ate at school. Then there was a widow lady down the street who always had some kind of job she needed help with and she fed me." He smiled and seized the opportunity for another bite. "I think she made up some of those jobs."

"Did she go to church?" Matt asked with heavy seriousness.

"Yeah, actually. Why?"

"Just curious."

"But you actually liked school food?" Ben asked "I've always heard it was terrible."

"I only stayed in school for the food," Doug admitted. "I hated school. Except math. I was good at math. And then in high school I had shop."

"Shopping class?" Ben crinkled his nose.

"No, wood shop. We built stuff."

"So that's when you decided you wanted to build houses?"

"Yep, because all the math jobs meant I'd have to read, too."

"You don't like to read?"

"It's too much work. With contracts and surveys, I have to get in my office by myself and really concentrate. Cass thinks I'm dyslexic or something."

Ben nodded. "Dad's good at math. So's Matt. They got that from you, huh?"

"Maybe." Doug got in three or four bites before the boys reloaded with the next round of questions.

"So you built your first house when you were nineteen?"

"No. I didn't build houses until I got out on my own. Before that, I hung drywall for a guy named Malcolm Leonard. He was a Marine drill instructor before he was a contractor."

"And that's why you're so tough," Ben said.

"I don't think I'm tough."

"Yeah, you do this squinty thing with your eyes that all the tough guys do. I bet you got in fights all the time."

"Actually that part's true."

"Really?" Ben's eyes grew wide again. "Were you a bully?"

Doug shook his head. "I never started anything, but I had a short fuse and didn't take anything off anybody."

"What'd they tease you about?"

"Ben, look, I'm not proud of it. Let's just forget it."

"Sure. No problem. We can talk about building houses, about the drill sergeant guy. Did he yell at you all the time?"

"No. He taught me a lot. How to work. How to be a man."

"Like what?"

"He told me I needed to be responsible and marry your grandmother, and he told me I needed to get out on my own so I could take care of my family."

"Sounds like a good guy,'" Ben said.

"He was."

"Was he a Christian, too?" Matt asked.

"I think so, why?"

"So was Jim Lowry, Dad's old boss, right?"

"Yes, Matt. What's your point?"

"It seems like there's been a string of people in your life who were there when you needed help and they're all believers. It's like God's been watching out for you."

Doug laughed gently. "If that's the case, He's dropped the ball the last fifteen or so years. No Christians around."

"What about us?"

"Where've you been, Matt? All of you? Everywhere, but here." Doug gulped from a bottle of water. "I think God finally got the hint and left me alone. Cass is not a Christian. Sandy, at the office, is not a Christian, and frankly, I'm happy with that."

Monday, September 14

Doug sat at the breakfast table, sipping a cup of coffee and scanning the morning paper. He kept one eye and ear on the small television on the kitchen counter, waiting for the weather forecast so he could plan his week just like he did every Monday morning.

This morning, though, he wrestled with an odd combination of satisfaction and bitterness. Matt's suggestion that they spend the day at Six Flags had been an excellent idea. He and the kids talked for hours in between rides and snacks. They wanted to know about him, about his work. They wanted to understand. Mark never did that, and Mark kept him from connecting with the kids all these years, and instead painted him as a caricature heathen in broad dismissive strokes.

He smiled as Cass glided by and kissed his cheek. "You're up early," he said.

"It's almost six-thirty."

He grinned but didn't tease her this time. "So Six Flags didn't wear you out?"

"I had fun." She grinned at him as she set a kettle of water on the stove. "And so did you, didn't you?"

"It was a good day. Oh, and my sugar's spot on this morning."

"Good, but you're still going to monitor closely today, right?"

"Yes, ma'am."

She crossed her arms and leaned against the counter. "So, I'm confused after yesterday. Why are we so evil again?"

Doug laughed. "Welcome to my world. Matt and Ben seemed interested in building houses so I think I'll take the kids over to the Davis site."

"I wondered what was on the agenda for today. It's kind of an in-between, calm-before-the-storm day. I guess I didn't know what to expect." The kettle began to hiss, so she got a cup and dropped a tea bag inside before pouring in the hot water. She dunked the bag a time or two then smiled. "Jane said your eyes get all gooey when you see me."

Doug smiled. "That obvious, huh?"

"I think she's just especially astute."

"A-what?"

"Astute. Intelligent, perceptive, with good judgment."

"Oh, she gets that from me."

Cass arched her eyebrows. "Does she now?" She rounded the counter and joined him at the table. "You know, all last night . . . I kept thinking the kids have made me realize there's so much . . . a whole other side of life really, that I've been missing."

"I'm doing everything I can to fix that."

Cass pulled a Diet Coke from the small refrigerator across from Sandy's desk, and looked out the window for Doug's truck. "He hasn't called, has he?"

Sandy laughed, and swiveled her chair around. "You honestly think he'd call me before he called you?"

"Point taken. And it's not even that late. Just anxious, I guess."

"You're not . . . worried, are you?"

"What? No. That's silly. There's nothing to worry about."

Sandy smiled gently and nodded. "He loves you."

"I know. I never questioned—"

"I mean, he loves *you*."

"Yeah," Cass whispered, but he didn't ask her along this morning. Yesterday, she and Jane seemed to really hit it off, and she thought maybe that was the icebreaker she needed, that it would create an 'us.' No, there was still a 'Doug and the kids' and a 'Doug and her.' There was no 'us.'

"He loves having the kids around," Cass said. "I wish you could have seen him yesterday." She took a drink from her can. "He's rediscovered a treasure that was even better than he remembered."

"You are his treasure."

"I haven't slept since he filed this lawsuit." She glanced out the window again. "Even if he wins . . . " She shook her head and crossed the room to her office doorway. "Sorry. I'm paranoid. Insecure. You name it."

"Honey, you're a woman. We're all like that. All the time." Sandy smiled. "And usually it's their fault."

Cass tried to smile. Once again she told herself it was only because the Davis site was still a hard hat area and he knew she hated hard hats. That's why he didn't invite her. Not because he was shutting her out. Not because the lawsuit was causing some weird intangible shift in their relationship. He was watching out for her, doing what he thought was best for her. She hoped.

"Here they come!" Sandy called, then laughed. "She's all hat!"

Cass had to smile as Jane skipped through the door, over-sized hard-hat dipping with every step. "Papa let me build!" she announced.

"You built the house?"

"With my own hammer and four nails!" she squealed.

Matt and Ben followed, minus hard hats with Doug last of all. He stepped around the kids and leaned forward to kiss Cass, but she was very conscious of Jane's eyes on her and turned her cheek toward him.

"Make sure Papa pays you scale for your labor," Sandy said.

Doug rolled his eyes. "Matt, Ben and Jane, this is Sandy Owen. She runs my office."

"Oh, he admitted it!" Sandy said. "I wish I had that on tape." She leaned down to shake hands with Jane, and then reached for Matt and Ben's hands. "I am so glad to meet you."

"You, too," Matt said.

"How's your afternoon look?" Doug asked Cass.

"I'm flexible, why?"

"Let's go grab lunch and hit the pool."

"Can't turn that down, can I?"

He shook his head. "Great."

"He never says that to me," Sandy said to Jane with mock aggravation.

"That's what happens when you're in charge," Doug said, then he grew serious. "Sandy, we have our first court date tomorrow, so we won't be in. The crews are all on track, so unless something comes up, it shouldn't make a difference."

"Right." She scribbled a note on her desk blotter.

"All right." He glanced around the office quickly. "I guess that's it. Let's go."

"You're really gonna leave me here when I know you're going home to your pool?"

"Sandy, someone has to answer the phone." He opened the door for the kids. "Now whether you're at that desk or you forward the calls somewhere else is your business." Then he frowned. "Actually, I guess it's still my business . . . you know what I mean."

"Where are we going?" Cass asked before he disappeared out the door.

"Oh . . . I don't know . . . where do you want to go?"

"The Grille. The kids should like that."

"Great idea. See you there."

Cass turned to Sandy. "I guess I'm done for the day."

"Honey, go home, enjoy the afternoon. Enjoy him. And above all, don't worry. When this lawsuit thing is over, you and Doug will be better than ever."

"I hope you're right." But from deep inside her came the faintest whisper, *what if she's wrong?*

Ten

Tuesday, September 15

Mark sat on the floor, his back against the end of the bed, his Bible resting on his knees. He laid a flashlight on the bed at his shoulder, and he read through First Peter once again in the early morning quiet. For most of the night he lay in bed, pretending to be asleep in the hopes that Julie would sleep. Somewhere across town, he knew his father was already awake.

Lord God, I'm struggling with bitterness bordering on hatred toward my father. He's arrogant, selfish. Help me remember that I was no different. Help me see him the way You do.

Yesterday, David Shannon gathered his church family to pray specifically for this hearing today. Mark knew that the churches in Mombasa and the villages, Paul Hammell's church in Italy, his first church in St. Joseph and so many others were all praying, if not for this hearing specifically, at least for the legal battle. God had to hear. He had to intervene.

That's exactly what he told Julie. She hadn't wanted to go to church yesterday morning, but he convinced her that it would be an encouragement, that she needed the renewed strength that would come from having everyone stand with them. She wasn't convinced, but she went anyway.

Father, I have a peace this morning. I just read to submit, submit to Your will. I know that this is just something we have to go through—a test before we move to the next ministry

*You have for us. Use this to strengthen my children's faith, and
ours, and we'll give You the glory.*

Maybe his dad had made his point, flexing his legal
muscle by grabbing the kids for the weekend. His dad liked
dramatic gestures. Maybe it was enough for his dad to drop
the suit completely. He could even imagine his dad wanting to
settle everything in a quick meeting without the judge and
lawyers.

Just then Mark heard the covers rustle and Julie called
his name. "I'm right here." He twisted himself up from the
floor, clicked off the flashlight and sat on the edge of the bed.
"I was just reading."

"Does it help?"

"I think so." He reached for her hand and managed a
smile. "It's almost over."

"I know I'm supposed to believe that."

"But?"

"I don't know. I have a bad feeling about today."

"But we've all been praying and God has amazing power—"

"Just because we prayed it doesn't mean He'll do it."
She sat up and leaned against the headboard. "Lots of people
pray and ask God for all kinds of things. He doesn't answer all
of them."

"Right . . . but He also works within His will. How could
it be His will for my dad to have our kids?"

She looked at him and blinked, then whispered, "You're
right. What purpose could that possibly serve?" She wiped her
eyes quickly. "I'm sorry. My faith is not where it should be."

"Where should it be?"

"I'm a pastor's wife, a missionary. My father and both
my grandfathers were preachers . . . I know better."

"Don't be so hard on yourself. This is a unique test."

"I'm going to get a big fat zero on it." She sighed. "I
know I'm supposed to be civil to your dad and that woman
today after what they've done to us. I know I'm supposed to
turn the other cheek and do unto others and all that, but

Mark . . . ”

    “It's okay.”

    “No. My mother could do it.”

    “Then call her.”

    “I can't.”

    “Why not?”

    “I just . . . I can't. I'll call her when it's over.”

    Julie paced in the hallway outside the family court hearing room. The air was stagnant and she could feel her underarms dampening. A single bead of perspiration trickled down her breastbone. She'd have to leave her sweater on now, which would only make things worse.

    Mark was seated on a nearby bench, his eyes glued to the door, watching for either the lawyers or his father. She turned back to the hearing room door, willing it to open, desperate to get inside before Doug arrived. She couldn't endure sitting in the hallway with him and that woman while they waited.

    It seemed odd that the hallway was deserted. No one crossed from here to there. No one passed. She and Mark were all alone. David offered to come with them, but Mark said there was no need. Honestly, she was glad it was just Mark and her. She didn't have to put on a brave face that way.

    She heard the heavy door open and spun around to see Chuck Molinsky coming down the hallway two steps ahead of Fletcher Durant. As promised, Durant was dressed in a dark suit, and even from that distance, Julie could see the dark tint in his glasses. Maybe he was hoping for some 'blind lawyer' sympathy points. She shook her head and sighed. If those two could get them through this, she would take back everything she said or thought about the lawyers.

    “Mark,” Chuck said, reaching out to shake hands. When Julie remained some distance away, he nodded toward her. “Julie, how are you doing today?”

"I'm okay," Mark said. "I have peace about it."

"I'm nauseous," Julie admitted.

Fletcher wheezed and then explained, "Mrs. Bolling, this is just an added step to your process prompted by the protective custody order." He nodded toward the hearing room door. "At issue is where the children will spend the next four weeks. The actual custody hearing is still next month, you understand."

"Yes, but we'll get the kids back today, right?" Julie asked.

"That is the intent."

The door to the hearing room opened and a middle-aged woman motioned to them. "Judge Whitmire will be ready in a few moments, but you're welcome to come in. Are both parties here?"

"Uh, no," Chuck said. "This is Mark and Julie Bolling, the respondents."

"Well, I'll tell you this much, Judge Whitmire won't wait around. If they don't show, this whole thing will be thrown out."

Julie looked at Mark with renewed hope. "Do we pray for heavy traffic?"

"If that's what it takes," Mark said, following her into the hearing room. They sat at the conference table furthest from the door, and waited. Julie crossed her legs, then uncrossed them, then tucked her left foot behind her right ankle. The brown carpet at her feet was like the carpet in church vestibules across the Midwest, but there were no coordinating threads. Just brown, some darker, some lighter, all brown.

Then the door clicked open. She expected the judge's black robes. No. A gray-haired man in a suit and red power tie strode in without bothering to glance their direction. He hoisted his briefcase to the other conference table. He unapologetically snapped open the fasteners and began stacking papers. They were doomed.

Finally, Doug stepped through the doorway, and at his elbow, gliding more than walking, was a striking blond woman. She was dressed in a beige suit that tastefully flattered her, which she complimented with a wide gold bracelet and a heavy gold necklace. Her perfect manicure set off the diamond ring she wore on her left hand. In spite of that, she didn't look like the type that was just after a man's money. Everything about her was stylish and elegant.

Doug's navy suit was perfectly tailored, set off by silk in his breast pocket coordinated with his tie. When he pulled out the woman's chair, his cuff links glinted. French cuffs. Doug Bolling. With just the right amount of gray at his temples, he looked like another high-powered lawyer. He pulled out his own chair, subtly nodded toward Mark, then took his seat between the woman and his attorney.

Julie's fragile confidence evaporated. They were sunk. Chuck and Fletcher had tirelessly reminded them that this wasn't about who could provide a better home for the children, but that Doug had to prove that they were incapable of providing a decent home for their children. With one look at the power couple and their slick lawyer, Julie knew they were in over their heads. They were on Doug's turf, playing by his rules, and he was playing for keeps. There was no grace or mercy in Doug's world.

Cass took a deep breath and closed her eyes. The abstract was now reality. "Mark and Julie" weren't just names punctuating one of Doug's rants. They were flesh and blood people, anxious, maybe even terrified parents, and she and Doug were here to strip them of their children.

She stole a quick glance at Mark and his wife. He wasn't the wild-eyed fanatic Doug had made him out to be. In fact, they had the very same eyes, but Mark's had a gentleness in them that showed through even now. Mark's face was narrow, just like Matt's. Ben's features were a blend of his parents', but Janie looked just like her mother.

For a split second, she could picture Jane snuggled on

her mother's lap. A wave of heat and nausea passed over her and she begged a God she wasn't sure she believed in to make this end quickly.

Julie's world stopped turning the instant Judge Henry Whitmire walked into the hearing room. In a blur of legalese, fogged by the distress of simply being in a hearing, she caught only bits and pieces. Doug's lawyer claimed that they were a risk to leave the country, and cited Matt leaving Doug's house as evidence. She knew Doug would use that against them. Mark claimed his father was worried. No, Doug was probably overjoyed because it played right into his plans.

The lawyer then demanded that they surrender their passports and that temporary custody be awarded to Doug, with only limited visitation.

And Fletched Durant and Chuck Molinsky sat there.

Neither man responded, neither defended them, or bothered to shoot accusations back across the room. Nothing.

Julie took Mark's arm. "Do something!" she whispered.

"It's not our turn," Mark whispered back.

She slumped back in her seat, and stared up at the ceiling to keep tears from spilling onto her cheeks. She hardly noticed when the attorneys protested strenuously that Victor Wiley was prejudiced against Christians and was leveling unfounded charges against their clients.

She did hear the judge say, "It has been my experience that a man's claim of religion has no bearing on his actions." It didn't matter that they were moral, upright, good parents, and good citizens without so much as a traffic citation. "I will grant the plaintiff's petition for temporary custody and visitation is set for Saturday afternoons noon to four p.m. at the plaintiff's home."

The gavel banged, and just like that, Julie Bolling lost her children.

"We lost," she whispered. Then she asked no one in

particular, "Where are they?" She stood and pushed away from Mark and Chuck. "I want to see my children! Where are they?" Charging across the hearing room, she grabbed Doug Bolling by the arm. "What have you done with my kids? I want to see them!"

"They're in a waiting room down the hall," he said firmly, then turned to his lawyer. "She can see them, can't she?"

"That's up to you," he answered, stuffing folders in his briefcase. "Take a bailiff with you."

Doug shook his head, turned and walked out of the hearing room and Julie followed at his heels. At the end of the hall, he opened a door. When Julie saw her sons and her baby girl, her knees grew weak and tears flowed unrestrained. She knelt down and Janie ran to her, flinging her arms around Julie's neck. She hugged Jane tightly, rocking her back and forth, crying, whispering to her, smoothing her hair.

"Are we going home now?" Matt asked.

Julie wiped her eyes, and swallowed hard. She stood slowly, taking Janie in her arms. "Matthew . . . the judge . . . "

Mark's arrival in the room cut Julie off. He hugged his boys, and kissed his daughter's cheek. "Did you tell them?" he asked quietly.

"I can't."

"We lost," Ben said. "We lost, didn't we?"

"It's only for a month," Mark said. "Just until the actual hearing."

Matt slumped into the nearest chair. "What did we do wrong, Dad? We prayed . . . we did everything God said. Why did we still lose?"

"I don't know, Matt. God's doing something I don't understand." Mark's voice was tired, his shoulders rounded.

"It was our lawyers," Julie said. "They won't fight for us. They let that other guy run everything, and couldn't answer him."

"Julie, that's not true," Mark said, an unexpected sharpness in his voice. She flushed, and clenched her jaw. Mark never spoke to her that way in front of the children.

"So what happens to us?" Matt asked, his head hung low as he leaned his elbows on his knees.

"Well, you go back to your grandfather's house, and we'll see you on Saturday."

"Saturday!" Matt jerked his body upright. "That's it?"

"For now, yes," Mark said.

"Dad, Janie cries every night," Ben said. "Doesn't the judge care about that?"

"He's doing what he thinks is best."

"You say everybody is doing what they think is best. When do we get to say what is best?"

"Ben, do you think I'm not upset about this?" He raised a hand and clenched his fist tightly, but a moment later he released the fist and ran his hand back through his hair. "I hate this, but we are under the authority of the government. I can't break the law just because I disagree with it."

"Doesn't this go against God's law, though?"

"No."

"Grandpa's a jerk," Matt mumbled.

"That's enough, Matt," Mark said.

"It's true," Matt protested.

"Your grandfather is in danger of dying without Jesus Christ, and if this is what it takes to bring him around then it's worth it," Mark said harshly. "We don't have a choice, all right!" He turned to face Julie. "I don't . . . I can't fix this," he said softly and walked out of the waiting room.

Doug sent Cass on ahead so he could speak to Mark alone. He couldn't leave the soulless exchange between strangers supposedly acting on their behalf as the last word. Plus there was that comment the other lawyer made during all that arguing over the passports . . . something about Mark leaving Kenya. Was that before or after the lawsuit? Before or after Jane broke her arm? Why was he hearing it now from a lawyer and not from Mark months ago?

When his son strode out of the waiting room, he stood a little straighter, and called Mark's name. Mark took two steps toward him, but said nothing.

He didn't owe Mark an explanation, but he'd offer one. "I want what's best for the children."

"But it's all lies," Mark said quietly. "You sat there and let that man lie about us just to get what you want. How could you turn on me like that?"

"It's not—"

"These are my children! You're claiming that I'm an abusive, neglectful father. That's insane! What would Mom say if she knew?"

"Leave your mother out of this," Doug growled.

"Is this your idea of honoring her memory?"

In a flash, before he had time to think, Doug slapped Mark across the mouth, the blow resounding in the empty hallway. He pointed at his son, but could only choke out the word, "Don't."

Mark stood frozen for a moment then slowly raised a hand and rubbed his mouth. "I'm sorry," he whispered.

Doug watched him turn and reenter the waiting room. A half hour later, Mark left the room with Julie and they walked to the far staircase to leave without even a fleeting look in his direction. Doug took a deep breath, straightened his tie and walked into the waiting room.

"Are you ready to go?"

Matt glared, but didn't speak. Ben took Janie's hand, and led her out of the room, stopping at the table by the door. He pointed to the box of tissues. She nodded, and he pulled two tissues out for her then followed Matt out of the waiting room.

***

Cass couldn't recall the last time she had been so anxious to leave a room. She felt hateful and unclean. As she waited in the Escalade, she tried to convince herself that Doug knew what he was doing, that this was just the way things had to be done, that it was the system. When she saw Mark's children trudge out of the Family Court building, all those notions were destroyed.

She wiped her eyes, then reached across to the driver's side and started the car. When Matt lifted Janie in, Cass tried to smile at them, to communicate that she knew there had to be a better way, but Matt refused to look at her. Even Ben climbed in the backseat without a word.

When Doug got in and began loosening his tie, she asked him, "Did you get everything you wanted?"

"Not now, Cass," he said, wearily. He leaned back to look in the rearview mirror. "Lunch?" There was silence. "Me either," he said, as he put the car in gear, then pulled out of the parking lot.

Eleven

It barely registered with Julie that she was in David Shannon's car with Mark headed out of downtown St. Louis. The hurt didn't register. The knowledge that she would spend the next four weeks without her children didn't register. All she felt was anger—blanketing, consuming anger.

Doug Bolling was evil. He was an evil, wicked man, and she hated him. *God, help me. I hate him. The way he breezed into the hearing room in that thousand-dollar suit, flaunting his wealth, his beautiful, blonde live-in . . . He probably took up with her just because he knew how much it would hurt Mark. God, how can You let him win like that? Where is Your justice?*

She saw Mark reach up and rub his lip. She was furious with him as well. Mark acted as though this was as natural as the seasons. It's only for a month, he said. She'd be dead in a month without her children. I can't fix this, he said. He hadn't tried. He gave up without a fight.

She'd prayed so hard for this to work out. Dozens of people prayed. How could God ignore all that? She'd always done the best she could, served God from the time she was old enough to understand what that meant. She had spent her adult life in ministry or on the mission field. Why was God abandoning her now?

Their lawyers were incompetent, but they were stuck with them. After all, it was far more important that they didn't offend David Shannon for hiring the lawyer than it was to actually get good representation for the family. Ben was right. When would they get to say what was best? When would someone fight for them?

Mark pulled into David's driveway, but left the car running. "Julie . . . "

"You can't help me right now," she said quietly. "No one can."

"I'm going to go for a drive, then. I'll be back later." Julie said nothing. He handed her the house key, and a telephone calling card. "Call your mother. Call whoever you need to." Then Mark backed out and left her standing in the driveway.

She eyed the credit card in her hand. Call somebody? Who? There was no one listening.

"God, I failed. I failed her. I failed my children. God, the looks on their faces. They needed me, and I couldn't do anything." Mark swiped at his eyes so he could see to drive. "I knew this was a test, and I thought I was ready for it." That gavel would echo in his memory for the rest of his life. And Julie, would she ever get over this?

All because he ran from a call. Oh, he covered it up with lofty, Godly work, but at its core, it was disobedience. Now there was a storm swirling all around him just like the raging storm that nearly wrecked the ship taking Jonah to Tarshish away from God's presence. The only way the sailors could stop the storm was to throw Jonah overboard. Mark sighed deeply. He was overboard now, drowning, and the only thing to look forward to was a fish's belly.

Mark pulled off the road into a parking lot and found a shady spot in the back corner away from other cars. In the pocket of his sport coat, he carried a small Bible his mother had given him. He flipped the pages to the second chapter of Jonah.

I cried out to the Lord because of my afflic-

tion,

> *And He answered me.*
> *Out of the belly of Sheol I cried,*
> *And You heard my voice.*
> *For You cast me into the deep,*
> *Into the heart of the seas,*
> *And the floods surrounded me;*
> *All Your billows and Your waves passed*

over me . . .

> *The waters surrounded me, even to my*

soul;

> *The deep closed around me . . .*
> *Yet You have brought up my life from the*

pit,

> *O Lord, my God.*
> *When my soul fainted within me,*
> *I remembered the Lord;*
> *And my prayer went up to You,*
> *Into Your holy temple.*
> *Those who regard worthless idols*
> *Forsake their own Mercy.*
> *But I will sacrifice to You*
> *With the voice of thanksgiving;*
> *I will pay what I have vowed.*
> *Salvation is of the Lord.*

God heard him. He had to remember that. And all this chaos, they were His billows, His waves. God was still in control. Mark took a deep breath and read the last verse out loud. "I will sacrifice to You with the voice of thanksgiving; I will pay what I have vowed. Salvation is of the Lord."

He laid the Bible aside and leaned his head back against the headrest. "Sacrifice with the voice of thanksgiving. Sacrifice. Give up something dear and precious to me. My kids? I've lost them temporarily. Isn't that enough?"

The next to last line read, *I will pay what I have vowed.* The vow he made to his mother, when he promised her he'd bring his dad to Christ. "I can't make that happen God. It was crazy to think I could. Just like it says, You're the only one who can bring him around."

He slouched in his seat and stared out across the parking lot. Think. What's going on? What's God doing? Salvation is of the Lord. The Lord . . . and not me. I can't fix it. It's the same message. Let go, submit, let God do it.

"Julie won't buy this. She thinks I'm sitting back and letting my dad and his lawyer have their way. How can I help her see it's You, that I'm letting You have Your way?"

He couldn't. The pronouns were all personal. Julie had to see it for herself, and right now she was too distraught. He'd have to be patient and hope she'd give him enough grace to make it through the next few weeks.

When Doug pulled into a visitor's parking place in front of Weston Elementary School, Cass was as bewildered as the children. School? What was Doug thinking? He didn't look at her, simply tightened his tie, then turned around to the kids in the backseat. "You guys can stay here or go in. It's up to you." Neither boy moved. "Jane, come with me," he said. "This is your school."

Matt spoke before Cass could. "You're making us go to school? Today?"

"You start tomorrow," Doug said. "You can't just sit at the house all day."

"We've never been to school, Grandpa," Ben said. "Mom's always taught us."

"All the more reason to get you in the system. Ben, unbuckle Janie's seat belt."

This was wrong. Cass knew it deep inside, but she had no part in the legal action. She was powerless. Then she looked back into Jane's eyes. "Janie, come on, baby. It'll be all right." She held a hand out and Janie slid out of her booster seat, then took Cass's hand. She steadied the little girl as she climbed over the front seat and out the passenger side door.

Cass knelt down and smoothed Janie's dress, and pushed a lock of hair behind Janie's ear. The little girl's eyes brimmed with tears. "I am so sorry," Cass whispered, taking Janie in her arms. "It'll be okay, sweetheart. This will work out some-how."

Doug rounded the car and knelt down beside Jane. "You'll like school. There are lots of girls your age to play with." He was trying his best to be the good guy, but Jane stiffened and pressed against Cass's body. "It'll be fun. You know they have a playground, don't you?"

She lifted her head just slightly from Cass's shoulder and shook it.

"Yeah, a really great playground. Let's go check it out."

She shook her head again.

Doug's voice tightened. "Jane, do you do what your daddy tells you to?"

She nodded without lifting her head.

"Well, the judge said that I am just like your daddy now. I know it's hard to understand, but that's just the way things are. If your daddy said you were going to go to school, would you go?"

Again she nodded.

"Then that's what you need to do for me. Listen to me, just like you listen to your daddy."

She turned her head, burying it in Cass's shoulder. "Come on, Jane." He took her arm and pulled her away from Cass. The little girl stretched to stay with Cass, tears stream-ing down her cheeks. "Cass, I could use some help," Doug muttered.

"Then let go," Cass said. She hugged Janie close, and whispered, "Will you go with me?"

Janie nodded slightly.

"I know it's hard, sweetheart, but you can do it." Cass fished in her purse for a tissue, and wiped Janie's eyes, then she covered the little girl's nose. "Blow. That's the way. All set?"

Janie wiped her eyes and nodded, but she wouldn't

look at her grandfather.

Cass stood and took Janie's hand, and walked into the school building with her, leaving Doug awkwardly trailing behind them.

———————————

Julie punched digits on the phone in the Shannons' guest room. The country code, the number, the credit card number, then she waited anxiously for the call to connect. Before Debbie Hammell could say 'hello,' Julie burst into tears. "Mom, we lost. We lost the kids."

"I thought the hearing was next month."

"Doug . . . we had to have a preliminary hearing after Doug stole the kids this weekend . . . Mom we were just finishing up dinner Friday and the deputy—" She squeezed down the fullness in her throat. "He had a protective custody order. He took the children for their protection. Took them away from me and gave them to Doug."

"I am so sorry. I'm so sorry I can't be there."

"Mom . . . I . . . my children . . . my babies . . . " Julie dissolved into sobs, unable to form words, in spite of her mother's attempts to comfort and console her. Singularly consumed, she lost her grip on the handset and it slipped to the floor. She labored to find the energy to lean over and pick it up again. "Mom? I'm sorry . . . I dropped the phone. We . . . today was a preliminary hearing." She swallowed again and took a deep breath. "The judge awarded Doug temporary custody until the hearing. We can see the kids Saturday."

She heard her mother take a deep breath, then whisper something. "How's Mark?"

Julie didn't try to stop a bitter laugh. "Mark let it all happen. He just absorbed it."

"Honey, I'm sure he did everything—"

"He did nothing! Nothing! He stuck us with these idiot lawyers—"

"Julie, honey, listen to me. You and Mark—"

"Mark won't stand up for us. He let his dad run over him again and we're all paying for it."

There was another pause, then her mother spoke with loving firmness. "Give me the number there and I'll call you back in a couple of hours when you've calmed down. You're not ready to hear anything yet. Cry, grieve, vent and then we'll talk."

"But Mom—"

"I don't know what else to do for you. I can be there in three or four days, but that doesn't help you right now. What about Jan? Is she there?"

"Jan's at work. I've got the house to myself. I'm glad. I don't think I could face anybody right now."

"Mark's not there?"

"Mark went for a drive."

"All right then, let's work through this. What's the worst thing right now?"

"I hate Doug Bolling's guts."

"Julie!"

"Mom, I do. God forgive me, but I do. He's not doing this because he wants to take care of my children. He's doing it simply because he can."

"I can't believe Doug is like that."

"No, you can't believe you were deceived by him."

Again, her mother's voice was soft and solemn. "Are you looking for help dealing with this, getting through it, or do you just want me to agree with you?"

"Mom . . . " She wanted a solution, a plan, a strategy. She was going to get a lecture.

"Julie, you have been called to be like Christ, and you know there is no place for hatred in your heart. You have to get rid of that first. Then you have also been called to stand beside your husband. You cannot abandon him now."

"I'm not abandoning him."

"You aren't with him now. He needs you more now than he ever has."

"He wanted to be alone."

"What will he come home to? Is he going to come home to the safety and security of a woman who loves him, or is he going to have to face another round of attacks?"

"Mom—"

"Julie, whose side are you on?"

"My kids' side, Mom. That's who I'm fighting for."

"Then make sure you know who the enemy is."

There was no doubt about that one, and Julie silently committed to do whatever it took to get her kids away from him. He'd better enjoy them, because when this was over he'd never see them again.

Ben pressed his forehead against the car's window. "Can he really make us go to school?"

"Apparently," Matt muttered.

"So do we cooperate or not?" He leaned back and looked at Matt.

"What do you mean?"

"We're only gonna be in this school for a month. How much do we really have to do?"

"We do the best we can to prove our way is better."

"Seriously?"

"If we don't, they're gonna be calling him, and he'll be on our case. They'll probably get the school psychologist to analyze us."

"They have one of those?"

"I don't know," Matt admitted. "But it'll be easiest if we don't draw any attention to ourselves."

"So we shoot for Bs?"

"I guess." Matt punched the seat in front of him. "This is so wrong."

"I thought you were the happy grandson?"

"Well, that was before I became a prisoner."

"I think it's worse for Mom. At least we're together."

"Mom's gonna lose it if we have to stay with him the

whole month."

Ben stared out at the red maple tree in front of the school. He missed the acacia trees that dotted the landscape outside of Mombasa. He missed the smell of the dirt and the color of the sky as night overtook day. That was home. This was a jumbled mess and he wasn't sure who the good guys and bad guys were anymore. "What happens if we lose again?"

"They take us away from our parents for good."

"Dad won't let that happen," Ben said.

"I didn't think Dad would let it happen this time," Matt said, then he motioned toward the school. "Here they come."

Ben pushed his door open and took Jane's hand, steadying her as she climbed across his lap to her seat, then he helped her find the buckle for her seat belt.

His grandfather got in and watched them in the rear-view mirror. "All set?"

Ben nodded, as if he had a choice.

"On to the middle school."

Cass got in the car and buckled her seatbelt without a word. Ben didn't know much about women, more than Matt probably, but even Matt could tell that the woman in the front seat was mad. She didn't look at Grandpa, she didn't glance back at any of them, and she didn't say a word. No one made a sound the whole time.

Ben noticed Janie's thumb slip into her mouth so he patted her knee, and tried to smile. She sighed deeply and closed her eyes as if she were going to sleep. Not a bad plan. Just sleep until next month.

When they rolled up in front of Clark Middle School, Ben saw his grandfather's eyes in the rearview mirror again. "Did she go to sleep?"

"Yeah, I guess," Ben said.

"I'll leave it running," he said but no one responded. "Come on, guys." He got out and stood by the driver's door waiting. Matt frowned and climbed out, so Ben did his best to get out without disturbing Jane in case she really was asleep.

"I hope they have a couple of spots on the football

team."

"Grandpa, we've never played football," Matt protested, and it wasn't his usual whine. He was serious. "I don't even know how."

"What do you do in Africa, then? Big game hunt?"

"We play soccer and cricket. That's what everybody does there."

"Well, you're here, and not there. Football will be good for you." His grandfather raised a hand to put it on Matt's shoulder, but Ben watched his brother dip his shoulder and twist away like his grandfather would pass on the plague if he touched him.

Instantly, their grandfather jerked Matt around by that same shoulder and pointed a finger right at Matt's nose. "I don't care if you like this, I don't care if you like me, but the reality is that I am your legal guardian and you will give me the same respect you give your father. Do you understand me?"

Matt glared and his jaw clenched. "Yes sir."

Ben stiffened as his grandfather turned to him. "That goes for you, too."

"You just took us away from our parents," Ben said. "You can't expect us to act like everything is all right."

"Ben, shut up," Matt said, "you'll just make it worse."

"All right, that's enough." His grandfather swept his arm back and pointed toward the school. "Now, we are going to go in here, enroll you in school, sign you up for the football team or the track team or something and you're going to start to live a normal life!"

Doug hit the garage door opener as soon as he turned onto the long drive up to the house. He couldn't take many more victories like this one. What he needed now was a handful of aspirin, a beer, and three or four hours to try and explain to Cass that he wasn't the jerk she thought he was.

He pulled into his spot in the garage, and eased the Escalade into 'park.' He looked at Cass, and saw a barely contained fury in her eyes. "Can I talk to you for a minute? Inside?" He dared to glance back at the kids and none of them moved to unbuckle their seat belts.

He got out and unlocked the back door, then held it while Cass pushed past him into the kitchen. She slammed her purse on the counter and unloaded. "That was despicable! That was the most reprehensible thing I have ever witnessed and here I was part of it! How could you? How could you do that to them?"

"I was doing what I was told to do."

"What you were told? So the grand strategy you and this lawyer cooked up was to traumatize these children, betray their confidence and then snatch them away from the only home they've ever known and cram them into a completely alien environment with no friends, no advocates, denying them any time to grieve or understand or even absorb what had happened to them?" She paced away hugging herself. "I feel so evil right now. I want to vomit."

"You're not evil."

"Tell that to those kids!" she said, waving her arm toward the garage. "Ben won't even look at me."

"Cass . . . " He took a step, but stopped short of touching her. "This wasn't what—"

"Explain to me how anything Mark does is so bad that this is better! Explain that to me."

"It will get better. It will work out."

"No, it won't, because you cannot have a rational conversation with your own son."

"I am not the one who cut off all contact between us! He did that!"

"Then call him. Bring him over here. Sit down and deal with it!"

"I can't do that," Doug muttered.

"You *won't* do that." She shook her head, then closed her eyes and whispered, "You know what? I'm going out."

He had enough sense to step aside as she charged past him, snatching her purse from the counter as she passed.

"Where—?"

"School supplies! The kids are going to school. They need school supplies."

All his energy faded when she slammed the door. She had never been angry with him but after years of living with Judy's anger, he felt a familiar bitterness welling up inside him. He couldn't give in to it.

He summoned the energy to loosen his necktie then he leaned over the counter. Victor Wiley painted a completely different picture of how today would go. The part about how everyone he cared about would think he was the biggest jerk who ever lived got skipped over in all the strategy sessions.

He shuffled to the refrigerator and got a beer. After a couple of gulps, he slouched onto one of the barstools at the counter. Being a jerk wasn't the worst part. He was used to that. The worst part was when Vic demanded that Mark surrender all their passports. He could still hear that other lawyer. "Your honor, Mr. Bolling resigned his position. He has nothing to go back to in Kenya."

Then came the clincher. He said, "Mr. Bolling began the process of moving back to the United States before this suit was filed. The plaintiff's case therefore has no merit and we ask that this whole proceeding be thrown out."

Mark was moving back. Before the lawsuit was filed. All this could've been avoided. If he had known. If Mark had told him. The question nobody was asking—nobody except for him—was why? Why would Mark leave Kenya and not tell him? The only thing he could figure is Mark hated him before the lawsuit was even filed.

Doug gulped the rest of the beer, dropped the bottle in the trash can then grabbed a second bottle on his way to his office. It didn't matter now. He was locked into this lawsuit. The only way out was forward.

Twelve

Cass paced the mudroom, trying to compose herself before facing the kids again. Anger made her cry. It always had, which in turn, made her angrier. It was a nasty frustrating cycle. Piled on top of that was a muddle of emotions about Doug she couldn't begin to untangle. She had never seen him like this, never dreamed he was capable of such cold-hearted tactics. She had never been angry with him. Perhaps most troubling was the fact that it wasn't just over something he'd done. This was the core of who he was. He was ruthless. That terrified her.

She didn't want to hear his rationalizations because she was afraid she'd believe them. This was wrong and she couldn't allow her love for him to cloud that. She did love him. That hadn't changed. But something had.

Years ago she spilled all of her deep dark secrets and he dismissed them with a wave of his hand and a declaration that he'd never leave her. This was just like those secrets. It shouldn't matter. So he was flawed. Everyone had flaws.

She took a deep breath, then one more. She had to pull herself together for the sake of the kids out in that car who had no one to lean on right now. Regardless of what they thought of her, she had to step up for them. It was good and right and decent and it was the only way she knew of to atone for her part in what happened today.

Cass found her keys, and a list Doug handed her last

Thursday. She had stuffed it in her purse without bothering to read it then. Saturday morning he talked about adding Jane's booster seat to the list. This was the list. Skateboards, bicycles, laptop computer . . . and then school things like backpacks. Had the lawyer told him to get a list ready or was it the project management part of his brain kicking in? For his sake, for their sakes, she would believe that he was trying to accommodate and provide for the kids. That was the Doug she knew. For that Doug she'd go finish out this list.

When she climbed into the driver's seat, Matt frowned and asked, "What now?"

"I think we need some space."

"Separate planets would be nice," Ben said. Cass adjusted the rearview mirror so she could see his face. He wasn't smiling.

"Anyway, we'll go shop for your school stuff, and see what else we can get into, maybe grab some dinner." She backed out of the garage and they drove in silence to Target. The boys gave her one-word answers as they chose notebooks and backpacks. She kept telling herself at least they were speaking. Janie only nodded or shook her head.

She took them to the sporting goods store so the boys could get their football gear, thankful for the salesmen who knew everything they'd need.

Their next stop was the electronics store where Cass stunned a salesman by asking him to pack up two laptop computers and a printer. "Two computers?" Matt asked.

"Look, he's paying for it," Cass said. "Take advantage of it."

"No offense, but I'd rather die than take anything from him."

"Matt," Cass sighed, "I'm not going to pretend that this isn't the worst day of your life, but I don't know what else to do except get through it."

"Can I ask you something?" Ben tilted his head, and squinted the way his grandfather did.

"Anything." Cass was relieved he was speaking to her.

"Whose side are you on? His or ours?"

How could she explain something she hadn't resolved in her own mind? "Ben, I love your grandfather. I know he's difficult—"

"So it's his." Ben folded his arms across his chest.

"But if you'll let me finish," she said firmly, "I don't know if he's doing the right thing."

"We might be able to turn this one from the dark side," Ben said to Matt, and Matt rolled his eyes.

"Oh, no. I am not going to let you play me against him," Cass said. "You're sadly mistaken if you think you can do that." Then she softened. "But I promise, I will do everything I can to make this easier on you."

Ben looked at Matt, waiting for him to respond. The teenager frowned slightly, then held out his hand. "Fair enough," he said quietly.

Cass shook his hand, and had to swallow hard to speak. "Thanks, Matt." She turned and shook Ben's hand, and lifted Janie into her arms. "Those guys should have your stuff by now." She shepherded them to the checkout register and then they waited while their purchases were loaded into the car. Once everyone was buckled in, Cass turned and asked, "To the mall?"

"What else do we need?" Ben asked.

"How many pairs of jeans do you have with you?"

"Three."

"I am not doing laundry every other day. We're buying more clothes."

"Do I have to try them on?"

"Of course."

Ben slumped back in his seat. "Any other tortures you have in mind?"

"Just dinner."

"If I live long enough to eat," Ben muttered.

"Once we find a brand that fits, we'll get two or three pairs of them."

"Once we find them."

"Are you hard to fit?"

"Like impossible," Ben said. "I'm not fat, but I'm not husky. If we fit my hips, the legs are way too long. Mom usually hems them."

"I know a few stores. I bet I can fit you in three tries."

"You're on," Ben said. "What do I win?"

"You haven't won yet." Cass drove to the mall and took Ben, with his brother and sister following, to the men's department in one of the upscale clothing stores. An older gentleman with a tailor's tape around his neck greeted her immediately. "Charlie, this young man is difficult to fit. Can you help me out?"

"Of course, Ms. Grayson." He pushed up his glasses, pulled the tape from around his neck and began measuring Ben with expert efficiency.

"Hey! That's a little close!" Ben protested when the man measured his inseam.

Charlie scribbled numbers on a small notepad he pulled from his pocket. "I'll be right back."

"Just jeans, Charlie," Cass said as he walked away.

"This is so cheating," Ben said. "You said *you* could fit me."

"I am using the resources available to me," Cass said with a wink.

Charlie brought back a stack of jeans and handed the first pair to Ben. "The dressing room is right this way."

"If I try these on, you're not gonna measure me anymore, are you?"

"No," Charlie smiled. "I have all the measurements I need."

"Matt needs pants, too," Ben said as he disappeared into the dressing room.

"I can buy mine off the rack," Matt called back.

Charlie turned to Cass while they waited. "Mr. Bolling is well?" he asked.

"Yes," Cass answered. "These are his grandchildren."

"I might have guessed. There's a strong resemblance."

Ben shuffled from the dressing room, eyes downcast. "Something wrong?" Charlie asked.

"No. They fit. First try," he muttered. "I still say it's cheating."

"We'll take four of them, Charlie." Then she smiled at Ben. "Look at it this way. We're done."

"Small consolation," he mumbled, turning back to the dressing room.

Cass followed Charlie to the register, with Matt and Janie close behind. "That's a lot of money for four pairs of jeans," Matt remarked.

"It's not for four," Cass said quietly.

"That's what one pair of jeans costs? My dad will die when he finds out you paid this much for Ben's pants!"

"I'll explain it to him."

"You'll have to be ready to catch him when he faints," Matt said.

After a few more stores, Cass mustered as much sincerity as she could and announced she was starved. She reminded the kids that none of them had eaten lunch and she steered them to a pizza kitchen for dinner. After placing their order, she looked at Matt. "Do you guys pray in restaurants, too?"

"Is that okay?"

"It's fine," she said and reached for Janie's hand. After Matt said a quick blessing, she reached for a packet of sweetener for her tea. "Matt, can I confess something to you?"

"I guess," he said.

"I didn't read Jonah like you told me to because I don't have a Bible. Would you let me borrow yours?"

"I can fix that. I'll be right back." He scooted out of the booth and disappeared. He returned carrying a small bag, just as the pizza arrived. He handed the bag to Cass.

"What's this?"

"It's a Bible. Nothing fancy, just a standard, basic Bible. There was a bookstore a few stores down."

"How'd you pay for it?"

"I have money," he said. "It's no big deal."

"Let me pay you back," she said reaching for her purse.

"It's a gift. You can't pay for a gift." He put a slice of pizza on his plate. "And you will offend the giver if you keep this up."

"Thank you, Matt," she said softly. "I'm touched. Deeply."

———

Mark had talked to David Shannon long enough to give him a quick summary of the hearing and to ask for wisdom. David said, "I can't tell you anything. I think I would be doing the same things you are." When he explained how hard the ruling hit Julie, David said his family would grab dinner out somewhere giving Mark and Julie some time. Mark hoped Julie could at least talk to him.

When Mark arrived at David's house, everything was still and silent, and he began to wonder if anyone was home. He unlocked the front door, and was startled to see Julie in the easy chair across from the sofa. "Why are you sitting in here with the lights out?" he asked, switching on a lamp.

"Seemed to fit," she said. Her voice was flat and emotionless.

He sat on the sofa. "Care to join me?"

"I don't think so."

"Julie, I need you right now—"

"And I need you, Mark! Where were you?"

He felt like she had just snapped a trap shut. She had been waiting for him all day, waiting for him to come home, and now she had him. "We agreed we both needed some time—"

"No, Mark, where were *you*? I don't know who that man in the hearing room was, but it was not the man I thought I married."

"What did you expect me to do?" He fought to keep his voice down.

"My children are my life! I thought you would at least try to keep your father from taking them."

"I did everything I could."

"You didn't do anything, Mark. Nothing." She stood and crossed the room, but then she turned back to face him. "You're a failure, Mark."

Her tone and her body language took him back to countless confrontations between his parents. Maybe that was what triggered his sarcasm. "Anything else you need to get out?"

"As a matter of fact, I think your father is the embodiment of evil."

"That's a little over the top."

"I hate him, Mark. I sat in the courtroom watching him. I could have choked him."

"I understand you're angry and you're hurt." He stood, thinking he could hold her, comfort her somehow, but her eyes flashed, making it clear she didn't want him anywhere near her.

"You understand? You?" Her eyes narrowed, and with her voice low, she spat out, "How dare you? How dare you suggest to me that you understand?"

"Julie, I lost my children today, too."

"It was your fault, Mark!"

"So I deserve to lose my kids?"

"You didn't deserve them in the first place. Or me."

"Now wait just a minute. I'm willing to take a lot because I know what we've been through, but that was uncalled for. Where is this coming from, Julie?"

She ignored his question. "I called my sister. She'll be here soon."

"You're leaving?"

"I can't stay here with you. I can't pretend everything is just fine in front of David and Jan."

"This won't get better if you leave."

She raised a hand and cut him off. "Don't, Mark. Just don't." She disappeared to the guest bedroom and returned with a suitcase. "I'll be back Saturday for the visitation."

"Can I call you?"

"I don't think you should."

"You're making a mistake, Julie."

"No, I'm undoing one."

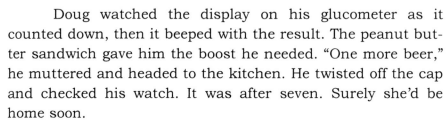

Doug watched the display on his glucometer as it counted down, then it beeped with the result. The peanut butter sandwich gave him the boost he needed. "One more beer," he muttered and headed to the kitchen. He twisted off the cap and checked his watch. It was after seven. Surely she'd be home soon.

She was right. They both knew that, but she had to understand—and she was the only one who could—why he had to see this through. He couldn't back down. He'd never backed down from anything. He took a long drink and made his way back to his office. The house was quiet, lifeless when she wasn't here.

She was so angry when she left. He didn't like how things happened either. It was a messy, ugly process. He would admit that. Even to Mark. But it would work out. The kids would be better off in the long run. That made it all worthwhile. If he had to play the villain to accomplish that . . . his shoulders were broad enough.

He took another long drink and thought he heard the garage door. "Thank God," he muttered. His instinct was to run to her, but he decided to wait until she found him, until she was ready to talk.

A half hour later, she appeared in the doorway. "Beer on a weeknight?"

"Not your typical weeknight." He set the bottle on his desk. "How . . . are things any better?"

"The kids are settling in. I think they're set for tomorrow."

"But things aren't any better."

"I don't see how they can be." She crossed her arms and leaned against the doorframe.

"What, uh . . . what about between us?"

"Things will never change between us."

It wasn't as reassuring as he would have liked. He studied her for a moment, as he sipped his beer. "Mark and I had words today."

"I can't say I blame him," Cass said. "Put yourself in his place."

"I hit him, Cass."

"You what?" she whispered. "How could you?"

"It happened before I had time to think," Doug said, rubbing his eyes. "I've never hit him. I never spanked him."

"Then you need to apologize. You told Matt it takes a man to admit when he's wrong."

"I know," he said, massaging his temples. "He knows . . . he knew exactly what to say. If he'd let loose with a string of profanity . . . that wouldn't have fazed me."

"Good grief, what did he say?"

"He said I was dishonoring his mother's memory."

Cass raised her eyebrows. "That's it? I don't understand."

"I can't explain it."

"I'll ask Mark, then."

"What?"

"She's obviously the key. You have to work through whatever issues are left over from her death. That was when your relationship with your son died."

"You're assuming we want to heal."

"Don't you?"

"That's up to Mark. He's the one who changed, not me."

"You really hate it, don't you? His religion, I mean."

"Cass, eighteen years ago, God declared war on me. Fighting is all I know."

"Was Judy this bitter when she got sick?"

"At first." Doug took a long drink from his beer. "I spent hours, days at the hospital with her. I did everything I knew how to do. It wasn't enough."

"You can't will cancer away." Finally her voice softened.

"It wasn't enough to keep her." He stared into the bottle. "She got her comfort from God, not me."

"I'm sure that's not true. I'm sure she needed you there."

"I was losing her anyway and He stole those last few months away. Then He got Mark, too."

"So are you trying to get the kids before God gets them? Is that it?"

"Sounds pretty stupid when you say it like that." He finished off the beer, and wiped his mouth on his sleeve.

"That's not your first beer, is it?"

"Three, I think. I usually can't handle four." He left his desk, walked over to her, and took her hands. "Don't leave me."

"I'm not leaving you."

"I mean it. Cass, you're all I have."

"We'll talk about this when you haven't had three beers."

"I'm not drunk, Cass. I know what I'm saying. Please . . . just promise me."

He wanted to ask her what was taking so long, but she looked in his eyes with soft sincerity. "I promise you. I won't leave you."

Thirteen

Mark sat at the kitchen table with David Shannon nursing a cup of hot tea. "You should go on to bed. There's nothing more you can do right now. I'll see if Julie will talk to me in the morning."

"We can go over there," David said. "Right now, if you want."

Mark shook his head. "She needs some time. She's never been angry like this. Completely irrational. It was my fault we lost the kids and that was the end of it." He sipped the tea, reliving that last door-slamming moment. "She's hurt, and she doesn't know how to handle that." He forced a smile. "Of course, I'm not handling it much better."

"There's a time of absorbing that has to come before the handling."

"Yeah, but a big part of the handling is accepting my responsibility for it."

"Now hold on—"

"David, sixteen years ago, almost to the day, I promised my mother I'd make sure my dad became a believer—"

"You can't expect—"

"I know. I can't make him, but . . . God help me, I would have rather done anything else than try to win my own father. And David, he knew. He knows I've never loved him like I should, I've never shown him the love Christ has. He called me on it right before I left. He said I'd go pour my life into people a half a world away when I wouldn't give him the time of day unless it came wrapped in a sermon."

"He was upset."

"He was right." Mark sipped his tea. "So I've spent seven years, hiding in Africa, avoiding my father, telling myself I had important ministry to do."

"You were doing great work in Kenya."

"I was. I quit. Resigned. Told Peter I was moving back here. If I'd done this when God told me to . . . if I had told my father . . . maybe we wouldn't be where we are today. I knew in April I was in the wrong place."

"So you mean to tell me, God let you labor there for, what? Seven years? In disobedience? I can't believe that."

"I'm pretty sure I have an ulcer because of it."

David gave him a wry smile. "If that's your only evidence, I know you're wrong."

Mark rolled his eyes and took another drink of tea.

"What was it like the first time Kenya hit you?"

"I was at a New Year's Eve service listening to a missionary talk."

"And?"

"I thought everybody in every picture was looking at me."

"And the first time you visited?"

Mark shook his head. "Part of my brain was making plans, the rest of me . . . I was wrestling with whether or not it was the right thing."

"What if it was the right thing at the wrong time?"

"My father-in-law said something like that."

"There you go." David smiled. "God still wants you in Kenya. He just wants you to resolve things with your dad first."

"I have to resolve things with my wife before I can do either."

"Julie will come around. Soon. Everything looks very dark right now because the shock and the pain are fresh."

Mark took a long drink from the tea. "You know what's

really strange? It was almost like my father's words coming out of Julie's mouth. 'You're a failure,' she said." He set the cup down. "And then the only word my father said to me after he hit me was 'don't.' Some of the last words she said were, 'Don't, Mark.'" He dropped his head. "Kind of ironic."

After a moment of quiet, David spoke. "You know, maybe you should talk to Chuck and his wife. They went through a bitter separation. Maybe they could help you out. I know they'd be glad to try."

"I hate to ask anything else from Chuck, especially after today. He was blindsided just like we were." He took a sip from his tea. "He was pale. Probably worse than I was." He glanced over at the wall clock. "I gotta let you get to sleep." He finished off his tea, and pushed away from the table. "If Julie's sister called Debbie and Paul, I may be getting a phone call in a couple of hours. Let's see . . . what time is it in Italy? Six, almost seven o'clock in the morning."

David yawned and stretched. "All right, you've convinced me. I hope they call. I hope they tell you they've talked some sense into Julie and she's on her way home."

"Thanks. For everything." Mark dropped his cup in the dishwasher and turned out the kitchen light. The prospect of sleeping alone was less than appealing so he settled on the sofa, figuring he'd hold out until he was exhausted and head to bed at the very last minute.

Would God really let him go back to Kenya after he'd made such a mess of things? Right now that was far too much to hope for.

Julie stood behind her sister, Jenna, as she unlocked her front door. The trip seemed to drag as they rode in quiet, but now Julie couldn't remember any of it. No landmarks, no highway signs, nothing.

Every time she closed her eyes, she could see Doug Bolling's profile, looking down his nose at paperwork on the table in front, the woman at his elbow, standing by her man no matter what. When the gavel shattered her world, Doug had this self-satisfied smirk. Then the way he turned and asked his lawyer if she could see her own children . . . unreal.

They had underestimated him and everything about this process. She needed to hire her own lawyer, one that would fight as dirty as Doug's lawyer. One that would get her kids back for her. The lawyer wouldn't do it for free, and she had nothing but a suitcase and thirty-seven dollars in her billfold. Fine, she'd find a job. She'd been to college. For two years. Without getting a degree. Without really ever majoring in anything.

She knew how to type . . . but not exactly how to use a word processor. Being a mother didn't require computer skills. She could organize and plan . . . and budget. She could play the piano, for what that was worth.

Tomorrow. She'd make a list tomorrow. There had to be something available. Springfield was a good-sized town. Surely someone had something for a woman trying to win back her children.

"You can have the bed," Jenna said as she held the door.

"Keep it. I won't be sleeping anyway."

"All right, we'll stay up then." She wandered toward the kitchen, dropping her purse and keys onto the table as she passed. "Want some ice cream? It's rocky road."

"I think I'd throw it up."

"Suit yourself." Jenna got the carton from the freezer and dug the scoop from the nearby drawer, then she frowned. "You think you might want some of this later?"

"Why?"

"Need to know if I can eat it from the carton or not."

"Feel free."

Jenna smiled and traded the scoop for a spoon, and dipped out a heaping spoonful. "So," she said, "you want to call Mom?"

"I already talked to her."

"And she said?"

"The usual."

Jenna frowned again. "And what exactly is the usual for when one's daughter has lost temporary custody of one's grandchildren? 'Cause I thought these were pretty extraordinary circumstances."

"You know what I mean. She said the usual Christian stuff."

"Like?"

Jenna hadn't asked any questions on the drive from St. Louis, and Julie thought she had escaped. The last thing she wanted after today was a grilling from her little sister, the aspiring psychologist. "She told me I had to be Christ-like."

"That sounds like her," Jenna said. "You sure you don't want some of this. I can scoop from this other side."

"No, I think I'm gonna get ready for bed."

"Two minutes ago you said you weren't sleeping. So whatever Mom said made you very uncomfortable and you don't want to discuss it."

"I don't want to discuss it."

"Let's talk about Doug then."

"Look, I don't want a therapy session. I mean I'm sure you're very good at it—"

"That is so dismissive and defensive. I want to talk about Doug, not you."

"All right, Doug is evil. He's a bully and a jerk."

"He's in business for himself."

"Yes, he's a building contractor. Builds big, fancy homes."

"And you're threatened by that."

"I am not."

"Fine." Jenna scooped out another spoonful of ice cream. "Have you seen his house?"

"No, but from the paperwork I know it appraised for a cool one and a half million dollars."

"Wow."

"Don't be impressed. He's evil. He stole my kids."

"Julie, didn't you say he started with nothing? I mean, you have to concede that a guy who starts from scratch and builds a business that allows him to have a home like that has to be a very sharp, very competent individual."

"None of that matters."

"And that, my dear, is your problem."

"My problem?"

"Yes." Jenna dropped her spoon in the dishwasher, then sealed the ice cream and returned it to the freezer. "You have totally different priorities."

Julie rubbed her forehead and sighed. "That's your expert analysis?"

"No. You want to hear it, though? Good, I thought so."

"I didn't say yes."

"Your eyes did." She leaned against the counter. "Doug wants validation. He's built this fabulous house to prove he is okay, that he has overcome his background, his beginnings, whatever."

"He stole my children because he needs validation? That's the dumbest thing—"

"There you go again. You're so dismissive. No wonder he doesn't like you."

"Jenna, I don't need this right now."

"Oh, but you do. Mom won't tell you because she's sweet and saintly and she's afraid you can't handle the truth. I know better."

"I'm not listening to this." Julie turned toward the living room.

"He's tired of hearing how you're right and he's wrong. He needs to hear that we're all wrong, but some of us have admitted it and done something about it."

"What?"

"Until you see that you are no better than he is . . . you're not gonna win."

"I'm not going to get my kids back unless—"

"I didn't say that. I'm sure you'll get your kids back as soon as it's legally doable. But you won't get through, or get over this—" She swept her hands in a circle in front of her. "Until you give him what he's after."

Julie rubbed her temples and desperately wished for quiet solitude somewhere. "How many years did you go to school for this?"

"Going on seven, thanks for asking."

"I think we need a spiritual solution, not a psychological one. Thanks anyway."

"This is a spiritual solution! We all grasp for someone to tell us we're okay because deep down we know we're messed up. But Doug has looked at your life and he's looked at Mark's life and from the evidence he sees, you may be worse off than he is. His way is passable, but your way is crazy, so he wants your kids to be on the right side."

"How can you . . . you don't even know him."

"Neither do you."

"That's ridiculous."

"Mom likes him."

"Irrelevant."

"He likes Mom. Bet he would have never sued Mom."

"Go to bed, Jenna."

"Only because I want to, not because you tell me to."

"Besides, the problem is not between me and Doug. It's with Mark and Doug."

"Oh, right. Mark. He's the reason you're here. I forgot."

"Are you like this with your clients?"

"With the ones who only want their schemes approved rather than seeking real transformational help, yes."

"I don't even know how to respond to that."

"Like this—'Wow, Jenna. You nailed me. How do I find that transformational help?'"

"You know what? You're not married. You don't have children. You have no idea what I'm going through right now."

"You're still being dismissive—Dad used to be like that too, by the way—but I'm going to bed. Tomorrow's my day off, though. We can spend the whole day together."

"I just need your car."

"Sure. But you need way more than my car, Julie Bolling."

Julie dropped on the sofa and pulled her knees up to her. Jenna was her sister. She was supposed to be an ally, not an accuser. Why was it wrong, why was she wrong because she was determined to get her children back? No, this was the right thing, and if she had any hopes of keeping her sanity, it was her only recourse.

Wednesday, September 16

Cass woke earlier than usual and stretched out a hand toward Doug's side of the bed. The sheets were cool. She rolled over and the sight of the perfectly ordered sheets and spread confirmed he had never come to bed last night. She checked at midnight and somewhere around two and he was still up, still haunting his office. She hadn't disturbed him either time.

She threw on her robe and headed downstairs. The door to his office was closed, but it was empty and dark. The aroma of fresh coffee filtered in from the kitchen, and the morning paper lay on the counter, but he was nowhere around. His truck was still in the garage. That meant the deck.

He sat on the step, his elbows resting on his knees. He was dressed in jeans and boots, so it looked like he was planning on going to work. He never moved when she slid the door open. "Doug," she said gently, "what's going on?"

He dropped his head but didn't turn around. "I'm not sure," he said.

She walked over and sat close to him on the step, wrapping her arm around his. "Let me help you carry it."

"I'm afraid."

"I saw that in your eyes last night. Afraid of what? That I'll leave?"

His jaw tightened. "I hit Mark before I knew what I was doing." He took a deep breath, then raised his head to look at her. "What if I do that again? What if I . . . ? What if it had been . . . someone else?"

"You'd never—"

"I never thought I would hit my own son." He blew out a deep breath, then stood and walked down the steps. "Is that who I am? Is that what I'm capable of?"

"It was a one-time event. The situation was unique."

"Every situation is unique, Cass. I can't excuse it. I've got to see Mark today. You think he'd talk to me?"

"I don't know. I don't know him."

"Me either." He shook his head. "Don't tell the kids, all right? About any of it." He had that panicked look in his eyes again.

"I won't. Are you sure you're okay?"

"I need to get this settled. Will you take the kids to school?"

"I figured that was my job now." She pulled herself up, and he kissed her on his way up the stairs. "I'll see you later, won't I?"

"Yeah," he said and strode into the house.

A moment later she heard his truck start. Just like that, he was going to see Mark. Was this what healing looked like? Healing shouldn't come with this disquieting uncertainty, with the sense that there was more going on than he was telling her. She watched his truck turn off their road and she wondered what it would take for him to admit he'd gotten more than he bargained for with this custody suit.

Mark had fallen asleep on David's sofa waiting for the phone to ring, and woke with his neck stiff and sore. The Hammells never called. Maybe Julie hadn't told them yet. Or maybe she painted such a picture of him as incapable of acting, of failing to protect his family that his in-laws had no choice but to believe her. He wouldn't put them in the middle, though. If they called, he would speak to them, but he wouldn't try to plead his case to them.

When the phone did ring, Mark nearly jumped off the sofa, but managed to snatch it up before the second ring. "Hello?"

"Mark . . . can we talk?"

It wasn't Julie or the Hammells. It was his father. Mark squeezed his eyes tightly shut then opened them. He was fairly sure he was awake. "Yeah, sure. Did you have a time in mind? Or a place?"

"I'm driving right now."

"You're coming here?"

"No, someplace more neutral. There's a McDonald's not too far from you. I'll meet you in the parking lot."

"I'll leave here in just a second." Mark hung up the phone, and rubbed his eyes. Seven-thirty. He was still wearing the suit pants and dress shirt from court yesterday. But his father was on his way. He wanted to talk. He changed into jeans and quickly shaved. It could be over today.

Cass wrote her cell phone number on three slips of paper and handed one to each of the children. "I'll be in my office all day. Call me if you need anything. Now have you got everything?"

"Backpack, lunch and stupid football gear," Matt said.

"Football may be fun. You may like it."

"You wanna play? I'll let you use my stuff."

Cass smiled at him and picked up her satchel. "Janie, sweetheart, are you ready?"

Jane stood silently, chewing on her bottom lip. Cass knelt down in front of her. "Three school days and you'll see Mommy and Daddy. Three more Wednesdays and this will all be over."

"You think Grandpa's gonna lose?" Ben asked.

"I never said that," Cass mumbled, taking Janie's hand. She led them out to the garage, but the boys stopped in their tracks just inside the door. "What?"

"Has this been here the whole time?" Matt asked, pointing at her Jaguar.

"Yes."

"Then why have we been riding around in his big black monster?"

"I don't know. We always take his car when we go together."

"I think we should drive separately from now on."

Cass rolled her eyes and shook her head. "Boys and cars." She unlocked the passenger door and helped Janie into her booster seat, then waited for the boys to get in. When she got in, she checked her planner. "Miss Jane, you are seven fifty-five to two-thirty, and the boys are eight-fifteen to four-thirty. Right?"

"Beats me," Ben said. "I'm just along for the ride."

"I will pick you up at four-thirty," Cass said.

"So how fast will this car go?" Ben asked as she backed out of the garage. "A hundred?"

"At least a hundred and ten," she said casually.

"Were you driving?"

"It's my car, isn't it?"

"Were the cops chasing you?" His eyes were wide, and for a brief instant she wanted to say yes.

"No, it was at a race track. They had a day where you could bring your car and see what it would do. The car could've gone faster, but I chickened out."

With that, she earned a respectful silence the rest of the drive to Jane's school. She parked as close to the front door as she could. "Come on, baby. I'll walk you in."

"It'll be okay, I promise," Ben said as Jane climbed over him to get out.

Cass helped Janie wriggle into her backpack, then took her hand. With each step, Cass could feel Jane slowing down, almost pulling her backwards. Cass stopped and knelt down in front of Janie. "Have your mama and daddy ever blown you a kiss?"

Janie nodded.

"Then there should be some kisses floating around up there." She took Janie's hand and held it open in her own hand, then she reached up and with a quick snatch, she pulled an invisible kiss from the air above Janie's head. She pressed it into Janie's hand, closed her little fingers over it, then pressed the hand to Janie's heart. "There's a kiss from your mama on your first day of school." Janie gave her a weak smile. Weak, but it was the first one since the hearing. That was a victory.

Janie kept the hand on her heart, so Cass guided her with a hand on her shoulder, and steered her into the office. They were both surprised to find Janie's teacher waiting for them. "Jane! I'm so glad to see you! My name is Mrs. Flynn." She leaned down and patted one of the office chairs. "Why don't you hop up in this chair for just a minute while I talk with Ms. Grayson, then I'll take you down to our room before the other kids get there."

She took a few steps away from Janie and Cass followed. "They filled me in just a little," Mrs. Flynn said. "I want to make this as easy as we can for her. Is there anything I need to know?"

"She's very shy," Cass said. "She doesn't talk very much, and she's had nightmares since we got her." Cass glanced back at Janie. "I hate this, all right. If we can get through these next few weeks, Janie will be back with her parents and this will be over."

"But aren't you suing for custody of her?"

"Her grandfather is. Just . . . please be understanding. She needs . . . she could use something good, something happy, you know?"

"Of course," Mrs. Flynn said.

Cass kissed the top of Janie's head. "Baby, I'll be right here at two-thirty. You'll do great today. I love you." She smoothed Janie's hair once more, and hurried out of the office so Janie wouldn't see her in tears.

When Mark pulled into a parking spot at McDonald's, he was surprised to see his dad leaning against his truck just a few spaces down. He wore the same style mirrored sunglasses he'd always worn and his arms were folded tightly across his chest.

Mark got out of the car, and walked toward his father without making eye contact just yet. Once he was close enough not to be overheard by casual listeners, he asked, "Are the kids okay?"

"The kids are fine." His father shifted away from the truck, and dropped his head long enough to take his sunglasses off. Then he cleared his throat and looked Mark in the eye. "I owe you an apology."

For the lawsuit? For winning? "Dad—"

He raised a hand. "Let me finish. I don't know what happened, what I was thinking. I just . . . reacted. You didn't deserve that."

He was talking about the slap. After all he had done, that was the only thing that bothered him. "But I deserve to have my children taken away?"

"That's a separate issue—"

"I don't see how it could be."

His father started toward the driver's side door of his truck. "I said what I came to say."

"That's it! Did you think this would fix anything?"

"It's too late for that."

"So you're content to write off your only son—"

"I have no son. My son abandoned me sixteen years ago." The longer he spoke, the faster the words came and the more forceful his hand gestures became as he jabbed at Mark. "When I needed somebody, somebody who understood what I had just lost. You turned your back on me."

"Dad, wait!" Mark rounded the truck, but his father gave him an icy glare then climbed inside and drove away. "That went well," he muttered as he scuffed back to David's car. "God, what was that all about? A little sucker punch to make me forget about Julie for a few minutes?" He was so stupid to think things could be over. No, his dad just wanted to dredge up the past, remind him of his failures then leave again. Maybe he should go find David and see how else he'd failed.

Then it hit him.

"Oh dear God, this is what my dad felt like. Everyone telling him he was a failure, that whatever he did wasn't enough. And Mom left him. She left him when they were married, but . . . once she became a believer . . . she was like a totally different person. Like Julie yesterday. Somebody I didn't even know . . . that's what my mother became to him . . . he couldn't reason with her . . . he was left bewildered and then alone."

He leaned back against the headrest, his hands icy cold, but his heart racing. "We're reliving it, Julie and I. I wouldn't see him, we wouldn't see him for who he really was and You've dropped us into his life."

It was nearly nine o'clock before Cass made it to her office at Bolling Developers. Sandy started on her before she got all the way through the door. "I expect this kind of treatment from him," she said.

"I know. I should have called you last night." She dropped her satchel against the short side of Sandy's desk. "It's been . . . we have some adjusting to do."

"But you won, right? You have the kids?"

"Temporary custody until the hearing, yes."

"Then I don't understand. He's not in here gloating. In fact, I haven't heard from him this morning."

"Doug was meeting Mark this morning."

"Oh, boy."

"Yeah."

"And how are you through all this?"

"I don't know. Court was horrible. The kids . . . " Images of Jane in the school office flashed through her mind and she turned away. Fixing a cup of tea gave her a convenient cover. "I took them to school this morning."

"I will say, when he decides on a course of action, he moves fast," Sandy said gently.

"He says the lawyer told him to get them in school immediately. The schools knew we were coming yesterday. I presume Mr. Wiley made certain of that."

"And you're going to try to be creative and artistic today?"

Cass laughed quietly. "If I get my email read today, it will be an accomplishment."

"Is he coming in?"

"Far as I know."

"But with Mark, all bets are off."

"Exactly." Cass sipped her tea, lingering at Sandy's desk a moment longer. "Have your ever met Mark?"

"A few times. The first time was in the funeral home after his mother died. I thought he was a really sweet kid. There were a few times I dropped off food at the house and he answered the door, but let's see . . . " She glanced back at the wall calendar. "His mother died in the fall, like September or October and come February, he was married and gone. Doug wasn't even back to work yet."

"Doug took off six months when his wife died?"

"Close to it." Sandy leaned back in her chair. "He was devastated, and then Mark left . . . he had nothing. I was worried about him. But then things thawed out and he gathered himself together and moved on."

"Did you know her?"

Sandy shook her head. "Dell went to school with her. Said she was a snotty brat." She smiled broadly. "Dell's not one to mince words." Sandy leaned up to her desk. "Neither am I as far as that goes. But I want to tell you something, because I hear this very subtle undercurrent in your voice."

"I don't know what you're talking about." Cass exaggerated shocked dismay.

Sandy rolled her eyes. "As I was saying . . . I saw him when Judy was dying, when he lived at the hospital . . . she never knew what she had in him until it was too late." Then she smiled. "I love him like a little brother, you know? And I am so glad he found you, because you see him, the real Doug Bolling and you love him. I'm not sure Mark ever has. I think that's their problem."

What if Mark had, though? What if the hard-nosed, spiteful Doug from the courtroom was the father he knew? She couldn't blame him for distancing himself from that. "Have you ever seen Doug angry?"

"How angry?"

"Cold, bitter anger. Callous, heartless, going-for-the-throat kind of anger."

Sandy pressed her lips into a tight line then reached for a stack of papers that suddenly needed straightening. "I'm not going to defend what he's doing, what he's done, but if he feels like he's been backed into a corner—"

"How do I get him out of the corner?"

"That I don't know."

Cass picked up her satchel from the floor. "Thanks, Sandy."

"Anytime."

She dropped her satchel in the floor by her own desk and settled in her chair, trying to get her bearings once again. The world had changed quite a bit since she'd last thought about the Rileys' tile countertops or the Sawyers' chandeliers. She was reading through emails and returning phone calls when her cell phone rang.

"Ms. Grayson, this is Carrie White at Weston. Jane is in the nurse's office. She threw up. Can you come and get her?"

"I'll be right there," Cass said. She clicked off her cell phone, then picked up the receiver for her desk phone, and punched in the speed dial for Doug's phone. He answered on the second ring. "The school just called. Janie's throwing up. I'm gonna go get her."

"Was she sick this morning?"

"No. Maybe it's just nerves or something. Listen, can you get the boys at four-thirty?"

"What? Yeah, four-thirty."

"Things didn't go so well with Mark, did they?" Cass asked gently.

"Nothing new."

"We can talk later."

"I'm tired of talking," Doug said. "Thanks for getting Janie, and I'll get the boys."

Cass dropped the phone in its cradle, and regathered her things. There had to be something else that Doug and Mark could build their relationship on besides this constant conflict. Someone needed to lock them in a room and not let them out until they'd made peace with the past, with Judy Bolling's death and with each other.

Ben leaned against the wall outside the coach's office while Matt paced. "I don't even know why we're here," Matt muttered. "Would he even know if we didn't play?"

"He'd find out somehow." Ben dropped his bag of gear and nodded toward the door. "I have this guy for math. He's not too bad in class. He's like Dad's age."

Just then the door swung open, and Coach Gentry motioned them inside. "Ben, right?"

"Yeah, and this is my brother, Matt." Ben leaned up to Matt's ear and whispered. "He didn't wear shorts in math class. He would've been much cooler." Matt frowned and waved him away.

The coach leaned against his desk and crossed his arms. "So tell me, how much football have you played?"

"Honestly?" Matt asked. "I can't remember the last time I saw a football."

"Then what are you doing here?"

Matt sighed and started the saga. "Our parents are

missionaries. We've lived in Kenya most of our whole lives. Now we're staying with our grandfather for a while and he thinks we should play football."

"Is he trying to get you killed?" the coach asked.

"That's a possibility," Ben said.

"You play soccer?"

"Yeah," Matt said and Ben nodded.

"Then I'll take you to the special teams coach. You can learn how to punt and place kick. That's kind of specialized, and you can keep to yourself in practice and not worry about what everybody else is doing." He grabbed a clipboard off his desk, and scribbled on it. "Ben, you'll be my JV kicker and . . . " He lifted his pen and looked at Matt.

"Matt."

"Matt can be my varsity man. Try to watch some football on TV."

"Thanks, Coach."

"You bet. Now get your gear on and I'll see you out on the field."

"All of it?" Ben asked pulling the pads from his bag. He held them against his arms, then decided they were probably for his legs.

"You guys are really starting out at the beginning." The coach stepped out of his office into the hallway. "Molinsky, get these guys a locker, and make sure they know what they're doing, then take 'em to Coach Wagner."

"Molinsky?" Matt asked.

"Jack. Do you know him?" Coach Gentry asked.

"I've met his dad," Matt mumbled then dragged his bag of gear into the hallway. The kid waiting for them wasn't much taller than Matt, but he was wide and he shaved already.

He used his helmet to point. "Locker room's down here."

Ben fell in step behind Matt and Jack. "So you're the adulterer's son?" Matt asked.

"Matt . . . really?" Ben moaned.

Jack stopped and turned slowly to face Matt. This was

the part where the new kids got pounded. So much for Matt's great plan to lay low and blend in.

"He didn't mean it," Ben said, hoping it wasn't too late already.

Jack looked at Ben, then at Matt. "It's true. Got any other smart remarks? I've heard 'em all, I bet." Matt didn't say anything. "Look, I know you're the missionary freaks. The way I figure it, we can show some solidarity like brothers ought to, or we can let the rest of these jerks see that Christians can't even get along with each other." Jack crossed his arms and leaned up against the lockers. "I'll let you make the call."

Matt, naturally didn't back down. "Your dad lost our court case. You'll have to forgive my bad attitude."

"Oh, I get it. It's *my* dad's fault you're here. Your grand-father had nothing to do with it." He turned to Ben. "Is your dad a jerk like this?" he asked, pointing at Matt.

"My dad is not a jerk," Ben said.

"My dad told my mom that he thought Mark Bolling was one of the finest men he'd ever met." He turned back to Matt. "Just so you know, my dad came home from your hear-ing and puked his guts out. He's hired you another lawyer out of his own pocket, and filed a motion to get your hearing moved up so you don't have to stay here any longer than you have to."

Matt pressed his lips together tightly and stood motion-less.

"My dad committed a sin, but he took responsibility for it and he works like crazy to make up for it. That makes him a great man. A greater man than somebody who thinks he's never done anything wrong." Jack turned to walk away.

"Hang on," Matt said quietly, and Jack turned back around. "I don't think that. I don't think I'm better than you." He clenched his jaw, but he couldn't stop tears from forming, from spilling onto his cheeks. "Two weeks ago, I was home. I was in Kenya and my life was normal. Now I'm in the middle of something and I don't understand what's going on or why." He wiped his eyes, and blew out a deep breath. "I'm tired of being

Saint Matthew and having things just get worse." He kicked his gym bag toward his locker. "Can we just start over?" He held out his hand. "I'm Matt, the missionary freak."

Jack smiled and shook Matt's hand, "I'm Jack, the adulterer's son."

Julie sat at Jenna's kitchen table working through a stack of employment applications from department stores, convenience stores, and even a few offices. Surely one of them had an opening. After all the hassle last night, Jenna hadn't said anything more about Mark or Doug. Maybe that was the end of it.

When the phone rang, Julie flinched and marked an errant line over the application. "Great," she muttered and started to ask Jenna for some white-out, but Jenna came in with the cordless receiver in hand.

"Sure, Dad, she's right here." Jenna smiled and held out the phone.

"I do not want to talk to him."

"I don't care."

"Tell him."

"No."

Julie groaned and took the receiver. "Hi, Dad."

"You want to tell me what's going on?" he said.

"Not really."

"So you understand you're wrong?"

"Excuse me?"

"You need to go home to your husband and work things out with him."

"Did Jenna call you?"

"Julie, listen to me—"

"No, Daddy, I've listened to you my whole life. You don't know what I'm going through or how I feel right now and I'm pretty sure you don't have any answers—"

"Julie—"

"I need my children. Mark won't do it. The lawyers won't do it. I have to."

"But this is wrong."

"Wrong? So you're going to pass judgment just like that? From five thousand miles away you can tell this? Of course. I'm not measuring up to your ideals, so naturally I'm wrong. Daddy, did you miss the part where Doug Bolling took my children? Why isn't he wrong? Why aren't you calling him? Why aren't you calling Mark and telling him to be a man and take care of his family?" She clicked off the phone and slammed it to the table.

"Easy," Jenna said.

"Did you put him up to that?"

"Oh, no. He's freelancing. Always has."

"Well, I'm not taking any calls from anyone."

"So I'm you're secretary now?"

"Don't pick up."

Jenna frowned and left her alone in the kitchen again. Good. She had work to do, and time was wasting.

"You really need to work on your people skills, Saint Matthew," Ben teased as he lugged his gear away from the practice field.

"I don't want to talk about it."

"You made a good recovery. I'm just sayin'." Ben suddenly dropped his gear, wrapped his arms around his brother and drove him to the ground.

"What'd you do that for!" Matt hollered and pushed Ben off his chest.

"Two reasons, well, three actually. First, I wanted to show you what I learned today. I think I'm a natural. Second, I wanted to see if you really are the 'turn the other cheek type.' And third, your pants weren't even dirty yet."

"You're such a child," Matt muttered, got to his feet and picked up his bag.

"Did you mean it?"

"Yes, you're a child."

"No, what you told Jack. Are you afraid we won't ever go back home?"

"Sometimes."

Ben nodded. "And you think it's the lawyer's fault?"

"I don't know whose fault it is anymore."

"Wow. I was pretty sure it was Grandpa's fault." Ben scanned the parking lot closest to the practice field. "I don't see the Jag."

"That's because he came, not Cass." Matt pointed to their grandfather leaning against his truck.

"So did you build some character today, boys?" Ben said, in a low voice, mocking their grandfather. Matt shook his head and shoved him.

Once they were close enough, their grandfather took off his sunglasses and smiled at them. "You look sweaty and dirty enough to be football players." Ben grinned at Matt while he slung his gear in the back of the pickup. "So what'd you think?" their grandfather asked.

"I hated it, every minute of it," Matt answered.

"Don't hold back, Matt," Ben said. "Tell him how you really feel."

"You'll get used to it." Their grandfather slapped Matt's shoulder pads, and reached for his gear but Matt climbed in the backseat of the truck, lugging his bag behind him. Ben shrugged and climbed in the front seat. When their grandfather got in, Ben asked, "Where's Cass?"

"Janie got sick at school, so she's home with her."

"Sick *at* school or sick *of* school?" Matt asked.

"Are you this smart aleck with your dad?"

"No. Did you push him around like you do us?"

"That's enough, Matt." Their granddad talked to the rearview mirror the way their mom did.

"Sorry . . . I had a bad day."

"It's going to be an adjustment—"

"I don't want to adjust. I want to go home. I want to *be*

home. I want to be with my mom and dad. I want my normal life back."

"You think living in Africa, converting the natives, is normal?"

"For us, yes. It's what God called us to do."

Ben sighed deeply. Saint Matthew was back.

"How do you know that? How do you know it's not some misguided boondoggle?"

"A what?" Ben asked.

"A waste of time and money."

Ben nodded. Boondoggle. He'd file that one away.

"We didn't just wake up one morning and decide to go to Africa. My dad did a lot of praying, studying, talking to people . . . "

"He didn't talk to me."

"You would have told him not to go."

"So he only talked to people who were going to agree with him?"

Ben shook his head. Matt, give it up. You're never gonna win like this.

"He talked to people who . . . understand what being a missionary is all about."

"Other Christians, you mean."

"I guess."

"You live in a closed society, Matt. There's no place for outside ideas."

"You're the same way. You don't want to hear anything about faith or the Bible."

"I've heard it all before."

"But have you ever listened?"

Fourteen

Saturday, September 19

Doug woke up with a splitting headache. Small wonder after the week he'd had—court, getting the kids in school, Jane getting sick every day, the boys trudging out of football practice. Not quite as smooth as he'd envisioned things. In seven hours, Mark would be here. At least he wouldn't want to talk.

He left Cass sleeping and fumbled through the drawers in the darkened bathroom looking for a bottle of Tylenol or ibuprofen . . . something. He found a bottle that looked promising, so he stepped back into the bedroom, and held up the bottle to catch a little more light. *There we go.* He snapped open the bottle and shook out three pills. He swallowed them, chasing them with a cup of water, and returned the bottle to the drawer.

He showered, shaved and dressed, savoring the early morning quiet. He grabbed his glasses from the nightstand and headed downstairs to his office. Switching on the desk lamp, he pulled out the court papers, and carefully reread them, especially the temporary custody order.

Regardless of what Vic Wiley said, Doug knew they won only because they convinced the judge Mark wasn't really leaving Africa, that he had misrepresented himself. Doug had trouble believing that. Yes, Mark deliberately withheld information from him—particularly when it came to the kids—but he wasn't a liar.

In the hallway outside the hearing room Mark accused him of sitting there and letting Vic lie just to get what he wanted. Doug refused to believe that. He never tolerated any kind of dishonesty. He never cheated any of his clients. He never fudged his taxes. He never even rounded up on an estimate. Vic said it was the way things are done, how they had to be done. He didn't know anything about law, so he had to trust Vic. Period. End of discussion.

He massaged his temple, and hoped the headache would fade soon. He double-checked a stack of paperwork he'd saved especially for this afternoon, guaranteeing minimal contact with Mark and Julie. He resolved not to bait them, and he'd try his best not to respond to whatever shots they might take at him.

Unless they started on Cass. He would not tolerate any snide comments about her. If they said anything beyond 'hello' to her, he would throw them both out.

***

At the red light, Mark double-checked the hastily drawn map and directions to his father's house. He bristled at the very idea that he needed directions to his dad's house. His own father, and he didn't know where he lived. So wrong. Of course, he shouldn't be headed over there for court-ordered visitation with his own children either.

He hadn't heard a word from Julie since Tuesday evening. Jenna took his calls, and promised to relay his messages, but Julie wouldn't speak to him. Debbie called Thursday and assured him that they had begged, prodded, encouraged and ordered Julie to go home, but even their pleas were falling on deaf ears.

David and Jan both said seeing the kids may make the difference for her, that she'd be ready to work with him to get them back as soon as possible. He wasn't so sure.

Left onto Ellendale. Mark wiped his palms on his pants

when he turned onto his father's street. The homes were beautiful, the obvious wealth intimidating. He strained his eyes watching the rearview mirror for another car, for Julie, but there was no one behind him. Maybe she was waiting for him. Maybe she was already there.

He drove the sweeping curve, and finally caught sight of his father's house, the last one on the road. The two-story brown brick home stood on the edge of a rolling, neatly manicured lawn. A broad driveway cut through the green grass and led to a three-car garage. Not another car in sight.

God, she promised me she'd be here. How am I supposed to explain to the children where their mother is? They won't understand. Don't ask them to carry this, too.

He pulled in the driveway and turned off the car. His watch showed eleven fifty-five. Was he legally required to wait until straight up twelve? But when twelve came, then what? Should he go on in without Julie? Would she be even angrier if he went alone?

He got out of David's car, and looked back down the road once more, hoping. This time there was a car, and it made its way down the road, past every other house. That had to be Julie. He waved, but she kept her hands on the steering wheel. Dark sunglasses hid her eyes. When she stopped and got out of the car, she left the glasses on. "How are you?" Mark asked.

"I'll be better when I get to see my children," she said as she brushed past him.

He reached for her arm. "Can't we talk?"

"This is my court-ordered time with my children. I don't want to spend it on anything else."

"Afterwards?"

"Yes, I have some things to discuss with you, Mark. We'll talk afterward."

"Are you going to tell the children?"

"Tell them what? That their father let them down? They know that already."

"Are you going to tell them that you left?" Mark

snapped.

"Not yet." Her tone softened the slightest bit. "Let's not tell them yet." She pushed past him to the front door and rang the bell without waiting for him to catch up.

Doug had barely gotten the front door opened when Janie blasted around him and into her mother's arms. The boys thundered down the steps right behind her. Ben nearly tackled Mark with a hug, while Matt hugged his mother even though she still had Janie in her arms.

Doug opened the door wide and stepped back. "Come in," he said, but no one seemed to hear him. Mark reached out and hugged Matt, but Janie wouldn't let go of her mother. She did lean her head out so Mark could kiss her, but then she nestled herself against her mother once again.

"Janie, I think you've grown," Julie said softly. "Have you been swimming?"

Janie shook her head.

"Then what have you been doing?"

"School," Janie said.

"School?" Julie said, looking first at Mark, then Doug. "Did you put her in school?"

"I enrolled them in school," Doug said. "They can't stay home all day, and they need to be in public school."

She glared at Doug, but only said, "That was fast." She carried Janie past him, and into the entryway.

Cass stood silently just inside the front room. Doug reached for her hand but positioned himself between her and Mark and Julie. "This is Cassandra Grayson," Doug said. "She's been a tremendous help to the kids and me."

Mark extended his hand, and Cass glanced at Doug before reaching around him to return the handshake.

"Thank you," Mark said. He sounded sincere.

Julie said nothing, and though Doug tensed, he remembered his promise to himself not to bait them. "The house is yours. I'll be in the office."

"Where to, guys?" Julie asked, looking to Ben.

"Back to the TV room, I guess."

"Lead the way," Julie said, following him through the house.

Once they disappeared down the hall, Cass followed Doug into the office. "I don't have to stay, do I?"

"No," Doug said. "I don't blame you for getting out of here."

"You don't need me for a witness or anything?"

"I can handle them. You need a break."

"All right. I'm going to the tanning bed and the gym." She glanced back toward the hallway and hesitated.

"Something wrong?"

"It's just uncomfortable." She pointed to the stack of papers on his desk. "What are you going to do?"

"Easements, permits and surveys," he said, slipping on his glasses.

"You're not gonna tempt me to stay like that."

"I would love for you to stay, but I was serious when I said you needed a break. We'll be fine. Go." He waved her out. "Get a massage or something."

"Not a bad idea. I'll be back about four-thirty."

Julie followed the boys down the hall, hoping it was as far away from Doug as they could get and still be inside. The kitchen belonged on a magazine cover and the overstuffed sofa and big screen television subtly underscored that he had won. She seethed, resenting the very fact that she had to touch the furniture in order to sit down.

"So how is school?" she choked out, trying her best to sound positive, even casual.

"Long. Slow. He's making us play football, too," Ben said. "The coach cut us a break though. We just have to kick, but he told us we needed to watch some football to get the hang of the game."

"What kind of classes do you have?" Julie concentrated on his eyes, and memorizing the way his unruly hair lay across his forehead. Mark sat perched on the edge of the cushion on the opposite end of the sofa. She refused to look at him.

"Math, English, science, world civilizations, P.E., and ummm . . . " Ben leaned back and stared at the ceiling. "Oh, art and Spanish."

"What about you, Matt?"

"It's pretty much the same, except for algebra, and American history. We didn't have a lot of choices." She knew that tone. He was upset. Who could blame him?

Mark thought this was his chance. "You came in late—"

"Are you guys gonna act like everything is normal the whole time you're here?" Matt blurted out.

"Matt," Julie swallowed hard before she continued. "I get four hours. I don't want to waste them being angry." She looked directly into Mark's eyes. "I have the whole rest of the week for that."

"So we should pretend everything is normal?"

"Let's give ourselves something good to look back on next week," Julie said. "I want to hear you talk. I want to hear you laugh, and sing, and tease each other . . . just like we were home."

"Can Dad explain football to us, then?" Ben asked.

"Of course," Julie said, then she turned Janie around on her lap. "Now, tell me all about your teacher."

Through the afternoon, in every sentence, every glance that passed among them, Mark sensed that each of them was afraid to bring up the topic they most wanted to discuss. So they ignored it, put on a happy face and killed the four hours before any of them realized it.

Finally, with the four o'clock deadline bearing down on

them, Julie sat down with Janie, and kissed her gently. She took Janie's hands and leaned in close. To Mark, that gesture seemed calculated to show him that he was excluded. "Janie, in a few minutes, I have to go," Julie said.

"No," Janie whimpered with tears already spilling onto her cheeks.

"This is going to be the hardest thing either one of us has ever had to do," Julie said, fighting tears of her own. "But I'm gonna try to be brave. Can you be brave?"

Janie shook her head.

"Oh, baby." Julie pulled her close. "We've already made it one week—"

"I want to go with you. Please, Mommy!"

"Not this time," Julie said. "It'll be a few more days—"

"Three more Wednesdays," Janie said.

Julie managed a smile. "That's right. How'd you know that?"

"Miss Cass told me."

Mark saw contempt flash across Julie's face, then it was gone. "Well, I want you to get some new library books, and keep reading, okay?" Janie nodded. "And I want you to say prayers every night."

"I do. Matt helps me, and Ben."

"You be the best girl you can, okay?"

Janie nodded again, and wiped her eyes.

"I'll try to fix this as soon as I can," Julie said, then she kissed Janie again and hugged her tightly. Julie set Janie on the sofa and then stood to hug and kiss her sons. "I think you're taller, Ben," she said quietly. Before she let go of Matt, she whispered, "Take care of them, Matt. They need somebody."

"Your games are Monday, right?" Mark asked Ben and Matt.

"Yeah, five-thirty and seven-thirty," Matt answered. "We're not any good, Dad. We don't know what we're doing."

"Doesn't matter. I'll be there." He looked at Julie, expecting her to add her assurances, too. She said nothing.

"Is that allowed?"

"It's a public place," Mark said. "I don't think it'll be a problem, anyway. Your grandpa will understand that I want to see you play football."

"We only have three more games." Matt said.

"Thank goodness," Ben interrupted.

"I love you guys." Mark hugged each of his sons. "I'm really proud of you. You're doing some amazing things."

"We're just trying to survive, Dad," Matt said.

"Right now, that's enough," Mark answered, then he lifted Janie off the sofa, and held her. "I'm proud of you, too. I'll be anxious for you to read to me next week." He lowered her gently to the sofa again, and kissed the top of her head. "It'll be easier if you stay here," Mark said. "Don't watch us walk out."

Mark looked to Julie but she immediately dropped her head and strode out of the room. He fell in step behind her and tried his best to keep up.

Mark paused at the office, figuring he should say something to his father, let him know they were leaving if nothing else. Julie, however, didn't stop. When the front door closed behind her, Doug looked up from his papers, and seemed surprised to see Mark in the doorway.

"Thanks," Mark said.

"The boys play football Monday. Ben at five-thirty and Matt at seven-thirty."

"Are you inviting me to the game?"

"I'm telling you when the games are. What you do with that information is up to you."

"Will I be allowed to speak to the boys?"

"Mark, I have custody—"

"Temporarily."

"What I was going to say . . . I have custody. I'm not a jailer. This is not prison. Come see their games. Call them on the phone. They'd like that."

"I'll do that," Mark said cautiously. "Thanks." He stood in awkward silence for a moment more, then turned and left.

Julie was waiting for him at her car. "You did great," Mark said.

"Mark, I've hired my own attorney."

Fifteen

A storm of thoughts, questions and defenses fired through Mark's mind. Not only was he a failure, but now she didn't trust him or his judgment. She was talking over his stupor, trying to explain.

"Wait, wait. Go back just a minute," Mark said. "You hired an attorney? What'd you use for money?"

"I've got a job."

"Doing what?"

"You think I can't handle a job?"

"Julie . . . " Mark rubbed his forehead. "Have you lost your mind?" His frustration was spilling out now. This could get bad.

"So now I'm crazy?"

"No! In two weeks time, you've gone from being a loving, supportive wife, to coming apart at court, to having complete scorn for me, to showing incredible strength in front of the kids just now—"

"I can't . . . I can't just sit back and wait. I have to do something."

"I thought we were. I thought we were working on this. Together."

"No," she said, quietly. "Not anymore."

"Did the lawyer tell you that?"

"Yes."

Mark paced away from her. She was two steps from divorce. Who was she listening to? Not her parents. Jenna? Jenna wouldn't . . .

"Can I ask you a question?" He turned back toward her. "Can I ask you a really sanctimonious, self-righteous question? Is this what God told you to do, Julie? Are you in the center of His will right now?" He clenched his jaw tightly to keep from dissolving in angry tears.

She hung her head. "I don't know where God is."

"He's right here! He's working in all this mess!"

"Was He working when you refused to tell your father you were leaving Kenya? Or when you dragged your heels for months giving him time to file this lawsuit? Was He working when you waited until the very last minute to shut things down, giving that slimy lawyer a cause to think we were a flight risk? So the judge would give Doug our children? Was God in that, Mark?"

The answer was yes. It had to be. She knew that as well as he did.

"Let's go someplace and talk—"

"After I get my kids back, we can sit down and talk about where we go from here."

"Where we go . . . ? What about the ministry?"

"God can keep His call." She opened the driver's side door of her car. "I've got no foundation anymore, no purpose."

"But you're walking away. You're choosing to go through this alone."

"I can't go through it any other way right now." She got in the car, and backed out of the driveway without looking at Mark again.

———————

Winding through Kirkwood on her way to the interstate, Julie alternated between gripping the steering wheel and wiping her eyes so she could see to drive. Her children were so brave. She was so proud of them.

Mark, though, was a different story. How could it be

possible to love him and still be so angry with him? On top of all he'd done to bring it on them, he'd shamed her because he'd found a way to cope with this disaster.

She was the missionaries' daughter, the missionary's wife. How could she not have the faith to smile her way through this? Her parents expected her to do that. Mark expected her to be right there beside him, quoting 'all things work together for good.' She couldn't. She couldn't because she didn't believe that.

She still believed in God. She was still sure that she belonged to Him, but she had been wrong about Him. God was unpredictable, unsettling. This wasn't the God she and Janie had sung about. This God acted with impunity in ways that defied explanation. For the first time, she understood why Doug Bolling didn't trust this God.

***

Ben lay across his bed, staring at the ceiling. It was like having some aunt and uncle visit today. Everything was weird. His parents. The visit. The dinner with his grandpa and Cass afterward.

"Well, that was the weirdest day ever." Matt shuffled into the room and sat on the end of the bed.

"Don't you have your own room now?" Ben muttered.

"Something's up," he said, scowling. "They never spoke to each other."

"You noticed that, too? They both said 'I' all the time and not 'we.'" Ben raised himself up and leaned against the headboard. "So what do we do?"

"Nothing, until we know for sure what's going on." Matt stretched out his legs, resting them on Ben's desk chair.

"So where are they?"

"Cass is helping Jane get a bath, and I guess he's downstairs."

"Do you think he likes this? I mean, he's gotta know we'd rather be with Mom and Dad."

"I think he figures if we're here long enough we'll change our minds."

"That's a pretty dumb plan."

Matt didn't respond, and Ben hoped he'd head back to his room.

"Do you think he'd let us go to church?" Matt asked.

"He wouldn't go with us."

"No, but you think we'd be allowed to go? You know, just to get out and hear something good for a change."

"Where are we gonna go? I don't know any churches around here except Pastor David's, and I doubt he'd let us go there."

"What about Jack's church?"

"You know where he goes?"

"No, but we have a phone."

This was the best idea Matt had come up with in a while. "It's worth a shot," Ben said. "What about Janie?"

"It's up to her. She can go if she wants."

Then Ben grinned. "You think Cass would go?"

"She just might," Matt said. "I'll go see."

Cass pulled her feet up on the sofa and nestled against Doug. He stretched out his legs to the coffee table, next to a half eaten bowl of popcorn. He draped one arm around her shoulder, while the other hung over the arm of the sofa, loosely clutching his beer bottle. To complete his Saturday routine, he'd found an old John Wayne war movie on television.

It was hardly a typical Saturday. All afternoon, she pictured Mark pulling in alone, his pleading gestures, and Julie's stiff avoidance of him. They weren't just parents trying to cope with the loss of their children. They were a husband and wife whose marriage was in trouble.

While she was at the gym, she wrestled with whether she should mention it to Doug. But when she got home, the kids seemed so empty, so lifeless, she went right to work making dinner for them. They picked at their food in silence then melted away to their bedrooms.

Now, she desperately wanted to talk with Doug, to tell him how uneasy she felt, but he'd probably rationalize it all away for her. They're adjusting, he'd say. It'll get better. That point was hard to argue. She couldn't see how it could get worse.

Thankfully, it was too dark for Matt to see her face flush when she noticed him, but she quickly sat up and slid away from Doug. Doug looked around and saw his grandson. "Oh, hey, Matt." He clicked off the television and sat up straight.

"Do you drink beer all the time?" Matt asked frowning.

Doug took a drink from the bottle, and set it on the coffee table. "What's on your mind?"

"Do you think it would be okay if Ben and I went to church with my friend, Jack, tomorrow?"

"Who's Jack?"

"He's on the football team."

"Already making friends? That's good," Doug said. "Yeah, sure. Janie's not going?"

"That's up to her. I wasn't sure what she'd rather do."

"I don't have to go, do I?"

"No, just drop us off, then come back and get us."

"That's silly," Cass said. "I'll go with you. I'd just get home, then I'd have to turn around and head back."

"You sure?" Matt seemed pleasantly surprised. After the day they'd had, that was priceless.

"I don't have to pick up any snakes or anything, do I?" Cass teased, crossing her arms across her chest.

"Not on your first time," Matt grinned. "So can I call Jack and get directions and stuff?"

"Matt, you don't have to ask to use the phone," Doug said, then he backtracked. "Unless you're calling Italy or Africa or something."

"Thanks. I'll let you get back to your movie."

After Matt was gone, Doug reached for the beer bottle

again. "We made it longer than I thought we would," he muttered.

"What?" Cass asked, settling next to him once again.

"Going to church. We made it . . . nine days."

"Listen, you have your rituals that bring you comfort and help you relax, like your Saturday beer, and the kids have theirs."

"But I don't go around telling everybody they should have a beer. I let people pick their own things."

"Did he say you should go to church?"

"Not yet. It's coming."

"Doug, you're impossible."

"Just watch yourself, tomorrow. Don't put too much stock in it."

"Are you afraid I'll get brainwashed?" she teased. "That's crazy, you know. Irrational."

He didn't return her smile. "Humor an old man, would you?"

"Don't worry. I'm only doing it for the kids."

———

It was after seven when Mark made it back to David Shannon's. He knew he'd been driving all that time, but he couldn't remember where he'd been, what streets he'd taken or what he'd seen. He had trouble recalling what he and the kids had talked about. It was all swept aside by Julie's declaration that she'd hired her own attorney.

David tried his best to help him sort it out and come up with some ray of hope, but Mark conceded they wouldn't find an answer tonight. David protested that he never slept the night before he preached anyway. Finally, Mark just came out and said he wanted some time, and David sheepishly slipped off to bed. Alone at the kitchen table, Mark laid his Bible open and begged God for answers.

You're the only one who knows what Julie's thinking. You're the only one who knows what she may do, and how this will all turn out. How can I help her? How can I even reach her? She's so closed right now. Father, I'm having a hard time not taking her words to heart. I've always trusted her advice, her take on a situation. God, if I'm wrong, I'll change, but I need You to show me. What do I do next?

Silence.

He sighed and flipped over to read First Peter again. This time though, the mention of Abraham and Sarah caught his eye. It had been a while since he'd read Abraham's story, so he turned over to Genesis and began to refresh his memory. In chapter twenty-two, he came to the story of Abraham's test of faith.

God called on Abraham to take his son, Isaac, the heir, the miraculous son born in Abraham's old age, and offer him as a sacrifice. In a move that defies explanation, Abraham set out early the next morning, determined to obey God's command. He went through all the preparations, and at the very last moment, the moment before he took his son's life, God stopped him.

Mark leaned back in his chair, letting the words sink in. Isaac wasn't just Abraham's son, he was the embodiment of all the promises God had made, the future and fulfillment of Abraham's purpose. Everything Abraham hoped and believed was wrapped up in that young man. And God said, "Give him to Me. Give Me your son, your hope, your very understanding of who I am and My plan for you. Give that to Me. Trust Me that I can do things you can't begin to conceive of, that I am limitless. Be assured that I know your heart well enough to know what I'm asking of you and that I know you well enough to ask for it anyway. Give it all to Me."

Sacrifice. That's what You want, isn't it? My marriage, my ministry, my future, my children. You're asking me to let go of all of it, and submit. But, how? I mean, go sacrifice your son is specific and straightforward. Do I just quit trying to hold on to them? Quit trying to get them back?

But, Julie . . . that would just make things worse with her. She was already accusing him of not acting, berating him for his failures. If he let go . . . she might . . . leave him for good.

No. He had to trust that God had Julie away for a reason, that his children were right where God wanted them. After all, they belonged to Him in the first place. A sacrifice has to be offered. It can't be taken. He had to do this willingly.

He read through the passage again, this time focusing on Isaac. Isaac had to carry the wood. He was participating, and not just a passive observer. He was going to worship, but this was worship unlike any he was familiar with. It didn't make sense to him. In all likelihood, he was physically strong enough to put a stop to the sacrifice, but he was just as willing as Abraham. He had that much trust in his father and in his father's God.

The sacrifice has to be willing, too. Matt, Ben and Janie have to submit themselves to whatever God was doing. God had to know what He was asking. They're all so young.

Abraham's wife, Sarah, wasn't part of the story. She had a different test. So did that mean God was doing something different with Julie?

He sighed deeply, then stood and stretched. He unlocked David's back door and stepped out into the yard. Even with the city lights, there were innumerable stars in the clear skies. God promised He would make Abraham's descendants more numerous than the stars. Then He asked for the sacrifice. The promise preceded the sacrifice, but the fulfillment came after. All right.

Mark closed his eyes and took a deep breath, then he looked up into the heavens. "Everything I have is Yours. Give me Abraham's peace and resolve, and help me explain this to the kids Monday evening."

Sunday, September 20

Cass stood in her closet, staring at the rack of clothes. What exactly does a woman wear to accompany three children—to whom she has no connection—to church? Especially when this particular woman has never been to church in her entire life?

They wear slacks in church now, don't they? Slacks and a sweater? Like what I'd wear to meet a client? Surely that's okay . . . and jewelry. Is what I normally wear "normal' for church people? Make-up! I completely forgot about make-up. Julie was wearing make-up in court, wasn't she? Well, that's not negotiable. Matt will just have to live with it.

She pulled out several combinations and held them in front of her at the mirror, settling on gray slacks and pink sweater. Classic. Can't go wrong. She would never admit it to Doug, but she was curiously anticipating the church service. For him to be so defensive about religion made her suspect that there may be something to it after all. What if he was wrong and Mark and the kids had a genuine connection with God, a real God? Wasn't that worth investigating?

At the other end of the hallway, Doug was helping Jane get ready. She tried not to betray her surprise when he stepped up and volunteered. She suspected if Jane asked him to go to church, he would go. Cass hoped he knew how much she loved him for that.

After one last check in the mirror, she headed downstairs to the kitchen. Matt and Ben were parked at the bar, and Ben was slurping the last bits of milk from a cereal bowl.

Cass smoothed her sweater, and pushed her hair behind her ears. "Do I pass inspection?" she asked, at least partly serious.

"Let's see," Ben said, "drop-dead gorgeous blonde with a Jag. You pass. Whatever it is, you pass."

"Drop-dead gorgeous?" Cass laughed. "Where did you ever hear something like that?"

"He's absolutely right," Doug said, strolling into the kitchen, with Janie trailing closely behind. He leaned over and kissed Cass on the cheek. "You know he's named after me. That's why he's so brilliant."

Ben rolled his eyes at his grandfather.

"Now seriously, Matt," Cass asked again. "Am I okay?"

"You look nice, but I don't think there's a dress code," Matt said.

"I want to blend in."

"You'll be fine," Ben said. "Just don't sit next to Matt."

"Why not?"

"Because he's a dork. He stands out." Matt punched him in the arm. "I need that arm," Ben said rubbing his bicep.

"Janie!" Cass said, kneeling down. "You look so pretty. Papa did a good job getting you ready."

"He just did the buttons," she said. "I did the rest."

"You're sure you want to go?" Cass asked.

"Uh huh."

"We're not going for Sunday school," Matt said. "Just church."

"I know," she said, "then we have lunch. Papa said so."

"Well, I guess we're ready," Cass said. She kissed Doug again. "I'll call you when we're done and we'll meet you."

"I thought I'd grill," he said.

"You're making lunch? I'm going to church every week."

"Never mind, then."

"Doug . . . I was kidding," Cass said.

"I wasn't," he said quietly.

———

Cass hustled the kids through the main doors at Preston Road Community Church just a few moments before eleven. Normally, as the adult, she should be the one to get her bearings and find where they needed to be. She was clueless though, and the kids were naturals, so she took Jane's hand and followed Matt and Ben as they confidently made their way into the auditorium.

She would have preferred a nice spot toward the back, but the boys strolled to a row much too close to the front. No slipping in and slipping out today. Once they were settled, Matt leaned over and gave her a quick rundown of what to expect. "How do you know that when you've never been here?"

"Some things are the same no matter what church you go to," he answered.

"Is your friend Jack here?"

"I haven't seen him yet." Matt turned and scanned the congregation. "Oh, wait. He's back there." Matt waved at a teenage boy sitting with a girl and a couple about Doug's age. The man looked vaguely familiar, then he turned his head, and she recognized him. The lawyer. Mark's lawyer. Matt's friend, Jack, was the lawyer's son. Of course. It all made sense now, but . . . how on earth would she get them all out of here without facing that guy? Warm anxiety flushed across her face and chest.

Doug warned her about church. Did he know? Surely he didn't know Matt's friend was the lawyer's son. Would he put an end to the friendship if he knew? She couldn't worry about that now. Matt was watching her, and she had to distract him.

"Is that his girlfriend?"

"His sister! Sick!" Matt said. "She's a year younger."

"And those are his parents?" she asked casually.

"Yeah. He's got two other brothers that are way older, so his parents are kinda old."

So they'd just pretend like neither of them knew who Jack's father was. "If he sits with his parents, he must be a bigger nerd than you are," Cass said with a teasing smile.

"Did Ben pay you to say that?"

"No, I did it for free," she said. "He said I was drop-dead gorgeous. I owe him." Just then, the music began and a man strode down the aisle past them and took a seat up front.

Matt nudged her. "The preacher," he whispered.

The preacher didn't look especially holy or anything. In the movies, they always had these big robes, and seemed untouchable. This one was just a regular guy, about Doug's age. He wore jeans with his sport coat and open neck shirt, which was exactly how Doug dressed when they went out to eat. So what was it about church types that set Doug off?

She watched Matt intently and followed his cues on when to stand or sit, and how to pray. The music was catchy, far more upbeat than she expected and she thoroughly enjoyed watching Janie sing the songs. The little girl seemed to blossom now that she was in a familiar environment. Apparently, church was church no matter where you went.

At last, it was the preacher's turn. He stepped up on the podium and opened his Bible, and Cass quickly got her purse and pulled out the Bible Matt had bought her. He glanced over and smiled broadly. At least she got this one right.

"Good morning!" the preacher said. "Welcome to our services. If you're visiting with us, I'm Pastor Glen Dillard and I sincerely apologize to you for getting here late and not introducing myself to you. Please make sure I get to speak with you before you leave." He spoke with an East Texas drawl, but somehow he reminded Cass of Mark. Maybe it was simply because they were both preachers.

"We have been looking at the life of Abraham, for the last . . . oh, eight or ten weeks, I guess, but this morning we have arrived at Abraham's final exam. Abraham is faced with the most difficult challenge of his life. He's already left his family and homeland, he's faced down foreign kings, he's become a father at the tender age of a hundred. But in Genesis twenty-two, God asks the unthinkable. Let's read."

Matt helped her find the story, and she began reading along with Glen. At first, she wanted to react like Doug, close the book and say, 'Child sacrifice. That's crazy.' But there was an earnestness in Glen's voice that kept her engaged through the climax of the story when an angel intervened, saving Isaac's life. Was this for real? A fable? An object lesson?

"Now God shows us up front what's going on here," Glen began. "It's a test. There are several things we can learn about God's tests from this story. First, God's tests defy logic. Why would God, the God who promised this son to Abraham, the God who miraculously brought about Isaac's birth, the God who made a covenant to Abraham that his descendants would outnumber the stars in heaven, why would this God ask Abraham to take the life of his one and only descendant? It made no sense. But Abraham passed the first part of this test. The Bible says he got up early the next morning and got started. He didn't argue with God. He didn't demand to know what God was doing with him before he obeyed. God said it, and he did it."

Matt shifted in his seat, and Cass glanced over at him. Was this a test for the kids? Being away from home and family for reasons they didn't understand. But what kind of God would put kids through something like that?

"And this wasn't just a test for Abraham," the preacher continued. "Isaac was coming face to face with his faith, too. A lot of commentators believe he was probably a teenager by now. He was strong enough to lug all that wood up the mountain. He could have easily overpowered his old man and put a stop to the test right now. Imagine being in his sandals. Here's Dad, tying him up, laying him on the altar with a knife poised above him. This was not what he signed up for! But Isaac submitted himself to it."

Question answered. Apparently, God did test kids. Did Matt understand this? Is that what prompted his change in attitude toward her? Was that what Mark had told him to get him to come back to Doug's house?

"Now the other significant thing about God's tests is that they are designed to prove your faith. Now think about this for just a minute. Does God have to test you to find out how strong your faith is? Is He looking for information? Of course not! He's God! The test is for us, to take us to the outer limits of our faith, to drive us to the point where we have no other recourse but to fall on our faces and say, 'God, I can't go any farther. I have reached the end of myself.' Then He steps in and says, 'It never was about you.' He won't work as long as we are still in there churning away."

Matt crossed his arms, and leaned back. Was this the first time he'd ever heard this? Was it helping him? She could see how Doug could equate faith with weakness. There was no room for self-reliance to exist alongside faith. Self-reliance was important to him. He admired it in her. Is that why faith was so foreign, so objectionable to him? It required a recognition that there were some things he could not do for himself.

"Abraham had already passed this test, too. He told his servants, 'we' will return to you, and he told Isaac that God would provide a sacrifice. Now he didn't have all the details worked out, but he knew God was going to do something."

Glen closed his Bible. "Now don't faint or anything, but there's only two points and a conclusion, not three points. Don't tell my seminary professors." He smiled and leaned on the podium. "If you are in the middle of something and you're asking yourself, 'What is God doing? I don't understand,' you, my friend, are probably in the middle of a test. If you hear yourself, saying, 'I don't know what else I can do?', it's time to turn that paper in. Tell God you've had enough. You're ready for Him to work."

He stepped back and slowly walked down the steps to the floor in front of the podium. "Some of you, though, haven't taken the entrance exam. It starts with one question. It's a two-parter. 'Have you ever recognized that you have done things that offend an almighty, holy God?' If your answer is yes, then you're ready for part two. 'Am I willing to do something about that?'"

As he spoke those words, he made eye contact with Cass. She swallowed hard and looked away. She hadn't ever done anything that offensive to God. Music began playing once again and Matt stood, so Cass followed his lead. Suddenly in that moment, she felt like her heart was being squeezed with hot, breathless pressure. Not knowing what was happening, Cass gripped the pew in front of her with one hand, then slid the fingers of her other hand over to check her pulse. *Is this what a heart attack feels like? I'm not even forty, yet.* Then one thought came to the forefront of her mind. *You're living with a man. You've lived with others. You've been with dozens more. That offends an almighty, holy God.*

Then it was over. The music had stopped. People were

rustling, gathering their things together. All three children were standing, waiting on her to step out into the aisle so they could leave. She took a deep breath to regain her composure, and dropped her Bible into her purse.

"What'd you think?" Ben asked.

"It was interesting," Cass answered. She swung her purse to her shoulder, and took Janie's hand, anxious to leave. Several people stopped her on her way up the aisle, each shaking her hand, and thanking her for coming. At last, she made it to the door with just the preacher standing between her and her escape.

He held out a hand and smiled warmly, "I'm Glen Dillard. Thank you for coming. You have a fine family."

"Oh," she said awkwardly, returning his handshake. "They aren't mine . . . it's . . . they're not mine."

"I didn't catch your name."

"It's Cassandra Grayson. And this is Janie and Matt and Ben Bolling." Glen shook hands with each of the kids. "The boys play football with Jack," she said, hoping that was explanation enough.

"Jack's a good kid," Glen said. "You're welcome back anytime. We've got some great stuff for teenagers, and little ones, too." He waved at Janie, and smiled again.

"My daddy's a preacher, too," she said, "just like you!"

"He is? What's his name?"

"Joseph Mark Bolling, except he's just Mark."

"I've heard your daddy preach, then. He spoke at a meeting I went to several years ago. Are you still in . . . Kenya?"

"Yes," Matt broke in. "We're just here for a little while. We enjoyed the service. Thanks." He took Janie's hand and steered her out the door. While Cass was glad to be out and away, she was bewildered by Matt's actions. What had Glen done wrong?

Once they were outside and away from the building, he knelt down in front of his sister. "People may think that Mom and Dad have done something bad if they find out we're staying with Grandpa. That's why I stopped you from talking to the pastor."

"But he was nice," Janie said.

"I know, but I can't risk it, okay?" Janie nodded. "The less you say, the better."

So not only were they cut off from any sense of normalcy, the lawsuit was robbing them of a sense of community, too. That cinched it. Cass couldn't tell Doug about Matt's friend, Jack. That connection was far too precious.

———————

When Cass and the children got home she found Doug on the deck, grilling hamburgers as he had promised. She smiled and kissed his cheek. "Everything smells great. What do you need me to do?"

"Sit here with me. Tell me how much you hated it and how you're never going back." He closed the lid on the grill, and took a seat in a nearby deck chair.

Cass took the seat next to his, and reached for his hand. "Doug, I love you, but I'm not going to lie to you."

Doug's jaw clenched tightly. He stood and leaned over the railing. "I swear, if I lose you, too . . . "

Cass joined him, threading her arm around his. "You're not going to lose me. I told you that. But . . . something happened in that church service. Something I can't explain."

"Like what?"

"I don't know. I was listening to the preacher—"

"I warned you about that," he muttered with a half smile.

"I wanted to understand," she said, "I was trying to figure out what the big deal was. What were the kids getting out of it? Why was it so significant to them?"

"And?"

"Then we got to the end, and I had this crushing sensation in my chest—"

"Then we're going to the ER," Doug said with panic in

his eyes.

"I'm in perfect health—"

"So was Judy." He turned off the gas to the grill.

"It's not like that. Will you listen to me for just a minute?" She took him by the arm again, and made him sit down. "What did Judy say happened when she decided that this was for real?"

"I don't know, just some . . . feeling or something . . . it didn't make any sense."

She dropped her head, considering her words carefully before she spoke them. "Doug, I'm afraid there might be something to this faith thing, and that you and I are on the wrong side of it."

Sixteen

Doug didn't respond. After several uneasy moments of silence, he walked over and began sliding the burgers off the grill. He grunted his way through lunch, avoiding eye contact with her. She couldn't tell if he was upset with life and the world in general or with her in particular, and honestly, she wasn't sure if it made much of a difference.

"I need to go put gas in my truck," he said as she cleared away the lunch dishes.

That was ridiculous. It could wait until tomorrow morning and in all likelihood the truck had a full tank. "Okay," she said. "I'll be here when you get back."

"That's the only reason I ever come back." There was a lifetime of frustration mingled with fresh fear in his eyes. He wasn't trying to get sympathy or manipulate her. He didn't play games like that. He was afraid of losing her to the unseen monster called religion, and he wasn't ashamed to admit it, at least in this quiet, private moment. But he ducked out before she could kiss him.

She watched his truck roll down the road before she went back to the dishes. If he had a little while to decompress, maybe they'd be able to talk. Maybe.

As she rinsed plates and loaded the dishwasher, Matt slipped around the corner and grabbed a Coke from the refrigerator. "Hey, just a minute. I want to talk to you." She dried her hands on the dishtowel, then rested them on her hips.

"This sounds like trouble." He inched backwards and set the can on the counter.

"Do you think perhaps I might have been interested to know who your friend Jack was? Who his father was?"

He dropped his eyes and bit his lip. "Would you believe me if I said that I never thought of that?"

"Yes, because you're a man."

He smiled.

She arched her eyebrow, and suppressed a smile of her own. "That wasn't a compliment." She dropped the last two plates in the dishwasher.

"I don't think you have to worry. Jack's a good guy even after I mouthed off to him. His dad's the same way."

"You mouthed off to both of them?"

Matt sighed deeply. "Yeah . . . his dad committed adultery—"

"Wait. What?" Adultery? A church guy. Was that . . . possible?

Matt nodded. "That's how Jack . . . " His face flushed. "Anyway, I was pretty harsh, and I got called out."

"So your dad's lawyer had an affair, and has a son as a result of it?"

"That's the short version, yes."

"Your dad knows this?"

"Yeah, Pastor David told us. Right before the sheriff came."

She should have felt guilty at that statement, but she was too busy processing. Mark cut off his dad for living with her, but he hired a lawyer who had cheated on his wife. It didn't make sense. No wonder Doug was confused and frustrated whenever the subject of religion came up. The rules seemed arbitrary.

"Anything else?" Matt asked.

"What? No. That was it."

He grabbed his can of Coke from the counter and headed back upstairs. Cass started the dishwasher, then wandered to her piano. At the keys, it wouldn't matter who she was or what she had done. Mark had to see the contradiction. He had to understand why that drove Doug up the wall.

There had to be a piece missing, something they were overlooking. She glanced at the clock and hoped Doug would simmer down and head home soon.

Doug turned into the subdivision and drove past a row of partially framed houses. On any other day, he'd inspect them, satisfied with the progress his guys were making. Today, he just parked the truck and stared out at the structures.

Cass wouldn't, she couldn't betray him that way. And that's what it would be, a betrayal, just like Judy had betrayed him, just like Mark had betrayed him. Religion was like a plague that infected everyone who came in contact with it. No one was immune.

What could he do, though? Cass was an adult. He couldn't forbid her to go to church or to ask any questions about religion. That was the same type of narrow-minded, intellectual bigotry he was trying to rescue the kids from.

No, he wanted her to keep talking. He wanted to know what she was thinking, where she stood. If he pressed her, she might write him off as irrational and shut down the dialogue.

He had to do something though. What if he married her? It might reassure her, and it would certainly rob Mark of his biggest weapon. What if he dropped the lawsuit? Mark and the kids wouldn't want anything to do with them. Then maybe she would lose interest in religion, and forget she had ever heard any of it.

Had he stirred an angry God by filing the lawsuit in the first place? Was God going to steal Cass away from him now? Doug rested his elbow on the armrest, and rubbed his eyes. If God did that, the fight was over. He had nothing left to live for.

But he did have her, and she was home waiting for him while he was out here pouting like an idiot. He started his truck and wheeled around and out of the housing development.

He found her at the piano, and for several moments, he simply leaned against the doorframe and watched her. Her fingers swept across the keys, her body leaned in or rocked backward as the music demanded. She was lost in her own private world, filled with the simple joy of creation. He didn't have the heart to interrupt her.

She sensed he was there though, because she stopped abruptly, then turned to face him. "I understand," she said.

"What?"

"Mark's lawyer, not the heavy-set one, the other one, he was at the church today."

He felt a tense shot of adrenaline. "Did he say something to you?"

"No. I don't know if he even knew I was there." She patted the bench and he slid in beside her. "Do you know anything about him?"

Doug shook his head. "Vic said he was a business lawyer. The other guy was the custody lawyer."

"He has a son who was born as a result of an extramarital affair."

"No kidding?" Then the dots connected. "So it's okay for the lawyer, but it's not okay for me to have you here."

She nodded and slid her arm around his. "That's what I meant. I understand your frustration with Mark. I don't see why one's okay and the other isn't."

Then that trip to church was the best thing she could have ever done. "Thank you," he said. "Thank you for seeing my side."

Monday, September 21

Mark pulled into the parking lot at Clark Middle School a few minutes after five o'clock, hoping to catch Ben warming up before the game. He rolled past high-end SUVs and crossovers, an indication of the school district's affluence. He had no idea what his father drove besides his work truck, if anything. Maybe the woman, Cassandra, had a car. She could certainly fit in with this crowd.

There was no doubt his dad would be here. Mark remembered his dad coming to every one of his junior high games in spite of the fact he rarely got to play. He hated football. He had no talent and weighed a hundred and twenty pounds soaking wet, but his dad said that football would be good for him. So he played. As far as he knew, the only football games his father had ever watched were those two dozen games.

He eased into a parking spot at the end of the row, got out and locked the car. David offered his camera, but Mark decided that when this was all over, neither he nor the boys would want to remember it particularly. He paid for his ticket and took a seat on the bleachers, hoping no one would sit close.

The team was lined up on the field doing warm-up exercises and stretching. With the boys in their pads and helmets, he had a hard time locating Ben. He was watching one boy intently, almost convinced it was Ben, when he felt someone sit down beside him.

"Dad, you made it," Matt said, then he scanned the rest of the crowd. "Where's Mom?"

Mark felt a heaviness settle over him. He hadn't planned on having this discussion until after the game, with both boys there. "Mom's at Aunt Jenna's." He pointed toward the boys on the field. "Which one is Ben?"

"There. Third row, second from this end. Number forty-seven."

"And what number are you?" Mark asked, noticing that Matt was holding a red jersey in his hand.

Matt held it up for his dad to see. "Nineteen." The junior varsity team finished their warm-ups and began their drills. "I don't have to dress until after halftime. Can I sit here with you?"

"Of course," Mark said. "Grandpa's here, isn't he?"

"He's coming, but I haven't seen him yet."

"Is he bringing Janie?"

"I guess. He knew you were coming, didn't he?"

"Yeah, he told me when the games were." Mark watched Ben set the ball on the tee and kick it into the net. "He's getting some power on it."

"Dad?"

Mark turned to face Matt. "What?"

"Ben and I know something isn't right. Are you gonna tell us?"

So much for thinking he and Julie could hide anything from them. "Yeah, after the game when I can talk to both of you."

"Does Grandpa know what's going on?"

"No, and I'd like to keep it that way for now."

Mark tried to fill Matt in on the game from time to time, but mostly they sat in silence alone with their thoughts. By halftime, Ben had been on the field to kick an extra point, and for a field goal attempt, which he missed. "It was a tough angle," Mark said.

"I gotta go," Matt said. "I'll be out as quick as I can after the game."

The second half dragged, but Ben got to kick another extra point and in the end, his team won fourteen to six. In between games, Janie found Mark, and came to sit on his lap. "Daddy! Ben only missed one kick! Did you see?"

"I did," Mark smiled. "I was here the whole time."

"We were late. Grandpa was working, and Miss Cass and I almost left without him!"

"It's good you waited for him."

"Daddy, we went to church yesterday, and the preacher knew you."

"You went to church?"

"Miss Cass took us. To Jack's church. Jack is on the football team with Matt."

"Who was the preacher?"

"Glen. He said he was from Texas, but he didn't have a

hat or anything."

"Maybe he doesn't wear it to church."

"Where's Mommy?" Janie asked.

"At Aunt Jenna's."

"But I miss her."

"She misses you, too. You're very brave, though."

"It's hard, Daddy. I cry sometimes."

He leaned down and whispered in her ear, "I do, too."

She patted his knee. "We'll be okay, Daddy." Then she snuggled in against him, and slipped her thumb in her mouth. Mark didn't say anything about the thumb sucking. They could break that habit again later. He found it harder to concentrate on the game, with Janie on his lap, but halfway through the second quarter, Ben joined them, dragging his gym bag with him.

"Matt said you needed to talk to us," he said as he slid down the bleacher.

"Matt needs to learn not to tell everything he knows," Mark said, with a scowl.

"It's not his fault. I can get it out of him." He looked out over the field. "So how'd I look?"

"Good, especially for a guy who's only been kicking for a few days."

Ben nodded slightly, pleased with himself. For the rest of the game, he settled back and said very little. Matt had one chance to kick and managed to slip it through the goalposts. The varsity team ended up losing the game after a late touchdown by the visiting team. Janie had fallen asleep, so Mark waited for the stands to clear out a little before he attempted to carry her down the bleachers.

"Do you see Grandpa anywhere?"

"Yeah, he's already over by the fence." Ben pointed toward the gate. Mark followed him to the spot where his father and Cass were waiting.

"Oh, bless her heart," Cass said once they were close enough to be heard.

"I'll carry her on out to your car, if you'll show me

where you parked."

"Sure," his father said. "You had a good game, Ben."
His father put a hand on the boy's shoulder as they walked
out to the parking lot.

"I missed the field goal."

"That's gives you something to work on in practice tomorrow."

Mark followed his father to an Escalade parked relatively close. His father unlocked the rear passenger door first,
then stepped out of Mark's way.

Mark eased Janie into her booster seat, and she roused
slightly. "Janie, I'm putting you in Papa's car."

"Okay, Daddy," she said in a dreamy voice, without
opening her eyes. "I love you, Daddy."

"I love you, too, baby. I'll see you Saturday." Janie settled against the seat back and soon was breathing deeply,
asleep once again. "I'd like to talk to the boys for just a minute
if that's all right," Mark said to his father, as he shut the car
door.

"We'll wait in the car. Matt should be out soon." Doug
opened the car door for Cass then walked around and got in
himself, leaving Mark and Ben alone.

Mark shoved his hands in his pockets and shuffled
away. It was almost easy talking to his dad. His defensive belligerence was gone, and it was the closest thing to normal they
had experienced since his grandparents were killed in a car
accident. It was a perverse mirage of normal though. His kids
were still going home with his father according to a judge's
decree.

"One down, two to go," Matt called out from across the
school parking lot.

"You did fine," Mark said. "Just what you were supposed to do."

"That doesn't make it any better," Matt grumbled. "So
what's up with Mom?"

Mark pointed to the concrete steps leading from the
parking lot up to the school. "Let's sit back here. That'll get us

out of Grandpa's line of sight."

"Sneaky." Ben took a seat halfway up the steps. "Mom can't take it, can she?"

"She's staying with Aunt Jenna for a little while. We need to talk through some things, but our primary concern is you guys."

"At least you're saying 'we' again," Ben said. "Saturday, it was all 'I' this and 'I' that."

They were too smart, too perceptive. "Saturday night, I stayed up late, reading and praying trying to find some kind of answer to all this. I want to help Mom all I can, but I'm not sure she even knows what she needs."

He looked at Matt and Ben, and his eyes began to tear up. "I love you guys, but I read the story about Abraham and Isaac—"

"The preacher preached on that yesterday," Ben said.

That little confirmation boosted Mark like nothing else had for weeks. God had them on the same wavelength. "You know the story is about a father giving his son back to God." He looked into the eyes of his sons, young men now, and he spoke with hard-won resolve. "God has you where He wants you. He's got a purpose in putting you with my dad, even putting you in this school. The bottom line is, you're His and not mine—"

"Dad, it's Cass," Matt said. "She took us to church yesterday, and it freaked her out. I think God's doing something with her."

"That would be awesome," Mark said. "But what I'm trying to tell you is I have to quit fighting God on this, and I'm asking you guys not to fight it anymore."

"We're not," Ben said. "Well, not really."

"Don't look at this like something to be endured, or wish you were someplace else. This is an opportunity that God is giving you. Grab hold of it."

Matt looked like Julie when he frowned. "Don't you miss home, though, Dad?"

"Of course, but if I'm really submitted to God, my greatest desire should be to be where He wants me. No matter where that is. I want you guys to look at it the same way."

"What about Mom?" Ben asked.

"God's doing something with Mom, too. She's so hurt. She misses all of you so much, but she's kind of lost sight of God. It's hard for her to see that He's doing anything. She feels all alone."

"Then why doesn't she come back?"

If only it were that simple and straightforward. "She's doing what she believes will help her the most. Can I just leave it at that?"

"So she's not gonna come visit us at all?"

"I don't know, Ben, but whatever she does or doesn't do, don't ever question how much she loves you."

"You love us just as much and you didn't flip out," Ben said, frowning.

"First of all, that's disrespectful to your mother. Second, everybody's different. Show her patience and grace, all right?"

"What about Janie?" Matt asked. "What do we tell her?"

"I told her Mommy was at Aunt Jenna's. That's all she needs to know. There's no reason to worry her. Besides, Mom may be back tomorrow for all we know."

Tuesday, September 22

Cass had had a full morning—dropping off the kids, a haircut, two stops to order a very particular countertop, and now to the Galleria in search of drawer pulls. Before she started on that quest, she stopped off for a latte. As she sat in the food court, sipping her coffee and reviewing her planner she noticed a janitor nearby. He smiled and went back to changing out the liner and bag for one of the trash cans.

She watched him a moment longer. There was something oddly familiar about him, but she didn't know any janitors so she passed it off. The next time she looked up, he had wheeled his cart a little closer and his eyes met hers again.

She quickly scanned the tables closest to hers to see who else was watching this develop, who else might come to her rescue, if necessary. No one. She reached in her purse for her cell phone, and called Doug, mostly for a pretense. He didn't answer. No doubt he was on a noisy job site.

She gave up on taking a break and closed her planner. Before she could gather her purse and stand, the janitor spoke. "Cassandra? I thought it was you. You look great."

"I'm sorry. Do I know you?"

He stood a little taller, and smoothed his blond hair and carefully adjusted his wire rim glasses. He smiled gently. "You don't recognize me? We knew each other years ago. In a past life."

Still nothing.

"I'm Donovan. Donovan Stone."

Seventeen

Suddenly breathless, Cass leaned back in her chair. "Don—but . . ."

"I'm sorry," he said. "I should have given you some warning, but I've been praying for an opportunity to talk to you, and when I saw you, I had to say something."

Donovan Stone. Of course, she didn't recognize him. He was thirty pounds heavier, and his eyes were clear for a change. His hair was neatly trimmed and there was no hint of stubble. His janitor's uniform was clean and unwrinkled. Oh, she knew Donovan Stone, but this guy was nothing like Donovan.

"You'll, uh, you'll have to forgive me. I'm a little stunned."

"I owe you a lot. I want you to know that."

Owed her? She sent him to prison. She obtained an order of protection against him, and had him arrested when he violated it. He didn't wait for her to ask him to explain how he owed her. Instead, he checked his wristwatch. "I'm on lunch, now. Can I sit down? And I understand if you say no. If you do, I'll never bother to you again."

"Um, yeah, sure."

He pulled out the chair across from her and sat down, and she instinctively eased her chair away from the table. "That lawyer, he really went to bat for me. I still had to do my time, but as part of the deal, he made sure I got treated by a competent doctor." He smiled and shook his head. "It changed everything."

"Good. Great. I mean, I'm glad you got the help you needed." She tried to sound sincere. She was sincere. She was glad he got help.

"No, you don't understand. For the first time in I don't know how long, I'd wake up in the morning not wishing and hoping for death before the day was out. I wanted to live. I just, I didn't know what to live for, right?"

She could only nod.

"It's Jesus, Cass. He gave me a second chance."

Jesus. The word was barely out of his mouth before she felt a wave of hot pressure in her chest, exactly like the one at the end of Glen Dillard's sermon.

"I don't know what to say, Donovan." That wasn't just a conversational filler. She truly didn't know what she was supposed to say. He clearly wasn't the same man she lived with years ago. He was positive and upbeat, seemingly healthy and he had a peace about him that defied explanation.

"I know it's hard to wrap your head around. My mother was the same way, but I'm telling you, Jesus is real. The changes He makes in you are real, and I hope and pray you find that out for yourself."

He said 'pray' again.

"You know, I thought going to prison was the end, but it was exactly what I needed. I had to lose everything before I was willing to hear the truth."

"I'm glad. I mean, not that you went to prison. I'm glad you're happy now."

He smiled again. "I wouldn't have bothered you if I was just happy." He scooted the chair away from the table. "I'd love to tell you more, but I can see I've freaked you out, so I'll take off."

"It, uh, it was good to see you."

"It was better seeing you. You still with Doug?"

"Yeah, actually. Not married, but . . . you know."

He gave her a wry smile and nodded. "I hope Doug

knows how blessed he is. Take care, Cass."

She watched him wheel his cart to a side corridor and disappear, and she suddenly felt spent. Of all the people in the world . . . of all the days to run into him . . . Doug would have a stroke if he knew. She glanced back at the chair where Donovan had sat. Was that even real? Donovan Stone? If Jesus could change Donovan . . . maybe it was just psychiatric medication. Maybe Jesus was just a coping mechanism.

Her phone chirped from inside her purse. Doug. "Looks like I missed your call. What's up?"

"Oh, I was . . . you want to get lunch?"

"Antonio's?"

"Meet you there." That's what she needed. A normal, ordinary lunch with Doug. No more radical transformations. No pains in the chest. Just salad and garlic bread. Yep. Have lunch and forget this whole bizarre conversation.

Doug met Cass just inside the door at Antonio's. He moved to kiss her and she turned her cheek toward him. She saw the squint, the intensity in his gaze. "What happened?" he asked.

She shook her head. "Not yet."

He frowned while they followed the hostess to a table, and while he dumped sweetener in his tea and while she pretended to scan the menu. "You have to promise me," she said. "Promise me that you won't get all bent out of shape."

"I don't like this," he said.

"Promise me."

"I don't think I can do that."

"Do you trust me?"

"Cass, what is going on?" He leaned up to the table. "Something has you shook up. Now, tell me what it is."

He sat totally still, his eyes locked on hers, and she blinked. "I stopped at the Galleria for a latte." She kept her voice low. "I ran into someone there. Someone I used to know."

Doug very slowly balled the cloth napkin in his fist. "That guy."

"Donovan."

"He never learns—"

"It wasn't like that. He . . . thanked me. He said Harry Crawford made sure he got treatment . . . he's completely changed."

Doug let a deep breath go. "Good. I was afraid you were gonna tell me he was all into religion now."

Cass tried not to choke on a sip of water. "Would that be bad?"

"It just comes off like one of those late night commercials, you know?"

"But you said Judy changed after she became a Christian."

"She found a way to help her cope with her cancer." He took a long drink from his tea. "Religion ruined Mark and me. If he'd never gotten mixed up in that stuff we wouldn't be like we are."

But religion did something for Donovan. The kids seemed to thrive in that church service. Doug would say it was because it was familiar, but she was starting to wonder.

"Do you believe in miracles?" she asked.

"What?"

"Do you believe there are some things that happen that defy a natural explanation?"

He responded with a weary sigh and a frown.

"So you don't?"

"I have a hard time believing there's not an explanation somewhere," he said.

"I don't know. I think the two of us finding each other defies explanation." She smiled and he shook his head. Doug was pragmatic, rational, the type of guy who had to experience something to really accept it. She was the same way, but she saw Donovan with her own eyes. She had lived with him for two years. She knew him, and he was a changed man. If it wasn't psychiatric medicine . . . what was it?

Wednesday, September 23

Julie sat in Jenna's kitchen, trying to angle the morning paper so most of it rested on the tiny table. Jenna stood watching the toaster as if that was necessary to make the toast pop up. When the phone rang, Jenna announced, "Eight a.m. He never fails." She picked up the receiver. "Good morning, Mark. Just a moment." She held the phone against her shoulder. "What lie shall I tell him this morning?"

"You don't have to lie, but I don't want to talk to him."

"Mark, I'm sorry," Jenna said into the phone. "I can take a message . . . I'll do that." Then she added, gently, "Hang in there, Mark. We're praying, too." She hung up the phone then came and stood uncomfortably close to Julie. "How much longer is this gonna go on? I can't keep talking to him every morning! It tears me up."

Julie decided days ago that silence was her best strategy.

Jenna opened a cabinet and pulled down a glass. "You have a perfect husband, you know that? Do you understand what you're walking away from?"

"That's not what I'm doing," Julie muttered.

"You're here. He's there. Looks like walking away to me."

"There's more to it."

Jenna poured a glass of juice, got the toast and took the seat across from Julie. "Educate me."

"Don't you have to go to work?"

"Wednesday is my day off. Now, I've had it with this. I took you in because I didn't want you on the streets somewhere, but I feel like an accomplice. Mom and Dad are mad at me, Mark's mad at me. I bet your kids are all mad at me, too."

"You're overreacting—"

"I am overreacting? I am? Back the truck up just a minute! I didn't just leave my husband over nothing—"

"It wasn't over nothing!"

"Then explain it to me. Simply and clearly, why did you leave your husband?"

"He did not do enough to keep his father from getting custody of my children."

"Okay, first of all, they're his kids, too. Second, you're saying Mark is a wimp. Is that it?"

"Mark won't stand up to his father. He never has."

"Mark is a gentleman. He has tremendous faith in God—"

"We have to take action. While Mark and the lawyers are waiting for God to do something, Doug is going to get my kids for good."

"So . . . " Jenna worked to chew the quarter piece of toast so she could speak. "So leaving your husband, and getting a cruddy job so you can hire a slimy lawyer is showing more faith—"

"This is not about faith!"

"Obviously."

"I don't owe you an explanation."

"Actually, you do. You're staying at my place, eating my food, and making me answer the phone when your husband calls." Jenna gulped down the juice, and set the glass down hard on the table. "Julie, here's what I see. You're the oldest, and you've always been the first, the best at everything. You got straight A's. You never got in trouble, and you always did all your chores. You think God owes you something for that."

"Jenna—"

"Wait, there's more. God let something bad happen after all you've done for Him and your whole belief system collapsed. Not only that, but Mark out-Christianed you. He's only been a Christian since he was nineteen. You've been doing this since you were five. How could he possibly have more faith than you do? Well, guess what? He does!"

"I don't have to listen to this." Julie pushed away from the table and stood up.

"So help me, Julie, I will throw you out of my house, if

you walk out of here!" Stunned by Jenna's threat, Julie sat back down. "I know you think that because I'm a twenty-three-year-old kid, that you don't have to listen to me, but I want you to get this with both ears. You have one more week. After that, I'm taking you back to St. Louis, if I have to drag you kicking and screaming and you're gonna deal with this."

Mark sat at the computer in David's family room trying to type a reply to an email from Peter Bakari in Mombasa. How much should he say? How much detail? Then he sighed and shook his head. He was putting his reputation and image first. That's what got him in trouble in the first place.

He took a deep breath, rested his fingers on the keys and typed the truth, the whole messy, inglorious truth. He hit send, and immediately felt lighter. The expectation of a reply would give him something to look forward to Thursday and Friday.

As Mark was shutting down the email program, David's phone rang. The caller ID showed Benton, Davis and Molinsky. Mark snatched the receiver from its cradle.

"Mark, this is Chuck. I just got off the phone with Fletcher. We got a prayer answered. They moved the hearing up to the sixth instead of the thirteenth."

"That's just two weeks away. That's great!" Mark said.

"I kind of expected to hear from you earlier in the week. How'd your first visitation go?"

"It was awkward."

"I'm sure. How'd your dad treat you?"

"Okay. He stayed out of sight during the visit, and then invited me to the boys' football games Monday evening."

"Good. That's a positive step. How's Julie?"

And now it would get sticky. "Julie told me she's hired her own lawyer."

"Did she say who?"

"Someone in Springfield."

"Springfield?"

"She's staying with her sister."

"I see," Chuck said with the knowing tone of a man who could fill in the details himself. "Has she filed anything?"

"Not that I know of."

"Do you know if she intends to pursue a separate agreement?"

"I don't know what she intends."

There was scratching in the background as Chuck mumbled, then he spoke. "I don't think this will affect anything between now and the hearing. We only have two more weeks."

"But?"

"This could impact the final arrangement."

"How so?"

"It depends on what she does, what she files. I'll call Fletcher, and another guy we're consulting with, but Mark, I'll be honest with you. If she makes this a three-way fight, it's anybody's guess what will happen.

Thursday, September 24

Cass ordered a latte and took a seat at the very same table in the Galleria food court where she sat on Tuesday. It was a few minutes before eleven, just like Tuesday. She sipped from her cup and scanned the faces in the crowd.

This was crazy. Crazy because she was trying to catch Donovan. Crazy because she had no idea what his work schedule or routine was. Crazy because Doug would never understand.

She wasn't entirely sure what she was doing. In some ways, she secretly hoped the Donovan she knew would show up today. If that was the case, she could write off Tuesday's meeting and go on with life. Another part of her was afraid she would confirm what she had seen—confirm that religion, faith and Jesus were more than she ever knew.

No, she should go. She should go back to the office and work on something. Before she could stand, she saw him, dragging his cart, changing the trash can liners. He looked up and smiled. When he worked his way to the nearest trashcan, he said, "This is getting to be a habit."

"That was quite a story you told Tuesday. I had trouble getting it out of my mind."

"I hope that's a good thing."

"I'm not sure."

He nodded. "How can I help?"

"I love Doug. I want you to understand that up front. I'm not trying . . . I'm not interested, okay?"

He laughed gently. "I'm not sure I'd want a woman who'd leave him for me. I've got nothing to offer." Then he dropped his eyes. "Never have."

That was the kind of manipulation she expected from him. She wasn't about to let him pull her in. "I've got one question for you."

"Okay, shoot. Figuratively, of course."

Another subtle little dig. "What makes you better than me?"

He laughed out loud. "Is that what you think?" He lifted a full liner from the hamper on the cart. "Cass, I'm nothing but trash." He dropped the bag again. "Look, it's not about who's better or worse. Truth is, we're all hopelessly messed up. The only thing I know is that you have to decide to do something about it."

She felt that squeezing heat again. It was like sitting through the end of Glen's sermon again. He used the very same words—are you willing to do something about it?

"What did you do?"

"You know that's another question, right?" He adjusted his glasses and grinned at her. "I prayed. I told God I didn't want be the way I was anymore. That I didn't want to be a sleep-around burnout head case. I wanted to start over."

Oh, brother. She took a drink from her cup. "So Jesus says, 'Sure thing, Donny. We'll call it all good and you get a clean slate.'"

"Um, yeah."

"That's utterly ridiculous."

"Yeah." He leaned on the handle of his cart. "But you wouldn't have come back here looking for me if you didn't believe there was something to it, now would you?"

Eighteen

Most weeks, Friday was the only day Doug was actually in his office before noon. But Cass had a list of stops to make today, and Sandy had a doctor's appointment, so he came in to hold down the fort. For him, that consisted of listening to the phone roll to the answering machine.

Since he was in, he hoped to get a jump on his stack of paperwork and maybe take off early tomorrow afternoon. The kids had done great this week. Jane didn't get sick at school. She only woke up crying at night once, and the boys had settled into a routine. That deserved celebrating. They hadn't got the boat out since the kids got here. If the weather held, maybe they'd even spend the night on it.

He left his desk for a refill of his coffee when he saw Sandy pull in. She didn't look at him when she walked through the door, and he felt a mild, but very familiar twinge. "Hey, what happened? I thought this was a routine doctor thing."

"It was. Everything was good. Normal." She kicked her purse under the desk, still not looking at him.

"Dell okay?"

"Yeah. Listen I've got some things I need to catch up on so—"

"It's none of my business."

She sighed and raised her head finally. "It's none of mine either."

"I don't get it."

"How long have you and Cass been together?"

"Eight or nine years. Why?"

"You love her and she loves you, right?"

"Yeah."

"Then let's drop it. Obviously there's been a mistake."

"Sandy . . ."

"No. I'm wrong. I have to be wrong. That's all there is to it."

"You saw her with somebody, didn't you?"

Sandy's face paled. "How did you know?"

"Tuesday . . . she said she ran into that guy. The head case." If that guy was harassing her again, he'd need more than psychiatric medicine to straighten him out this time.

"There has to be a logical explanation. She wouldn't . . . she's not that type . . . she loves you."

Doug nodded. "I'm sure she'll tell me what's going on. I mean, she told me at lunch that same day. It rattled her."

Sandy folded her hands on her desk, and spoke very gently. "Doug, this was not a woman rattled by a run-in with an abusive ex-boyfriend." She blinked several times. "They were clearly enjoying themselves."

"I'm not worried."

"Good."

"We have no secrets."

"You shouldn't."

"She talks to people all the time," he said.

"Naturally."

"I'm gonna go back to work."

"Is she meeting you for lunch?"

"I guess, but I'm not going to bring this up."

"You shouldn't. That sounds paranoid."

"Exactly. We'll just . . . we'll just let it go. Unless she says something."

"Good plan." Sandy scooted her chair up to her desk, leaving Doug to wander back to his office. Cass wasn't meeting that guy. There was a simple explanation. She was in the Galleria all the time and more often than not, she grabbed a latte. She didn't want to drink it in her car. Who could blame her? Then that guy probably sat down and she was too polite to tell him to get lost. End of story. When he had a chance to talk to her, she would lay it all out for him, and he would remain very low-key and never mention that Sandy saw her. Nothing to worry about at all.

Cass glanced at the clock on her dashboard as she wheeled out of the Galleria parking lot. Good grief, it was almost noon. She quickly dug through her purse until she found her cell phone, and dialed Doug. "I am so sorry. Things took longer than I expected. You want me to pick up lunch for us and Sandy?"

"Sandy says she ate, but if you want to grab me a sandwich, that'd be great. I'm at my desk all afternoon."

"Me, too. Well, until time to get the kids." Out of nowhere, a surge of guilt washed over her, bringing her to the brink of tears. How could she . . . ? How could she get so wrapped up in talking to Donovan that everything else seemed to fade away? "I should have called," she said quietly. "I just . . . time got away from me."

"Things happen. I understand. See you soon."

She dropped the phone back in her purse and took a deep breath to clear her head. Donovan . . . it was like talking to that preacher. He drew her into his story of bottoming out and surrender and finding hope. He made her want that hope, too. But she had a wonderful life, and she told Donovan so. Doug gave her a love and security she'd never known before.

"It won't be enough," Donovan said. "Now that you know you're missing this, you won't be able to rest until you fix it."

"You don't understand. I cannot tell Doug . . . I mean his wife told him that she needed God, that he couldn't, that he wasn't enough. And he never got over it. To this day, it tears at him. I will not do that to him."

"But Cass—"

"No, this is not embracing Christianity. It's rejecting him. I can't."

That's where they left it. She stopped and got a sub for Doug and a salad for herself on the way back to the office. Sandy barely looked up when she passed by on her way to Doug's office. "Thanks," he said clearing a spot on his desk. "Listen, I'm gonna try to get everything done today so I can get the boat out tomorrow afternoon. I thought the kids would like it. Maybe we could spend the night."

"The boat?"

"Yeah, we haven't had it out since August."

"Are we allowed to take them on the boat?"

"Why wouldn't we?"

"I don't know. Custody laws are funny sometimes."

"Cass, are you all right? You seem nervous or upset maybe."

"Do I? Just getting here late, I guess."

Doug nodded silently.

"You know, I'm not sure I'm up for the boat tomorrow. But don't let me stop you from taking the kids out."

"I wouldn't want to go without you," he said. She hoped she was imagining the chill in his voice.

"You know I love you, don't you?"

"I never questioned that."

"Don't. Never question that."

Saturday, September 26

Doug poured himself a cup of coffee and walked out to the deck. He gazed out across the backyard and watched a deer bolt from the tree line and head toward the country club. When Judy's cancer came back, the worst part was the powerless knowing. The disease progressed on its own timetable, but at every turn, it asserted that there would be an end, and that end would be very bad. He and Judy both knew that, and they couldn't do anything but live it.

He gulped his coffee and let it slowly burn its way down his throat. All night Thursday, all day Friday and all last night, he felt that same powerless knowledge. Something had undeniably shifted.

Cass said she loved him and he needed to believe her. She promised she would never leave him. He turned, leaned against the railing, and at stared the balcony for the master bedroom. That's when the thought hit him—there were worse things than losing his wife. Much worse.

Mark pulled into his father's driveway just before noon. When he didn't see Julie's car, it confirmed his fears—she wasn't coming. It took every bit of resolve he had to keep from driving to Jenna's, dragging Julie back and making her talk to him. Surely, knowing that she was missing seeing the kids was having some effect on her. Maybe this week, he'd see some breakthrough with her.

He got out of the car, surprised by how warm it was for late September. His dad met him at the door. "The kids are out in the pool."

"Thanks." As he stepped through the doorway, he noticed his father scanning the street. "Julie's not coming."

Only a slight raise of the eyebrows betrayed his father's surprise.

"She's hired her own lawyer, and has been advised not to go along with the present arrangement."

"Her loss." His father closed the door. "Listen, Cass is out there . . . never mind."

"I won't bother her." Mark walked back through the house, through the kitchen and out onto the deck. "Daddy!" Janie called and ran with little penguin steps to him. Matt and Ben swam to the side of the pool and pulled themselves out.

"Here, Janie." Cass handed her a beach towel. "You

don't want to soak your daddy."

Mark nodded at Cass, and she gave him a faint smile. Janie threw the towel around her shoulders, but Mark took her in his arms and hugged her tightly. "Are you going to swim, Daddy?"

"Not today."

"Where's Mommy?"

"She's still at Aunt Jenna's."

"When is she coming home?"

"Soon, baby." He turned to Matt and Ben, and hugged each of them. "Hey, guys."

"You may as well swim now, Daddy," Janie giggled. "You're all wet anyway."

He led her to the edge of the pool. "Show me how you can swim underwater." She grinned and jumped in the water, and he didn't even flinch when she splashed him.

"I'll leave you alone," Cass said quietly as she slid her feet into her flip flops.

"You don't have to go," Mark said. "I'm sorry I make you uncomfortable."

"Ben and Matt! Come on!" Janie called.

"Go ahead," Mark said, nodding toward the boys. "Go play."

Before the boys could get in the water, Mark heard his dad come out on the deck, huffing with aggravation. "I'm going to have to go. I've got a crew arguing with some city guys about digging for a water line."

"You're leaving with me here?" Mark asked.

"I can trust you, can't I?" His father's eyes narrowed, then drifted toward Cass. "Even though you're a free man, now?"

Mark didn't respond.

His father turned toward Cass. "I'll be back as soon as I can." Mark heard the sliding door close and a moment later the truck pulled out of the garage.

"I'm sorry," Cass said. "That was uncalled for. He's been on edge the last few days."

"Don't worry about it." Mark pulled a lounge chair over and sat on the end, watching his kids play.

"Has he always talked to you that way?" She moved over to the chair beside his.

"Or worse."

"Daddy! Watch me!" Janie called from the diving board. She held her nose, and jumped high off the board into the water. When she popped up, Mark clapped his hands for her.

"He learned that sharp tongue from my mother," Mark continued. "I've heard her rip him mercilessly, and he would just take it."

"You're kidding. I've heard him criticize you for taking what he dishes out."

"I think in some weird way, he's trying to help me out. He always took everything, and he doesn't want me to do that."

"Was your mother like that to you, too?"

"Yep. Always on my case about something. But after she became a Christian, that changed. I'd go see her in the hospital and she'd listen to me. She was encouraging. She had this gentle spirit about her." He waved to Janie again. "I loved talking to her." He sighed. "But when I became a believer, too, that made me a mama's boy."

"Oh," Cass said, her eyes wide. "I've heard him call you that."

"I should stop. I don't want you to think bad things about my dad." He took his eyes off his children for a moment, and turned to face her. "I want to thank you for taking my kids to church. That meant a lot to them, and to me." Mark risked a grin. "You may have noticed, my dad doesn't want much to do with church or religion."

She smiled broadly. "I got that vibe."

"It goes back to my mother. She was this refined, elegant woman. He couldn't believe she married him. He worshiped her."

"And she got sick," Cass said quietly.

Mark nodded. "He couldn't come to terms with the fact

that this perfect woman could get sick and die. He took it personally. It was an attack on him, so his strategy was to hit back. He's had this little war with God for years now. Since he can't attack God directly, he goes after me."

"He's very dismissive when anyone brings up faith."

"He's deceiving himself," Mark said. "If he doesn't discount it, then he has to concede that God is sovereign and can do unexplainable things like let my mother die."

She nodded slowly, turning his statement over, and his instinct was to press her. Instead, he let it go. "Matt said it was kind of your first time."

"Yeah, believe it or not."

She reached and made a show of straightening the stack of towels on the nearby table, so he changed the subject. "Are you from St. Louis?"

"Richmond Heights. My parents are living the retiree life in Phoenix, and my brother is in Tampa. I've traveled all the way to Kirkwood."

"Julie has a brother down around Tampa. It's nice down there."

"We went down for Nick's wedding last year." She let her eyes drift out across the yard. "I doubt we'll make the trip again anytime soon. Nick and I aren't close."

"I'm sorry to hear that," Mark said. "It's a real strain when there's conflict in a family."

"Especially when they bring it upon themselves."

He deserved that he supposed. "Sometimes . . . people draw a line in the sand, and even if it's a stupid line that never should have been drawn in the first place, they drew it. And they can't admit it was stupid, so the only thing they can do is hold that line. They'll hold it no matter what it costs . . . until it costs everything. By that time, they don't remember why it mattered so much or how to erase it and start over."

"You know your father pretty well."

"I wasn't talking about him." He looked her in the eyes. "I owe you an extreme apology."

She glanced at the kids splashing in the pool. "I'd say

we're even." She stood and picked up the book that lay on the lounge chair nearby. "Mark," she said, "this is none of my business, but I hope things work out between you and Julie very soon."

"Thank you," Mark said. "They will. I'm not sure how, yet, but they will."

———————

Cass loaded the dishwasher and wiped down the stovetop and counters following dinner. At least the kids ate this week. She, on the other hand, had trouble choking down any of it. She already suspected Doug was wrong about Mark's religion, and after this afternoon, she was sure he was wrong about Mark. Cass waited until she was sure the children were asleep, then she caught Doug in the TV room. "Can I talk to you?"

"Always," he said. He gulped the last of his beer and turned off the television.

She joined him on the sofa, and with her heart pounding, she said, "I want you to drop this lawsuit."

He frowned and shook his head slowly. "I can't. You know that."

"No, you *won't* drop it." She didn't bother to hide her irritation. "You could call that jerk lawyer of yours right now and put a stop to it."

"Nothing can be changed until we go to court again." He pulled his feet off the coffee table and straightened up. "Did Mark put you up to this?"

"That's just a little patronizing." His eyes narrowed. "The lawsuit is wrong. Mark is a good man, and he's a wonderful father. You should be proud of him, not his chief persecutor. Did you know his marriage is in trouble?"

"Yes."

"And that doesn't have any impact on you?"

"Julie leaving him is a good thing."

"How can you say that?" She yelled at him as she stood

and paced in front of the television. "I don't know how much longer I can stomach this."

"It won't be that much longer. The hearing got moved up to the sixth."

"I'm not going back to court. I refuse to be associated with this anymore."

"It's a little late for that!" he shot back. "I distinctly remember you telling me before all this started that you were in it for the long haul."

"I meant the relationship! Do you honestly expect me to go along with everything you say, no questions asked? No disagreements?" Then it made sense. "That's why Mark drives you up the wall, isn't it? Because he *is* man enough to disagree with you. He doesn't need your blessing or your approval, and he does it with a clear conscience."

Doug stood up, his jaw tightening. "How's your conscience?"

"Excuse me?"

"As long as we're talking about how saintly Mark is and how rotten I am, what about you sneaking around meeting that head case?"

Her voice caught in her throat. "How . . . "

"Sandy saw you," he said, his words accused her with pain rather than anger. "She didn't want to tell me. Neither did you, apparently."

"This is exactly why I didn't tell you. I knew you wouldn't understand."

"Answer this, then. Do you want to be with him?"

"Of course not."

"Then what . . . the second time wasn't an accident."

She felt a heaviness in her heart. She had to tell him the truth. "He's . . . he's a believer, a Christian now. I wanted . . . I wanted to hear—"

"No!" he shouted. "I will not tolerate—"

"STOP!" Every muscle, every nerve tightened. "Stop right there. You won't tolerate? No, you get this. I will not have you dictate to me who I can talk to and what we can talk about—"

"Do you love me?"

"That doesn't buy you the right—"

"Do you love me?" It was louder, more desperate.

"Yes! Yes, I love you!"

"Then respect my wishes."

"When you respect mine."

In the instant after she stormed from the room, in a flash, before his brain could engage, Doug snatched up the closest thing, the television remote, and threw it across the room. It shattered into a dozen plastic pieces against the stonework around the fireplace.

For a moment, he stood frozen, staring at the chip in the stone, processing what he'd just done. He'd yelled at her. He'd raised his voice in anger at her. What was he doing? What was he thinking? He was demanding and overbearing . . . because he was afraid. He was going to lose her. He lost Judy . . . and Mark . . . and he was going to lose her.

He dropped to the sofa, buried his face in his hands, and for the first time in years, he sobbed.

Sunday, September 27

Cass paced the master bedroom, fuming and muttering, "This is exactly how he treats Mark. Exactly. He makes an unreasonable, demeaning demand, and you have to respond with belligerence and it all spirals out of control until they'd said things they didn't mean." She wished she could take it all back.

Tears brimmed then spilled onto her cheeks. It was like Mark said. He'd drawn a line and even though it was a stupid line, he'd hold it at all costs . . . until it cost everything. He wouldn't let it destroy their relationship. He wouldn't let it go that far. He wouldn't.

The hours passed, and Doug never came upstairs to bed. Now as morning light filtered into the bedroom, Cass wrestled with just how significant the argument was. There were only days left before the hearing, and she was certain he would lose. The kids would go home with their parents, and they would go back to their lives.

What exactly would they go back to? She knew living with him was wrong. She knew that trying to take Mark's children was wrong, and she knew that everything Doug believed about his son was wrong. Could she go on as if none of this had happened? Was he worth lying to herself day after day? Maybe for a while, but it couldn't last.

She threw the covers back and sat on the bed. She reached over, lightly ran her hand over Doug's pillow, and burst into tears. She loved him, she would always love him, but she knew this was the beginning of the end.

⸺

Doug woke up in the desk chair in his office stiff and disoriented. His back hurt, his head throbbed and he felt sick. He pulled himself up and got the spare meter from the downstairs bathroom. Low. He needed to eat something. Soon. No insulin, right? He rubbed his forehead and tried to remember the numbers. No, he was low. He was sure he didn't need insulin. He'd have to check it every hour or two today.

He never intended to sleep. The third beer. Stupid, stupid decision. He swallowed three aspirin, put the meter away, and headed back to his office. The notepad on his desk was filled with illegible scribbles, the fruit of his all-nighter. He wracked his brain, trying to find a way out of the mess he'd created, but every option—whatever they were—involved admitting that Mark, or worse, Mark and Julie, were right.

If they could make it a few more days. If they could make it that long, then he would take Cass to the Bahamas again or Hawaii maybe. They'd go on vacation and he would ask her to marry him. Maybe even get married there on the beach. Just start over.

A knock on the open door of his office startled him, and he swiveled around. Cass stood there dressed, her make-up and hair were perfect. "I'm sorry," he said, shaking his head, crossing the room to her. "I'm so sorry."

"For what?" she asked.

"For raising my voice with you and . . . I just . . . I'm sorry."

"Listen, I was thinking," she said, her eyes darting between his eyes and the floor. "After this is settled, we should take a few days."

"I was thinking the same thing," he said, smiling uneasily.

She nodded and glanced behind her. "I'm gonna take the kids to church again."

"Good. They need that."

"You want to meet us for lunch?"

"Sure. Just give me a call." He watched her walk away. No kiss, no goodbye, no 'I forgive you.'

"Did we do something wrong?" Ben asked when Cass pulled into the church parking lot. "You didn't say anything all morning."

"I didn't sleep last night," Cass said. "I'm not awake yet."

"Grandpa wasn't talking either."

"Yeah, I think he slept on the sofa last night."

"Did you have a fight?"

"No," she lied. "He was watching a movie."

"Well, Matt won't let you sleep in church. Believe me, I know."

She managed a smile for Ben as she got out of her car and locked it, then took Janie's hand. Walking to the church building, she checked her watch and hoped the preacher was running late like last week. They found seats on the far aisle, and Matt sat beside her once again.

She couldn't concentrate on the church service, and not knowing the routine yet, she felt a step behind. At least when the preacher started, she could just sit and stay seated. She pulled her Bible from her purse in order to make a good show, and waited while Matt found the passage for her.

"Last week, just at the tail end, I asked a two-part question," Glen Dillard began. "The first part was 'have you ever done anything to offend an almighty, holy God?' and then the second part was 'are you willing to do something about that?'"

Cass's chest tightened. She vividly remembered his words.

"The first thing you do is tell God what He already knows, what you've realized. That you've offended His holiness. We call that sin. Then comes the doing something about it part. You ask Him to remove that sin, and replace it with a new eternal life. Now while you're still living, that life may look the same on the outside, but the insides have all been re-done."

Cass thought of Donovan, and Mark talking about the change in his mother, how her demeanor changed. Is that what Glen was talking about?

"Finally, and this is what we're going to talk about today, as proof of that investment, you determine to live God's way. We call that discipleship. And to find out about discipleship, it's best to consult the source, Jesus Christ. So in Matthew ten, starting at verse thirty-two, it reads—"

Cass tuned him out, and her mind drifted back to Doug. He looked positively shell-shocked this morning. He had the same shame and terror in his eyes that he had after he'd hit Mark. Was his unresolved grief, pent-up for years, going to vent itself in violent anger? Was that reason enough not to stay with him?

How could she leave him though? After talking to Mark, after seeing him this morning, Doug was not the strong, self-confident man he strove to assure everyone that he was. He desperately needed her approval, her reassurance. She had replaced Judy as the idol in his life.

" . . . Now this 'set against' here," Glen continued. "That's completely separated. I won't torture you with Greek, but think 'dichotomy.' Mutually exclusive, contradictory even. Alienated. If you choose discipleship, there are people you will alienate, and there is a very strong possibility that some of those people will be the ones you care about the most."

That was exactly what had happened to Mark. He had chosen discipleship, and he had cut himself off from his own father. A man wouldn't do that for something that had no substance. If Judy loved Doug half as much as he loved her, she couldn't tolerate a division between them unless . . . unless everything she and Mark and the kids believed about Jesus was absolutely true. If it wasn't true, then it was the cruelest of hoaxes, leaving shattered relationships in its wake. If it wasn't true, then Doug was justified in his bitterness. But if it was true . . .

Matt shifted and stood, snapping Cass back to the present. She'd have to work all this out later. Right now, she had to get ready to face Doug at lunch.

"Where is lunch?" Janie asked.

"I don't know," Cass took Janie's hand to walk out with her. "What sounds good to you?"

"Spaghetti."

"I think I can work with that," Cass said.

When they reached the back of the church Glen Dillard smiled and shook Cass's hand. "You came back," he said. "Thank you."

"I enjoyed it. You make things plain and simple." At least the part she had heard was plain and simple.

"The gospel is, ma'am." He reached in the pocket of his suit jacket, then handed her a business card. "If you'd like to hear more sometime, my wife and I would be thrilled for the opportunity to explain it to you."

"Thank you." She dropped the card in her purse. "I may take you up on that."

They met Doug at Olive Garden for lunch, but with the bustle of the restaurant and the chatter among the children, there was no opportunity for conversation. On the drive home, Cass looked over at Matt in the passenger seat, staring absently out the window.

"Is it worth it, Matt?"

"Is what worth it?"

"Is going through all this, being away from home, from your parents, is it worth it?"

"The truth?" He glanced back to Ben, who nodded for him to answer. "The truth is, I know it has to be, but sometimes it's hard to see that."

"So this is a test? Like Abraham last week?"

"That's what my dad said. You been thinking about this all week?"

"Off and on. Doesn't that tick you off that God makes things hard?"

"Kind of, but I don't want to be lazy and useless, either. It's like playing ball. They'd fire the football coach if he didn't make us sweat. We'd never make it through a game."

"So life is just a game?" she asked with a smile. "I should have known with boys that it all comes back to sports."

"Okay, then we'll talk about shopping. Isn't it worth driving all over the city to find the perfect pair of pants? I mean it takes forever, and it's in and out of the car, and trying them on—"

"No!" Ben said. "It is totally not worth it."

"I'm not asking you!" Matt said, then he turned to Cass. "But once you get the pants, it's kind of cool what you had to go through to find them. It makes 'em more special."

"Shop a lot do you?"

"My mom likes to shop and she won't buy anything that isn't just right and on sale. That's one reason Ben hates it so much."

"So do you know what the test is for, or what you're supposed to learn going in?"

"No. Hardly ever. That's what makes them hard."

"Matt, would you pray for me? I think I've got a test coming up real soon."

Nineteen

That afternoon, Doug retreated to his office again. Cass wouldn't look at him through lunch, and hadn't spoken since they had gotten home. He ached to talk to her and clear up things between them. Something was going on, something bigger than just the lawsuit.

His first instinct had been to blame Mark, to believe he had poisoned Cass's mind somehow. In reality, he knew Cass was too smart for that. He clung to the promise she made him, the promise that she wouldn't leave. She would keep that promise. She had to.

"Hey," Cass said. She spoke softly, but he flinched nonetheless. "How's your sugar? You want me to make you some dinner?"

"I'm not . . . no, I'll get something later. Things are messed up today." He swallowed hard and looked in her eyes. "Are you still angry with me?"

"No," she said with a sigh.

"Then what is it?"

"Can I be a typical woman and say 'I don't know'?"

"You have never been a typical woman, Cass." He was able to smile and she gave him the slightest smile in return.

"Maybe not." She dropped her head, and looked at the floor in front of her. "I'm wrestling with some things inside, Doug, and I don't think I understand them well enough to talk about them yet."

"I know what you mean." He waited for her to look up at him. "Do you still love me?"

"I will always love you."

Monday, September 28

Doug splashed cold water on his face after he finished shaving. Immediately he felt a sting on his chin. He dried off, and checked the mirror to find the nick. He never found a cut, but he looked into his own eyes. The longer he stared at himself, the angrier he got.

You know what? You make me sick. You get your act together and start acting like a man. When he walked out of the bathroom, he nearly ran into Cass. "Good morning," she said. "Is everything okay?"

"Fine. Why?"

"Nothing. You seem a little tense."

"It's Monday. I've got a busy week."

"You remember the boys have a game tonight."

"Yeah, I've got a five o'clock. I'll meet you there." He got a shirt from the dresser drawer and pulled it over his head.

"Did I say something wrong?"

"Of course not. I'm just telling you what my day looks like."

"Do you want me to bring you a sandwich or something at the ball field?"

"I think I can handle getting dinner. I'm not completely worthless."

"Who said you were worthless?"

"Just drop it, all right?"

"It's dropped."

He checked his watch and jammed his billfold in his back pocket. "I'm gonna take off."

"This early? What's up?"

"Don't you trust me?"

She pressed her lips into a thin, tight line. "So is this

how it's going to be? Guilty as imagined?"

"Did I ask you where you were going today? Who you were meeting with? No, I didn't. You told me you didn't want to be with that guy. You told me you loved me. That's the end of it, right?"

Her eyes lingered on his for a moment, but then she turned away and began putting in her earrings. "Don't wait on me for lunch."

Cass dropped off the kids and headed straight for the office. If the rest of the week shaped up like this morning, she wasn't sure she wanted to face it. Doug was insufferable this morning. Unreasonable. Totally out of character. Or maybe it wasn't. That was what gnawed at her most. What if this was the real Doug? What if the last few years had been the fairy tale and now harsh reality was all that was left.

No, she'd rather believe that he was afraid, afraid of losing face, afraid of losing her, afraid that he might be wrong after all. That had to be it. He was afraid and so he was lashing out. Maybe they could talk after the football game tonight. Maybe if he had some space and the day to simmer down, they could have a conversation. If not . . . well, she didn't want to think about the alternative.

Right now, she had another issue to deal with.

She took a deep breath and strode through the door at Bolling Developers. Sandy was at her desk, but she barely raised her eyes from the computer screen. "He's not coming in this morning. We need to talk."

"Got your story straight?" Sandy crossed her arms and scowled.

"Donovan Stone is a Christian now. His whole life has turned around. I wanted to hear the details. I knew how Doug would react, so I didn't tell him. End of story."

"If you hurt him—"

"I'd rather die."

"He will die."

Cass wasn't a football fan, but she understood enough to know Ben sailed through his game, making two extra points and a field goal. Matt wasn't so fortunate. He trotted on the field to kick an extra point. The snap was good, and the holder got the ball down. Matt, however, bounced the kick off the goalpost.

"For cryin' out loud, Matt!" Doug muttered. He frowned and scowled the rest of the game and shot out of his seat and down the bleachers as soon as the game was over. Cass was a half dozen steps behind him by the time he made it to the parking lot. She reached him as Mark, Ben and Janie walked up to them.

"Nice quiet weekend?" Doug's voice had the bite of patronizing sarcasm.

"What do you mean?" Mark asked.

"With Julie not there, I figured you finally got to enjoy your weekend. Do what you want for a change."

"Not in front of my kids," Mark said.

"They're gonna find out the truth sooner or later."

"Not now." Mark took a step in between the children and his father.

Doug jabbed a finger toward his son. "You want a restraining order? I don't have to let you see the kids here—"

"That's right, you're a saint," Mark said sarcastically.

"Ben, get in the car," Doug said. "Janie, you too."

"We rode with Cass—" Ben said.

"I didn't ask you who you rode with. I said get in the car." Ben raised his eyebrows and started to hug his father. "You have a hearing problem?"

"No, sir," Ben said, and Mark nodded for him to go ahead. "Come on, Janie. I'll buckle you in. Bye, Dad."

"Love you guys," Mark said.

"Bye, Daddy!" Janie said, waving at him, and blowing

kisses.

Once Ben had shut the car door, Mark said, "Don't take this out on my kids."

"Mark, I've got nothing to say to you." He pointed across the parking lot. "In fact, there's no reason for you to hang around."

"I'm going to say goodbye to Matt."

"I think he needs to go straight home after that kick he screwed up."

Cass had listened to the exchange in disbelief. Where was all this hostility coming from? She reached out and touched Doug's arm. Immediately, he snapped around to face her. "Cass, stay out of this."

"Stay out of what? What is with you?"

"Nothing." He waved a hand angrily in Mark's direction. "I'm not gonna let him take advantage of me."

"He's not trying to—"

"So you need her to take your case now?" Doug asked Mark, his voice edged with contempt. "Or are you trying to come between me and Cass? Is that it?"

Mark shook his head and crossed his arms across his chest, but said nothing.

"Good, here he comes," Doug muttered, seeing Matt crossing the parking lot.

"Hey, Dad!" he called.

"Matthew! What happened out there?" Doug asked, frowning.

"What are you talking about?"

"You missed a kick! A gimme. What was the problem?"

"I don't know. I just missed."

Doug swore under his breath. "One thing," he said, holding a finger up in Matt's face. "You got one job on this team. How hard could it be?"

"You wanna try it?" Matt shot back.

"Matthew!" Mark said.

"I can handle this." Doug shot a glare Mark's direction, then he turned back to Matt. "You think you've been living in a prison? You're grounded to your bedroom. I don't want to see your face except at meals. You understand me?"

"For missing a kick?" Cass asked.

"No, because he's a disrespectful, smart-mouthed punk." He turned back to Matt. "Now, get in the car." Doug climbed in his car without another word to Cass or Mark, and drove away as soon as Matt shut his door.

Cass turned to Mark with wide-eyed disbelief. "I have no idea what's going on. He's never . . . "

"Mr. Hyde? It's a cycle. He'll calm down. Eventually."

As Cass drove home, one question kept running through her mind—what if he doesn't? Something was eating at him, but he couldn't keep spewing this venom at the children. They were innocents and she had to do her level best to shield them.

Doug was only a few minutes ahead of her, but the house was already dark and still when she arrived. She found him in the office, his favorite retreat of late. His chair was swiveled so that his back was to the doorway. "What can I do to help?" she asked gently.

"I don't need any help," he replied without turning around.

"Have I done something?"

"Of course not," he said, turning around, his voice finally softer.

"Who set you off?"

"Nobody."

"Then ease up. You were too hard on Matt."

His shoulders tensed, and the sharp edge returned to his voice. "How many boys have you raised? I know what I'm doing."

"I'm not going to let you talk to him like that—"

"Let?! You . . . aren't gonna let me? I seem to recall you telling me you didn't want to have anything to do with this."

"Doug, I love those kids—"

"And I don't?"

"This is not an attack on you!" She dropped her head and sighed. "You have got to make peace with this . . . this . . . whatever before it tears us apart."

"You're the only one who can tear us apart."

Wednesday, September 30

Julie sat in her sister's car in the parking lot of Nina Breckinridge's law office. Just walk in there and sign papers. That would begin legal action to get her children back. Five minutes tops. It had to be this way, and once the kids were back, everyone else would understand that.

Lord, I pray Your blessings on this meeting, and I ask You for quick resolution to all this. Bless my children and protect them from the influence of their grandfather and from any lasting damage from this ordeal. In Jesus' name.

Not that she thought God was listening. It was just a habit, deeply ingrained in her. It was what she was supposed to do, exactly like the other shallow, sunshiny notions she built her life on that were useless when put to the test. She had no faith, no real faith anyway. She was like that seed that landed in shallow ground. It sprang up quickly, but withered once the hot sun beat down on it.

She had done worse than wither. She had attacked Mark. Could he ever forgive her? How much damage had she caused in their marriage? Would there be anything to go home to once this was over?

Once inside, she was shown into the lawyer's office quickly. "Julie, how are you?" Nina said, standing to shake hands across her desk. She was just a few years older than Julie, but she was tough and accustomed to winning her cases. Not bad for grabbing a name out of the phone book.

"We have everything we need. You know, your husband's lawyer was so helpful, I almost hate to do this to him," she said with a laugh.

"Oh, he's a nice guy," Julie said.

"And we all know what happens to nice guys," Nina said, opening the folder on her desk. "Now, I need to clarify a few points. Has your husband ever spanked your children?"

"A few times."

"Excellent," Nina said, making a note. "Has he ever berated the children or you? Used words like 'stupid' or 'crazy'?"

"What are you getting at?"

"Honey, depending on what we have to work with, we need to establish a pattern of behavior in support of the claim of mental and or physical cruelty."

"Mental or physical cruelty?"

"You want your kids back, right?"

Julie nodded in spite of a rising uneasiness.

"And it is my job to make that happen. Now, from what I've read of your case, your father-in-law took action because of the decisions your husband made. If we separate you from him . . . I think we have a slam dunk."

"Separate me? I have to leave Mark? I can't do that."

"Julie, honey, you already have."

"No, I . . . " She didn't leave Mark . . . she just needed some time . . . some space . . .

"It's perfectly natural to have difficulty accepting the end of your marriage—"

"No." Julie grabbed her purse and stood up. "Send me a bill. I'm through here." She rushed out of the office and by the time she made it back to Jenna's car, she was nauseous and shaking uncontrollably.

When her hands finally steadied, she drove back to Jenna's place, and let herself in. The end of her marriage? That wasn't what she wanted. That was never . . . she just wanted her kids. Her stomach rolled and quivered again. Hopefully, Jenna had some 7-Up or ginger ale or something in the refrigerator. Instead, she found a note taped to the gallon of milk.

"And you will seek Me and find Me, when you

search for Me with all your heart. I will be found by you, says the Lord, and I will bring you back from your captivity. Jeremiah 29:13-14.

Your week is up. Better be packed when I get back from the store.

Love,
Jenna

P.S. You might read Jeremiah . . . or Jonah . . . or something . . . anything."

She heard the front door open. "Julie! I don't see your suitcase!" Jenna bustled into the kitchen, and slung two bags of groceries up to the counter.

"How'd you get to the store? I had your car."

"It's a half-mile away. I rode my bike." Then she pointed at Julie and squinted the way their father did. "You're changing the subject, Missy. Suitcase. Where is it?"

"I just got back. Honest. Just walked in the door."

"All right, but I am completely serious. We are going to St. Louis, and early enough that I can get back home at a decent hour—"

"Jenna, I fired my attorney."

Jenna raised her hands and spoke to the ceiling. "Hallelujah, thank you, Jesus!" Then she looked at Julie. "In therapy we call this a breakthrough."

"I'm not in therapy."

"I can fix that. I can set you up with one of my colleagues."

"You know, you're too young to have colleagues."

"And you're too old to be acting like such a brat. Now, back to the lawyer. What happened?"

"She thought . . . I mean, her strategy . . . " She rolled her eyes up to the ceiling and let a deep breath go. "She thought my best option was to . . . to divorce Mark."

"See! Slimy. I tried to tell you." She started unpacking the grocery bags, handing off a carton of eggs, cheese and lunchmeat to Julie. "Here, put these in the fridge. So what now?"

"You're making me go back to St. Louis."

"All right, hold it right there," Jenna raised a hand. "You have to get beyond, 'I'm making you go.'"

"But you are."

"Julie, what is the most important thing in your life right now?"

"Getting my kids back."

"Good. Now, where are your children? This is not a trick question."

"St. Louis."

"At?"

"Doug's house."

"There you go. You want your children. He has your children. He's the one you need to deal with."

"Out of the question," Julie said.

"Why? Because he intimidates you?"

"He does not intimidate me."

"Then what is it?" She pulled out a package of cookies. "Want one? They're oatmeal."

"Yeah, actually. I didn't eat breakfast." Julie took a cookie then got the gallon of milk from the refrigerator.

Jenna handed her a glass. "So, go on. Doug . . . he doesn't intimidate you."

"I can't stand him."

"You told Mom you hated him."

"All right, fine. I hate him."

"Now we're getting somewhere." Jenna pulled out one of the chairs and sat at the kitchen table. "Why do you hate him?"

"Because he's a jerk."

"Specific behaviors, please."

"He's obnoxious."

"Behaviors, Julie, not more adjectives. I don't think you hate him to the core of his humanity. You couldn't hate anyone like that. What does he do?"

"He bullies Mark."

"And?"

"He treats Mark like a brainless little kid."

"And when will those behaviors change?"

"They won't."

"Two breakthroughs in one day." Jenna nodded and smiled. "My point is, you cannot change anything about Doug Bolling. All you have control over is how you respond to him. As long as he provokes this emotional reaction, he owns you. How does Mark deal with him?"

"He doesn't."

"Explain. Like Doug says something insufferable about Mark being a missionary. What does Mark say? How does he react?"

"He doesn't. He goes right on like he never heard it."

"Exactly. Mark has learned he is not responsible for his dad's attitude, only for his response to it."

"You're good." Julie reached for another cookie.

"Thank you." Jenna said, buffing her nails on her shirt-sleeve, and then blew on them.

"So what do I do?"

"I can't tell you that. My job is to help you frame your problems clearly and rationally. But, I will say, Mark knows something you don't about dealing with his dad. You need to suck it up, beg him for forgiveness and then ask him to help you."

Ben lay on his bed letting the blood rush to his head. With Matt grounded, it was like prison for Janie and him, too, so he decided to work on hanging upside down. Building up his tolerance would have to come in handy for some future cool job.

"Looking for a new perspective?" Cass startled him and he jerked himself up off the bed.

"Training to be a jet pilot," he said.

"Good luck with that," she smiled and started to walk away.

"Hey, you have the inside track. Grandpa's been, like, a jerk all week. How much longer is this gonna go on?"

"I don't know. He's not talking to me very much."

"He's mad at you? I didn't think he ever got mad at you."

"I don't think he's mad at me. I'm not sure he even knows." She checked her watch. "Better get to bed. Whatever it takes to keep the peace, you know." She smiled and headed on down the hall.

Ben lay back on his bed. Whatever it takes. Sometimes a man had to take matters into his own hands. He swung his feet around, got out of bed and slipped downstairs. He found his grandpa holed up in his office. "Grandpa?"

He looked up from a stack of papers. "Isn't it past your bedtime?"

"Yeah, I know."

"So are you here to ask me what my problem is?"

"Nope."

"Then what are you here for?"

"How'd you meet Grandma?"

He took off his glasses and laid them on his desk, then leaned back in his chair. "Not now, Ben."

"Okay. So . . . are you still mad at her?"

"Mad at her? What are you talking about?"

"If I loved somebody and they left me, I'd be mad."

"She didn't have a choice. She was taken away from me."

"Yeah, that doesn't make much sense."

"No, it doesn't." He put his glasses back on, and picked up the top sheet from the stack.

"But you have Cass. She's pretty terrific."

"She is."

"I've never been in love before. Girls . . . some of 'em still have cooties, you know."

"That won't last much longer."

"That's what my dad tells me, too." He thought for a moment. "Is it worth it?"

"Worth what?"

"Is being in love worth . . . maybe losing somebody?"

"I've been trying to answer that question for sixteen years."

"I think it would have to be."

"Oh, yeah?"

"Otherwise, what's the point? Why get up in the morning?"

"Ben, what are you getting at?" his grandpa asked with a sigh.

"I don't know. You don't have to act tough. It's okay to miss Grandma. It's okay to not understand it."

"Do you understand it?"

"Nope. If I did, I'd be God. And I'm not."

"I'm not either."

"What would you do if you were?"

"I'd stop people from dying."

"Then where would we get our heroes?"

"What are you talking about?"

"'Cause heroes always die. That's what makes 'em so . . . heroic."

His grandpa smiled finally. "So your grandma was a hero?"

"She was my dad's hero. I bet she was yours, too."

"I never thought of it like that."

"She had to be pretty tough, you know. Knowing she'd never get to see my dad get married, or see us kids. Plus she had to worry what would happen to you without her."

"I don't think she worried about me."

"She was a mom. She worried about everything. I promise." He got a half, no, a quarter of a smile out of his grandpa.

"She would have loved you, Ben."

"Yeah, I'm pretty lovable," he nodded. "She loved you a lot, I bet."

"Not until the end. I . . . uh . . . I'm not too lovable, I guess."

"Not the last few days, that's for sure," Ben muttered.

"Midlife crisis."

"What's a midlife crisis?"

"It's when a man takes stock of his life, and realizes time is short and he gets afraid he's on the wrong track."

"Hmmm," Ben said. "You're probably not gonna fix that one tonight."

"I didn't expect to." He leaned back in his chair and did his tough guy squint. "I used to believe the world was pretty straightforward, black and white. But I'm finding out it's all gray. And getting grayer."

"Do you care if I pray for you? You know, just that you'll figure it out?"

"Sure, Ben."

Thursday, October 1

Julie crossed and uncrossed her legs, then gave up and began pacing again. Doug's office was a mess. Stacks of papers and folders on the desk, on the bookcases, on the file cabinets. How could he ever find anything?

She was pleasantly surprised when Doug's secretary let her wait in the office, but Sandy said she had no idea when he might be back. The longer she waited, the less of her carefully crafted monologue she remembered. If he didn't get here soon, it would all be gone.

She had to deal with Doug before she could face Mark. In fact, she and Jenna had argued all the way from Springfield yesterday, because she insisted she needed another day before she saw Mark. While she appreciated Jenna's help for the last couple of weeks, and the rental car, and the night in the hotel last night, Jenna didn't know Mark. She only knew the carefully cultivated image of Mark.

The real Mark didn't know where God wanted him. He'd spent years in Kenya, avoiding his father, not following God's call. The real Mark had no idea how to deal with his father or how to respond to him. And honestly, she wasn't positive the real Mark would take her back.

However, if she could somehow, someway, reach an agreement with Doug, and end this custody nightmare, she and Mark could work everything else out.

If.

She heard a heated exchange outside the office door and her stomach tensed. An instant later, the door burst open, and a red-faced Doug Bolling thundered, "Get out of my office! Now!"

Twenty

Julie swallowed hard and stood her ground. "Not until I say what I came to say."

"When you walked out on Mark, that ended any responsibility I have to you. I don't owe you the time of day."

"You stole my children," she shot back. "You owe me plenty."

"I didn't steal your children. The court took a good look at how they were being raised and the judge gave them to me." He sat in his desk chair. "Now, what do you want?"

"My children. What will it take? Please." She was begging.

"It's tough when you lose everything you're living for, isn't it?"

"Then you understand. Can't we work something out?"

"Not as long as Mark is letting you call all the shots. I'd give him the kids tomorrow if he'd divorce you."

"So this is not to hurt Mark. It's to hurt me."

"Actually it's not, tempting as that is. It's to protect the kids from your narrow, bigoted way of looking at everything and from the life you're forcing on them." He leaned forward resting his elbows on his desk. "It may be too late for Matthew. He's the most arrogant, self-righteous kid I've ever seen."

"Then you don't know Matt at all. He's a wonderful young man."

"No, he's just like you," Doug pointed at her. "When he

talks, I can hear you saying every word, every condescending, judgmental word that comes out of his mouth."

"Do you think, maybe, just maybe, he's a little upset by what you've done? You've torn him away from his home and his family. Did you really expect him to embrace this with open arms?"

"I thought Christians thrived on adversity, you know, that persecution was good for you," Doug answered sarcastically. "Didn't you teach him about turning the other cheek?" Then his eyes narrowed. "Or about loving your enemies?"

He had baited his trap and he was waiting for her to bite. No way. "I'm sorry you see us as enemies. I guess that's why you've never understood how much Mark loves you. You've never recognized what a good man Mark is."

"Mark is not a man," he sneered. "I don't see him fighting to get his kids back. He's letting you fight the battle for him."

"He's a gentleman."

"Gentle," Doug smirked. "He won't stand up to me and he won't stand up to you. He would have never done something as idiotic as moving to Africa if you hadn't put him up to it."

"Mark was following God's call."

"Mark was following you. You run his life. His mother ran his life before, and now you do it, all under the pretense of love, all the time pushing him, telling him he's not good enough."

"I have never said Mark wasn't good enough—"

"You walked out on him! In that one act, you've told the kids and everybody else what a failure you think he is. He didn't live up to your expectations so you shamed and humiliated him." He stood and leaned across his desk. "You wrap yourself in sanctified holiness, but you don't have any more love and grace for him than I do. See, Julie, I know your type. With you, love is conditional, performance-based, withdrawn on a whim."

"Mark knows I love him."

"Have you seen Mark lately? Does he know you're here?" Julie flushed in silence. "That's what I thought. Your actions don't match what you say. I think that's called hypocrisy."

"And you genuinely love Mark?"

"At least Mark knows what to expect from me, and I have the nerve to own up to it. I haven't deceived and betrayed him."

"You took our children! If that's not betrayal . . . you're delusional—"

"Am I? The truth is, I know exactly what you're doing because I've done it myself for years. See if this sums it up. God doesn't behave the way you want Him to, and you lose the most important thing in your life, so you come back with bitterness and anger. You can't touch God, though, so you unload it on Mark."

"No," she said quietly.

"The truth hurts, doesn't it? Here's another truth for you." He leaned forward, his voice low and intense as he spoke. "You are no different from me. You're angry, resentful, vindictive, and devoid of any compassion. You carry the same poison, just in a different bottle." He put his glasses on and opened a folder lying on his desk. "Now, get out of my office before I throw you out."

Julie stood with her lip quivering in awkward silence as Doug ignored her. She had no defense and certainly no rebuttal for his tirade, so she was left to rush back out to the rental car. The only shred of dignity she escaped with was the fact the he didn't see her cry.

He was right. All the things he said about how she had treated Mark were true. The horrifying reality was that she was just like Doug. That made her want to scream, and vomit, and sink down into the dirt and never crawl back out. The anguished shame and bitter sorrow were beyond anything she had ever experienced. Losing a baby didn't hurt like this. Not even losing her children hurt this way.

Unable to hold back any longer, she lay across the center console and sobbed. The tears flowed until she was weak, dizzy and breathless. Then words spilled out in a voice she barely recognized. "Dear God, I am so sorry . . . I was so blind, for so long. I've failed You. So self-righteous . . . and my marriage. I've broken my marriage vows. I promised to honor Mark. He was obeying You, and I . . . I've done everything I could to undercut that. Mercy, forgive me. Help Mark forgive me."

Exhausted, she pulled herself up, and gripped the steering wheel. She had to get out of Doug's parking lot. She stretched a hand out level, testing it, making sure she was steady enough to drive. Not great, but passable. She was too ashamed to face Mark yet, so she drove aimlessly down one major street then looping back on another. Soon she saw a sign for the Galleria and mechanically changed lanes. The mall was safe and anonymous. She could fade into the background as she tried to sort out where she could go from here. That is, if she still had any options left.

She bought two packages of Tylenol from the vending machine in the ladies room. Next, she got a large coffee and found a table in the food court away from the foot traffic. She sipped her coffee and dug through her purse for her small Bible. She had carried one with her constantly since she was twelve because her father suggested she needed to be prepared in case the Lord opened a "door of opportunity." The doors didn't get much wider than this.

Mark had been reading First Peter, and he was weathering this storm, so maybe the answers were there. She flipped to the epistle and read through it slowly, but nothing struck her. Now what? Maybe Peter was still the key. She turned to the Gospels and began reading all the passages about Peter. She made it as far as the tenth chapter of Matthew, when a verse stopped her.

He who loves father or mother more than Me is not worthy of Me. And he who loves son or daughter more than Me is not worthy of Me.

That's exactly what she had done. She worshipped her

children, or rather, being a mother. That consumed her time and energy and devotion. She had knocked God out of His rightful place, and set up mothering her children as the god of her life.

She sighed deeply and took a long drink from her coffee. A few chapters later, she hit one of the key exchanges between Peter and Christ. Jesus asked the disciples who they thought He was, and Peter immediately answered, 'You are the Christ, the Son of the living God.' Jesus called him blessed because God Himself had revealed that to him. Moments later, though, Jesus called Peter Satan.

> From that time Jesus began to show to His disciples that He must go to Jerusalem, and suffer many things from the elders and chief priests and scribes, and be killed, and be raised the third day.
>
> Then Peter took Him aside and began to rebuke Him, saying, "Far be it from You, Lord; this shall not happen to You!"
>
> But He turned and said to Peter, "Get behind Me, Satan! You are an offense to Me, for you are not mindful of the things of God, but the things of men."

She reread the passage, looking for what had changed. Peter stopped depending on what God was revealing to him and went with his instincts, his own assessment of the situation. He was dead wrong.

God couldn't make it much plainer. She had been Peter her whole life. Always relying on herself to come up with the right answer, the expected answer. All these years, she'd mistaken self-reliance for faith. Real faith is waiting on God, trusting in God.

She found a slip of paper stuck in the back of the Bible and she quickly jotted down some notes before the thoughts slipped away—things she wanted to tell Mark, things she hoped he could forgive. The list grew, filling margins and even the white spaces between the lines as she continued to read through Matthew and Mark and most of Luke's gospel.

As Jesus gave the last instructions to his disciples before His arrest, He delivered a sobering message to Peter.

And the Lord said, "Simon, Simon! Indeed, Satan has asked for you, that he may sift you as wheat. But I have prayed for you, that your faith should not fail; and when you have returned to Me, strengthen your brethren."

With those verses, Julie was overcome with tears of guilt again. She had been sifted, all right. But . . . that meant Jesus prayed for her, just like He'd prayed for Peter. Simon was Peter's given name. He wasn't Peter until he met Jesus, his name change symbolizing a fresh start. Jesus knew Peter was about to deny Him, and that he would suffer the bitterest shame and humiliation because of it, but He was confident that Peter's faith would hold. Her faith was in shambles for sure, but it was still there, and she was ready, oh so ready, to return to Jesus Christ.

She winced as she choked down the last gulp of coffee, now cold and bitter. She stood and tossed the cup in the trash, debating whether she should try to eat a little something. Maybe that would ease her headache. She had just reached for her billfold when she heard her name.

Doug's girlfriend stood at the corner of her table. As Julie struggled to remember the woman's name, she spoke gently, "I understand if you don't want to speak to me."

"It's not that," Julie admitted wearily. "I've drawn a complete blank. I know you told me your name, but it's gone."

"It's Cassandra. Cassandra Grayson." Her eyes dropped for just an instant. "Cass, actually."

Julie reached her hand out. "I didn't have the decency to shake your hand before. That was wrong. I'm sorry. I hope you don't hold it against Mark or the children." Cass shook her hand and smiled awkwardly.

"Can we sit down?" Cass asked, pointing to the table.

"Please," Julie said.

"I should be apologizing to you." The woman's eyes

darted back to her hands, never lighting on Julie's for more than an instant. "Doug . . . the lawsuit is wrong. I wish I could do more to help." She swallowed hard, and her eyes finally settled. "You have amazing, remarkable children and they are doing so well in the face of all this."

"Thank you. They . . . have their father's faith."

"It's so natural, so genuine, in all of them. I mean, their faith isn't just something they believe, it's who they are." Cass leaned forward. "I took them to church." Her eyes began to glisten. "Matt, he explained everything to me. He bought me a Bible even."

"Did Matt explain what salvation means? What being a Christian is about?" It was a reflex. That was the question she was supposed to ask, but once it was out, her insides seized. Was God really doing this? Was He going to allow her the opportunity to explain salvation to someone? After all she had done wrong?

He was. As far as He was concerned, she was already home.

Cass shook her head. "It's not Matt's fault. Doug is so hostile to it. I don't want to antagonize him, or make things difficult for Matt."

"Are you afraid of Doug?"

"No," Cass answered, "but the most hurtful thing I could ever do to Doug is become a Christian." She sighed deeply. "I know what he's done to you and Mark, but I love Doug so very much. I would rather die than bring him more pain. He still, after all these years, he still grieves for his wife, and he grieves for Mark."

"He's a complicated man." Julie could concede that much. Christ-like love for her father-in-law was going to take some more work.

"Anyway," Cass continued, "the thing is, I know this is real, but can I become a Christian without losing Doug?"

"I can't answer that," Julie said. "I was just reading a little while ago, that Jesus sometimes causes divisions in families—"

"Wait!" Cass snapped upright in her chair. "That's what the preacher said Sunday, that you may alienate the people you care about most." She raised her hand to her mouth. "I have to choose," she said softly. "I have to choose between Jesus and Doug."

"Cass, there is no choice. Doug is a human being. He's fallible. He has weaknesses. Jesus Christ is God. Even though Doug can offer you a wonderful, comfortable life now, someday this life is going to come to an end. Then what? Life goes on after death, and it goes on either in God's presence in heaven or it goes on apart from God . . . in hell."

"You really believe in hell?" Cass asked.

Julie nodded. "Jesus did."

"Tell me how this works, then."

Julie quickly explained the gospel, that Jesus' death on her behalf satisfied God's requirements for justice, but that she had to own her sins and had the responsibility to choose to accept that death as the full payment for them.

"Sins," Cass said, "like living with Doug?"

Julie nodded.

"The first time I took the kids to church . . . I felt it. The guilt . . . and I felt like I couldn't breathe, like my chest was being crushed." She took a deep breath. "If I do this, will I be able to sleep again?"

Julie smiled. "I think so."

"And I just have to pray?"

"Yes. You tell God you understand that you've broken His laws and you want His forgiveness because Jesus died to make that possible. Then you tell Him you want to live in obedience to Him."

"That's it?"

"That's it. It's simple, but it changes everything."

"That's what a friend told me, too." She bowed her head, and spoke softly. "God, I know that living with Doug is a sin, and I know that's not the only one. I want Your forgiveness because Jesus Christ died for me. I believe that. I know it's real." She dissolved into tears and Julie reached across the table and squeezed her hand. "Thank you," she said, wiping her eyes.

"Oh, here you go, ma'am." An unopened box of tissues slid across the table. Julie looked up, and a man winked at Cass then walked back to a custodian's cart parked close to a nearby trash can. Cass turned around and gave the man a thumbs up. He smiled broadly and nodded.

"He . . . his name is Donovan," she said. "We knew each other years ago. I ran into him last week . . . a week ago, actually, and he told me this amazing story of how Jesus changed his life." She opened the box of tissues, and snatched the first one then pushed the box across to Julie. Cass wiped her eyes. "I guess I've been getting it from all sides lately."

Julie smiled. "God is relentless like that sometimes."

Cass let a long, slow breath escape. "I feel a hundred pounds lighter."

"I know what you mean. You cannot imagine what this did for me."

Cass sat up straight again. "It just dawned on me—you're back in town. So you and Mark . . . ?"

"Not quite yet," Julie said. "I made the mistake of going to see Doug first."

She dropped her eyes again and almost apologized. "He's been on edge for the last week. He . . . it's wearing on him, I think." Cass glanced at her watch, then smiled. "Did you drive here?"

"I have a rental."

"Listen, I came in here to check on a special order at Eddie Bauer's. Let me run up and do that, then I'll take you to see your kids."

"Are you serious?" Julie's eyes began to brim with tears.

"It's almost time to pick them up from school. They would be thrilled to see you."

"What about Doug?"

"He'll never know, but it doesn't matter. This is the right thing to do."

Forty minutes later, Julie stood outside Cass's car, her eyes glued to the door of Weston Elementary School. She took Cass's advice to wait outside just to be on the safe side. The less the school personnel knew, the better. Julie heard the bell ring and soon children streamed out of the building. She stretched and strained trying to find Janie in the crowd.

She spotted Cass first, and at last she saw Janie holding tightly to Cass's hand, and tears brimmed. Janie looked so tall, so old. Had she really changed that much in two weeks?

Then almost in slow motion, Janie turned her head and their eyes met. She left Cass, backpack and lunchbox behind and ran. "Mommy!"

Julie bent down and Janie jumped into her arms. She held her little girl tightly, whispering through tears, "I love you, baby. I've missed you so much."

"Miss Cass said she had a surprise, but I thought it was ice cream!"

Cass joined them carrying Janie's backpack and lunchbox. "Better than ice cream, huh?"

"YES!" Janie said. "Can we go home after we get the boys?"

"Baby," Julie said, "I'm not supposed to be here, and if the judge finds out, we could all get in trouble. Miss Cass may still get in trouble with Grandpa."

"She can handle him," Janie said.

"Even so," Julie said. "We need to make it as easy as possible for her since she did this for us."

"So don't tell anybody?" Janie asked.

"Don't tell anybody."

"Janie, hop in your seat so we can go get the boys," Cass said.

"Are we gonna surprise them, too?"

"You bet!"

"Mommy, sit in the back with me." Janie patted the seat as she climbed in. Julie slid in the back seat beside her, and helped her get her seat belt buckled. "We do this every day," Janie said. "Sometimes we go get ice cream, but sometimes we have to go back to Miss Cass's office, or to the new houses or to the stores, but just until the boys finish with football, then we have to get them. Then we go to Grandpa's house and we make dinner. Then the boys goof off until Grandpa makes 'em do their homework. Except Matt doesn't goof off now, he has to go straight to his room after dinner."

"Matt got in trouble?" Julie asked.

"He smart-mouthed Grandpa at the football game after he missed his kick."

"It's a long story," Cass said. "We won't waste time on that right now."

"Did you hear what Matt said?" Julie asked Janie.

"No, Grandpa made me and Ben get in the car, but Matt told Ben and Ben told me so I wouldn't keep asking where Matt was."

Cass pulled up in front of Clark Middle School, and turned around to Julie. "I'm going to get the boys."

"But it's not four-thirty yet," Julie said.

"Some things are far more important than football practice," Cass replied with a wink. "I'll be right back."

As soon as Cass shut her car door, Jane looked at Julie with wrenching seriousness. "Mommy, I missed you Saturday. Daddy came all alone."

"I'm sorry, Janie. That was wrong. I hurt Daddy's feelings, and yours and the boys', too."

"Are you still mad at Daddy?"

Julie felt a twinge of shame. "No, and I never should have been. Daddy was right. I was so sad that you had to stay with Grandpa, that I couldn't think straight. I forgot God was still taking care of all of us."

"But now you remember?"

"I think so. Aunt Jenna helped me a lot, and I spent a long time studying my Bible today."

"We only have to stay with Grandpa till Tuesday. That's what Matt said."

"Matt's probably right," Julie said. "We can make it until then, can't we?"

"Here they come!" Janie pointed toward the school.

Julie smiled and got out of the car. Matt and Ben broke out in wide smiles as soon as they saw her, and left Cass behind. They hugged Julie tightly, and she kissed them both through tears.

"Where's Dad?" Ben asked.

"I haven't been to see your dad yet," Julie said. "I ran into Cass and she offered to bring me to see you."

"Dad will be glad."

"I'll be glad to see him," Julie said. She looked to Cass. "Where can we go?"

"Why don't I take you back to the Galleria?"

Ben climbed in the backseat with Janie, and Matt took the front passenger seat. "Cass is pretty cool, isn't she?" Ben said. "She's like a double agent."

"Yes, thank you, Cass. I really appreciate everything."

"It would have been pure torture at Grandpa's without her," Matt agreed. Cass smiled without taking her eyes off the road. "So what's gonna happen now?"

"After I leave you guys, I'm going to see your dad, and hopefully he and I can work things out."

"But right now?"

"I guess we just hang out at the mall until it's time for you guys to go home." She reached over and patted Janie's knee. "Maybe we should get that ice cream." Janie smiled and nodded.

Inside the Galleria, Cass made an excuse about another order she needed to check on. She promised to meet them in the food court in an hour.

Julie bought ice cream, then she and the kids found a table. The boys filled Julie in on school and their football games, and Janie jumped in regularly to redirect the conversation. In mid-sentence, though, Janie's face clouded. Cass was headed their way. "Now, baby, don't," Julie said.

"But we just got here."

"I know, but this was a bonus."

"I guess," Janie muttered, a pout already settling across her face.

Cass pulled a chair over to the table. "I need to talk to you guys before we go home." She looked at each one of the children and smiled. "Your mother explained everything about Jesus to me this afternoon. I believe it. I'm one of you, now."

Ben grinned. "I knew you would!"

"Well, I couldn't have done it without you guys. Especially you, Matt. Thank you."

He smiled then rounded the table and hugged her tightly. "This is a great day."

Cass took a deep breath, and suddenly grew very serious. "Knowing what I know about Jesus . . . I can't stay with your grandpa anymore."

"You can't leave us!" Janie cried, tears beginning.

"I'll stay until after your parents visit on Saturday. I don't want anything to jeopardize that."

"Grandpa won't understand," Ben said.

"No, he won't," Cass said, as her own eyes began to brim with tears. "I expect he'll hate me. But I wanted you guys to know . . . to know how special you are and how much I love you."

"You're pretty special, too," Ben said. He hugged her, and then looked around. "All right. Enough mushy stuff."

"Now, we do need to go, so hug your mama one more time," Cass said.

Julie embraced and kissed each of her children, but then she turned to Cass, and hugged her tightly. "Thank you. Thank you for letting me see the kids. Thank you for helping them. They are so blessed to have you there."

Cass tried to smile. "Pray for me. Pray for Doug, too. I think he's miserable because he knows."

"Of course, we'll pray. You may be the one who can reach him."

"If Judy couldn't—"

"You're an extraordinary woman, Cass," Julie said.

"God will do great things with you and through you. Wait and see."

———————————

Mark pushed David's lawn mower back into his shed, and checked his watch. Twenty minutes to spare before David got home and at least forty-five before he expected Jan and Maddie. David would give him a hard time for cutting the grass, but fresh air and physical activity were a welcome change. Mark had studied and read all he could stand.

Jenna hadn't answered this morning when he called. As he mowed, he tried to reason through where she might have been. If Jenna had to go in to work or something, Julie wouldn't have answered the phone. It was probably something that simple. He didn't know her work schedule, but surely she would be home later this evening. Calling in the evening might be enough to catch Julie off guard and at last, he could convince her to talk to him.

He locked the shed and as he walked back toward the house, he caught sight of a car slowing down in front of the house. He didn't recognize it. Before he could make it around the house from the backyard, he heard the car door open. He picked up his pace, but once he made it to the front of the house, he stopped dead in his tracks. Julie.

She walked toward him, with tears in her eyes. "Mark . . . I am so sorry . . . can you forgive me? Can I come home?"

Twenty-One

Mark ran to his wife, took her in his arms, and kissed her as she sobbed on his shoulder. "It's okay," he murmured. "Everything's going to be all right. You're home. You're home now."

Her words spilled out in a jumbled mess, but there was a constant refrain. "I'm sorry, Mark. I'm so sorry."

He let go of her, pushed her hair away from her face, then leaned his forehead down to touch hers. "None of that matters now. You're home." He smiled at her through his own tears. "It doesn't matter anymore," he whispered. He hugged her tightly. "Everything's gonna turn around now. We're gonna win."

"Mark, Cass . . . she's a Christian now. I was there. I prayed with her."

Mark laughed out loud. "Do you know what this means? He's not far behind."

Julie shook her head. "She's going to move out. I promised her we'd pray."

"Wait a minute. When did you see Cass?"

"It's a long story. Can we go somewhere and talk? I don't want David and Jan to come home in the middle of this."

"Sure." Mark sniffed his shirt. "I don't think I'm too smelly from cutting the grass." Julie smiled at him and he felt the weight of the world melt away. "I'll leave David a note," he said pointing toward the front door. "Don't leave."

"I won't, Mark. Never, ever, ever again."

———————

All the way home from the Galleria, Cass had reminded Janie that she could not, could not say anything about seeing her mother today. All right, yes, technically it was a lie, but then Matt said something about Rahab and the spies. Whatever that meant. It didn't matter. It worked. Janie promised not to say a word.

Doug would be home in a half hour or so. She wasn't sure she could be any more deceptive than the children. She needed help. She needed an approach, a lead-in that would prevent him from that reflexive animosity. She wanted to explain it to him. She wanted him to have the peace that she felt. More than anything, she wanted him to understand that Jesus' love made sense because of the way he loved her.

At five-thirty, Cass heard Doug's truck, and moments later, he came in from the garage and walked straight through the kitchen, then took two steps back to kiss her cheek. "I'll be in the office."

"Bad day?" she asked.

"I had an unscheduled appointment," he muttered, glancing around for the children. "Where are the kids?"

"Upstairs. Ben's room, I think."

"Julie stopped by. 'Can I have my kids back?'" He sarcastically mocked her.

"She came alone?" She hoped she could pull off playing dumb.

"Yeah. She's got a lot more nerve than Mark." He jerked the refrigerator open. "And Sandy let her just walk in there! What if she'd had a gun or something?"

"Sandy didn't know. It's perfectly natural to let your daughter-in-law in your office."

"Not mine." He pulled out a can of Diet Coke and opened it. "I know we go back to court Tuesday, but I'm this close to getting a restraining order or asking for somebody to supervise the visitation," he said, holding his finger and thumb less than an inch apart.

"She's probably through with you."

"I wish. Mark will take her back though, so I'll never be rid of her." He gulped the Diet Coke. "Wonder what it would take to get him to divorce her. A million?"

"Dollars? That's beyond despicable, Doug."

"I wasn't serious," he mumbled, and took another long drink. "Anyway, Sylvan Hills—or whatever stupid name they gave it—is ready to be subdivided, so I need to go over the surveys before we turn it over to the realtors. Call me when dinner's ready."

Cass turned on the water and began scrubbing potatoes to bake for dinner. Irritated was an improvement from the bitter anger of the last few days, but she felt queasy. He needed her, and she . . . was getting ready to abandon him. He was struggling. How could she love him, and still push him over the edge? If he wouldn't listen to Judy or Mark, why on earth would she listen to her? Then there was the question she hadn't dared to ask—how was she going to get out of sleeping with him the next two nights?

Mark drove Julie's rental car to a park not too far from David's house. "I discovered this the first week you were gone," he said and Julie felt the heat of guilt. It would get a lot hotter before they were finished. He parked and quickly came around to her side of the car. She hesitated when he reached for her hand. Now he'd know how damp her palm was. He didn't mention it as he pulled her to a bench.

"Now you were going to tell me how you ran into Cass this afternoon." He smiled with gentle love.

She took a deep breath, and swallowed to force down the rising emotion. For the next two, almost three hours, she talked. She told Mark everything, even the most disgraceful details of her conversation with Doug. Mark interrupted only to scold her for apologizing.

Finally, she took Mark's hands. "I learned something from Cass today. She loves your dad unconditionally. She doesn't want anything from him. She gets thoroughly put out by the things he does, but she just loves him."

"That's the way it's supposed to be," Mark said.

"Yeah," she dropped her eyes and gathered a last bit of resolve for one more confession "Mark, I haven't loved you that way. I've been in love with you, I've thrived on being a partner in ministry, but I don't know if I've ever loved you, Mark, the way I should."

"Julie—"

"I'm serious. God convicted me of so many things today. I want you to teach me, or help me find somebody else to teach me. You deserve this. You deserve to be loved the way that you give love."

"I don't know if I ever 'learned' it," Mark said. "It just kind of happened."

"Then you have a gift," Julie said. "The other thing is, while your dad was ripping me up one side and down the other he let something slip. He needs that kind of love. Desperately."

"He always has, but I'm not sure if he ever realized when my mom changed, when she finally loved him unconditionally. He thought it was probably because he was taking care of her. She said he was so insecure—"

"Your dad?" Julie asked in disbelief.

"It's all a show, Julie. All the loud . . . belligerent . . . arrogance is a cover."

"Then what's going to happen to him when Cass leaves?"

"I'm almost afraid to imagine." He checked his watch, holding it toward the street lamp to make out the numbers in growing darkness. "It's almost eight-thirty. Are you hungry?"

"The ice cream with the kids is all I've had today," Julie admitted.

"Let's find some dinner somewhere then." Mark leaned

over, draped his arm around her shoulder and pulled her close, then he kissed her. "I am so glad you're home," he whispered.

That night, after getting the kids settled in bed, Cass stole back downstairs, mentally making a list of things to do, anything that would put off bedtime. Doug found her loading the dishwasher. "Hey," he said, then he came and leaned against the counter close to her. He smiled that shy boyish grin of his. She couldn't remember the last time she'd seen it.

"Hey, yourself."

"I was watching you at dinner tonight. I don't think I've ever seen you look so beautiful."

"All right, what'd you do?" she teased.

He took her hand and pulled her closer. "I'm serious. Your eyes sparkled. Your smile . . . listening to you talk . . . " He leaned in and kissed her neck. "It was like seeing you for the first time."

She melted against him. "I had a good day, that's all." He was back, the Doug she loved, not the bitter, angry man he'd become.

"I need to make sure you have those more often," he said, sliding an arm around her waist. "It made me realize how crazy things have been lately, what a jerk I've been." He kissed her again, and slid his hand under her sweater to the small of her back. "How much I've missed you . . . "

She missed him, too, and she ached to follow his lead. But . . . "Doug, the kids . . . "

"Our room is on the other side of the house."

"But what if—"

"We have a lock on our door."

They did. They absolutely did. He kissed her again. If she pushed him away, it might trigger another explosion from him. It would be a rejection. None of them could live with him when he was like that.

But just this once . . . the scent of his cologne . . .

She couldn't. What excuse could she give him? Wouldn't matter. He'd never believe it. He knew her too well. "I know we both want—"

"Papa! Miss Cass!"

Janie.

Cass jumped back away from Doug the instant before Jane staggered around the corner. "I had a bad dream."

Doug scooped her up in his arms. "You're okay now." He wandered over to the sofa with Jane, and Cass slumped onto one of the bar stools. She wiped her trembling hands on her slacks. Apparently divine intervention came in the form of a seven-year-old's nightmares.

"I have bad dreams sometimes, too," Doug said. Cass froze, not wanting to interrupt or intrude.

"About kidnapper dogs with shiny eyes?"

"Not exactly." He stretched his feet out to the coffee table. "Mine are about being all alone."

"I dreamed I got lost from Mommy and Daddy at the airport one time. And I got on the wrong plane, and the people were giants and they talked weird and I couldn't tell them who I was or where I belonged." She nestled in closer to him. "Tell me yours. Ben says they lose their power if you say them out loud."

"My mom left when I was a kid. In the dreams, she always told me it was my fault before she left."

"She sounds more like an evil queen than a mommy."

He didn't respond for a long moment. "Anyway, I'm pretty sure there are no kidnapper dogs with shiny eyes—"

"Not yet, Papa! I can't go back yet!"

"Oh . . . how long does it usually take?"

"Sometimes till tomorrow."

"Jane, honey, I don't think we can sit up all night again."

"What if I come up and lay down with you?" Cass asked.

Jane's head popped up over the back of the sofa. "Yes!"

Doug smiled with gentle resignation. "Can we finish our discussion later?"

"It will have to be later," Cass said, as she stood and reached for Jane's hand. "Kiss Papa goodnight." Jane did and scrambled around the sofa. Before she walked away, Cass leaned over and kissed Doug. "I love you," she whispered. "I'm so sorry."

"It wasn't meant to be."

He had no idea.

"There will be other nights," he said, swinging his feet down from the coffee table. "Tomorrow, for instance."

Friday, October 2

Cass stood at the back door and gazed out across the pool to the point where the glow from the house was overcome by the darkness at the tree line. The kids were settled in bed, the kitchen was spotless, and all that was left was facing Doug again.

Last night, she lay awake in Jane's bed, staring at the ceiling. All his nightmares were about being left alone. She cried in silence until she was exhausted. She spent the morning staring at a sketch pad, trying to come up with some way, any way, she could get out of this without crushing him.

Then they went to lunch. Thank God it wasn't Antonio's. She couldn't have sat through lunch at his favorite restaurant. It was just like it used to be, though. Easy, comfortable, natural. Faith couldn't come between them could it? She was moving out. She had to, but couldn't they stay together?

He would marry her if she asked. Maybe that—

"Finally! This was the longest day of my life!" He swept into the kitchen and pulled her into his arms.

"Doug . . . " She pushed away from him. "I can't."

"Can't? What's wrong?"

"I just can't. Can we leave it at that?"

"Did I do something?"

"It's me. It's all me."

"You want to talk about it?"

"I don't think you can help me."

"Me either, but I think I'm supposed to offer at least." His half-smile tore her heart in two.

"I'm sorry," she said with a deep sigh. "You know, I would rather die than hurt you."

"Cass, it's okay." He took her hands in his, then raised them to his lips and kissed them gently. "There's no pressure."

"I hope you understand, Doug. I hope you never question that I love you."

"I don't."

"No matter what else happens—"

"Cass, what's going on? You sound like you're getting ready to give me some bad news."

"No, I just . . . life is short. You never know what's coming next. You understand that better than I do, even."

"Have you seen a doctor or something?" Doug asked with rising alarm. "How do you feel? You know, you said something about chest pains the other day."

"Doug—"

"When was your last check-up?"

"Stop," she said. "It's nothing like that. Don't you ever . . . have you ever sat down and taken inventory of your life?"

"Well, yeah. A lot lately."

"Somehow, I think there's more to life than what I've had up till now."

"More?" The lightness is his eyes faded. Oh, no. It would come out tonight. Now.

"I love you, Doug Bolling. Promise me, you will never forget that."

"But you want more." His voice was cold and hard, his eyes were narrow and dark. "That guy?"

"No! Good grief, no." She turned and took a step or two away from him. She was messing this up so badly. "All right." She stood for a moment, her back to him and she took a deep breath. "Doug, I haven't . . . I mean . . . I . . . " She turned to face him. "I know everything Mark and the kids believe about Jesus Christ is the absolute truth."

"You what?" It was something between a hiss and a growl.

"I believe it. I prayed. I became a Christian."

"How could you do this to me?" His voice was low and intense. "You know what it did to me when Judy left me. I wasn't enough . . . I wasn't good enough for her either."

"You are good enough. I love you. That hasn't changed—"

"No!" He stabbed a finger at her. "You can't possibly love me and then betray me like this. That's what this is! Betrayal!" He started to pace. "I trusted you. I thought you understood."

"I do understand. I've agonized over how to tell you, trying to figure out a way to do it without hurting you."

"Well, you failed," he said sarcastically. "I wish you had just cheated on me. I could have handled that."

"I see," she said with resignation. "If you still feel this way in the morning . . . I'll pack my things."

Twenty-Two

Doug's knees buckled under him, but he managed to summon enough presence of mind to grasp the armchair before he went to the floor. He twisted and dropped into the chair. This was his worst nightmare—the absolute worst thing that could happen to him.

How could she? She knew exactly what she was doing. She was betraying and rejecting him, just like Judy and Mark before her. Deep down, he knew it was coming though. He could sense something was up almost from the time the kids got here.

The kids. He'd brought them here. It was his lawsuit.

He had brought it all on himself.

He had engineered his own ruin.

Upstairs in the bedroom, Cass began to pack. She knew there was no question how Doug would feel in the morning, how he would feel next week or ten years from now. Barring a miracle, of course.

That wasn't how she wanted to tell him. It wasn't a rejection of him. He was a good man, such a good man, and she had never loved anyone like she loved him.

She hugged herself tightly and dropped onto the bed. *I love him. Don't let this be it.* She sighed deeply and pulled herself up.

She wiped her eyes, and began to gather her make-up and things from the bathroom. She would just get what she needed for a week or so. By then, she would have a place . . . and a job. She surely couldn't work for Doug anymore. Maybe, she should take some time and . . . heal. Visit her parents in Phoenix. In fact, Phoenix was a nice place. A nice place to start over.

Saturday, October 3

Cass decided the earlier she got out, the better. It would be easier on her if she didn't say goodbye to Matt, Ben and Janie. They knew she was leaving. The timing would be the only surprise. Even if Doug made visitation difficult, they would be back with their parents Tuesday. She could see them again after that.

As soon as the sky lightened, she took one last look around the bedroom, then swallowed hard, picked up her suitcase and headed downstairs. Doug wasn't in the office, but she soon found him in the TV room. His back was to her and he never moved when she stepped in the room. "Doug?"

He slowly turned around, then stood to face her. He looked older, worn down. His eyes were dark and she couldn't recall ever seeing him unshaven. "You promised me you would never do this," he said quietly. "I asked you, specifically, and you promised."

"The woman who made those promises is dead."

"That's the dumbest thing I've ever heard," he said, shaking his head. "That's just an excuse to break a promise."

"All right. You're welcome to believe that." She moved to pick up her suitcase again.

"Wait! Don't do this. Please . . . I'm sorry. Be a Christian. I can live with that."

"But I can't live with you. That's wrong."

"We'll get married . . . today . . . or Monday . . . as soon as we can." Not because he loved her. Not because he was committed to her. Because he was desperate. Desperate and afraid.

"How long do you think a marriage will survive if it's built on manipulation? Even if it's fifty years, I'll always know you only did it because you didn't want me to leave." He forced her to a place she never intended to go. "I've lived with you for seven years and I was never good enough to marry until this moment."

"I told you . . . I was afraid if I married you . . . that somehow I'd end up losing you."

"That's brilliant logic. Just like the way you reserve your most bitter hatred for the ones you claim to love. How long before you hate me, too, Doug? How long before I become the target of your bitterness? Before you blame me for costing you the kids?"

"It won't happen."

"I'm not so sure. I've seen a rage and a seething hostility in you that I never knew was there and quite frankly, it scares me."

"You're right." He was panicked now. "How can I reassure you?"

Not help me get rid of it. How can I cover it? How can I distract you? If she left now, she would be the villain . . . but she would still love him. That's what it came down to. She had to leave while she still loved him. Before bitterness came and chipped away at every good thing. Before the memories were clouded by a host of slights real or imagined. Unless . . .

"Come with me right now. We'll go see the preacher from this church I've gone to. I want you to listen to him explain the gospel. Give him a fair hearing. You don't have to believe him, just listen to it."

Doug was crestfallen. He dropped his head, and closed his eyes. "I . . . I can't do that," he said, almost whispering.

"Then I can't stay," she said, thankful she didn't have to look him in the eyes. She picked up her suitcase, but when she reached the door to the garage, she turned back. "I'll send for the rest of my things. My resignation will be on your desk Monday morning."

Doug couldn't watch her leave. He heard the door shut and then her car started. Moments later the garage door raised. The sound of the garage door closing was loud, stark, like the closing of a bank vault or a prison door. Or maybe a tomb.

He stood dazed, unable to focus his mind enough to make his body move, unable to begin to consider what to do next. When Judy died, he had months to prepare, not just for her death, but to come to grips with the fact that she had drifted away from him, that the connection between them was broken. Even with Mark, he knew for months before his son left home.

Twelve hours ago, he was the luckiest man alive. Now he had nothing. Judy was taken from him, but Cass had chosen to leave. She chose. He had done the best he could—again—and it wasn't enough. She said she loved him, but it wasn't enough to keep her from leaving. He had failed again.

He blinked, slowly reorienting himself as if he were trying to regain consciousness. It was Saturday. There was a backpack on the floor by the television. A backpack. Ben's backpack. The kids. He couldn't take care of the kids. Not anymore.

He ran his hand back through his hair. His arm still seemed to work. Maybe his legs would, too. He trudged upstairs to Ben's room and woke the boy. "Pack your things, all of them. The stuff you brought and the stuff you've got since you've been here. I'm taking you home."

"For good?"

"Cass left this morning. She's not coming back. It's over, Ben."

"Grandpa, I'm sorry."

Doug took his keys from his pocket and handed them

over. "Go ahead and put everything in the car. I'll be in my office."

———————

Ben stared at the car keys in his hand. They were going home. Today. As soon as they could get packed. He threw the covers back and headed down the hall to Matt's room. "Hey!" he said, pulling out the pillow from under his brother's head.

"Ben!"

Before Matt could yell anymore, Ben held up his hand. "Grandpa said to pack. Cass left this morning."

"I didn't think she was leaving till tonight." Matt climbed out of bed.

"Yeah, well, something must've happened. He said 'it's over.'"

"Ben, why doesn't he just give in? You know, he's fighting God, making himself miserable."

"I don't know. Maybe this is his last stand. I'm gonna get Janie up, help her pack." He walked to the end of the hallway and woke up his little sister.

"Is it breakfast?" she asked, rubbing her eyes and yawning.

"Miss Cass left this morning. Grandpa's taking us back to Mom and Dad."

"Back?" Janie broke into a wide smile. "I need to get dressed!"

"Yeah, but we need to pack all our stuff. This is it."

"We'll never see Papa again?"

"I didn't say that. We just won't be staying here anymore."

"I don't want to not see Papa again."

"Get dressed, then I'll be back to help you pack."

Matt and Ben packed their gym bags, backpacks, and filled garbage bags with the overflow. "Anything else?" Matt asked as he surveyed Janie's room.

She pointed to the bed. "My sheets."

"I guess we should put the others back on," Matt agreed. He found the original bedclothes on the shelf in the closet. Ben and Janie helped him make the bed, and then they folded the unicorn bedding and dropped it in a garbage bag.

"Now, are we done?" Matt asked.

"I think so," Ben said. "I double-checked my room already."

"Let's start loading the car, then. Janie, you can just wait downstairs." Matt grabbed two garbage bags and headed downstairs with Ben following.

———————————

Janie trailed behind them, but she stopped and checked every room looking for Papa. Finally, she came to his office, and its closed door. He had to be in there. There wasn't any other place to look. She turned the handle as slowly and quietly as she could and inched the door open. The room was dark, not a scary dark, just a no one was in there kind of dark, so she almost didn't see Papa. He sat at the desk, his face in his hands, elbows resting on his desk. He was still like a statue, even when she closed the door. Maybe he was asleep. She tiptoed to him, ducked under his arm, and climbed onto his lap.

She laid her head against his chest, and whispered, "I love you, Papa."

He didn't say anything, but he wrapped his arms around her. She felt him kiss the top of her head. She felt a drop on her cheek, then another. Papa was crying. She had seen Daddy cry, but Papa never made a sound.

Soon a tear trickled down her own cheek to Papa's shirt. She didn't mean to cry or to get his shirt wet. It sneaked out. Maybe he hadn't meant to cry either, and the tears sneaked out. That's why there was no sound. Or maybe he didn't want anyone to know he was crying. Sometimes boys get embarrassed when they cry. Maybe Papa was that way.

If he was, then she would pretend she didn't know he

was crying. After sitting for a very long time, Papa wiped his eyes and coughed quietly. "Are you ready to go?" he asked.

"The boys were loading the car."

He nodded and lifted her off his lap, then he stood up. "Let's go."

The boys were waiting in the kitchen and without a word, they followed Doug out to the garage. "Are you sure that's everything?"

"We double-checked," Ben said.

Doug nodded, and climbed into his car. He reached for his sunglasses, even though the skies were overcast. Ben helped Janie up into her seat and buckled her in, then sat beside her while Matt took a seat up front. They rode in silence until Matt spoke. "Grandpa, I don't want to say anything stupid—"

"Then don't," Doug said.

"Okay," Matt said, quietly.

"Thank you." He drove through a residential neighborhood, then made a left turn onto the street where the Shannons lived. "This is it, isn't it?"

"Yeah, it's down there on the right," Matt said, pointing. Doug stopped in front of the house but left his car running. He got out, raised the lift gate, and began setting bags and backpacks on the curb.

"Dad will want to talk to you," Matt said, helping Doug unload.

"I don't want to talk to him."

"Please?"

Doug took a deep breath, and gambling that this would buy him privacy and solitude later, he gave in. "Just your dad. Not your mom."

Matt nodded, picked up his bag and motioned for Janie and Ben to follow him. He stepped up to the door and rang the bell, glancing back at his grandfather while he waited.

When Jan Shannon opened the door, her face showed a mixture of surprise, confusion and excitement. "Matt? What's going on?" she asked as she opened the storm door and let the children in.

"He brought us home," Matt answered simply. "Is my Dad here?"

"Of course." She stepped back toward the kitchen. "Mark! Julie!"

When his dad came in, with his mom close behind, he smiled broadly. "Is this it?"

Matt nodded.

"Thank you, Jesus." He crossed the room and hugged each of them tightly. Matt and Ben hugged and kissed their mother before she scooped Janie up in her arms.

"Papa is very sad," Janie said.

"Cass left this morning," Matt explained. "He said he would talk to you, Dad."

"Say a prayer," Mark said as he crossed the room and walked outside. His father leaned against the rear bumper of his car, his head down, his arms crossed across his chest. He didn't change his stance as Mark approached, and gave no indication that he even heard him. "Dad? Can I do anything?"

"No." He raised his head slightly. "I'm through, Mark. There's nothing left to fight for." It seemed to take all his energy just to speak.

"You still have custody of the kids until Tuesday."

"Well, then, it's my decision where they stay. I can't take care of them." He sighed and dropped his hands. "They're good kids. You've . . . you're a good dad, Mark. You sure didn't learn that from me."

"Dad—"

"No, I know what I am, Mark. I can't lie to myself any longer."

"You're grieving. Everything looks bad."

"It's bigger than that. I drove your mother away. I drove you away, and now . . . " Unable to finish the sentence, he shook his head slightly, and swallowed hard. "I think that's a pattern."

"I'm still here."

"Then you're a bigger fool than I am." He pressed his lips together tightly, and pushed himself away from the car bumper. "I'll see you in court. I, uh, I don't expect to win, but if the judge is that incompetent, I'll take care of it."

He pulled a checkbook from the back pocket of his jeans, and putting his foot on the bumper, he laid the checkbook on his thigh and began to write.

"What are you doing?"

"I've cost you a month's salary and five plane tickets."

"You don't have to—"

"Mark," he said through clenched teeth. "I swear, if you don't take this." He tore out the check and held it out to his son. "You asked what you could do. This is it. Take the check."

Mark took the check and folded it without looking at it, then slipped it in his pocket. "Thank you. Thank you for bringing my kids back."

His father nodded without speaking, then walked away. Mark watched him get in the car and drive off, then he picked up as many bags as he could carry, and brought them into the house.

"How is he?" Julie asked, with Janie still in her arms.

"Bad," Mark answered, setting down the bags. "Worse than when Mom died." He motioned to Matt and Ben. "There's a couple of bags outside still." The boys headed for the door.

"Maybe it won't last."

"He's in a battle, maybe for his very soul." Mark frowned and shook his head. "He's either going to find God at last, or this is gonna kill him."

Doug found an open liquor store and bought a case of beer on his way home. As he backed his car into the garage, a thought crossed his mind. *I should just stay out here.* He watched the garage door close and he knew all three of the doors sealed tightly. *I could have the catalytic converter off in two minutes. Start the car, drink the beer till I pass out, and just never wake up.* No one would really miss him until he failed to show up for court Tuesday. There was three-quarters of a tank of gas. More than enough. He lowered all the car windows, and slid his seat all the way back.

But Cass would never get over it. She would blame herself, probably forever, and he couldn't bear that. If it hadn't been for her, he would have ended it all long before now. These years with her had been the best in his life. He loved her far too much to hurt her.

He switched off the car, grabbed the case of beer and went inside. He put the case in the refrigerator, pulled out a cold beer and twisted off the cap. As he took a sip, he heard the low rumble of thunder off in the distance. When he stepped out on the deck, he could see the western skies were black and threatening. The wind had picked up and the air carried the freshness of nearby showers. He leaned over the railing, and watched the leaves blow past. The thunder was louder, sharper.

He took a long slow drink from the beer as lightning flashed across the sky. *Maybe God can just show me who's boss and strike me dead. Or maybe I can at least catch pneumonia.* Heavy raindrops began to fall, and then it came in cold, pelting sheets. Doug never moved, except to raise the beer bottle to his lips every few minutes. He had to squint to see the lightning in the driving rain. Water dripped from his elbows, his chin and his fingertips. His shirt was plastered to him, and water soaked through his jeans.

"So what's it gonna be, God?" he asked, looking up in

the sky. "Now's Your chance," he said as he spread his arms wide. "Let's just end this right here and now." He gulped the beer and wiped his mouth on his shirtsleeve. "I don't have anything left! You can't do anything else to me!"

Lightning flashed, followed immediately by a crackling boom, and Doug couldn't help flinching. "You want the house? Go ahead, burn the house down. Make sure You get the garage while You're at it." He finished off the beer and threw the bottle out in the yard.

"You know, my son prays for me," he said, pointing up in the sky. "Do You ever listen? Did You ever hear Judy when she prayed for me? Because I sure can't tell You ever hear any of it." Lightning flashed again, but the thunder came several seconds later. The storm was moving on.

"I get it," Doug said. "It'll be worse for me if You let me live. Of course. It makes perfect sense." He pushed his hair back off his face. "We can't keep this up. We gotta come to some kind of an arrangement." The thunder rumbled again, and Doug held up a hand. "I'll be right back. I need another beer."

He dripped and squished his way in to the refrigerator and back, opening the beer once he got back outside. "All right. I've lost. I admit that, but You won't kill me. Now what?" There was a low rumble, and he gulped from his beer. "No, don't send any angels or stupid visions or anything like that. I'll believe You even less than I do now." He pointed toward the sky with the bottle. "And that's not much."

He pulled a deck chair around and slouched into it, propping his feet up on the railing. The rain continued to fall, causing him to blink as the drops stung his face. "You know what? I'll even concede that You brought those women into my life. I know I sure didn't have anything to offer either one of 'em. But You took 'em both away. I knew You were gonna take Cass eventually." He wiped his eyes, and his voice dropped, stripped of its bravado. "That's why I never loved her the way I should've, the way she deserved. Because I was afraid. Because I knew this is what I had to look forward to." He swept his arm in a wide arc.

"See, I loved Judy with everything I had, and You took her. So I changed my strategy. I refused to let Cass have my whole heart. Didn't change how she felt, though." He sipped the beer as a new wave of pain washed over him. "And it didn't change how You operate."

He finished off the beer and pitched the bottle over the railing and out into the yard beside the other one. "Okay, how about this? Cass left me because I refused to give You a fair hearing. I got Judy's Bible in there. Now I'm willing to read the thing. Are You willing to bring Cass back if I do?" He waited for a moment, listening, but there was nothing but the sound of rain. "Not gonna commit to that one? Well, I'm gonna read anyway." He stood up and squeezed water from his shirt. "After I dry off," he mumbled.

Twenty-Three

Sunday, October 4

Cass never slept well in hotels even in the best circumstances. Last night, every time she closed her eyes, she saw Doug's face, the pleading desperation and then the unfathomable resignation. Yesterday, she made it as far as the gas station before she had to stop and throw up. That became the order of the day, every few miles, every few minutes, she had to stop and find a restroom.

Why did he have to be so hard-headed? Why did he push her to do the one thing neither one of them wanted? A trip to see Glen Dillard would have taken twenty minutes. For twenty minutes, she would have stayed with him. Married him even. But he refused. That wasn't stubbornness. That was insanity.

She talked with her mother yesterday afternoon, and although her mother made an excellent case for driving to Phoenix now, Cass decided to wait and fly out next weekend. She wanted, she needed to give Doug a chance to call. She had to give herself that much hope. Maybe tomorrow, after spending the weekend alone, he would come around. Or Tuesday, after the hearing, when he lost his case for good.

This morning, though, she was going to Glen Dillard's church. Alone. Maybe Glen would pray for her, for them, and maybe God would have pity.

****

Doug woke up, but nothing had changed since yesterday, except for the splitting headache. That was new, but that,
like everything else, was his fault. Three beers was his absolute limit. There had been plenty of times he wanted to drink
more, but his metabolism and his diabetes always kept it in
check.

Yesterday, he went over his limit and his body was
making sure he paid for that. He opened his eyes to let the
smallest sliver of light in. That was too much. He raised his
hand to shade his eyes before trying to open them again. He
could see enough to tell this was not the bedroom. Not his
bedroom, anyway. Ben's? Or Matt's? No, it was Ben's. He
sighed and slowly pulled himself up, yawned and rubbed his
eyes. This probably made a lot of sense last night.

Let's see, there was the storm. That was before noon.
Then he changed clothes. And he read. He read Judy's Bible.
Where? In his office. But he had four more beers—he was fairly sure it was four—so that made . . . six altogether. Six. He
was an idiot.

He checked his sugar. He remembered that. And it was
low, so he ate something. Cereal. He had two, no three maybe,
bowls of cereal. Then he knew he was going to crash . . . but
he couldn't stand sleeping in his bed alone . . . so he came in
here, rather than pass out in the bathroom or the hallway.
That was ten or twelve hours ago.

He rubbed his face, and was surprised by the stubble.
He never shaved yesterday. Another day wouldn't kill him. His
sugar might, though. As appealing as that was, he had some
things to take care of first. He forced himself to his feet and
made it to the downstairs bathroom. He tested his blood. Low.
He skipped his insulin and had two more bowls of cereal and
chased them with a big glass of orange juice.

He glanced up at the ceiling. "I'm gonna finish reading,
don't worry. I keep my promises."

REFINED   303

Cass slipped into the church service as the music began. She hoped she knew the routine well enough to follow
along without Matt's help, and that the stomach flu, or whatever it was, had run its course. She found a seat on the far
aisle and had just settled in, when she felt a hand on her
shoulder. Glen Dillard was reaching to shake her hand.

"You're all alone this morning," he said.

"The children are back with their parents."

He nodded. "I'm glad you came."

"I became a believer Thursday." She managed a smile.
"Isn't this where I'm supposed to be now?"

"Absolutely." His smile was broad enough for both of
them. "I'd love to hear how it happened. Would you care to
hang around after this is over?"

"Actually, I was hoping for a chance to talk to you."

"My office is across the hall, right outside that door." He
pointed to a back door across the auditorium. "Give me a few
minutes to shake hands afterwards, then I'll be right there."
He smiled at her again. "You made my day."

Cass watched him make his way to the front, trusting
he had some answers. Since Doug wouldn't hear the gospel,
was he hopeless? Would God keep giving him opportunities?
She was terrified now that something would happen to him,
and she'd be separated from him for all eternity. She understood the frantic anxiety that must have clouded Judy Bolling's last days. How could she die in peace, with Doug's future unsettled?

The worship service was different from the ones she at-
tended with the children. Instead of crushing pain in her
chest, each song touched her heart. Each prayer was mean-
ingful. She felt like she belonged instead of being a spectator.
For these few moments, she was able to put all the turmoil
aside and simply soak it all in.

When Glen stepped to the podium, he smiled and
raised his hand as he opened his Bible. "Now I know y'all will
find this hard to believe, but not only does this sermon not
connect with last week's, but it doesn't begin a new series or

anything. It's just a stand-alone message."

He grinned at the light chuckles from the audience. "All day Friday, I could not get these Scriptures out of my head, and this ole boy's slow, but I do catch on eventually. So I threw out my outline and figured I better preach what God told me to preach."

He stepped out from behind the podium, and slipped his hands into the pockets of his jeans. "You know, one of the most difficult things for us as believers to live with is when someone you love rejects the gospel, and as a result they reject you." He dropped his eyes and there was a sweet sadness in his voice. "My oldest brother, Paul, is that way. We were raised up in church, but when he turned eighteen, he left the church and the rest of the family far behind. Even now, when we talk, it's strained, because there's a division between us." He pulled his right hand from his pocket, and pointed out over the crowd. "Some of you have loved ones that are hardened, angry Christ-rejecters."

Cass snapped upright in her seat.

"But I have hope for my brother, Paul, and for anyone who is hostile to the gospel, because of the apostle Paul. We're gonna read his story in Acts and then we're gonna read his comments on it in Galatians, and I'll show you where the hope comes in."

He stepped back behind the podium, pulled a pair of glasses from his breast pocket and slipped them on. "All right, in Acts chapter nine, we have the story of Paul's conversion. Now, I can read. I know it says 'Saul,' but after he was converted, he went by 'Paul.' Saul is a Hebrew name that means 'great.' 'Paul' means 'small.' I think Paul was trying to say something about his change in attitude." Glen smiled and began reading the story of Paul's trip to Damascus to arrest and persecute any believers he found there. On the way, Jesus Christ appeared in the form of a blinding light.

"Now Paul did a complete one-eighty," Glen said. "Immediately. And if you'll pick up in the middle of verse nineteen with me."

*Now for several days he was with the dis-
ciples who were at Damascus, and immediately
he began to proclaim Jesus in the synagogues,
saying, "He is the Son of God." All those hearing
him continued to be amazed, and were saying, "Is
this not he who in Jerusalem destroyed those who
called on this name, and who had come here for
the purpose of bringing them bound before the
chief priests?" But Saul kept increasing in
strength and confounding the Jews who lived at
Damascus by proving that this Jesus is the Christ.*

"Isn't this the guy who 'destroyed those who called on
this name'? Quite a change, wasn't it?" Glen stepped back
from the podium, and began filling in the background on Paul.
As he recounted Paul's consenting role in Stephen's martyr-
dom, Cass began to see the parallels with Doug. Doug's actions weren't as extreme, but the emotion was just as intense.
Christianity was a threat to Doug, and to his way of thinking.
If somebody like Paul could change . . . could Doug?

"Now in Galatians chapter one," Glen continued, "Paul
says something about his conversion, something critical to
understanding how God works. Okay, Acts, Romans, First and
Second Corinthians, then Galatians. It's just a little book. In
chapter one, starting at . . . oh . . . verse thirteen."

*For you have heard of my former manner of
life in Judaism, how I used to persecute the
church of God beyond measure and tried to destroy it; and I was advancing in Judaism beyond
many of my contemporaries among my country-
men, being more extremely zealous for my ances-
tral traditions. But when God, who had set me
apart even from my mother's womb and called me
through His grace, was pleased to reveal His Son
in me so that I might preach Him among the Gen-
tiles, I did not immediately consult with flesh and
blood, nor did I go up to Jerusalem to those who
were apostles before me; but I went away to Ara-*

bia, and returned once more to Damascus.

"The key is 'when it pleased God to reveal His Son.' There was a moment in Paul's life when it just clicked. All his arguing and opposition disintegrated, and he embraced the Savior he had resisted so vehemently for so long."

Cass caught Glen's eye as he looked out over the crowd, and she gave him a subtle smile. This was what she needed to hear. God could change Doug. God was willing. It was simply a matter of timing. Paul knew the gospel, and no doubt, Doug had heard it from Judy and Mark. Maybe Judy knew this already. Maybe that was how she could face death.

Glen finished his sermon and the invitation music had barely faded when Cass heard her name. She turned, and immediately little arms wrapped around her. "We knew you would come!" Janie Bolling squealed.

Cass picked Janie up in her arms and hugged her tightly, fighting tears. "I've missed you."

Matt and Ben were close behind Janie and they hugged her as tightly as Janie did. "I told Dad you might be here this morning." Matt pointed behind him where his parents were trying to make their way through the crowd.

"You're with your parents?"

"Grandpa took us back Saturday morning," Matt said.

"How was he?" Cass asked quietly.

Matt hesitated, shifted away from her. "My dad talked to him a little. He was just . . . tired, you know?"

Cass nodded as Mark and Julie finally got close enough to give her a hug, too. "The kids were so hoping you would be here," Julie said. "They couldn't imagine not seeing you again."

"I would have figured out some way to see them again, I promise," Cass said. "Mark, how's Doug? The truth."

"He's . . . he brought the kids back because he said he couldn't take care of them."

"I'm sorry. I'm so sorry," Cass whispered.

"I know, Cass, I know."

"He's in a battle, isn't he? He's fighting so hard."

Mark nodded. "I don't know if he can do it any other way. I think it's like Glen said. God's gonna have to make this click for him."

"Glen!" Cass said. "I almost forgot! I'm supposed to meet him."

"We won't keep you, then," Mark said. "That's an important meeting."

"Listen," Cass smoothed Janie's hair, her eyes tearing again. "I'm flying out to Phoenix Saturday morning. Can I see you and the kids sometime?"

"Of course," Mark said. "We'll plan on Thursday or Friday."

"Great," Cass said. She kissed Janie again, and hugged the boys. "Thank you."

"No, thank you," Mark said. "He's gonna come around. I think you mean that much to him."

"I don't think I could live with myself otherwise." She made her way across the auditorium, to the hallway, to Glen's office. She paced waiting for him to arrive, and moments later, she saw him escorting a woman down the hallway.

He waved, and walked a little faster to close the distance between them. "Miss Grayson, I asked my wife to join us. I hope that was okay." Cass nodded. "A minister can't take any chances in this day and age." He opened the door and motioned her inside his office. "Now, to make this official, Miss Grayson, this gracious, long-suffering saint is my wife, Laurie."

Laurie Dillard smiled and reached out her hand. Her handshake and smile were warm and friendly. "Glen doesn't give himself much credit," she said gently. "I'm pleased to meet you."

"Your sermon answered most of my questions," Cass began, taking a seat.

"Good," Glen said, as he and Laurie sat down. "It's a lot easier if God answers them." He smiled and folded his hands on the desk in front of him. "You were gonna tell me how you became a believer."

"All right. There's some background here. The kids . . . I came with them actually. They're Mark Bolling's children. I guess you know Mark." Glen nodded. Cass dropped her eyes and continued quietly. "I was living with Mark's dad." She glanced at Glen but his expression never changed. Relieved, she continued. "Doug filed a lawsuit for custody of Mark's children. He claimed that since the children were being raised by missionaries in Africa, their welfare was somehow endangered. Doug won temporary custody of them until the actual hearing. The hearing is Tuesday." Glen nodded.

"So, the children asked if they could go to church, and I offered to take them. Doug has no use for religion. He lost his wife sixteen years ago, and the short version is he blames God for it."

"A lot of people do that," Glen said.

"Anyway," Cass said, "I think God had already been working on me through the kids and then in that first church service, I don't know, something happened. I knew then that this was for real, that Doug was wrong, that I was wrong. Matt answered some of my questions for me and let me process things and then I ran into Julie Bolling at the Galleria. She explained everything to me, and helped me pray."

"Julie did?"

"Yeah, even though we were kind of legal enemies."

"Isn't it remarkable how God works?" Glen said. "That's tremendous."

"Here's the thing," Cass said. "I left Doug. He was furious with me. He said I'd betrayed him, but then he begged me to stay. He offered to do anything, get married, whatever. I asked him to come with me to see you, to listen to you explain the gospel, just listen." Her voice dropped to a near whisper and her eyes brimmed with tears. "He refused, and I left."

"That was an extremely courageous thing to do," Laurie said.

"It wasn't courageous. I know what it did to Doug." She wiped her eyes. "But I got from your sermon that he's not hopeless."

"As long as he's living, there's hope," Glen said. "We'll be praying for Doug. It sounds like he needs a Damascus road experience."

"He needs something," Cass muttered.

After a quick shower, Doug brewed a pot of coffee and carried a large cup to his office. Judy's Bible lay open on his desk to the book of Job. His glasses lay off to the side. He held up the ends of the Bible comparing what he had read with what he had left. "Not bad."

Read was probably stretching it. He did his best to look at each page for what seemed like an appropriate amount of time before turning to the next. Whatever answers Judy and Mark found in the Bible certainly weren't there for him. Most of it made no sense.

What was priceless, what kept him reading, were the little notes Judy had made in the margins. Sometimes they were dates, the dates she read that section, he guessed. More often there were comments—"how true," "needed this today," and so on.

Then he found a slip of paper tucked in toward the back. She had rewritten a section with his name in it. "I do not cease to give thanks for you, Doug, while making mention of you in all my prayers. Every day, many times a day, I pray that God would give you a spirit of wisdom and of revelation in the knowledge of Him. Doug, I pray that the eyes of your heart may be enlightened, so that you will know the hope of His calling, the riches of the glory of His inheritance, and the surpassing greatness of His power toward us who believe."

He could almost hear her saying it. In his mind, he could visualize her taking his hand, and looking in his eyes and saying, "Doug, I pray for you." He knew she did. She told him she prayed for him, but now he knew what she said. It was a glimpse into her heart.

"He didn't answer your prayers either." Was Cass praying for him now? Wouldn't matter. He was a lost cause.

He took a long drink from the coffee, then slid on his glasses. As he read the first chapter of Job, he nodded, identifying with Job's losses, and the seeming injustice of it. However, final words in the chapter made Doug stop and lay the Bible down.

> *"In all this Job did not sin nor charge God*
> *with wrong."*

Not charge God with wrong? He took another drink from his coffee. Job had to be made up. Nobody could just take what God was pouring out that way. His head began to throb as he worked to follow the conversation between Job and his friends, trading accusations and rebuttals. Then in chapter eleven, another section stopped him cold.

> *"If you would prepare your heart,*
> *And stretch out your hands toward Him;*
> *If iniquity were in your hand, and you put*
> *it far away,*
> *And would not let wickedness dwell in*
> *your tents;*
> *Then surely you could lift up your face*
> *without spot;*
> *Yes, you could be steadfast, and not*
> *fear;*
> *Because you would forget your misery,*
> *And remember it as waters that have*
> *passed away,*
> *And your life would be brighter than noon-*
> *day.*
> *Though you were dark, you would be*
> *like the morning.*
> *And you would be secure, because there is*
> *hope;*
> *Yes, you would dig around you, and*
> *take your rest in safety.*
> *You would also lie down, and no one would*
> *make you afraid;*

Yes, many would court your favor.
But the eyes of the wicked will fail,
And they shall not escape,
And their hope—loss of life!"

How to forget my misery . . . that's all I ever wanted. He
rubbed his eyes and sighed. "And you would be secure, because there is hope." Hope. He had no hope. But Cass, he
could see it on her face. It radiated from her. Even the kids
had it. Judy had told him many times that she was not afraid.
She dreaded the physical pain that her cancer would bring,
but fear was not part of the dread. She had that 'rest in safety.'

What did he have? Nothing. Absolutely nothing. That
part he understood. There was nothing of worth or value in
him. Judy, Mark, Cass and the kids . . . they were good people. He could see how God would want them. He was a hard,
bitter, failed old man.

'If you would prepare your heart . . . ' How? What did
that mean exactly? Would that end the misery, the despair,
the hopelessness? He grasped that last line, however—death
was all he had to look forward to.

Monday, October 5
Sandy was used to an empty office. Before Cass came, if
she saw Doug two hours a day, it was unusual. But he always
called. There was always a message waiting for her Monday
morning, explaining where he was and when he'd be in the
office later. Then always by nine a.m., he would call and talk
to her in person.

There was no message this morning.

Things seemed good Thursday, and better on Friday, so
she assumed that his and Cass's relationship had righted itself. The nosy, gossipy part of her hoped to catch him when
Cass was out and get the details. She and Doug had been
through far too much for silly things like privacy. She smiled

to herself and scanned her desk for a handwritten note he'd left. Nothing.

She put on a pot of coffee and checked out the window. No trucks or cars turning in. Quarter after eight. She sat down at her desk and dialed his house. The machine picked up. She hung up without leaving a message. She called his cell, then Cass's. Nobody answered.

"All right. That does it." She turned off the coffee pot, locked the door and drove to Doug's place in Kirkwood. She peeked in the garage and saw his car and truck, but Cass's spot was conspicuously empty. "Oh, no," she whispered.

Doug wouldn't answer the front door even though she held the doorbell button in for three solid minutes. "Doug! I know where you keep your spare key!" She didn't really, but there were a limited number of places it could be. She'd find it. She walked around to the deck. Two beer bottles lay in the yard.

She tried the back door and it slid open. "Doug? It's Sandy." She tiptoed through the kitchen. "Doug? You can call me out for worrying about you, but you always leave a message." There were more beer bottles in the kitchen trash and four bowls and spoons in the sink.

"Doug?"

She found him slumped over his desk.

"DOUG!"

"What?" He slowly raised up to his elbows and rubbed his eyes. "What time is it?"

"Twenty till nine."

"In the morning?"

"Yes. Monday morning."

He leaned back in his desk chair. "She left. Saturday morning."

Right now she didn't have time to grasp the searing heartbreak in that simple declaration. He needed intervention. "Have you been drunk all weekend?"

"Just off and on."

"How's your sugar?"

"Manageable. I've been eating."

"Yeah, I bet. I'm gonna make you some breakfast."

"I don't want anything."

"Then I'm calling an ambulance."

He squinted at her and frowned.

"Eggs it is."

"Thanks," he muttered.

"Been sleeping in your chair?"

"Just last night, I think."

"Can you stand up?"

"Yes," he grumbled then proved it, and she got a better look at him. The right side of his shirt was tucked in, but that was all. His eyes were dark and he had three days' worth of stubble.

"So what have you done all weekend?"

"Slept. Not slept. Drank some beer. Ate a lot of corn flakes."

"Want some coffee?"

He sighed with a lifetime of weariness. "Yeah."

She heard him shuffling behind her so she got to work as if this was the most normal thing in the world. He slouched onto one of the bar stools. "It wasn't that guy."

"Good." Sandy couldn't look him in the eyes. Instead, she rummaged through the cabinets until she found the coffee.

"I took the kids back to Mark."

"Probably a good decision."

He nodded. "Then I read. Judy's Bible."

"Did it help?"

"No." He rubbed his chin slowly. "You know, ever since I was a kid . . . " He gazed past her for a long moment. "Never mind." He stood, but kept a hand on the counter. "I'm gonna get a shower and shave."

That was the reassurance Sandy needed. He was bad, very bad, but he'd get himself together. She wouldn't have to call Mark or Cass. She could leave him the dignity of private grief. He deserved that much. She washed up the dishes, and checked the food in the refrigerator. If he was living on cereal, he'd be out of milk by evening.

Fifteen minutes later, he was back in the kitchen, and she scooped scrambled eggs from the skillet onto a plate for him. "There's tabasco in the refrigerator," he said.

"Yes, sir."

He scowled when she slid it across the counter to him, but he ate like he'd survived the weekend on beer and corn flakes.

"You've got a couple more eggs in there. Want me to fix them up?"

He shook his head. "Gotta see how these process first."

They sat in awkward silence while he ate, until she couldn't stand it. "I would be glad to listen."

He pushed the empty plate away and leaned back in his chair. "There's nothing to say. I did this to myself." He gulped the rest of his coffee, and set the cup down hard. "Thank you for being the one person who never abandoned me."

"Doug—"

He waved her off. "Now, I've got a couple of meetings today. Court's tomorrow and I'm about out of beer."

Tuesday, October 6

Mark, Julie and the children waited in the hallway outside the hearing room in the family court building. Yesterday at school, Matt, Ben and Janie said goodbye to the friends they had made, anticipating the judge's decision today would make their return to their parents legal and official.

Just as the clerk opened the hearing room door, Chuck Molinsky led Fletcher Durant through the doorway to the stairs "Sorry," Chuck said, shaking Mark's hand then Julie's. "We're running behind."

"We haven't been here long," Mark said. "There's no sign of my dad, though."

"He's got a few minutes," Chuck said, glancing at his

watch. "Fletcher?"

Fletcher leaned on his cane and lowered himself onto a nearby bench huffing and puffing as he maneuvered. Once settled, he looked up at Mark and Julie. "Mr. and Mrs. Bolling, we were delayed because something has come up. Something that may affect your case."

Mark saw fear flash across Julie's face and he reached for her hand.

"I received a call that Judge Henry Whitmire met his maker late last night." Julie gasped quietly. "The details are scant, but he left an establishment sometime after midnight, and police found him in his car early this morning. His wife . . . has a lot of unanswered questions." His eyes were magnified by his thick glasses as he looked at Mark. "What this means for you, is that your father may be given the option to start this process over."

"Start it over?"

Fletcher nodded. "They usually want to keep the same judge on a case from beginning to end and bringing a judge in just to make the final ruling could be contested."

Mark felt Julie's grip tighten. "We'll be all right. I don't think he'll fight it."

Julie gave his hand a little squeeze. "You're right," she said. "This is going to be over today."

Fletcher smiled and leaned forward so he could whisper. "I know it will."

Chuck offered Fletcher a hand. "We can go on in. Are the kids sitting in this time?"

"Unless you don't want them there," Mark said.

"It should all be good today," Chuck said with a smile. "They may want to hear it."

Julie hung back for just a moment. "Mr. Molinsky, I owe you an apology."

"No." Chuck shook his head. "You reacted like a mother who had just lost her children. You don't need to apologize for that."

"Mr. Molinsky, I acted like a woman who had no faith in

God or her husband. That was completely wrong. I do appreciate all the work you've done for us, and for your sacrifices on
our behalf." She held out her hand.

"If I shake your hand, will you call me 'Chuck' from now
on?"

"Of course," she said. After the handshake, Chuck led
them into the hearing room to their seats at the table. The
children sat behind them on folding chairs.

At precisely ten a.m., a distinguished older woman en-
tered from one of the side doors and glanced around the hearing room and frowned. "Are all the parties here?" she asked.

Just then Mark saw his father slip in. He nodded slightly to the woman and took his seat. "I'm sorry," he said quietly.
He never glanced in Mark's direction. There was no silk in the
breast pocket of his expensive charcoal gray suit and no
French cuffs today. His hair seemed grayer, his square-
shouldered confidence had given way to beaten-down fatigue.

"Mr. Douglas Bolling?"

"Yes, ma'am."

She turned to Mark. "Mr. and Mrs. Mark Bolling and
counsel?"

"Yes, Your Honor," Mark answered, as they stood.

"Very good," she said and stepped behind the table. She
wore a pair of glasses around her neck on a chain, and as she
opened the folder on the table in front of her, she slid on the
glasses. "Please sit," she said as she took her seat. "I am
Judge Margaret Swift. While it is the policy of Missouri courts
for you to keep the same judge throughout the family court
proceedings, unfortunately we will not be able to do that.
Judge Whitmire has died unexpectedly."

Julie slipped her hand in Mark's.

The judge shifted in her seat, "Mr. Bolling, you filed the
original action. The court will grant a postponement, a review,
or a rehearing in view of the extraordinary circumstances. Do
you wish to continue today?"

"Yes." His father's voice was quiet, lifeless.

"Mr. Molinsky, do you and your clients wish to continue?"

"Yes, Your Honor," Chuck answered.

"So noted," the judge said, then she folded her hands and Mark was glad he wasn't the one on the receiving end of that glare. "Mr. Bolling, in my opinion, your case should have never gone beyond filing. It has no merit, no evidence to support it and is clearly motivated by a personal vendetta. For an attorney to advise you to proceed with this borders on malpractice." Mark saw his father stiffen.

"Therefore," the judge said, looking toward Mark and Julie, "this court rules that Matthew Bolling, Benjamin Bolling and Jane Bolling remain in the permanent, physical custody of their natural birth parents." She banged the gavel, then allowed herself a slight smile.

The echo of the gavel was still fading when Julie flung her arms around Mark's neck, then she twisted and took each of her children in her arms. Mark hugged his sons and lifted Janie up to hug and kiss her, then he even pulled Chuck into a hug after shaking his hand. Fletcher blushed as Julie hugged him.

Out of the corner of his eye, Mark saw his father move. He grasped the table in front of him and stood slowly, then pushed in his chair. Mark made his way around Chuck and his family to get to him.

"Dad, how are you?" Mark asked.

His father ignored the question. Instead, he reached inside his suit jacket, pulled out an envelope, and handed it over. "The lawyer said you should have a copy of these."

"What are they?" Mark asked taking the envelope.

"Just some papers. So I guess you're heading back to Kenya?"

"My plans aren't set yet. Can we get together? The kids will want to see you."

"I don't think so, Mark."

He turned to walk away, so Mark blurted out the one piece of information that might keep him there, talking. "I saw Cass yesterday. She loves you."

His father sighed. "I've had my chance." He raised his hands, and a little energy returned to his voice. "I blew it. It's my own fault."

"God gives second chances all the time."

His father held out his hand. "Goodbye, Mark. You're a good man."

Mark shook his father's hand, then stood there, stunned by his words, unable to formulate a response. At the last moment, just before his father stepped through the door, Mark called, "I love you, Dad." His father gave him a half-smile, a weak nod, then he was gone.

The envelope.

Mark opened it, unfolded the papers inside and his stomach immediately tightened. It was his father's will, rewritten yesterday. It gave Sandy a quarter of a million dollars, then it named him as a joint heir with Cassandra Grayson of the remainder of the estate.

As soon as they got back to the Shannons' house, Mark pulled Julie into the kitchen away from the children. "My dad gave me a copy of his will today. He gave Sandy a big chunk then split the rest between me and Cass."

"I watched him in court. That was not the same Doug Bolling who put me in my place Thursday morning."

"This is worse than when my mother died. I'm going over there." Mark slipped off his tie, and unbuttoned the top button of his dress shirt. "The will, and the check Saturday. Something's not right." Then he dared say it out loud. "Julie, I'm afraid he might be suicidal."

"Do you want me to go with you?"

"He won't talk to me if you're there."

"Do you want me to call Cass?"

"Not yet. If . . . " Mark said with tears in his eyes. "If he . . . I don't want her to . . . see him, you know?"

Mark rolled through stop signs and cut through parking lots to avoid red lights and any other delay on his way to his dad's. He got out of the car and peered through the garage window. The Escalade and the truck were both there. He walked around front and rang the doorbell, but his father wouldn't answer.

"Dad!" Mark banged on the front door. "I just want to know you're all right!" There was no movement inside the house, not a sound.

Mark drove to the nearest pay phone and called his dad. It rang and then rolled to the answering machine. "Dad . . . please . . . just let me know you're okay." He heard the phone click and then the line went dead. His dad had picked up the receiver and dropped it back on its cradle.

Mark called back immediately, but got a busy signal. The phone was off the hook. Now what? Go back to his dad's with the police and have them break the door down? Find Cass and see if he'd talk to her? Hope this is normal grief?

He hung up the phone and shuffled back to the car. He'd give his dad one more day. If things hadn't changed, then he'd try more aggressive intervention.

Doug slouched on the sofa, with his arm hung over the back. He held a beer bottle loosely in his hand. Two empty bottles lay in the floor, and there were nine more in the refrigerator. A realtor was coming Friday to put his house on the market. He'd made a call to Jim Lowry about selling Bolling Developers. Jim, surprised but interested, had offered him two and a half million dollars. He'd go in to the office tomorrow and see if it was decent offer. He didn't care. He'd take any offer, but it would go into the estate, so he was looking out for . . . for Cass and Mark.

Once that was taken care of . . . if diabetes didn't kill

him soon enough, he had a fresh box of rounds for his favorite pistol. Doug sighed, raised the bottle to his mouth and drained it. Then he laid his head back, closed his eyes and wished for death.

Twenty-Four

Wednesday, October 7

Cass sat in a small exam room waiting for her doctor to come in with some answers. She'd battled this stomach flu for almost a week now, since the day she left Doug, and nothing would touch it. This morning she had arrived just before eight and the nurse had drawn blood, taken urine samples and even swabbed her throat for a culture. Now it was just a matter of waiting for the doctor to finish her rounds at the hospital, then she would make the diagnosis, write a couple of prescriptions and Cass could get out of here. Being sick at a hotel was miserable enough, but she couldn't bear the thoughts of flying with the flu.

Dr. Lynn Foster opened the door, then closed it behind her. She was in her early forties, with an easy manner that always made Cass relax. "How do you feel right now?" she asked.

"Honestly, I'd like to go throw up."

"Do you want me to give you a few minutes?"

"No, just tell me what this is, and how to make it stop."

The doctor pulled a seat over and gently asked, "Cass, when was your last period?"

Cass stepped down from the exam table, and pulled her datebook from her purse. As she flipped the page back, she felt a dizzy heat as it all came together. "Thirty . . . eight days ago," she whispered.

The doctor nodded. "You're pregnant. This is morning sickness."

Cass eased into another chair close by. "Oh, no . . . Doug . . . "

"This wasn't planned, was it?"

"No . . . I was taking birth control pills . . . how?"

"It could be anything. A bad lot of pills. Vitamins. OTC meds." She reached for Cass's wrist. "You look pale. Do you need some water or something?"

"No," she said, leaning her head back against the wall. "Pregnant . . . now . . . " Cass blinked slowly, then turned to the doctor. "How far along am I?"

"Not very. You're looking at mid-June." She laid Cass's folder on the exam table. "This is a shock, obviously. Take some time. Talk it over with Doug and decide what you want to do."

"What do you mean decide?"

"Decide whether you and Doug want to keep the baby."

Her mind still reeling, Cass couldn't even register the suggestion that she might abort the baby. It was lost in a swirl of confusion, regret and uncertainty, then tears began to spill onto Cass's cheeks. "I left Doug last week."

Sandy took her eyes from the front door just long enough to check the clock. She hadn't heard from him yesterday. His home phone was busy and he wasn't answering his cell. If he wasn't here by nine o'clock, she was calling the police. It was eight forty-five.

Then she heard a familiar truck pull up outside. Doug came in, and waved to her. "Morning, Sandy. I've got a meeting with Jim Lowry tomorrow and Sue Bracken from the realty company will be here Friday."

"Okay," she said. He seemed like everything was normal. Maybe she was just overreacting. "You had a few messages, but things have been quiet."

"Good," he said, taking the message slips from her. "Is there any coffee left?"

"Yeah, do you want me to bring you some?"

"I'll get it." He stepped over to the counter and poured a large mug full of black coffee. As he passed, he said, "I've got to get some information together for Jim, so if you wouldn't care, hold my calls."

"Sure. Let me know if I can help you." She hoped he understood she was talking about much more than office work.

"Thanks, Sandy." He understood.

———————————

Doug closed his office door, then he dropped the message slips in the wastebasket, and took a seat at his desk. He turned on his computer and swiveled his chair around to set his coffee cup on his desk. That's when he saw the envelope.

Mr. Doug Bolling, Bolling Developers.

The energy he pretended to have vanished. He picked up the envelope gently as if were made of delicate china. He carefully slit it open with his pocketknife. The letter inside was dated Sunday.

> *Mr. Bolling,*
>
> *I am resigning my position with Bolling Developers effective immediately. In lieu of the customary two weeks' notice, please feel free to withhold my final paycheck.*
>
> > *Cassandra Grayson*

He held the letter for several moments, and then in a burst, he tore it in half, and in half again. He walked to the wastebasket and slammed the pieces into it. As he stood there, he realized his hands were shaking and he was sweating. He held onto the edge of his desk to steady himself. His heart pounded inside his chest. He managed one last thought before he blacked out. *Please, let this be it.*

Mark answered the phone on the second ring, pen in hand, ready to take a message. "Hello, this is the Shannons' residence."

"Mark! Thank God!"

Cass was panic-stricken. "Cass—"

"Sandy just called me. They took Doug out in an ambulance. They're taking him to St. Joe's—"

"What happened?"

"I don't know. He collapsed. I don't know if it was a heart attack, or . . . "

After yesterday, Mark wouldn't let his mind drift to other possibilities. "Where are you?"

"I'm on my way to the hospital."

"I'll be right there." He quickly got Julie and the kids, and a street map of St. Louis. St. Joe's. He'd never been to St. Joe's. It was in Kirkwood. Julie kept him focused on driving as she read off the streets and gave him directions.

If his father was at the office, then it couldn't have been anything he did to himself, could it? *God please don't let this be the end. Please give him the grace of another chance. Cass needs him. I need him. Father, keep him in Your hands.*

"There," Julie said, pointing. "On the right."

"Got it." Mark pulled up to the emergency entrance.

"You go," Julie said. "I'll park the car."

"Thanks." Mark kissed her, then rushed inside.

Cass sat in a corner of the emergency room waiting area, her arms folded tightly across her chest. She wanted to go throw up again, but she was afraid to leave, afraid she'd miss seeing someone who might have a scrap of information.

Sandy paced nearby. A veil of blame hung between them, and Cass was willing to accept it as her punishment for leaving. At least Sandy called her. She couldn't thank God enough for that.

She ached to tell Sandy about the baby, to beg her for-giveness and hear her reassurance that Doug would take her back. She couldn't deal with a baby without him. He had to be okay. He had to.

She crossed her legs and hugged herself a little tighter. What would Mark think? And Matt? And Glen? They'd kick her out of church. Maybe not. Maybe she'd get a pass since it happened before . . .

She couldn't go to Phoenix. She couldn't leave until she knew Doug forgave her. She wouldn't tell him about the baby until then. She should have agreed to marry him. This was her fault.

"He seemed better this morning." Sandy muttered it to herself more than to Cass. "I thought he was better."

"Better?" Cass dared to ask. "What was wrong with him?"

Sandy paled, then she took the seat next to Cass and grasped her hands. "You did not hear this from me, all right?"

Cass nodded. "He blames me, doesn't he?"

"It's bigger than that. Much, much bigger." She glanced at the double doors and the outside doors. "Judy didn't know. Mark doesn't know. He doesn't want you to know this or he would have told you himself. The only reason I'm telling you now is so you understand how it all fits together."

"How what fits together?"

"Everything. So you know it's not just you." She almost smiled. "See, Doug had a younger brother, and when they were kids . . . his brother drowned."

"Oh, how awful."

"I only know because my sister was in the same grade as Doug and Dell. I remember when it happened. It was in the summer, not long after school got out. He never, never talks about it because, well . . . his mama blamed him because he was there with him when it happened. I guess she thought Doug should've saved him or something."

"That's why his mother left?" Cass didn't try to stop the

tears welling up in her eyes.

Sandy nodded. "His dad lost his will to live and crawled in a bottle." She pointed toward the double doors. "Now Doug is a mellow drunk, but Dell said John Bolling was an angry, violent drunk, and if he was awake, he was drunk."

"So Doug's been rejected and blamed at every turn, his whole life."

Sandy nodded.

"And I left him." Sweet Jesus, have mercy.

"But honey, you have to understand, you have to see that he has kind of a warped view of things. He thinks the worst about himself. He can't see any good in himself." She jabbed a finger on the arm of the chair. "He sees every circumstance, every single one, as confirmation of that."

"But he's such a good man, and he's worked hard and made a good life for himself, for us."

Sandy did smile this time. "It's never enough for him. And he never relaxes and enjoys it—he came close with you, closest I've ever seen—but he's just waiting for it all to fall apart."

"And it did."

"But you came back," Sandy said. "That may make all the difference in the world."

"I hope and pray you're right." She raised her head and looked around for a doctor or nurse, but there was nobody. "Surely they know something by now. Or at least they could just tell us what they're checking."

"I expect it's his sugar," Sandy said. "He wasn't eating like he should."

"That's easy to fix, right? They just admit him and monitor it real close for a day or two, right?" She was grasping. "Till he gets back on track."

Sandy nodded. "I'm sure that's all it is."

Cass stood and looked down the long hallway, trying to will someone to come through the heavy double doors, and give her some confirmation—yes, he would be okay, yes he would forgive her, yes he would take her back.

Instead, she heard her name and turned to see Mark charging through the doors. "What's going on? What happened?"

"Sandy thinks it's his sugar, maybe."

He immediately got with Sandy and they began comparing notes—Saturday, Monday morning, Tuesday at court and this morning in the office. They recounted conversations, commented on body language until Mark looked at both of them. "He rewrote his will Monday. Sandy . . . is there any way . . . could he . . . is there any chance . . . he's done this to himself?"

That's when Cass lost it. Her resignation was on Doug's desk. He would have found it first thing. That pushed him over the edge. And she was pregnant.

She realized Mark was on his knees in front of her, and Sandy was pushing a cup of water toward her.

"Cass, I'm sorry. I shouldn't have said anything. I was thinking out loud."

She slumped into the closest chair, buried her face in her hands, and sobbed.

"Cass . . . what is it? Do you know something else? Something you're not telling me?"

"I . . . " She raised her head, and swallowed hard. "Mark . . . I'm pregnant."

Well, he wasn't dead. Judging from the way he felt, he wasn't even close. Doug sighed and moved to cross his arms, but it pulled the IV line, so he frowned and lay his arm back at his side. The emergency room. He couldn't remember anything, so he guessed Sandy called an ambulance. Then she probably called Mark. And maybe Cass.

A young man in green scrubs stepped around the curtain. "How do you feel, Mr. Bolling?" he asked.

"I feel pretty good now. So can I go?"

The doctor smiled as he made a note on Doug's chart.

"You were a very sick man, Mr. Bolling. We're going to keep you a couple of days." The doctor laid Doug's folder on the end of his bed. "Your blood sugar had dropped very low. Dangerously low. It's a miracle you're alive much less awake and arguing to go home. Did you check it this morning?"

"Yeah, it was low."

"Take any insulin then?"

"No, because it was low."

"Do you have trouble with low sugar in the morning?"

"Not typically."

"Any ideas what might have caused it to dip? Diet change? Recent illness?"

Doug sighed deeply. "Life events and a case of beer."

The doctor frowned and scribbled on the chart. "At least you admitted it," he muttered. "Tell me about your alcohol usage."

"One or two light beers on a Saturday." He started to cross his arms again, forgetting the IV momentarily, but stopped in frustration when he felt the tug. "This was . . . out of character."

"All right, I'm going to believe you because you were up front about it." More scribbling, then he laid down the pen and spoke quietly. "Mr. Bolling, life events happen to everybody. There's no shame in getting help dealing with them."

"I'll take care of it."

"Again, I'm going to believe you." He picked up his pen and wrote again. "You've had two rounds of glucose intravenously but if your next check is okay, we'll get you something to eat. Do you remember how you felt before you passed out?"

"Dizzy. Heart pounding. My hands were shaking, and I was sweating."

"When was the last time you ate?"

Doug let a deep breath go. "Tuesday sometime, maybe, I don't know."

The doctor shook his head. "All right, after the blood test and a piece of toast or something, we'll get you in a room and see how you do with lunch. Once you get in a room your family can come—"

"I don't want to see anyone," Doug said, cutting him off.

"That's your choice, of course." He picked the folder back up, pulled out his pen and began making more notes. "Can I give your family an update?"

"Yeah, whatever," Doug muttered.

"I'll check back with you soon." The young man disappeared around the curtain.

"Great, just great," he mumbled. "You make no sense at all," he said, looking toward the ceiling. "I can't even die. You had me right there! Is there a reason You won't kill me. Do You want me? Is that what You're trying to tell me? That makes no sense. I've got nothing. Why would You want me?" Doug's chest tightened, but the machine monitoring him didn't register any changes. It wasn't that kind of tightness. It was the same kind Cass felt after she went to church. He knew it was. Two weeks later, she converted.

He closed his eyes, and he could see her face. He was tired . . . so tired of fighting, of being miserable. So very tired.

Cass watched in utter surprise as Mark took both her hands and smiled gently. "Congratulations. He will be over the moon thrilled when he finds out."

"Won't they kick me out of church or something, though?"

"Do you want them to?"

"No, but I thought—"

"Only a graceless jerk who lost sight of his own sinfulness would do something like that. Trust me. I know what I'm talking about here."

"Thank you," she whispered, and wiped her eyes with the heel of her hand.

Sandy slipped an arm around her shoulder and squeezed. "Mark's right. He will be downright silly. Wait and see."

The double doors swung open and Cass jumped up to intercept the doctor. "How's Doug? Doug Bolling. Did you see him?"

"Mrs. Bolling?" the doctor asked, looking at Cass.

"Yes," Sandy said, "and I'm his sister. How is he?"

"He was hypoglycemic—"

"But he's okay?" Cass asked.

The doctor nodded. "Hypo is low blood sugar. He indicated that he hadn't been eating like he should."

"Beer and corn flakes," Sandy muttered.

The doctor raised his eyebrows, but went on with his update. "We're going to admit him just to be on the safe side, but I expect everything to line out very soon."

"Can I see him?" Cass asked.

The doctor's eyes darted to each of them in their huddle. "He asked not to have any visitors."

"Does he know we're here?"

"Yes," he said. "I'm sorry."

"No," Cass said, and Mark reached out for her hand. "It's not your fault." She took a deep breath, regaining some composure. "Thank you for the information. At least he gave us that much."

The doctor tightened his lips. Maybe he thought that counted as a smile. Cass watched him stride back down the hall and heaviness settled back over her. "He hates me," she said.

"He doesn't," Mark said. "I promise you, he loves you. He just doesn't know how to cope with anything."

"I have to see him, Mark. I have to talk to him, and beg him to forgive me."

⁓

"At least it's a private room." Doug frowned and took the hospital gown from the nurse.

"You lucked out. We're not very full right now." He stepped in the restroom to change and she said, "You know, you could have somebody bring you pajamas and a robe. Might make it a little more bearable." When he came out of the restroom, she pointed to the bundle of clothes in his arms. "You have a phone?"

"Yeah."

"Then call somebody. Who wouldn't help out a guy in the hospital?"

He could think of a few who wouldn't. The only numbers he had in his phone were Sandy's and Cass's. He dialed Sandy. She answered before the second ring. "Hey, they're gonna admit me. I need some things from the house."

"Gimme a half hour," she said.

"Thanks." He gave her the room number, then laid his phone on the bedside table and settled in the bed. The nurse attached leads from the monitor to Doug's chest. "Since you reported palpitations and you're in that magic age group he wants to make sure there are no cardiac issues. They're bringing breakfast up." She checked her wristwatch. "Actually it will be lunch. Can I get you anything in the meantime?"

"No, thanks. I'll just settle in here and stare at the walls."

"You do have a television." The nurse smiled and pointed to the set hanging above the end of the bed.

"Thanks, but I'm good." He waited until the door clicked shut behind her. His phone was right there. Cass would come if she knew he was in the hospital. "I'm not praying," he said. "You've burned me too many times with that. But . . . " He shook his head. "I'm not even gonna ask. Never mind."

———

"It'll be all right," Sandy said as they drove toward Kirkwood. "I promise you."

"He didn't want to see his *wife*," Cass made air quotes for Sandy's lie.

"He didn't know his *wife* was here. That was too much for him to hope for."

Too much to hope for. Cass understood exactly how he could be afraid to hope.

"He has no idea." Sandy winked and patted Cass's knee. "But I think there is a part of his brain that knows." She glanced over and smiled. "See, I don't have a key to the house. Mark doesn't have one, and he never mentioned where he kept the spare. He never told me what to pack for him. Deep down, I think he knows you're here."

They pulled in the driveway and Cass felt a strange, sad nervousness. As she stepped inside, the familiar scent of home hit her and she teared up.

Her piano sat off to her right. Years ago, Doug hired a special crew of expert piano movers to bring it in. He sat on the bench with her as she played it for the first time here in the new house, their house. She walked over to the piano, lightly running her hand along the case. "Would you mind if I played? It's therapeutic, I guess."

"By all means," Sandy said.

Cass pulled a book from the bench and flipped it open to a piece she'd played only once or twice. It was "Amazing Grace," the only hymn she knew. Before long, amid the words of grace, healing, restoring, saving grace, she heard singing, and a moment later she realized it was her voice, a pure spontaneous offering. She wasn't playing for herself anymore. It was for the savior who gave the gift of music, who gave all gifts.

"The Lord has promised good to me,
His Word my hope secures;
He will my Shield and Portion be,
As long as life endures."

She stopped playing, and leaned away from the keys. That was enough. There were more verses, but she'd heard enough. The Lord had promised good. She believed that. In spite of the doubts and unsettling uncertainties in this moment, the Lord, her Lord had promised good to her.

Cass looked over and Sandy had tears in her eyes. "That was perfect," Sandy whispered. "I haven't heard that song in I don't know how long."

"I don't know if I've ever really heard it before now."
Cass laid a hand gently on the bench beside her. "You know
sometimes . . . if I pretend I don't notice . . . he'll sing. He has
a beautiful voice." A voice she wanted to hear again, regardless
of what he said. She closed the piano cover. "I'll get his things
together."

Cass clutched the overnight bag on her lap. She packed
everything he could possibly want or need—pajamas and a
robe, his comb and razor, toiletries, his cologne, even his
glasses and the top files from his desk. She also dared to pack
Judy's Bible in the side pocket of the bag, whispering a prayer
that he wouldn't see it as overstepping, or violating some sa-
cred bond between Judy and him.

"I think Mark should take the bag in," Cass said as
Sandy parked in the hospital lot.

"Don't you want to see him?"

"More than anything," Cass said.

"Then you take the bag in. That way he knows you did
it for him."

"Thanks, Sandy." Cass squeezed her hand. "For everything."

"You bet." Sandy winked and opened her car door.
"Now, we know how impatient he is on a good day. Let's get
this stuff up to him before he has a meltdown."

Cass shifted the bag from one hand to the other as she
walked, thankful she could just follow Sandy. Mark stood
when they reached the small waiting area on Doug's floor.
"Have you seen him?" Cass asked.

Mark shook his head. "I was waiting for you." He smiled
gently. "I thought we could go together. You know, we'd outnumber him that way."

Julie hugged her tightly, "Congratulations," she whispered. "I'm going to predict we get two more pieces of good

news today. That will make three. Good news always comes in threes."

So did bad news.

Cass hugged Janie, then Ben and finally Matt. "I think this is my test, Matt."

He grinned. "Nope. You already passed that."

"Pray anyway."

"Sure. And just so you know, so's Peter in Kenya and our grandparents in Italy."

"No pressure." Cass rolled her eyes.

"That's the whole point of praying. No pressure." He rolled his eyes, in a dead-on impression of her.

"You're such a punk," Cass said with a smile. She took a deep breath and smoothed her sweater against her. "All right, Mark. Let's do this."

He nodded and led her down the hallway to Doug's room. Cass took one more deep breath before stepping into the hospital room. This was it. Her whole life hung on these next few minutes. Could they heal? Could they make a life together after everything? She stepped carefully around the curtain, and looked into Doug Bolling's eyes.

———————

There are a handful of memories Doug carried with him his entire life. At the top of that list was the sight of Cassandra Grayson rounding the corner of that curtain in his hospital room. The only prayer he'd ever had answered in his life . . . and he'd been too afraid to pray it.

"It's really you," he said softly. "You look incredible."

"I'm a wreck," she said, with a half-smile that made the rest of the world melt away. Her hair was tucked behind her ears, and her eyes shined. She crossed the room to him. When she got close enough, he reached out and she slipped her hand into his. It was warm and soft. She was really here. "Doug, I—"

"Shhh, let me go first." He raised her hand to his lips

and kissed it. "Help me sort this out. I don't want to be bitter . . . and hopeless . . . and miserable . . . and alone. I'm tired, Cass. Tired of all of it."

She pulled the chair closer without letting go of his hand. "I don't know if I have your answers, so I brought some backup." She motioned behind her, and he saw Mark standing in the corner by the curtain.

"Mark, God made more sense when He was taking things, people, away from me," Doug said. "I deserved that." He shook his head slowly. "I don't understand why I woke up today. I heard the numbers. I know what the paramedics said. I should be in a coma or dead."

"He loves you, Dad, and He's been pursuing you for years."

"Why?"

"That's what He does—"

"No, why me? Why Doug Bolling? I'm nothing."

"Because He chooses to."

"I can't buy that."

"Did you still love me Saturday?" Cass asked.

"Of course."

"And Sunday, and Monday and Tuesday?"

"Yes."

"After I left you . . . after I hurt you . . . so deeply. You chose to love me. Don't you see?"

A flush of heat passed over him from his cheeks to his chest. "I wanted to die," he whispered.

"I'm so sorry. I should have never . . . I'm sorry . . . " Tears spilled onto her cheeks.

"I think that's what I needed. I needed to face the truth, the truth that I had ruined my own life, that I'd squandered everything I'd ever been given, that I was worthless."

"Doug . . . "

"No, I read . . . " He glanced at Mark. "In your mom's Bible. In Job, I think. It said, 'if you would prepare your heart, and stretch out your hands to Him.' I couldn't do it. Not to a God who took everything and then wouldn't kill me." He smiled at Cass and then at Mark. "But when I woke up in the emergency room—" He kissed Cass's hand again. "And you came back . . . " He looked at his son. "Mark, tell me how to do this."

"Sure. Check the drawer behind you, Cass. See if there's a Bible in it."

"Oh, I packed one." She looked at Doug, as if she expected a recrimination. "I hope you don't mind."

"I love you," he whispered.

She pulled Judy's Bible from the bag and his glasses. Mark reached for the Bible and carefully turned the pages. "Let's just go to Job, since you read that."

> "If you would prepare your heart,
>   And stretch out your hands toward Him;
>   If iniquity were in your hand, and you put
> it far away,
>   And would not let wickedness dwell in
> your tents;
>   Then surely you could lift up your face
> without spot;
>   Yes, you could be steadfast, and not
> fear;
>   Because you would forget your misery,
>   And remember it as waters that have
> passed away,"

Doug had no idea how Mark found the verses, but he did. He read them slowly and carefully, but they sounded different this time. Instead of a hopeless sentence being passed, they contained a way out.

Mark laid the Bible on the tray table and Doug slid on his glasses. "Two things, Dad. Preparing your heart is recognizing where you stand before God. It's knowing you have violated His moral law."

"I understand that."

"Then the second thing is the putting iniquity away."

"You know, I had to look that word up. Sheesh."

Mark smiled. "Putting it away means you commit to living in obedience to God's commands. It's a life of following after Christ."

"But the misery is gone, right?"

"That's not saying you'll never have hard times again, but the kind of misery you've felt these last few days will be gone forever."

"All right, I'm in."

"Well, hang on. Job didn't know about Jesus yet. Actions carry consequences, and our sins against God carry a death penalty. But Jesus Christ willingly died and paid that penalty for anyone who would accept it. So, you've violated God's law. Jesus took the penalty. You accept that payment and you commit to live as a follower from now on."

"That's what I want." He closed his eyes and for a split second wished Judy was here. He felt Cass squeeze his hand. "I don't want to live like this anymore. I've made myself miserable, but You've given me a second chance I don't deserve. Forgive me for fifty-six years of bitterness toward You. Jesus Christ paid my penalty. The years I have left are Yours. You've proved . . . you brought my family back. You brought Cass back. I can never repay that."

Cass hugged him tightly before he could even open his eyes. "I love you," she said. "You know, it was easy for me to embrace the fact that God loved me because of the way you love me. You didn't care about anything in my past. You valued me and wanted me to share your life."

"I do love you."

Doug saw Mark wipe his eyes. "What?"

He shook his head. "Not now."

"No more secrets, Mark."

"It's not like that. I just . . . I wish Mom was here."

"Yeah," Doug said, even as he squeezed Cass's hand. "She prayed for this. I read it in her Bible." He flipped to the back and found the sheet with Judy's prayer.

Mark's eyes filled with tears. "I promised her . . . right before she died. I failed. Her and you, Dad. I am so sorry."

"Mark, you know, we've all done enough to spend the

rest of our lives apologizing to each other. Let's just . . . drop it." He held out his hand and Mark smiled and shook it. "Now, I have a very important matter to take care of."

He sat up as straight as he could without stretching the wires to the instruments. He took both of Cass's hands in his. "You'll have to imagine I'm down on one knee, okay?"

She laughed and let go of his hand just long enough to wipe her eyes.

"Cassandra Grayson, I am a fool. I love you. I have loved you from the day I met you and I will love you until the day I die. Will you please, please allow me the greatest joy I can imagine and become my wife?"

"Yes! Yes! I love you! Yes, I'll marry you. Yes!" She threw her arms around his neck and kissed him.

"Thank you," he whispered. "Thank you for coming back."

"I shouldn't have left."

"Doesn't matter. We're starting fresh."

"About that. There's something you need to know." She scooted extra close to him. "I saw a doctor this morning."

Fear shot through him. "Cass—"

She lay a finger on his lips. "I'm pregnant."

For a long moment, he didn't move, didn't even breathe. He opened his mouth but words would not come. Finally, he blinked, and managed to squeak out, "For real?"

Cass nodded. "She said mid-June."

"How's Friday?"

"Friday? What are you talking about?"

"For the wedding. Where's the doctor? I gotta get out of here. I've got a life to live."

Friday, October 9

At exactly six-thirty, Cass walked down the staircase. She paused a moment at the full-length mirror in the hall closet. Thankfully, the suit still fit. It was ivory, with a beaded satin jacket, elegantly tailored, just the thing for a woman who had moved beyond taffeta and lace.

Doug gave her his shy, embarrassed smile when she admitted how long it had hung in the closet, her hopes hanging there with it. "You should've knocked me upside the head," he said. Maybe, but she was happy with how things worked out. Yes, a little sooner would have been nice, but Doug was marrying her because he wanted to, because he loved her, and that assurance was worth the wait.

The hairdresser managed to squeeze her in this afternoon after the morning sickness subsided, and delivered an elegant upsweep. She checked her make-up one last time. The diamond in her brand new engagement ring sparkled each time she moved her hand.

One final look. One more deep breath. This was it.

She met Matt in the entry hall, and he handed her the bouquet the florist delivered at the last minute. "Grandpa's gonna flip when he sees you," Matt said, offering her his arm. "You look exactly like a bride should look."

"Thanks, Matt. Are you ready?"

"I'm not the one getting married. But you should know you're being beamed worldwide."

"What are you talking about?"

"Well, Dad, Ben and I all have laptops equipped with webcams. We called your dad this afternoon and got him set up. Peter and my grandparents were already good to go, so through the magic of technology, they're all watching."

"No pressure."

"None whatsoever."

She took a deep breath and tugged at her jacket and smoothed her skirt. "All right then. Let's do this."

Matt offered her his arm and walked with her very slowly, his back straight, and his chin held high. In the living room, Julie and Janie waited to Mark's right. Janie clutched a basket of flowers with one hand and waved with her other. A beaming Ben Bolling stood up with his grandfather. Sandy and Dell, and Glen Dillard and his wife, Laurie, were off to the

side as privileged observers. Chamber music from a satellite
radio station filled the room, barely covering the click and whir
of Julie's and Sandy's cameras.

Across the room Doug stood a little taller. When their
eyes met, his lit up, and he smiled at her. She would carry
that smile in her heart for the rest of her days.

No doubt everything Mark said was beautiful and pro-
found, but she didn't hear any of it. She was soaking in the
moment, the moment she had longed for, and all but given up
ever experiencing. From time to time as Mark spoke, Doug
gave her hand the subtlest squeeze, or he winked or simply
smiled at her.

Julie touched her arm, and handed her Doug's wedding
band, his first. Judy never gave him one. That was oddly reassuring.

"Cass, place that ring on Dad's finger and repeat after
me," Mark said.

"If it's okay, Mark, I can take it from here." She handed
her bouquet to Julie, and quickly wiped her eyes, then she
turned to face Doug. "I, Cass, take thee, Doug, to be my wedded husband, to have and to hold from this day forward, for
better, for worse, for richer, for poorer, in sickness and in
health, to love and to cherish, till death do us part, according
to God's holy ordinance. Thereto I pledge my love."

Doug leaned over and kissed her cheek.

"You're not supposed to do that yet," she whispered.

"What's he gonna do," Doug said, nodding toward Mark,
"stop the wedding? I couldn't help it."

Ben tapped Doug's shoulder and handed him a ring.
"Your turn, Grandpa." Then he leaned up and whispered in
Doug's ear, loud enough for Cass to hear him. "Just so you
know, if you don't marry her, I will."

"You're out of luck," Doug said, slipping the ring on
Cass's finger. "Mark, you better prompt me." He looked at
Cass and solemnly repeated his vows with strength and confi-
dence in his voice.

"I, Doug, take thee, Cass, to be my wedded wife, to have

and to hold from this day forward, for better, for worse, for richer, for poorer, in sickness and in health, to love and to cherish, till death do us part, according to God's holy ordinance. Thereto I pledge my love."

It was almost too much. He did love her as much as she loved him, and now everyone else knew it, too. No matter what happened the rest of her life, God had granted her this one perfect moment.

At last, Mark glanced around the room and said, "I now pronounce you man and wife. You may kiss your bride." The little group burst into applause before Doug could pull Cass close. When she managed to open her eyes after he kissed her, he had the same dreamy-eyed look he had after they kissed the very first time on a riverboat on New Year's Eve years ago. A lifetime ago it seemed.

He tore his eyes away from hers. There were hugs and congratulations all around, until Doug raised his hands. "We made dinner reservations for everybody," he said. "It's some fancy place Cass picked." Then he grinned. "The food's probably good."

She shoved him gently.

He held out his arm. "Shall we, Mrs. Bolling?"

Mrs. Bolling. Always and forever Mrs. Bolling.

Epilogue

Thursday, August 12, en route to Mombasa, Kenya

Mark eased the airline seat all the way back and closed his eyes. His father had insisted on buying the tickets, and Mark had to admit first class had its perks. It had been exactly one year since Julie got that phone call from David Shannon that a lawsuit had been filed. It seemed much longer.

After the lawsuit was resolved, and after the wedding, his father asked them to come and stay. How could he refuse? He had no direction, no plans, and he finally had his dad. So after his dad and Cass honeymooned in Key West, Mark moved his family into the Kirkwood estate. The following Sunday, he saw his father and Cass baptized. In that moment, he was overcome by conflicting feelings of 'mission accomplished' and 'now what?'

His father felt the same kind of restlessness. Before the trip to the hospital, he had contacted Jim Lowry about buying Bolling Developers. Of course, none of them knew then that it was part of a plan to get his affairs in order. Even after the honeymoon, his dad said he wasn't sure if he wanted to build houses anymore. They talked and prayed, then consulted with Jim, and with their new pastor, and after Sandy assured him whatever he decided was okay with her, he chose to go through with the sale and retire.

Ironically, that's when things got busy for Mark. He put his accounting background to use as they worked through the details of the sale. They inventoried equipment and materials, tracked down purchase receipts, figured depreciations, and sorted through tax records. On January 1, after twenty-nine years, Doug Bolling hung up his hard hat. In the end, he said he couldn't waste the second chance he'd been given. He was determined to pour his energy into his faith and his family. Mark hoped the world was ready for a sold-out Doug Bolling.

When the deal was finalized, his father rewrote his will yet again. This time, he left Sandy out, but he paid her the quarter million dollars as a retirement bonus. Dell was able to take an early retirement. They were still deciding whether to move closer to their daughter, or buy an RV. When Sandy saw firsthand the peace that faith brought into his father's life, she embraced it too, and so did Dell.

Cass decided she'd work for Jim on a case-by-case basis. That way she could feed her need to create, but on her terms. Mark smiled. Everything at that house was on her terms. Like the baby's room.

Mark and the boys helped his dad put the nursery together. They changed paint five, no, six times, repapered twice and tried four beds and dressers before she was satisfied. A first-time mother who happens to be an interior designer with an unlimited budget proved to be a dangerous combination.

Jonah Ross Bolling came on June eighth, two days after his dad's birthday. Jonah was a little early, but he and Cass were fine. Ross was his father's middle name and Jonah was for the second chance—a perfect name. Jonah looked like his dad, and like Ben, and so far he was an easy-going baby. They deserved that. Mark's kids were still trying to wrap their heads around the idea of a baby uncle.

"What are you thinking?" Julie asked as she took his hand.

"Anxious to get back to work." He preached the morning Cass and his father were baptized, and being back in the pulpit energized him. He accepted other invitations to preach around town, and each time felt more like home. He thought maybe God was moving him toward the pastorate again. But then his heart started to ache for Kenya. By Easter, he was sure of God's genuine call and his father's blessing. No ulcers this time.

"It was a good thing Peter never followed through with shipping our things back," Julie said.

"I think he knew all along."

"How long before your dad comes to visit?"

"He was talking about Christmas."

"They're going to travel with the baby?"

"Yeah, but get this. He's going to stop in New York, and London. I think it was gonna take a week to get here. He thinks it will be easier on Jonah to break the trip up."

"That may backfire."

"I guess we'll find out." He squeezed Julie's hand. "You think things have changed much in Mombasa?"

"I don't know about there, but we sure have changed," she said.

"Fiery trials will do that. Leave you refined."

"No kidding." She swept her thumb across the back of Mark's hand. "Listening to your dad . . . he has this sense of urgency about him. Like his time is short."

"He's not even sixty yet."

"I know. Maybe he just feels like he has a lot of lost time to make up for." She glanced across the aisle at Ben and Jane, then peeked through the seats at Matt. "You know, I was thinking . . . your dad knew what kind of trials believers have to face sometimes, but he still came to Jesus."

"Maybe he figured it couldn't be any worse than what he'd already been through."

"I bet nothing will shake him. Whatever it is. I bet he'll walk right through it. Calm, sure, resolute."

***

"Fear not, for I have redeemed you;
I have called you by your name;
You are Mine.

When you pass through the waters, I will be with you;
And through the rivers, they shall not overflow you.
When you walk through the fire, you shall not be
burned,
Nor shall the flame scorch you.
For I am the Lord your God,
The Holy One of Israel, your Savior;"
   Isaiah 43:1-3

Please enjoy this preview for Resolute,

Book Three in the Foundations series

Book Three: Foundations Series

PAULA WISEMAN

Tuesday, May 11

The directions to the doctor's office were just gone. Doug Bolling gripped the steering wheel of his car in frustration. He'd been there dozens of times, last week even, but today, he couldn't remember the first turn.

He could miss the appointment, and claim he forgot it. Forgetting the appointment wasn't as bad as forgetting how to get there. Or he could make up some excuse for Cass to drive him. No, he wasn't ready to tell her about the lapses, not without proof.

He pulled out his cell phone and thanked God that the doctor's number was on his contact list. Then he thanked God that he still knew how to use a phone. "Karen, this is Doug Bolling. I've got a nine-thirty. I, uh . . . I need directions to the office . . . I know, Karen. Just please . . . help me out, here."

He carefully copied everything into the notebook he carried with him everywhere. It had become his lifeline. He read the directions back to the receptionist double-checking every detail before he hung up.

Doug paid careful attention to the street signs, the red lights and stop signs, and made it with time to spare. Before he got out, he bowed his head and whispered, "Please God, let it be anything else. Anything."

He didn't have a chance to pick up a magazine before the nurse called him to an exam room. This was a bad sign. The nurse weighed him, took his blood pressure and asked for his latest glucose readings. She dropped his file in the door's slot on her way out.

He hated the exam table, always had, and wouldn't sit on it until the doctor made him. Instead, he eased into the metal and vinyl chair in the corner. He got his notebook from his back pocket, slid on his glasses and read his list for the day. Today was easy—doctor, post office, then pick up the boys. He knew how to get to the post office and the school. Completely manageable.

Dr. John Stansbury swung open the door, and shook hands with Doug before pulling a stool over. "How are you today, Doug?"

"That's what you're going to tell me."

"How old are you now?" The doctor laid Doug's folder on the exam table and flipped it open.

"I'll be sixty-eight next month."

"And how long have you been married?"

"Almost twelve years."

"Just the two boys?"

"No, I have a son from my first marriage. Is this some kind of test?"

"Actually yes. So far, so good. Can you count backwards from a hundred by sevens?" He scribbled on the folder's top sheet.

"Yeah . . . uh . . . ninety-three . . . eighty-six . . . sixty, I mean, seventy-nine, seventy-two . . . sixty-five . . . "

"That's good enough," Stansbury said, waving him off. "We got the results back on the CT and MRI."

"It's Alzheimer's, isn't it?"

The doctor laid his pen down and that's when Doug knew. "Yeah, it looks like it. We can't be a hundred percent sure until—"

"Until the autopsy. I read that much." Doug dropped his head and looked at the list he was still holding. His boys' names caught his eye, and his stomach tightened. "How much time am I looking at, John? I mean, good time."

"A year, maybe two. Of course everybody's different, and we can look at medications to slow things down, memory techniques . . . you can stretch that out."

"My boys . . . my boys are little. Jonah's not eleven yet, and Noah's nine."

"They'll learn to cope, Doug, just like you will, just like Cass will."

"I haven't told her, John."

"She hasn't noticed anything?"

"If she has, she never mentioned it . . . or I forgot it." He smiled for an instant, then thoughts of telling his wife squeezed his heart. "I guess I can't put it off."

"Bring her in Thursday or Friday, and we'll talk about what to do next." He made another note in the folder then closed it. "You've got a lot going for you, Doug. You exercise. Your overall health is fantastic."

"My brain is self-destructing, though."

"You have structure and a routine and you've got tremendous family support. Those will all help slow this. I've got you at stage three, but I think you're closing in on four. We need to get you in with a neurologist."

"I don't need a neurologist. I trust you, John."

"I appreciate that, but they can help you more than I can. I'll handle your sugar and everything else, but let them manage your brain."

Doug turned a page in his notebook, and took the pen from his shirt pocket. "Okay, tell me again."

Cass's car was in the driveway when Doug got back home, but he had to be sure his knees wouldn't buckle under him before he went inside. This was going to devastate the woman he loved. Now he understood what it was like for his first wife when she came home and had to tell him it was cancer.

"Cass!" he called as he came into the kitchen from the garage. He called for her at the staircase, but the house was silent. He finally found her on the deck, relief replacing his dread for just a moment. All that returned as soon as he looked into her eyes.

She was not yet fifty, her blonde curls pulled back in a loose ponytail. Mark's son, Ben had called her drop-dead gorgeous when he met her years ago. It still fit her. Their age difference never bothered her, even when they got the occasional odd look when they were out with the boys. She walked away from a career as a successful interior designer to be a wife and mother.

He came to faith in Christ because of Cass. His first wife, Judy, became a believer after she got sick, but he was so angry and bitter, he wanted nothing to do with a God who would strike that way. With Cass, her conversion came after he had the nerve to sue for custody of Mark's children. He won temporary custody, and while the kids lived with them, everything in his life unraveled. Cass found faith, and moved out, and he nearly destroyed himself. God intervened, though, and gave him a blessed second chance at everything.

He married Cass, sold his construction business and poured everything into his new family and his growing faith. These last twelve years had been the best of his life. Now it was the beginning of the end. He prayed the foundation they had built was strong enough to get them through what lay ahead.

"I wonder what the poor folks are doing today," he said, teasing her for lounging by the pool.

She laid her book aside and swung her feet around off the lounge chair. "I knew you'd be home soon, so yes, I was taking a break."

"You should spend your life reading by the pool. That's why I built it."

"You built it, because it would improve the resale value of the house, Doug." She pushed her sunglasses up on her head, and smiled at him. "How'd did it go? Free from doctors for six more months?"

He sat on the edge of the deck chair and took her hands.

"I don't think I like this," she said, frowning.

"Cass . . . " How was he supposed to do this? Was there any way to soften this?

"What's wrong, Doug?"

"Cass . . . I, uh . . . I have Alzheimer's disease."

She squeezed his hands and whispered, "No, you don't."

"I wish . . . "

She pulled away, stood and paced away from him. "What gave John such a ridiculous idea? Because you forget a name here and there? I do that! That doesn't mean anything!"

"Here." He handed her the notebook from his pocket.

"What? What's this?" She flipped through it. "Doug! Making a to-do list is brilliant. So?" She snapped the notebook back to him.

He opened to the front. "Do you see this? These are directions . . . to John's office, Cass. I had to call . . . the girl . . . with the phone . . . " Not now. He couldn't lose words now. He had to be able to explain this to her.

"Karen, the receptionist."

"I had to call her for directions, because I couldn't remember how to get there."

"Everybody forgets things, Doug. I hate to break it to you, but you are almost seventy—"

"Cass, I've had a CT scan and an MRI. There's visible damage." It spilled out. He hadn't told her about the tests, and he watched her face pale, her eyes brim with tears.

"You did this without telling me?" she whispered. "How could you keep this from me? How could you do that to me?"

"Because I wanted things to be normal as long as they possibly could. I hoped it was something else."

"How long have you known?"

"I've suspected it since late last year. I saw John early last month about it."

He slipped his hands around her waist and pulled her close, but she was stiff, resisting him. "I have been in your place, Cass. I know what it's like to hear news like this, and I am so sorry." There was no sound, but he knew she was crying. There was never heaving or sobbing. She did it with dignity, like she did everything else.

CPSIA information can be obtained at www.ICGtesting.com
Printed in the USA
LVOW130901060613

337262LV00002B/284/P